THE GILDED OBSESSION

The Gilded Obsession

The Beautiful Destruction
Series Book Two

ATHINA FERNWOOD

IngramSpark

TRIGGER WARNINGS

WARNING

THIS BOOK CONTAINS AND IS NOT LIMITED TO

Violent subject matter.

Mature Language.

Discussions about things including self-harm, thoughts of suicide, and emotional, physical and sexual abuse.

Explicit sexual content

Sexual content may include, but is not limited to spanking, bondage, blindfolding, impact play, oral sex, temperature play, humiliation, triple penetration, knife play, degradation, breath play, dacryphilia, foursomes, begging, sensory play, orgasm control, squirting, anal play, the use of various types of sex toys, role play, exhibitionism, consensual non-consent (CNC), and masturbation.

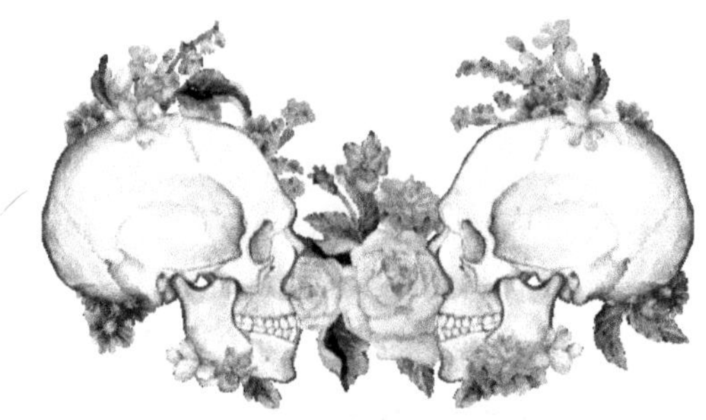

The reason you fall for the villains over the heroes of the story is because the hero will choose the world over their love.
The Villains will burn it down for her.

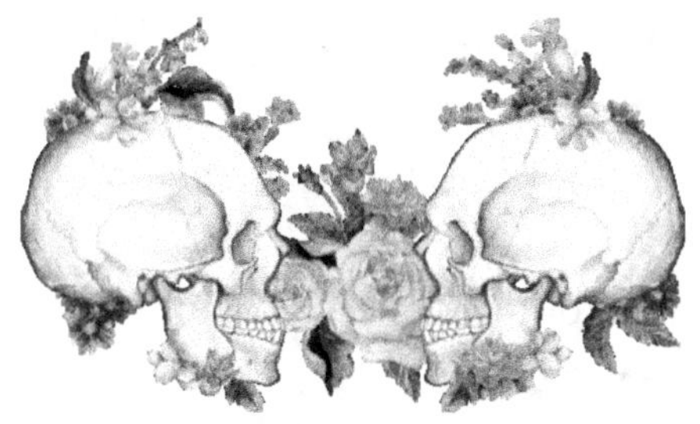

~ One ~

Hazel

I show no shame as my eyes fall to the lacy black bralette holding her breasts, giving me an eyeful of cleavage along with it.

The buds seem to harden further under my watch alone, and when I meet her gaze again, I see nothing but pure desire waiting for me. It wasn't planned, but I can't stop myself as I move in, pulling her waist to me and smashing my lips against hers. Hazel's mouth parts for me instantly, and I take advantage of that as I slip my hand around her back, unsnapping the clasp on her bra and guiding the straps down her arms.

The hard peaks press against my chest, skin to skin, and I swallow her gasp while she swallows my moan when her fingers grip onto the roots of my hair. Hazel uses my body for balance as she kisses me back just as fiercely, rocking her hips against my erection. I can't wait to be inside of her, but there are so many other things I have planned first. Things that I know she's going to love. Grabbing her neck and pulling back slightly, I say against her lips, "Finish undressing and go braid your hair. Once that's done, you're going to come stand in front of me." She blinks once before she steps back, panting slightly as her fingers begin to make quick work of her pants and underwear.

I make sure she knows that I'm watching her, smiling to myself as she gets all flustered under my eyes.

Hazel holds my gaze as her hands part her blonde strands into three sections, braiding it back into a simple tie. It's so much easier like that, and I love the way her baby hairs fall loose to frame her face the way they are now. Pulling down a set of handcuffs hanging by a chain from the ceiling, I watch her intrigued reaction as she steps in front of me like I asked her to.

"Hazel." I say, grabbing her attention from the restraints and down to my eyes.

"Arms up." She automatically positions her hands inside of the cuffs for me, making my job quicker as I fasten the clasps on them. The position raises and pushes her breasts out, making them look even more perfect and irresistible. Rounding Hazel's slightly shaky body, I allow two of my fingertips to remain on her stomach, dragging them against her soft skin as I loop around.

Her legs are pressed tightly together, though I can still smell her arousal quickly filling the space around us.

It's enough to get me high off of her, walking away with excitement coursing through my bones. I hear the chains rattle as her head turns around to look at where I'm going, and I allow it.

I allow Hazel to watch as I move my hands across the rack of equipment close by, specifically stocked with things to administer unique forms of pain.

I want to see how much my girl can not only handle, but how much of it she'll beg for. Tracing my fingers slowly over the paddles, the whips, and the canes, I allow my eyes to flick back up to

Hazel, noting how her thighs pressed tighter, but her body tensed at what my hand was hovering over now.

"You are no longer allowed to look at me unless told otherwise." I say, doing this for the prime reason of building up her thoughts.

I know Hazel is scared, understandably so, but I want to show her just how delightful pain can be.

She'll get the exact same rush when receiving my hits as I will delivering them, and once again this all boils down to trust.

Wrapping my hand around the handle of the black flogger, I remove the loop from the nail and familiarize the weight of it in the palm of my hand. This wasn't the one her eyes caught on, but it will achieve the same effect; just a little more equipped for getting her used to the sensations.

I'm tempted to spend the next hour punishing her for not turning her head quick enough, but I need her in the correct headspace right now, especially since I know she easily falls into subspace during pain play.

Just the thought of it has my cock hard and straining against the material of my pants.

Making sure to keep my steps audible, I take in every part of Hazel's body as goosebumps line her otherwise smooth skin. I know she wants to turn around to see what I've brought with me, but she fights it, causing immense satisfaction to pass through my mind.

I absolutely love this part of training; when she finally starts to submit both consciously and unconsciously, her body aiming to please me without even knowing it. It's beautiful, and over half of the appeal of this lifestyle.

Walking until I'm standing only a few inches away from her back, a dark smile forms on my face as Hazel reacts to me, sharply inhaling as my warm breath fans over her shoulder and neck.

My head is angled slightly downwards to near her skin, becoming slightly foggy from her intoxicating smell. Noting the way her eyes fall shut and her arms loosen slightly above her, I allow my lips to drop down to the top of her shoulder, planting a single kiss there.

Her skin feels soft against mine, and I end up moving slightly to her side as I continue to kiss a path towards her neck, feeding off of the sound she made as I trailed the long straps of the flogger up the back of her thigh lightly.

There was no pain, but it was enough to tell Hazel what I was about to do to her.

I was going to break her in the best ways possible. I wanted her to scream, and cry, and come harder than she ever has before without me even touching her with my own hands. I want her every thought to drift away, every part of her being focused on me and her and this room.

Reaching that moment is one of the most satisfying things a person can experience, and I'm going to be one of three who gets to show that to her over and over again.

Sucking slightly harder on a particularly sensitive spot-on Hazel's neck, I enjoy the little shiver that runs through her body, likely from the combination of my mouth and the leather brushing gently against her skin.

The preparation beforehand is just as important as actually knowing how to use a flogger, and only when a calm sigh leaves Hazel's mouth do I sharply step back, raising my arm before extending it slightly, allowing gravity to do most of the work. It wasn't hard by any means, but it was just enough impact for Hazel to get a sense of the weight and the slight, promising sting of it.

My eyes dropped down to her ass as each of the strips came down on her skin, causing her body to jolt forward in surprise and a throaty gasp to fall from her lips. I knew her eyes would have flown open by now, and I have to fight down the urge to walk around for the sole reason of watching her face.

Adjusting my position again, I brought the flogger down on her left ass cheek this time, and I wasn't nice about it either. I knew it would hurt, and I watched as Hazel embraced the feeling, her body twitching at the jolt of pain, and no doubt pleasure, that was forming in her body.

When her legs shifted and clamped shut, I gently, but quickly kicked them apart, catching sight of the glistening wetness beginning to leak to the space where her thighs begin. Bringing my mouth down to her ear, I place one hand on her shoulder to keep her grounded as the one with the flogger whips around, angling purposely to the side so that the leather straps loop around to her front, hitting the skin right below her breasts.

A loud whimper leaves her body as her knees buckle, but I give her two seconds to regain her focus.

"If you move your legs again, I'm going to whip the insides of your thighs five times each." I promise, letting my hand soothingly trail her skin, despite the pleasurably harsh actions to come, "And I promise you the skin there is more sensitive and I will not be merciful with it either." Like expected, she keeps silent, the slight shake in her muscles the only indication that she understood.

I will almost always give a single warning first before delivering a punishment, and I believe my words are enough in this case to keep her still. Now that I've allowed her the introduction to these new feelings, I know she's ready for more. I made sure my next hit bit harder, landing over the already reddening skin of her round ass. Unlike the times before, I didn't give her a chance to recover.

Moving quickly and precisely, I directed the flogger to come down against the backs of both of her thighs, craving the way she sounded as she cried out. Her voice was like music to my ears, and I needed more.

"Do you like this, my submissive?" I coo, allowing the glorious sting to spread across her skin once again.

When she was too lost to respond, a cruel smile formed on my face as I moved slightly to her left.

The next swing curved so only the tips of the leather strips curved around her body, landing across her right breast along with her aching nipple.

This time when she cried out, I pulled away from her body entirely, admiring the angry red of her ass and thighs. She truly was a vision from the back, but I wanted to see her face now.

Not only for my pleasure, but for her safety.

I know Hazel hasn't spaced out yet, but it will be easier for me to know when she does if I can read her expressions. Subspace can be extremely dangerous if it's not monitored, so as I loop her body, I watch her face as I trial the tail of the flogger against the side of her leg, over her stomach, and across her breasts.

Hazel's eyes are down on the ground right now, remembering my order earlier that she wasn't allowed to look at me. If only she remembered to respond to my most recent question.

Walking up close to her, I pressed my hand against the nipple I whipped, smirking at how she gasped and moved away, even though her body silently begged for more.

"Tell me, sweetheart. Do you think it's okay to remain silent when I ask you something?" I say, moving my hand from her chest and slowly gliding it up to stroke the side of her cheek.

"I'm sorry, Daddy." She says, her voice quiet and genuinely apologetic.

"I didn't ask if you were sorry, I asked if you thought it was okay to ignore me?" Looking down at her bowed eyelashes, my cock grows impossibly harder at how utterly submissive Hazel looks right now.

Her body is entirely restricted, her head lowered, and her skin glowing from both the beautifully reddened skin and the thin glean of sweat that has formed. I can smell her arousal nearly every time I breathe in, and I can't wait to drop to my knees and force her to come all over my tongue. I don't want things to be pretty with Hazel; I want them to be shattering, and destructive, and all-consuming.

"No, Daddy... It's not okay." She finally answers my question, and I can see the slight buildup of tears forming in her eyes. I can tell how badly she wants to come, and considering I haven't touched that soaked cunt of hers once tonight, I'm sure she's absolutely aching.

"What shall I do with you then?" I hum, stepping back and noting the tremble in her muscles.

"Maybe I should play down here for a bit?" I suggest, allowing the flogger to tease the insides of her thighs. My heart speeds at her reaction, knowing she wants this just as much as I do. I don't allow Hazel the time to overthink this as I bring the flogger down in a way that hits multiple spots on her right inner thigh all at once.

This hit would have been the most painful one yet, and when her mouth parts in such an immense combination of pain and pleasure, I wouldn't be surprised if she were to come just from my lashes.

I would allow it too. Watching her body jerk in reflex, I grin at her helpless, destroyed state. The only thing that's missing right now are the tears I can visibly see Hazel holding back. Her body, and every one of my instincts are telling me she wants more, but it's times like this when checking in can never hurt to do.

"Colour?" I ask, taking a long stride forward to close most of the small distance between us.

"Green, Daddy." Hazel lets out a small sigh in contentment when my left hand drops between our bodies, aiming for the gap between her legs.

The second my fingers brush against her inner thigh, they become slick with her arousal. She is quite literally dripping, and it has my blood humming in desire as I bring my hand back up towards my mouth.

"Look at me." I say surprisingly softly, encouraging those striking green eyes to watch me lick her wetness off of myself. This was mostly me giving her body a short pause to all of the new sensations, but with her gaze now fixed primarily on me, my need for complete and utter control took over.

My arm snapped out quickly, sending the leather strips forward and making contact against her breast.

I just as quickly repeated the action to the other side, loving the sounds of sudden cries leaving Hazel's lips.

I soon fell into a continuous pattern of strikes, lashing her body over and over again until she was shaking in desperation and her clit was swollen from the lack of attention.

I felt my mind clear itself of every consuming worry as my body began to feel lighter from the power and control and confidence overtaking me.

Everything about this was freeing for both of us, and only once I noticed Hazel's attention begin to go almost sedated and warm did I ease up a little. I saw that she was just on the edge of completely falling into subspace, and there was no better feeling than watching as she allowed every last ounce of her strength and trust to transfer over to me.

"You're doing so good, sweetheart." I praise, bringing the flogger down on her left thigh without warning. Like I expected, her knees bowed in from the blow at the same time she cried out. I knew that right now, every hit would not only send her further and further into that headspace, but it would also be intensified by all of the heightened emotions.

"I bet you could come just from this, couldn't you?" I cruelly tease, knowing she's on the edge but not able to get anywhere unless I allow it. I think I will.

"Spread your legs for me, sub." I order, wanting access again not only to her thighs, but to her clit as well. It takes Hazel a long moment, but she eventually does what I ask.

Aware of her foggy state of mind right now, I lessened the force of my next two swings, hitting her thighs both times. With this, a single tear fell down her cheek. It was beautiful as her glistening eyes met mine, before more spilled. That was a release in itself for her, and it only had my cock hardening impossibly further.

"That's right, sweetheart. Cry for me." I didn't hold back with my next hit, watching her face as the strips hit hard against her leg, suddenly coming up with my arm and swinging against her stomach and the undersides of her breasts. Hazel became a mess after that, and it had me wanting to unhook her right now and slam my cock so deep inside of her, she'd be able to feel me for days to come.

"Please, Daddy!" Hazel begged, the words falling off of her tongue on a choked gasp.

"What are you asking?" I say, curling the flogger to the side so it curled to hit her already sore ass. Hazel tried to bite her lip, but was too far gone to care about the noises falling from her mouth.

"Harder." She whimpered, and it was the only word she was able to get out. If I went any harder it would cause her skin to welt, and I knew it would be crossing both of our limits to do so.

Tossing the flogger to the ground, Hazel wasn't even given the chance to process the action before I was dropping to my knees before her and pulling her hips towards me with my hands. She threw her head back with a gasp when I gripped her ass tight, intentionally sending sparks of pain all throughout her body.

"Fuck." I curse under my breath from the sight of her. Hazel shifted and is now watching me with every inch of her focus as I slowly raise her left leg, hooking it over my shoulder. It leaves her completely spread open for me and I can't hold myself back as my mouth moves forward and my head dips down.

"Shit!" Hazel swears when my tongue lashes against her clit harshly, licking and sucking and flicking it with my mouth. I knew the suddenness had her head going even more floaty, which is why my free hand pulls back and lands a hard slap to her burning ass. Hazel's screams are addictive as I draw them out of her, and it only provides as further encouragement for me. My arm wraps around the thigh over my shoulder, holding tightly as my tongue moves down to her entrance.

"Oh god!" She cries as her tears drip down her face and her legs tremble around my head. My eyes are on hers the entire time as my tongue moves inside of her, fucking her with it roughly. I hum as her taste floods my mouth, every one of my senses consumed by

Hazel. The tremble in her body tells me she's about to climax, and I'm more than ready to devour her when she's ready.

"Go on, sweetheart. Come for me." I say against her pussy before latching onto her clit. Hazel screams as my teeth scrape against the sensitive bundle of nerves, and I can't help but smirk when I spank her one last time.

The pain and pleasure all channel into one massive orgasm that sends Hazel's body spiraling.

"That's it." I encourage, my tongue lapping against her in lazy strokes as both of my hands have to hold her still. I don't allow a single bit of her release to go unnoticed, consuming every part of her.

Hazel's face is soaked in tears, her eyes bright from the wetness of them. Her skin is red, her body is trembling, and she has never looked more beautiful.

I see the way her muscles loosen entirely, and the physical shift of all of her worries and stresses freeing themselves from her mind. I don't stop until Hazel becomes overly sensitive, pulling my mouth off of her core and turning my head to place one single kiss to the thigh over my shoulder.

I just realized I had been unconsciously running circles with my thumb to slowly bring her down from her high, but I continued to do it as I rose from my knees and towered over her once again. Neither of us say a word as my arms raise upwards, my fingers making quick work of the shackles around her wrists. As predicted, the second her hands were free, Hazel began to drop, but I was quicker than that. Wrapping both of my arms around her body, I pick her up and allow her head to fall tiredly onto my shoulder.

"You did so good, sweetheart." I praise, walking over to the couch and sitting down with her body now straddling mine. I'm already seeing some very minor indicators of a sub drop coming on, but I do everything I can to keep on top of it, one of them being reaching down to grab a warm, thick blanket to wrap around her now shivering body.

"I'm very proud of you, Hazel." I honestly say as I press her chest to my body and lean both of us back slightly. I end up wrapping the blanket around us both. I help Hazel to slowly retap into all of her senses, doing what I can to keep her grounded.

Her head is tucked into the side of my neck, the scent of my body wash no doubt apparent to her sense of smell. I continue speaking words of praise and encouragement, running my hands soothingly down her back and against her neck. Today was a lot of new for both her and myself, and that's one of the reasons why right now is so important. I think I've successfully brought Hazel down for now, but I don't rush anything as the two of us just sit here together.

"Carter." Her quiet voice murmurs against my neck, the caress of her warm breath sending a heated feeling through me. "Mhm?" I say, noticing the way her hips shift forward so she becomes flush against my bare chest.

There's a small pause between us, but then Hazel repeats the same words that I've said to her more than once before.

"Thank you." In return, I held her a little tighter, not allowing myself to yet think about the deeper meaning behind her words.

"Always."

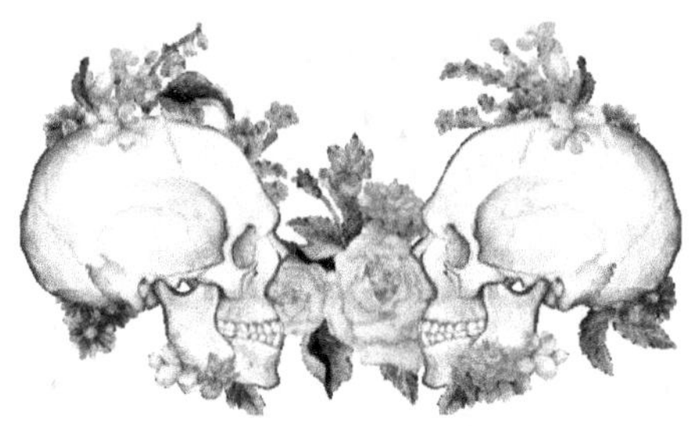

~ Two ~

Hazel

I feel really, really warm right now. It took me a long time to realize I had been moved into Carter's lap, but now that things have come back into focus, I just feel warm and secure and genuinely happy.

Always. That one single word was spoken like a promise and it had my heart racing a little quicker than it had before. Everything about today has only confirmed just how strong my feelings are for Carter, and right now, no matter how close my body is to him, I needed more.

"Daddy." I say, angling my head and planting nothing more than a ghost of a kiss to the side of Carter's neck. I want him so bad, and the hard length pressing between my thighs tells me the feeling's mutual.

"Hazel." Carter counters, but his hands drop to my hips, stopping them as I move to grind forward against his erection. "Mhm?" I hum, darting my tongue out and teasing the sensitive part of his neck before sucking lightly on his pulse point. "We can't do this tonight... not when you were just completely spaced out and shaking only minutes ago." I took my one hand and ran it through the dark hair at the base of his neck.

Tugging hard, I tried to show I had control over my body again, even though my muscles burned and my skin still felt hot from the flogging.

"I want you, Daddy." I say, moving my attention up to the hard line of his jaw and the perfectly trimmed stubble on his cheek. I knew my words hit a spot because his grip on my hips loosened just slightly as a deep groan fell from his lips. Within the same second, a surprised gasp came from my own as my braid was suddenly curled in Carter's fist and yanked back. Forced to look at his face, eyes that were nearly black stared back at me, his jaw visibly flexing and unflexing in contemplation.

"You want me to fuck you?" Carter asks what we both already know the answer to. When I nod, his free hand moves to rub against my ass, the skin heating and tingling from the multiple lashes it's already taken today.

"Then beg for it." Carter says, causing the small, desperate rocks of my hips to cease entirely.

"What, now you choose to stop teasing me?" I really don't know what to say, but somehow I end up muttering a single, "Please, Daddy." I mentally wince at how pathetic that sounded, well aware that that was not what Carter had in mind when I was told to beg. The corners of Carter's mouth turn up slightly as a soft chuckle falls past his lips.

"In subspace, I guarantee you would have been pleading me a lot louder and better than that, sweetheart." Carter says into my ear, his hand letting go of my hair and moving to trace down the side of my body.

It took me a moment to understand what his words meant, as well as why he was suddenly touching me again, but I then realized that asking me to beg was a test.

Carter knew me well enough to know that if I were completely in control of my thoughts, I would have acted the same way I just did: holding myself back due to embarrassment and uncertainty. Once I realize that also means Carter isn't going to hold back anymore, things begin to heat up and my heart starts to speed once again in desire.

"Though," Carter says, pulling me forward by the waist and angling my hips down in the process, "I still want to hear you beg for my cock." That had me squirming in his lap, and my eyes broke contact with his as I nervously bit my lip.

"Don't overthink it." Carter helps, kissing the corner of my mouth before guiding my hips away and back forward again.

My clit brushed against the material of his pants with every movement, causing my core to tighten and wanting more.

"Please, Daddy." I begin again, keeping my eyes down to where our bodies meet, "I need you so bad." Carter moans as I continue to rub myself against his covered length, the sound vibrating straight to my clit and causing my face to grow flushed once again.

"Tell me what you want, sweetheart." He says before rocking his hips upwards, grinding myself down to rub ourselves against each other. I still feel sensitive everywhere from earlier and I can't help but gasp as my clit is dragged over Carter again and again.

"You." I squirm, but Carter doesn't let me move far, "I don't care how, I just want to feel you inside of me."

I know my cheeks are likely bright red in embarrassment, but the carnal look of desire in his eyes has me soaked and highly distracted.

"You want my cock, is that it?" Carter asks in my ear, causing my head to spin from the deep, sensual tone of his voice. I don't answer quickly enough, and in punishment, a hard slap is landed on my ass, causing me to jerk forward and rub harshly against the rough material of his pants.

Yes, Daddy." I whimper, moving my hands down the stunning ink covering this body until I reach his waistline.

"Alright slut. Since you asked so nicely, go on and finish undressing me." I don't have to be told twice as I slide off of his lap and sink to my knees on the ground. Carter's legs part to make space for my body in response. Looking up through my lashes, I teasingly run my palm over his crotch before dragging my fingers up to his belt buckle.

Lust pours out of me as I drag his zipper down, but when my eyes look to where my hands are, I quickly realize that Carter isn't wearing any underwear. I know the smirk on his face is because he knows how turned on I am, but I plan to make it drop as my hand reaches into his pants and pulls out the hot length of him. Holy shit. My eyes widen and look up at Carter to see that his smirk has only grown.

"Tell me, sweetheart. Have you ever taken someone who's pierced before?". K I don't know why I'm so surprised, but the metallic piercing protruding the tip of his cock caught me off guard. I guess until now, I've never really touched Carter in this way, but now that I have, I don't want to stop.

Precum was spilling from his leaking tip, but when I dipped my head to taste him, a hand reached down and gripped onto my hair demandingly.

"I don't believe that's what I told you to do." Carter says, causing dread to flow through me.

"Stand up and go lay on the bed." He orders, and on shaky limbs, I do. God, please tell me he's not changing his mind to punish me.

My clit has begun to hurt from how hard it's throbbing, and all I want is him. I end up on my back, my hands crossing over my stomach as I wait for Carter to join me. He never said I couldn't look at him, so I took advantage of that, turning my head to watch as he pulled his pants the rest of the way off, his dick raised and resting against his lower stomach.

Fuck, fuck, fuck.

His girth looks big enough to genuinely hurt, but yet again, I'm probably going to enjoy myself even more because of it. It doesn't mean I'm not worried though.

It doesn't help when I can't tell what Carter's intentions are as his knee is placed on the bed, the mattress dipping slightly under his weight.

Was he going to do this now? I know I practically begged for him to fuck me, but my legs remained clenched tightly together, making no move to accommodate the width of his large body. Carter doesn't care as his knees nudge mine far apart, forcing my legs open as his waist fills the space between my thighs. A small amount of his weight presses down against my chest as he inches forward, a hand being placed on either side of my head. I couldn't move anywhere now, and Carter knew that as a sinful look appeared across his face.

"Trust me." He says, leaning forward and licking a line across my bottom lip that had my legs tightening around his waist. "You're too big—" I began, but my words were swallowed by my gasp when two fingers were suddenly plunged inside of me. I was already so wet that I could not only feel, but hear each movement he made.

"As much as my ego loves to hear you say those words, I can assure you that I'm going to fit." I can't even argue as he continues to stroke me, pressing against my g-spot over and over again as he works up my body.

"Daddy, please." I whimper when his thumb presses hard against my clit, before retreating slightly and running in feather light circles. It's much worse than the harshness of the former, because his gentle teasing somehow only made everything more sensitive.

"You look so pretty right now." Carter says against my lips before purposely brushing against them, "I can't wait to see your

face as you shatter around my cock, but I need to prepare you first."
Prepare me?

"F-fuck." I curse when a third finger is added, all of them pumping upwards at a much faster pace that has me moaning and squirming uncontrollably.

"Hm, does that feel good?" He asks, knowing damn well it does. Just laying on my back hurts from all of the lashes I've received, and I think that's why things are building up so quickly. Everything hurts. Everything feels so so good. My hips try to buck up into Carter's touch, but he doesn't let me, so instead, I place a hand on the base of his neck and smash my lips against his. Kissing Carter is definitely one of my new Favorite things to do, and when he moans into my mouth as I tug his hair, I turn molten beneath him.

"Daddy... I—"

"Don't come. Not yet." He counters, not giving me a chance to protest as his mouth claims mine again. I could feel myself tightening around his fingers, and I knew that my orgasm was approaching when a familiar knot tightened in my stomach. I wasn't allowed to come, but every single factor was against me.

My whimpers and movements in protest only caused Carter to go harder and to work me up that much quicker. He didn't make a single thing easy for me, and just as I was about to start begging, his mouth pulled away from mine.

No words were said as Carter simply watched as my face contorted in pleasure.

"You've been so good for me tonight." Carter smirks, and while his tone was praising, I knew there was an ulterior motive behind his statement.

"Good behavior deserves to be rewarded." Then why won't he let me orgasm? My legs are shoved farther apart, so that my knees are propped up and spread to fit his large frame between them. Looking down between our bodies, my legs begin to shake. I can't help it as I stop fighting my climax when I see Carter pumping his cock with his own hand while watching my face.

"Come now." He says before pulling his fingers out of me abruptly. It didn't matter because I was already orgasming, but I barely had time to comprehend what was going in their place before I felt the tip of Carter's dick nudge my entrance.

"Fuck!" I screamed as my mouth parted and Carter slammed all the way inside of me while my climax was only beginning. "Oh my god—" My words were completely drowned out when two fingers were shoved in my mouth, my release coating them and drool spilling down the corner of my mouth.

"Jesus, Hazel." Carter groaned, not moving but remaining inside of me to the hilt. He hurt so bad, but that was half of the pleasure as I continued to spasm and clamp down on his length, moaning and trembling through every second of my orgasm. I couldn't even speak as my lips closed around Carter's fingers, sucking my come off of them the same way I would his cock. Painfully and slowly, he pulled his hips back only to slide back in, hard enough that my body had moved up the bed slightly. I could feel his piercing drag against my walls with the action, and that single thrust broke both of our control.

Replacing his fingers, Carter's mouth met mine in a searing kiss. Our lips and tongues were clashing against each other in a mess, but when Carter let out a deep moan of pleasure, I knew I was done for.

Aftershocks of my orgasm continued to spark within me, but I was brutally fucked through it. I could barely even think as both of my feet hooked around his waist, pulling Carter into me and forcing him to push back in.

At the same time, my hips thrusted upwards, meeting his and taking him deeper inside of me.

Carter didn't like me having even that smallest bit of control though, biting my lip hard before pulling away and placing a hand on my neck to pin me down.

I nearly cried as I felt him pull all the way out until only his swollen head was being swallowed by my cunt. My first instinct was to protest the loss of contact, but my words got lost when Carter's free hand reached back and slid over the skin of my thigh.

I let out a breathy gasp as he grabbed my left leg, untangling it from his body and stretching it up so that it rested on his shoulder, placing me into something like a vertical split.

The movement had his cock slipping from my body entirely, but with his chest now pushing my leg between our chests, I could only look at him in confusion as the hard length of him was grabbed in his hand.

"Dominic wasn't lying. You really do feel like heaven and hell all at once." Carter mutters, his voice gruff.

They spoke about me? Before I could even ask about it, my thoughts were replaced by a whimper as he rubbed the head of his cock against my extremely sensitive clit. My body jerked as his piercing torturously massaged the bundle of nerves causing me to groan out something inaudibly.

"Yes, sweetheart?" He smirked in question, amused by my desperation and inability to form cohesive sentences.

"Just fuck me already... Daddy," I dutifully added at the end.

My head had angled to look at Carter's eyes, and a rush of heat ran through me before he did as I asked, sinking deep back into me.

My pussy swallowed him inch by inch, and at the last moment, Carter's hips jutted forward hard. I quite literally felt like I was being split in half from this new angle as my breath caught in my throat.

I couldn't even cry from the feelings flooding me, the pleasure too intense to allow my brain to comprehend even the simplest of thoughts.

"Is this what you wanted, my sweet submissive?" My senses were highly aware of him watching and soaking in my every expression, but I couldn't meet his eyes as mine rolled to the back of my head.

With my left leg being pressed against my chest, it opened me up in an entirely different way, Carter taking advantage of how much harder and deeper he could thrust into me. With every movement,

Carter pulled out until only his tip remained before slamming back in, his tight hold on my body preventing me from escaping these overwhelming sensations.

Over and over, I was left nearly empty, only to be filled to the hilt within the next second.

The sounds coming out of me were no longer human as my body was used and teased and manipulated in the most beautiful ways until I thought I was going to break.

My eyes had fluttered shut a long while ago, but with Carter's hand cupping my cheek, his voice soon forced them back open.

"Look up at me with those pretty eyes so I can watch you struggle, sweetheart." His voice was pure sex as he said it. And struggle, I did. Pulling hard at my already sore nipple, Carter's action drew my eyes open to look at him, water forming at the edges of them. I could barely keep up with anything around me as my hips were raised slightly, triggering yet another earth-shattering orgasm.

His black eyes held my body as much as his hands did, fucking me to the point of no return and turning my brain to absolute mush.

I knew Carter had to be close, but he never stopped ramming into me, giving me no break or reprieve from the overstimulation.

"I can't! I can't!" I cried softly, trying to move away, but finding nowhere to go. Right after, I felt warm, wet tears begin to spill down my cheeks, seeing Carter smile through my blurry vision.

"What's wrong, can't take it?" Carter taunted, his large hand playing and kneading my breast painfully, "Where'd all that fight go, sweetheart? You were begging for my cock only minutes ago." His tone was cruel, but it only caused clamp down harder around him in desire.

"I-It's too much." I sobbed, no doubt a mess, but the way Carter was looking at me right now made me feel like the most beautiful person in the world.

"You can take it." Carter doesn't allow room for anymore conversation, bringing his mouth down to the crook of my neck and placing open mouthed kisses against the skin there.

His tongue lathed against my shoulder as my muscles shook beneath him, praying that this moment could both last forever and end now, so my body could get a break.

"Please, Daddy." My breath hitched on a choked breath as I felt Carter's hot mouth nip at the spot right below my ear. "Come for me, sweetheart. Be a good girl and make a mess all over my cock." I couldn't stop nor handle myself as I dove headfirst into a pool of euphoria, my body giving out on me and going limp as Carter chased his own release. With a deep roll of his hips, I began to gush uncontrollably, crying out and bursting with pleasure.

Carter's moans blended with mine as we lost ourselves in each other, his dick swelling and twitching inside of me. Letting out a strained cry from my own mouth, Carter's head fell into the crook of my neck at the same moment. His thrusts soon lost their rhythm and became erratic as he continued to use my body for his own pleasure, my pussy soaking him with every movement. I screamed as he thrusted one final time, slamming all the way inside of me and remaining there.

Carter's groan rumbled throughout my entire body as he too shook as he came. I felt his release coat my walls, the two of us undoing each other and holding our trembling bodies for support.

While Carter held himself just above me, I could still feel the rapid beat of his heart matching mine, heavy pants leaving both of our mouths.

Rowan

"Rowan, no." Hazel protests, but this is something I'm not going to budge on.

"You're sore and you need a break." I say again, my eyes flicking over her body.

"But that means I won't see you again until next week." Even though that's not what I had planned, I did make the decision to not spend the night with Hazel in the playroom today.

Yesterday with Carter was a really big day for her, and I know that considering she was teetering on the edge of sub drop last night, it's safest to wait a full twenty-four hours before we try anything again. However, not seeing her at all today isn't something I want to give up either.

"Or you could just stay here to hang out for the day with the promise of many orgasms in the morning." I wink as she eats the last bite of her sandwich.

"That wasn't why I didn't want you to cancel tonight's scene." She flushes, standing from her spot on the couch and moving to place her plate in the dishwasher. I know.

"Then stay for the day," I offer, following behind and placing my plate next to hers, "I have to work, but you're more than welcome to keep me company." It takes her practically no time to agree, but I can tell she's still a little disappointed about our first individual scene being postponed.

I would've loved to try a game out with her with much less clothes and darker lighting, but I'll just have to save it for tomorrow.

"So you'll stay, darling?" I inquire, smiling at her inhale when I close the washing machine door before moving to pin her between my body and the counter.

"Of course." Hazel's expression matches my own as her head tilts up to meet mine.

"Though I am still very sad about the no orgasm thing." She fake pouts, her one hand on my bicep and the other moving to caress the back of my neck. Smirking at her obvious intentions, I lower my head so that my mouth hovers right overtop of hers.

"Maybe this will make it better, darling." I play along, happily taking advantage of the lack of distance between us. Dipping my head that extra inch, I instantly grow warm at the feeling of her soft lips pressing against mine. It's gentle and slow, but it has me instantly enraptured in Hazel's touch.

"If that's what working qualifies as, then count me in." Dominic jokes as he walks into the living room to our left, causing Hazel to turn her head. The pink on her cheeks makes it seem as if we were caught doing something we shouldn't have, and it brings amusement to course through me.

"And what exactly have you done for work today, Dominic." Hazel counters, her eyes looking over his shirtless form. It's clear he's just left our personal gym and has done very little business work so far today.

"This body doesn't come for free, princess." Dominic makes a dramatic show of showing his muscles before looping the counter towards Hazel.

At some point, she had moved beside me, but her body grew stiff as Dominic continued to walk right towards her. I smile because I already know what my friend's intentions are, and the look on Hazel's face shows she knows it too.

"Wait!" She laughs, her eyes looking for the quickest escape.

"I meant it when I said count me in." Dominic teases, taking quick steps towards where the two of us are.

"You're covered in sweat, and I'm willing to bet you stink too." Hazel laughs, causing me to smile along with her. Her green eyes look up at me for any kind of support in this, but I just wink at her as she goes to grab my body as a shield.

"Are you kidding? I'm not kissing him for you." I say, pivoting so that Hazel is now in front of me, Dominic extremely close by.

"Traitor." Hazel lets out an amused mumble under her breath before bolting away. I watch as Dominic follows, moving in to grab her, but he makes the mistake of dropping his guard entirely.

Hazel sees the opening and manages to catch Dominic off balance with a quick bend of the knee, her body dipping away from his before running away with a giggle.

The sound of her laugh truly makes me happy, and I can't remember the last time myself nor Dominic have smiled like this.

"No!" Hazel shrieks as Dominic quickly recovers, catching up to her with three long strides. Her body is picked up by the waist, and naturally, Hazel's legs wrap around Dominic's body for support and balance. Her arms move over Dominic's shoulders as he brings his head down to kiss her, holding her tight despite Hazel's true claims of him just coming from his long workout.

"Now I'm all gross too." Hazel's nose wrinkles, her hands playing with Dominic's dark curls as her eyes move over to me. The corners of her eyes are crinkled in happiness, a wide smile across her face. Fuck, she's gorgeous.

Even that in itself is an understatement.

"I guess I'll just have to clean you up then." Dominic plants yet another kiss to her cheek, and I can't help but agree. Dominic's hair is nearly soaked right now and I can't imagine Hazel wants to spend the rest of the day smelling like someone post workout.

"Go shower." I encourage, stepping away from the counter, "Though, feel free to join me in my office when you're done." I say, giving her a wink as Dominic moves to carry her up the stairs and likely to his room.

This is, of course, despite Hazel's protest that she can walk herself. I just grin at her stubbornness, knowing Dominic is probably going to do all of the cleaning for her too.

Though, I doubt she'll have any complaints about that. Once their muffled conversation fades out completely down the upper hall, I make my way over to my office, making sure to clean up any mafia related work from Hazel's vision. As usual, I find myself completely lost in my work until the soft knock of a hand sounds from my door.

"Come in." I call, already knowing it's Hazel as I turn my spinning chair to face the entrance. A second later, I see the handle twist and the door crack open to reveal a wet haired, smiling Hazel.

"Darling." I say in greeting, gesturing for her to close the door behind her. I have to admit, it's extremely weird having someone else other than Carter and Dominic in here, but it's a good kind of weird more than anything.

I already find myself smiling as Hazel walks in and awkwardly stands beside me, noting that there's only one chair in this room and it's currently being occupied.

Twisting myself, I grab Hazel's wrist to spin her before bringing her back to take a seat on top of me. I plant a kiss on her temple when she hisses in discomfort from her ass, only confirming that it was a smart move to postpone our night together. Hell, I can't really complain about this though, can I? I can already feel myself growing hard beneath her as Hazel continues to squirm and shift in my lap. I can't stop it, but I feel her freeze when she notices it.

"Sorry." She lets out a slightly embarrassed mumble causing me to chuckle. I'll never get over how such little things cause her to get worked up.

"How was your shower?" I smile, wrapping an arm around her waist and pulling her back flush against my body. Her head ends up naturally falling against my shoulder.

The very fact it was a reflex for her had me wishing I could somehow bring Hazel even closer to me.

"It was good." She answers, her squirming finally coming to a full cease, "I've never even seen a shower head come from the roof though." Hazel chuckles, referring to the waterfall shower head that's built into the ceiling.

"Yeah, it was quite the shock for me too when we first built this place." I respond, remembering how different so many things were before I met Jolene, Dominic, and Carter.

The sudden thoughts of my past are something I instantly shove down, holding Hazel a little bit tighter for the support she doesn't realize she's giving me.

"Who's that?" Hazel asks after a pause, noting the image of a man currently opened on my screen.

"Work." I say, bringing my mouth down slightly to her ear, "This stuff is really private and only things Dominic, Carter, and I really ever see. I need your word you'll keep this entirely to yourself." I see the corners of her eyebrows furrow at this, but she turns slightly, her eyes meeting mine.

"I promise." She agrees in curiosity, trying to figure out what she's looking at on the screen. I fill in the blanks for her the second she turns back to my computer.

"This is the profile of a person applying to become a VIP member at Rush." I tell her, my eyes flicking over the man in his mid forties known as Carson Law.

"Why are you showing me this?" Hazel asks in interest.

"One, it means I get to spend more time with you." I begin, liking the way her expression shows that feeling is more than mutual, "And two, I thought this might make you feel a little more comfortable around the club." Once again, she shifts. "How so?" Hazel questions. Moving my mouse with my hand, I click "open file", the screen showing endless amounts of personal information on Carson Law.

"Every single member of our club has to go through extremely in-depth background checks before their application is accepted." I explain, "Hired professionals by us complete these screenings, and then a general report is sent over to me, the one who makes the final decision." I quickly skip over things like name, address, personal cell, and things like that, scrolling right to the section I was searching for with all of the findings and results. I zoom in just slightly for Hazel to see.

"This man has no concerning matters on his criminal record nor social media, he's educated, trained through our business in the beginners course to becoming a slave, and based on his credit history and current income, it's clear there will be no problem with him paying us his fees." I watch as Hazel's eyes widen slightly at all of this information. The facts I voiced are barely even the beginning of just how detailed every report is.

"To answer your question, darling, I just wanted you to see for yourself that not just anyone with money is able to attend that section of the building. Every bartender, security guard, paying member, and janitor, they're all hand chosen by myself personally or someone I know is trustworthy." I see understanding pass over her features, now knowing the vast extent of safety measures that are in place and consistently maintained. I want Hazel to feel more than comfortable everywhere she is with us, the club being especially high on the list of locations.

"So that's your job then? Hand selecting the new members of Rush?"

"One of many." I say, my eyes quickly wandering over all of the clean records scored for various things in this man's life, "This isn't the most exciting part of what I do, but I figured it would give both of us a chance to relax for a little while before later." "Later?" Hazel's eyebrows raise in question, her pretty eyes locking on mine.

"Well since you're going to be at work all night, I figured we could maybe take you out for an early dinner before you start?" I watch as her eyes light up and a small smile tugs at the sides of her lips.

"I'd really like that." Hazel says, planting a small kiss to the line of my jaw before turning back to look at my computer screen. I was a little surprised by her act of affection, but I wasn't complaining in the least. I love how easy things are feeling with her. It's like nothing else matters but me, her, and my two best friends. Honestly, it's a feeling I thought I'd never get to indulge in.

"Good," I smirk, shifting slightly beneath her, "Because I'd really like that too." I walk into the living room to spot Carter and Dominic leaning against the railing of our balcony connected to the side. I can tell things are tense between them, but it's been that way since Carter's decided to start keeping secrets.

Sure, I'm a little hurt that he won't tell me, but even more, I'm concerned about how big this information must be for Carter to keep it from the two closest people in his life.

My plan was to talk to both of them before we left, but seeing as they're already deep in conversation, I decided to go upstairs to see how Hazel's doing instead. She said she wanted to head upstairs to lay down for a little before we headed out, and I last saw her an hour ago where she'd gotten comfortable under the covers of my bed. It's very clear that yesterday had drained her, which is yet another reason why I canceled our scene for today.

I do know, however, that with the proper continuous care, she'll be more than ready to meet with me tomorrow as a substitute for tonight. Moving up the stairs two at a time, I turn down the hallway and take a couple of steps towards the door to my bedroom. It doesn't take me long as I quietly open my door and find a heap of Hazel's golden blonde hair splayed out across my pillow, a content breath coming from her body.

The sight affects me in so many different ways, but the most prominent one is me wondering what the hell I did right to deserve the privilege of calling this woman mine?

Ever so quietly shutting the door behind me, I walk inside and towards Hazel's form. I find half of her face buried in my pillow and the other half showing her eyes pinched together and her eyebrows narrowed slightly. Is she having a nightmare? Stepping towards her side of the bed, I move over the sheets in front of her and lay down to look at her beautiful features showing both relaxation and something else, but I'm not sure what. Just as my hand reaches up to her face to wake her, a small moan escapes her mouth causing me to freeze entirely in surprise.

Her lips are parted ever so slightly, and a smirk pulls up across my mouth as I realize what kind of dream she's really having.

Instinctively, I notice how Hazel's leg finds mine in her sleep, hooking over my shin just to have some form of contact with me.

"Sir, please," I hear a small whimper fall from her mouth, and I silently groan at how hot she is before I get an idea. Smiling to myself, I feel my own cheeks grow warm as my hand breezes over Hazel's collarbones, chest, and stomach before finding the waistline of those teasing little shorts she put on this morning. They made it very easy for me to slip my hand past the stretchy material, beneath the simple underwear she has on, and straight to her heat.

The second my fingers found her slit, they became soaked as more noises of pleasure fell past Hazel's slightly parted lips. My eyes were full of desire as I watched her, sinking two of my fingers inside and curling them up to tease against her spot. Hazel was already so turned on from the dream that her walls were clamping down and tightening around me, her body seemingly ready to orgasm from just a few strokes.

She very well just might. Thanks to her leg hooked over my own, it leaves her spread open just enough that my thumb can come up to find her clit. Her hips began to rock in small, desperate circles, seeking out my every touch with every movement, but something was missing.

I wanted her awake when she orgasmed, I knew that for certain. Sinking my fingers deeper inside of her, I added just enough pressure to her clit to have her eyes fluttering open and meeting mine in a slight daze. Her eyelashes followed as she glanced down before pinching shut again in pleasure.

"Come." My voice is a quiet demand, but it's one Hazel happily obliges. Her release quickly found my fingers as I continued to pump them upwards, moving in to kiss her bottom lip that was begging to be taken as her mouth parted in pleasure.

I soaked up every second of her orgasm, smiling as I nipped at her mouth, kissing her even though her mind was too foggy to do anything but lazily meet my actions. Her chest pants heavily as her eyes slowly open back up, blinking as she meets my icy blue gaze.

"That was one hell of a wake up." Hazel lets out a small smile as she shifts closer to me, "Is it time to go?" She murmurs against my mouth after a moment of breath. I seem to need to catch my own as her thumb mindlessly traces over my jaw as if it has a brain of its own controlling it.

"Whenever you're ready." I answer, wishing we could just lay like this forever. I honestly think if I could, I would. A small sigh leaves Hazel's body as she forces herself up from her reclined position, untangling the leg she just realized was wrapped over my own. I roll onto my back and watch as Hazel steps off the bed and over to the mirror mounted on the wall. Her small fingers idly play with the strands of her hair, moving them back into place on either side of her middle part. Unlike other times, I just noticed she wasn't wearing any makeup today.

I also saw there was a small indent on the side of her face from where her cheek rested against the crumpled pillow, and I couldn't help but smile to myself at how relaxed she looked. "What?" Hazel grinned as her eyes met mine in the mirror. She had caught me staring.

"Don't you remember what I said the first time I was with you at Jolene's?" I answer a question with a question. It takes her a second, but the moment I see her cheeks flush, I know she understands what I'm referring to.

"I like to look at nice things." Hazel is not a thing by any means, but she is breathtakingly stunning and I'm reminded of that every single time I even think of her. Instead of responding to that, Hazel turns towards me, her eyes glancing over my attire.

"Should I be changing into something more... formal?" She asks with a tilt of her head. In the previous times we've gone out, we've all been in suits and Hazel dresses. Today however, my grayish-blue pants and black shirt were as fancy as I planned on getting.

"No need. I figured we'd just grab some burgers and shakes from a place downtown and then find a quiet place to park and eat." I say.

"Really?" Hazel's smile widens immensely at my words causing a chuckle to fall from my mouth.

"Yes, really." I wink, "You didn't really think we just ate at posh restaurants all the time, did you?"

"Can you blame me?" She says, walking over to the bed and jumping so she lands on her stomach right next to me, "These are your casual clothes, and I'm willing to bet your outfit is at least a couple hundred dollars all together." She's not wrong. "Well I can assure you that all three of us have a large weak spot for good fast food, just as much as five course meals." Hazel seems to really like the idea of going out to something less fancy, and honestly, I feel the same way.

Places like the River Cafe are amazing every once and a while, but listening to music and driving down a highway is just as good for me. There's a small pause between us before a teasing grin

forms on my face, my eyes glancing over the sight of her laying in nearly the same position as the one I woke her up in. "What were you dreaming about?" I ask, noticing the way her face flushes to a deep shade of pink, her eyes dropping from mine.

"We should probably head downstairs. I'm sure Carter and Dominic are wondering where we are." She diverts, flipping over and moving to get off of the bed.

"Oh I don't think so, darling." I say, and before she can move another inch, I'm on her. Hazel says my name as I move her onto her back, my hands grabbing hers and pinning them above her head. Her hips go to buck up to move away, but I beat her to it, straddling her so she can't go anywhere I'm not.

"Now I'm even more curious since it's something you won't share." I grin as Hazel realizes I'm not letting her get out of this. "Rowan." She says again, trying to move her hands but failing with every attempt.

"What was the dream about, Hazel?" I ask again, my light hair hanging over my forehead as Hazel's splays beside her.

"Just things." "Things?" I repeat her unhelpful response.

"Mhm." She hums, defiance in her eyes, "And stuff too."

"Stuff and things?"

"Glad we're on the same page." She quips, amusement lacing her every word.

My free hand cups the side of Hazel's face, my thumb trailing over her bottom lip.

"I wonder what kind of motivation you need to open up then?" I say, thinking of ideas as her eyes flash in slight uncertainty, "I could punish you for not answering me the second I asked, but I really did think Dominic and I's demonstration from a couple nights ago was enough to show you what happens when you disobey." Unless a safe word is called, I'm going to get to the bottom of this. I've already decided that.

"Though, I'm feeling a little generous today." I smirk at how just my tone alone has Hazel becoming turned on again, "Tell me what I want to know now and my urge to tie you up as Carter, Dominic, and I use you for nothing more than a pretty sight to look at will fade away." Hazel's reaction to my words has me hardening fully, and I can instantly tell I broke through to her.

"Okay." She says, her arms no longer trying to fight me as her cheeks flush in embarrassment. I wait patiently for her to form her words, my eyes watching every feature on her face.

"We were in the playroom." Hazel begins, biting her cheek for just a moment before continuing, "You were behind me." She says.

"And..." I smile, my thumb absently encouraging her as I hold her face in my hand.

"And Carter was at my front while Dominic was to my side." There's a small pause before she said, "I was taking all three of you at once, but just as I was about to orgasm in my dream, I woke up to a real one instead." Hazel didn't look at me during her answer, but the flush on her face told me enough. I'm going to make sure that dream of hers comes true one day, but right now, she really was right earlier when she said we were keeping the others waiting.

"Good girl." I praise, bringing my lips down to kiss her in approval that she was willing and trusting enough to go out of her comfort zone at my request.

Her body naturally arches to meet mine, and I find myself wanting to take her right here, right now, not only to just be with each other, but to also reward her. Instead, however, I find myself pulling away before I forget how to act like a gentleman and dismiss the idea of dinner all together.

~ Three ~

Hazel

When Rowan told me they were taking me out for burgers, I think I really misunderstood just how much these men enjoyed this joint downtown.

Each of their orders doubled mine in size easily, and they even bought extra so they could have some leftovers for lunch tomorrow.

I got a chocolate shake with sweet potato fries and a BLT hamburger, while each of them had their own regular order that they've apparently gotten every single time since they moved to New York.

I took their word for it, enjoying the light conversation we all engaged in on the drive out to god knows where.

Dominic was the one driving today in one of their convertibles, as usual, speeding at a rate that made my skin tingle with an edge of adrenaline.

We'd spent about fifteen minutes driving around after grabbing our food, but Dominic promised that we'd be pulling over any second now.

I didn't mind though. Honestly, I enjoyed laughing with them all, especially when it came from Rowan and Carter's bickering and constant jabs thrown at each other.

They spoke like siblings would, and mostly, it was just straight up entertaining listening to Carter's mixture of seriousness and amusement, and Rowan's humor and personality.

I was smiling until my face hurt, but I had a feeling that wasn't going to end anytime soon, nor did I want it to.

"Wait, this is where we're going?" I ask, my eyes flicking over the trees now on either side of the much narrower road. There weren't any streetlights on the side anymore, and the sound of cars on the main roadway had become nothing more than a distant hum after a few minutes.

"I figured some privacy might be nice." Dominic said, pulling into a massive circular clearing with the trees surrounding us on all sides.

The only noise to accompany were the crickets in the grass, the birds singing from the trees, and the low hum of the mostly quiet engine.

"How do you guys find places like this?" I smile, unbuckling my seat belt and twisting to find that we're completely alone here.

"When you've lived here for as long as we have, you tend to get bored of the same old scenery and never ending busyness of the city." Rowan says from the front seat. So far I love New York, but I feel like after a year or two, I might very well develop the same itch to find new places— places like this.

I simply hummed in response, grabbing a hold of the three bags of food, passing the one up to the front which Rowan happily took.

The one full of their leftovers was placed at my feet while Carter passed over the cups containing the chocolate shakes we all ordered.

I have to admit everything smelt great, and the low rumble of my stomach seemed to agree.

"I think this is yours," Dominic says from the front, and I pass him his burger in exchange.

I notice Carter looking at me from my side, and when I turn to him, I don't find him smiling but he does look happy. A grin tugging at the corners of my mouth, I lean over and plant a kiss to Carter's cheek, smiling even harder that I caught him off guard.

"Thank you for dinner." I say, since he paid for it. I pulled away to move back to my seat, but Carter didn't give me the chance. Tugging my waist, I was slid over until my hip and thigh met the side of his.

"You're welcome, sweetheart." He murmured in my ear for only me to hear, reaching over and placing my burger and box full of fries on my lap.

Rowan and Dominic were talking to each other from the front seat, so they were mostly oblivious to the butterflies fluttering in my stomach as Carter placed one arm around and over shoulders. I shifted as I leaned into his touch, moving to unwrap the burger I got.

They're all so good to me, and I can't help but feel like the luckiest person in the world as the four of us all sit in the middle of nowhere, smiling like we've known each other for years.

"Like I didn't already know that." I snicker at Rowan's mock offense.

"I'd watch that pretty mouth of yours if I were you, darling." He counters causing my legs to tighten from where I'm still under Carter's arm.

"You can't punish me for stating facts, Cal." I flash a teasing grin, feeling a little light headed from how much I've been laughing in these last few hours.

"No, but I can for earlier." His grin copies mine, but his is more promising and sinful. I had a feeling he would mention my dream to Dominic and Carter at some point, but I can already tell this is going to be an interesting conversation based on the three sets of eyes I can heavily feel on my body now.

"That hesitancy of yours is going to land you in quite a bit of trouble with us, darling." Rowan says, causing my heart to speed up a little bit.

"Maybe, but you already said you weren't going to touch me tonight. I can't help it that my body felt the need to take matters into its own hands." My inner brat is thriving right now off of this feeling, as well as the looks I got from all three of my doms. Typically, I try to suppress her to save me some pain, but now that I know how good it can be, I think I'm finally going to let her out to play.

"You'd be surprised at how creative we can be, sweetheart." Carter says into my ear, his hot breath sending tingles all throughout my body and down to my core.

"But first," Dominic starts, "You're going to tell us what Rowan's talking about." Shit, I didn't think this part out. While a part of me craves this thrill, another is scared shitless because with Dominic being who he is, he's going to figure out that I lied to Rowan earlier.

"Don't suppress any details either, princess." Fuck. I have two options. One, tell the truth, even though Rowan's going to instantly realize I lied. Two, play around with them for a while and take whatever punishment I know will come later. I've been itching to ruffle up all three of their controlling demeanors, and I don't think I can resist when such a perfect opportunity has arisen.

"Well since you guys no longer feel like giving me orgasms, I guess you could say I had a dream to make up for it in your absence." I explain, even though I damn well understand why we're not doing anything today.

While Carter has been giving me soothing creams— mostly for my ass— all throughout the day, I'm still too sore to do a full scene tonight.

At my words, Rowan smiles, Dominic's eyes flash with challenge, and Carter... Carter places his free hand on my thigh, moving it until it's on the inner, most sensitive part of it. I gasp when his hand tightens, but then he lets go, his thumb rubbing soothing circles on the skin there.

"Please do continue, sweetheart." He says, "I believe you were just about to tell us what happened in this dream of yours that you felt we aren't capable of giving you." I swallowed nervously, but the adrenaline in my veins overpowered that sensible part of me by a long shot.

"Oh, and we want the truth, darling. Not that pathetic excuse for a lie that you spewed to me earlier." Rowan said, his eyes locked on mine as he spoke.

He knew.

He knew I was lying this whole time and let me get away with it?

"You seem to be taking after Dominic a little too well." I simply say, trying to shift as Carter continued to touch me, but there was nowhere for me to go. We were literally in the middle of fucking nowhere.

"You don't do what we do and not know how to read people, sweetheart." Carter says, causing my heart to race even more. There's that indirect hint of what I like to call their side business. I'm almost certain they're a part of some kind of gang type thing, but there's still nothing I have that confirms I'm right.

"And what was it you said you did again?" I keep my voice neutral to cover just how desperately I was wanting an answer. "We're people of many talents," Carter simply says, sliding his hand up my leg slightly, "Especially on reminding brats of their place when they forget that it's submitting to the people who can turn them into a pathetic mess in a matter of seconds." His words sent a shiver down the spine of my back, goosebumps appearing across my skin. With the slightest motion of his head, Dominic steps out of the car silently, very clearly demanding that I watch him as he moves and opens the trunk.

I can only focus on my breaths as a plain white bag is pulled out and brought towards me.

"You're very very lucky that you're still recovering from last night, princess." Dominic's voice is low but dominant as he speaks. His hand reaches in and rummages through the solid plastic bag, clearly taking his time on purpose, much to my disappointment.

"You're also very lucky that we know how to temporarily improvise." Rowan adds, no comfort to his voice at all. Shit.

I turn my eyes to look at him, and I can tell that he was displeased by my untruthfulness.

But Rowan wasn't just upset about my lying. No, he was fucking pissed. I'm smart enough to keep my mouth shut right now, but it doesn't stop the frantic beat of my heart as all three men seem to have a silent conversation in contemplation. It's Carter who breaks the pause, though it's not his words, but his actions that elicit a gasp from my lips.

Not bothering to ask, Carter hands both drop down to my waist and twist my body so that I'm kneeling on the padded seat of their convertible. Before I get the chance to ask what he's doing, his hand is placed on my lower back, forcefully pushing me down so that I'm bent over the back of their car.

My hips become tilted upwards from the small bump of the headrest I'm angled on top of.

"Such a bad girl. Lying to her dominants." Dominic tuts, tossing the bag to Rowan who's currently moving into the backseat beside me. My legs are pressed tightly together and my gaze remains down, even though I can see Dominic's outline as he takes a seat on the back of the car, right beside where my head was.

"You know, Hazel," My body tenses as I feel cool hands toy with the waistband of my shorts. Whether it's Carter or Rowan is a mystery, "I thought we were making progress with your training." Dominic says, causing unexpected shame to pass through me.

I can tell all of them are really angry with me, and I don't want them to be.

I just can't tell them what my dream was about. I don't know why I dreamt it, but it's too embarrassing to say out loud to anyone, even myself.

"We meant it when we said there would be no scene tonight, so here's how this is going to go." Dominic began, but my focus was partially grabbed by the two men behind me.

Rowan's fingers hooked into my waistband, pulling down my shorts and underwear in one movement, while Carter's rough hands began roaming my body in the most teasing yet calming ways.

Even in disappointment, they're trying to soothe me.

It caught me off guard, but I knew that despite that, nothing but my safeword would be strong enough to get me out of this.

"We had this ordered to play with sometime next week, but it would be a waste to wait when it's the perfect addition to the beginning of your punishment." As if he were waiting for Dominic to finish speaking, the second that last word was out, Carter's hand wound at the roots of my hair.

My mouth fell open and my scalp throbbed as my head was jerked back, my eyes rolling up to meet Dominic's angry green ones.

"I'm sorry." Was all I could think to say, but none of them wanted that.

"No," Rowan's voice sounds in my ear, the cold air meeting the space between my thighs as he nudges them apart with his hands, "But you will be." The sound of a cap opening from behind me has me tensing, but Carter's other hand running circles along my back counters that feeling.

"We bought you a new toy to play with, brat, and you're going to be a good little slut and let Rowan do as he pleases with it." The cold, slick feeling of lube is rubbed in circular motions around my rim, the feeling still unfamiliar enough to have me unrelaxed.

"That is of course while you look me in the eyes and tell us every dirty detail about your real dream." Dominic shows very little expression now other than control.

"I can't." I blush, my hips trying to move forward and away from Rowan at the feeling of his fingertip pushing inside of me. The surprise at how much more easily it felt this time showed on my face, my eyes widening a fraction as Dominic grabbed my face with one hand.

"What has you so hesitant from telling us the truth, princess?" Dominic asks, shocking me slightly by his question, "Is it embarrassment... or perhaps fear?"

Both. I tell him that too, forcing my eyes to remain open at the feeling of a second finger being nudged into my ass. "Mm..." Dominic hums in thought, "Maybe you just need some encouragement then?" Carter's tight grip on my hair releases, my head falling into Dominic's steady hands.

A moment later, I can hear the sound of a box opening, and then an object being removed.

"Trust." Carter leans to murmur in my ear before his hand comes around to show me a teardrop shaped silicone toy in his hand. I whimpered as Rowan sunk two fingers inside of me in one fluid thrust, my body squeezing him and fighting the urge to squirm.

"Do you trust us, Hazel?" Dominic asks, and my heart calms because I know I do, but starts to speed again because I know this is me giving in.

It's me praying to god they would find my dream more amusing than questionable. I chose to focus my thoughts on my next words, instead of the fact that Carter just showed me a butt plug intended to be used on me within a few minutes.

"I do, Sir." I say as my eyes look up to meet his, and a long breath comes from my body, "I don't really know where to start." I admit, subconsciously knowing Carter has moved back to the backseat. I quietly moaned when his finger began to circle my clit, making me aware of just how wet I am despite my fears of punishment.

My unsure response didn't seem to anger Dominic thankfully, his hand stroking the side of my cheek. I'm not even sure he knows he's doing it to be honest.

His eyes are entirely locked on mine as he seems to memorize every inch of my face.

"How about you start off by telling us where you were?" Dominic helps, and my heart races because I know I have to tell the truth about everything.

"In the playroom, Sir." My eyes fell shut when Rowan and Carter both moved just faster enough to make it noticeable. They were both being really gentle with me I realized, even as Dominic's voice was firm as he told me to look at him.

"I was on my back on the bed," I continued, my face red as they all listened with complete interest, "My arms and legs were splayed out, tied to each corner of the bed." A slight smirk began to tug at Dominic's lips as I spoke, trying to keep my head sharp, despite the two men behind me.

"You were punishing me." My voice was quiet, trying to find ways to stall from the real details, but not sure where to find them. Dominic gave me an encouraging nod to continue, though it didn't calm me.

"I don't remember why I was being punished, but... you guys were pretty much using me for your pleasure and never for mine for the whole night." A small smile appeared on Dominic's face at my words, as if that's something he'd want to do. I heard Rowan re-adjust from behind me before I felt his fingers start stroking me at a new angle that forced a moan past my lips.

The pleasure of it caused my knees to bow inward from surprise, but as if he was already expecting that, Carter's hand was there to push them back open.

"Go on, darling." Rowan speaks for the first time in a while, "Sounds to me like we were just getting to the fun part." We were. But we weren't. Carter seems to agree with Rowan's statement as a deep hum in agreement came from him.

"You guys... you had finished all over my body multiple times, with always one of you fucking me." I took a short breath in encouragement before continuing, "But you always made sure it was too brutal and too quick to bring me enough pleasure to come." I could feel my ears turning to fire in embarrassment, but I was soon more focused on the fact that Rowan pulled his fingers out of me after my words.

My heart raced at the sound of a cap opening yet again, but this time, I knew it was for more than fingers.

I squirmed in response, but Carter placed a hand on my lower back and pressed hard enough to keep me pinned still.

"You're doing really good, sweetheart." Carter suddenly spoke, as if sensing I needed that extra bit of comfort. I did. Especially when I felt a cold, wet toy meet my back entrance, running in circles just like his fingers did at the start. Rowan didn't push in though.

Not yet.

Because of this, my focus was sent entirely back to Dominic and what he was asking of me.

"You all said really horrible, degrading things to me, and then continued when you saw that your words only made me more turned on." It was true, but I was also stalling.

"Anything in particular?" Dominic tilts his head with a smile, though I had no answer for him this time.

"Sorry, Sir, but I don't remember now." I say truthfully. Dominic can tell I wasn't lying, and Carter and Rowan seemed to believe me too.

"I bet I praised you for being such a good little slut, just like you are now." Rowan says, causing myself to clamp down on nothing, with only Carter's light circles on my clit to bring me pleasure.

Fuck, I swear they're even hotter when they're angry.

"Seems to me like we used you as our own personal fuck toy." He continued, Dominic giving a cruel smile at the idea.

"Was that it, Hazel? Did we use you like you were nothing but a set of holes for us to fuck, while you had no choice but to lay there and take it?" I moaned and told him yes in response, gasping as more pressure was added to the toy and Rowan began to prod just the tip into me.

"Mmm, I thought so." I swear I could hear a satisfied smirk come from behind me, "What else?" Rowan asks, making me aware of just how screwed I now am.

There's nothing left to say, but the thing that brought me to lie. Dominic could sense the change in me, but demanded it of me nonetheless.

"Princess, I guarantee whatever you're about to say, we've heard worse. You should know by now that we would never judge you, but all three of us are already thinking of the best way to punish you for your lies. I wouldn't suggest tempting me to add to it for making us wait." Fuck, fuck, fuck.

"I really don't know why I dreamt it, Sir." I said, stalling and praying for him to drop it, even though I know he won't. Just as I opened my mouth to speak again, my words were replaced by a sharp gasp and a strangled moan as Rowan pressed forward suddenly with the toy.

The shape and texture of it didn't allow for a slow entry, my body welcoming it inside easily and buzzing happily at the full feeling of it.

"Oh my god." I whimpered and my legs tried to shut themselves, but they didn't even move an inch. The slight shake of my muscles was the only movement I was capable of right now.

"Good girl." Rowan mumbled, but I was too lost to say anything.

The feeling of the plug in my ass was so intense, I couldn't even fathom what it's going to feel like when one of them is inside of me. I think Carter was thinking the same as he groaned at the sight.

"Now finish what you were going to say and then we're going to drive you to work." Dominic says, pushing me back so that I fall fully into the backseat and right into Rowan's lap. I can feel how hard he is, and he groans when I adjust myself from the unexpected feeling of the toy.

"Please, I can't—" My words fall short when Carter's thumb drags through my folds, bringing my arousal up to my clit to rub in hard circles now.

There really isn't a lot of room in the back of their car for all of us, but Dominic remains seated on the trunk and Carter and Rowan make do with me on top of them.

"You just added to your punishment, darling. Don't make us ask again, because you really won't like what happens if you do."

"Tell us what demented things that pretty little head of yours was dreaming about." Carter said, his dark eyes capturing mine and holding them as his thumb moved fast and harshly.

Sparks of an orgasm began to appear, but I didn't dare ask if I could come. I already knew that answer.

"You," My mouth parts as Rowan's hot breath fanned over my neck and ear, "Carter, you..." Fuck, it's so stupid. "Youpeedonme." My words came out as one, my head turning away and trying to bury itself into Rowan's shoulder. .K I was red hot in embarrassment, and I didn't know what to say.

I do know, however, that I just caught everyone completely off guard, Carter's thumb no longer touching my clit. I couldn't bring myself to look at them, but Rowan's hand came up to my jaw and twisted my head to look at him.

I didn't know what to expect, but the look on Rowan's face wasn't one of anger or disgust, but one of... amusement.

The asshole is trying not to laugh. When I turn to look at Dominic and Carter, I see that they share nearly identical expressions.

It's silent for a moment, but then I can't stop it as a smile pulls up onto my face and my body begins to shake with laughter.

I seem to set off a chain of dominoes because once that first giggle leaves my mouth, all four of us end up laughing as my face re-hides itself against Rowan.

"He peed on you?" Dominic says through heavy breaths from laughing so hard. I can't.

"Shut up." I murmur against Rowan's chest, barely noting that someone put my shorts back on for me.

"I don't think you're in a position to be making demands, sweetheart." Carter's eyes are crinkled at the corners, and despite his words, I don't think I have ever been more relieved in my life.

"If that's something you're interested in—" He begins, but I shut it down before he can even finish his sentence.

"It's not." I assure, truly having no interest in the idea at all, "It's still very much a hard limit." It's clear they believe me, so there's that, but I know I've wound myself into a lot of trouble with them nonetheless.

None of us could stop smiling, and when Rowan lifted me so that I was sitting in between him and Carter, Dominic gave me a wink as he hopped off of the car and rounded to the front seat.

"Wait, we're leaving?" I ask, still very much aware of the butt plug and my throbbing clit.

"I may not be as upset with you as I was before, but there are very few things that I hate more than lying." Dominic said from the front seat, the hum of the engine coming to life beneath his feet.

"In other words, your punishment has only just begun, and I highly suggest you text Jade because you won't be coming home tonight."

Riley was back today, my ass is still sore, and it turns out that being on your feet for hours with a butt plug inside of you is just another form of never ending edging.

Today, or I guess technically yesterday, Dominic dropped me off at Rush for my night shift.

While I had stupidly assumed they were just going to leave, all three walked me inside of the building, and didn't stop to wait as I moved to get dressed.

A fresh uniform had been found waiting for me in my locker, one in which I gratefully slipped on, before applying my makeup in the small employee's bathroom.

Within the short amount of time I had to get ready, I soon found myself walking out to the bar to begin my shift.

And guess who was there waiting for me? Carter, Rowan, and Dominic like a group of overbearing mothers sat there the entire night as I worked, only ordering two drinks each, all of which were demanded to be made by me.

While they spoke to each other and had a good time, they also found enjoyment in the fact that every time I moved, I had to stop myself from moaning, or simply collapsing to their feet in apology.

Hour by hour, I watched as the minutes on the clock ticked by until my shift came to a tiring end, and I gratefully left to punch out.

I was tired, turned on, and frustrated all at once, and I'm willing to bet every bit of that showed on my features as I left through the back exit.

Unsurprisingly, my men looked as attractive as ever as they stood by their car waiting for me.

Nobody spoke on the ride home, but it was clear that while I was uneasy, Rowan, Dominic, and Carter were relaxed and content with the silence.

I was exhausted, but I knew that walking around work all day with a toy inside of me was not even the tip of my punishment.

I'm supposed to be sleeping at Jade's right now, but instead, I'm riding back with my boyfriends so they can play my body in whichever ways they want for as long as they want. This silence continued once we were in the house, as well as when Rowan led me upstairs to remove the teardrop shaped toy I've grown to form a love-hate relationship with. It's just the two of us in the bathroom right now, and my toes curl in warmth as they come into contact with the heated flooring. Rowan's eyes are softer now as he tugs his shirt over his head, discarding the dark material to the counter top. His hands move to my body next, long fingers dipping under my shirt before dragging it up and over my head. My eyes were heavy from exhaustion, putting up no fight as Rowan slowly dropped to his knees at my feet.

My stomach sucked in, yet my back arched forward as a gentle kiss was placed on the curve of my hip before my shorts and under-wear were slowly dragged down my legs as well.

I placed a hand on each of Rowan's shoulders as I lifted my feet one at a time, stepping out of the stretchy material. It was hard to keep my eyes open as his gaze settled on the bare skin of my body, his breath causing the short hairs on my legs to rise in response.

It was short lived, though. Slowly rising from the floor, Rowan ends up towering over me once again, his eyes fixed on mine.

"There are makeup wipes in the middle drawer if you're inter-ested." His voice is low as he speaks, and I find myself entirely lost in the mere sight of him. It takes my brain a solid minute before I understand what he's saying.

"Right, thanks." I mutter, truthfully forgetting I had applied mascara and such before work. Rowan steps away from me, giving me some space to move as he walks over to their ridiculously fancy shower.

A control panel was built into the exterior of the glass contain-ment, soon having the lights dimmed to a dark blue and water running from the ceiling like rain would during a storm.

While I shuffled over to the sinks soon finding the soft wipes, Rowan turned to look at me from the shower door and through the mirror.

My attention snagged on him as his fingers dropped down to the buckle of his belt, my eyes following the movement. At the same time, I subconsciously cleared my face of the eyeliner, lip gloss, and light contour I'd applied previously in the night. I was less focused on my own task, though, as Rowan's belt came undone, his zipper soon following suit.

The sharp V of his hips became more prominent under this new lighting, and I couldn't help but bite my cheek as a faint line of hair began to show, trailing down past his boxers.

"I wouldn't look at me like that if I were you." Rowan says, his voice a low rumble as he speaks.

Turning away from his reflection and looking at him in the eyes, I can feel my cheeks flush as I take a step towards him.

Rowan's hand moves to open the glass door for me, steam swirling around me as I step into the hot stream of water. He remembered from last time how I liked it.

Turning and watching as Rowan strips down the remaining clothes on his hips, he smirks as his eyes travel across my own body.

"Darling." He says, stepping inside and letting the door swing closed behind him.

The second he's close enough, I practically slump against him, following his lead as he moves us back and under the water.

A sigh escapes my body the second the heat meets my skin, turning it slightly pink as it eases all of the tension from my muscles.

Luckily for me, Rowan did all of the work, pouring a decent amount of shampoo into his hand before massaging it into my scalp.

My eyes fell shut at the feeling of his fingers working their magic, and he let me use him as support as my hand grabbed onto his arm.

I think Rowan was the most upset with me today because he was the one being lied to, but he still took care of me and every last inch of my body.

When he began to rub soap down my legs and to my feet, a small shiver of pleasure shot up and into my veins.

Every one of Rowan's touches pushed me further and further into exhaustion, my brain nothing but a puddle of mush under his hands.

Before I knew it, nearly every part of my body had been lathered in a fresh smelling body wash, my head tipping back under the water and allowing the controlled rainfall to caress from the top of my head to the lilac painted nails of my toes. "Hazel," Rowan's voice brought my eyes to slowly open, drinking in the sharp edges of his face and the icy blue swirls of his irises.

"No more lies, okay." He says, and I worry he's mad, but there's only a relaxed expression painting his face, "Even if it is something as dirty as getting—" Nope, we are not reliving this. Even foggy, my brain can agree with me on that.

"If you promise to never bring up what I told you again, then no more lies." I promise, cutting him off before he can bring more embarrassment to my already mortified soul.

Assurance sparks within him before Rowan tips my chin up with his finger.

"Good." He reveals a small smile, blinking away the droplets of water gathering on his eyelashes.

"Then let's finish cleaning up here, and I'll let you sleep." And Rowan stayed true to his word. Once both of us were fresh and mostly dried off, I somehow ended up drowning in one of Rowan's hoodies, only wearing that and my underwear to bed.

My brain is still slightly foggy when I wake up, but the first thing I notice is that my body is no longer sore from what I did with Carter two nights ago.

The second thing I become aware of is the change in my attire, Rowan's hoodie somehow becoming replaced with a light blue nightgown of sorts that reminded me of a sexy version of a hospital gown.

Pulling myself up from the large bed, I find that while I'm entirely alone in the playroom, the layout of it has changed.

To my right, a slightly inclined examining table had been added to the room, causing my eyes to widen and my heart to race in both realization and the many more questions to have arisen in my head.

Swinging my legs off of the mattress, I curiously, yet nervously walked over to the padded seat, my eyes flickering over the cuffs and straps attached to where a person's arms and feet would rest.

The understanding that this was going to be my punishment shot through me so quickly I nearly stumbled, looking to the locked door but finding that it's still just me.

Turning back to the seat that seems to be interchangeable as my own personal torture device, this time I notice a small white note laying on the black table.

To our sweet submissive, If you're hungry, we have already prepared pancakes and berries for you downstairs in the fridge. If not, you will fold your clothes neatly and place them on the usual desk, presenting by taking a seat on the chair, and waiting for us to find you.

Let's put that five under the role play category to good use, shall we? My core clenches from the mentioning of the BDSM checklist we filled out what feels like months ago, though it's only been a few weeks.

If their intentions weren't clear before, they sure are now.

I'm to be their patient and test subject while they get to ruin and punish me to their heart's desire.

The very idea of the scene I've placed in my head has me moving.

Knowing I'll be able to get food afterwards, each hurried step of mine to the washroom matches the thumping beat in my chest. I have to admit, I'm a little scared.

Not of them, but I do know that this is going to be my first serious punishment.

The instances before were more teasing, but this time, I can already tell things are going to be different.

They're going to try and break me, and I think I'd let them too, knowing they'll be right at my side to pick me up and place the pieces back together.

My toes brushing against the heated floors, I take no more than two minutes to wash my face, brush my hair and teeth, and use the washroom.

I was unsure if I was still supposed to be braiding my hair back for today, but as I said before, this scene seems very different from all of the others.

I decide to leave it down for now, knowing it can be a quick fix if they ask otherwise.

By the time I exit the bathroom, feeling much fresher might I add, my heart feels like it's going to explode from the inside out. At third glance, the examination table looks a hell of a lot more intimidating over compelling than it was before. Apart from this role play type idea, I have absolutely no clue as to where this scene is going to go. I suppose there's only one way to find out.

Before I've even presented in the way they asked, I begin to hear the rhythmic beeps coming from the door, indicating that someone on the outside is unlocking it.

My heart leaping from my chest, I push my worries aside and practically throw myself at the padded cushions, taking a seat before I can even realize that the gown is still on me.

Oh fuck.

We haven't even started yet, and I'm disobeying orders.

Before I can scramble to fix my mistake, all three of my men walk into the room and I practically gape at their figures. Rowan, Dominic, and Carter are identically dressed in all white, from their white pants to the tight fitted t-shirts that left very little to my imagination.

I mentally wince as their eyes drag over my own form, noting how it's still clothed and not following their instructions. They don't miss a beat though, closing the door behind them and all walking towards me with unfaltering unity.

"Our patient appears to already be quite aroused, though she does seem incompetent to understand that her clothes should be folded and not on her body." Rowan says, and to say my eyes widened is an understatement.

He spoke about me like I was nothing more than a stranger, and I can't deny that his words only heightened my increasingly apparent state of need.

I shifted in my seat, my eyes trying to keep track of all of their movements, but failing to do so as Dominic walked around to my left, Rowan at my feet, and Carter to my right.

The look in their eyes silently tells me that this is going to be good.

I can clearly see that all four of us are excited right now, even if I'm also scared shitless.

I flinch from the cold of Rowan's hand as it comes down to my ankle, small goosebumps causing the hairs on my legs to rise.

I probably need to shave, but it's not exactly like I had all the time in the world last night to do it.

I keep silent as each of the men grabs some part of my body, placing it in the perfect position to be tied down.

Both of my ankles are spread apart to either end of the table, Rowan quickly fastening them down, but not touching me in any other manner.

The exact same goes to both Dominic and Carter, them only touching me for the sole purpose of restraining me.

"Breathe, princess." Dominic whispers quietly in my ear, his arms reaching to one last thing I failed to notice before.

The sight of the thin strap being secured around my waist didn't help the uneven rise and fall of my chest, the smooth leather tightening until I quite literally couldn't move apart from the slightest bit of my knees and head.

A final loop is fastened beneath my breasts right afterwards.

Fuck, this shouldn't be turning me on as much as it is, but it is.

With no undergarments to provide any false sense of dignity, the tips of my nipples poke through the near sheer material of the gown.

Even the slightest of movements threatens to leave me exposed, the cool air finding its way past the thin fabric.

"Let's remove this pretty thing before we begin, shall we?" Carter says more so to himself, his eyes scanning over my body before reaching into one of the drawers attached to the examining table.

At first I was curious, but then, my pulse spiked and my mouth went dry.

"Her heart's beating quite quickly right now," Rowan smiles, and only then do I notice his fingers on my wrist counting my pulse, "We've barely even started and you're turning into a needy mess." I wanted to lean into his touch for more contact, but I simply couldn't.

That frustrated me just as much as it aroused me.

I suppose the same could be said for the small scalpel currently in Carter's hand, though, the blade poised right at the dip in the neckline partially covering my chest.

My arms and hips moved to squirm, but they quite literally aren't able to even make it a single inch.

Oh God.

The sharp tip of the knife was brought to rest against the center of my throat, threatening to part my skin like butter if I dared to move in even the slightest way.

Carter wore a dark smile on his face at my fear, his only sign of breaking character.

I did learn something just now, though. I think I very might have a fear kink as well, because I can physically feel how soaked I am between my thighs right now.

My eyes pinched shut the second the knife began to cut, but it was never my skin the blade tore in half.

No, it was only the sound of the fabric tearing beneath Carter's fingertips that I had recognized.

With every deep rise and fall of my chest, I focused on the tip of that knife, dragging threateningly down the planes of my stomach and just faintly over my pelvis.

It wasn't until right before the blade dragged over my clit that Carter pulled back, assessing the torn material only covering the back portion of my body now.

A small gasp fell past my mouth as Rowan's hands moved under my ass to raise me no more than a centimeter upwards before Dominic grabbed onto the fabric and tore it clean from my body in one movement. The sleeves that were once secured around my shoulders are now nothing but crumpled material on the floor. "Much better." Rowan smirked, removing his hands from my body and merely using his eyes to feel me. "Sir, I—" "You're not allowed to speak unless spoken to, or it's a safe word." Dominic cuts me off, his voice leaving no room for debate. Swallowing my sentence, I simply lose my mouth and look at each of them, hoping for some form of information from any of them. "As you will soon know, today is all about punishment, where we will perform a manner of different experiments on you to see how your body reacts to each one." Carter says, my head flicking to him and watching as he tucks the knife away for safe keeping. "There will be three stages taking place, one conducted by each of us, but we've decided to throw in some rules as a sweetener." My head now turns to Rowan. "It's quite simple, really. For every time you exceed our predicaments, you get a reward. For every time you fail, we will add to your punishment." My knees try to bend in towards each other, but because of how straight they were pulled, I couldn't move them anywhere near far enough to help ease the intense ache between my thighs. But how do we know when it ends, I want to ask, but I know I'm not allowed. "Your actions, or lack of, will ultimately determine how this entire thing plays out, though there will be a guaranteed three tests whether you succeed or not." So in other words, I have to do better than what they think I can handle for three times at a minimum. Sounds easy... Not! The expressions worn on their faces look as though they want to break me right now, and the worst part is that I think I want them to. Ultimately I did lie, and if this is how they've decided to forgive me, I'm more than game. This entire scene has me hot and terrified all at once, but at the same time, we all know I wouldn't have it any other way. "Carter will be performing the first stage of our experiments, beginning with stimulation examinations." Dominic says from my side, my heart racing from his words. Within the next second, the dark haired man walked behind my head before wheeling over a metal table with a stainless steel instrument tray attached to the top. It contained a number of different items, some of which I recognized as vibrators and others in which I've never seen before. Both the known and unknown of this all has me soaked and already hypersensitive, my body trying to arch itself further into Carter's hand as he gently brushes the skin across my stomach. "The question to this experiment is how long can our patient restrain from making noise as her body is stimulated in a preset number of ways and time periods?" Carter holds my eyes the entire time, silently demanding for me to look at him. His words have me trying to squirm in protest, but there is no escape for me other than facing this head on. But how can they expect me to stay completely silent when they're going to use those toys from the tray on me? Not even a whimper or a moan? Now my heart is racing for an entirely different kind of fear, because I don't think I can do it. "My prediction is that she can last ten minutes without making a sound." Carter says, looking at me cruelly as worry fills my body. I can't do that. There's no way in hell I can go that long without any noise. "Under the circumstances that the patient is unable to exceed this time limit, there will be no punishment. We will simply restart the timer and retest until she reaches the predicted outcome." Carter's words had clear double meaning to them. Restarting as many times as it takes is the punishment. Up until now I've felt more than warm, but realizing how hard this is going to be has my blood running cold. "If you may begin the timer, we'll begin." Carter says to Rowan, though he looks at me as he speaks. The smallest flicker of warmth in his dark eyes is the only comfort I receive before the watch on Rowan's wrist is fiddled with, soon indicating that the ten minute countdown has begun.

Moving from the end of the examining table, I watch as the blond walks around to where my head is before taking his hands and gently brushing back a few handfuls of my hair behind my ears. A few of my blonde strands fall into neat waves along my shoulder blades, but those too are soon pushed away so that they hang on the sides of my arms instead. At the same time, Carter's hand currently resting on my stomach slowly drags up the length of my body, the calloused feeling contrasting the softness of my skin in a way that makes me shiver. Mindful of holding my tongue, I allow my muscles to loosen as Carter's hand drags up and down just a few times, causing my heart rate to slow just enough for me to relax. It was a false sense of security though, because then Carter's eyes moved from mine to Dominic. "We will begin with full body stimulation, the target points being her neck, nipples, and clit." Carter states, taking his hand off of my body and walking with the tray to where my legs have been forced apart. Rowan takes his friend's previous position, looking down at me with a sinful smile that has my body melting into his perfect test subject, despite my worries. Looking down, I find that the examination table is raised enough that my neck is in perfect reach for Dominic's mouth, the same way my clit is easily accessible to Carter's wandering hands. Shit, this is definitely going to be hard. I've been absently counting the time in my head, but it's been no more than a minute and I already want to moan or gasp or quite literally anything that can be used as a release. The most noise made is the heavy breaths leaving my body, trying to keep my focus as Dominic's warm breath fans across the curve of my neck. My body shivers as heat spreads straight to my core, drawing a slight tingle to my skin. Angling my head up just slightly, I silently plead for Dominic to touch me, one he happily obeys. For the most part, my neck has healed entirely from the bruises and marks these men have left behind, but with the light graze of Dominic's teeth against my skin, I know I'm merely a blank canvas for him to paint all over again. I nearly forget that this is a punishment until I feel two fingers take my nipple between them, applying a rapidly increasing compression around it. My eyes fly to Rowan and then his hand, finding that he doesn't intend to let go nor ease up as the pressure becomes increasingly more painful with every second. I have to take my lip between my teeth and force down the whimper building in my throat, channeling the pain into tensing my muscles instead. Only once Rowan seems satisfied that I've spent enough time in silence does he let go, his thumb instantly swiping and flicking across the painfully hardened nub. Paired with Dominic's lips and tongue skillfully nipping and sucking at the sensitive spot on my neck, I nearly break beneath their fingertips before this has even started. I would like to think it's been at least three minutes by now, but there's no way for me to know and Rowan's too far away for me to get a good look at his watch. To make things harder, I suddenly feel both of Carter's hands touch the skin on the insides of my calves, sliding them upwards to the slight bend of my knee before continuing his path towards my heat. My hips went to move up, but the strap effectively kept me pinned down and immobile. There was utterly nothing I could do to distract myself from this, and the second the rough pad of Carter's thumb swiped across my clit, I couldn't hold back the small sound that escaped my mouth. It was near silent, but Rowan caught it, taking his hands off of my nipples and stopping the timer on his watch.

I nearly wept in disapproval as Dominic too pulled away, Carter's finger now only a mere hover over my core and denying any relief I had hoped to receive. "Our patient lasted a total of three minutes and fifty-seven seconds for attempt one." Rowan read before his eyes flicked back up to mine. He never said it, but his look was clear. This is going to be a long, long process if I don't get it together. At the same time, he seems to be happy that I folded so easily, me feeding into this punishment perfectly for them. "We'll begin again in thirty seconds." Carter says, staring up at me with hungry eyes. All it takes is one glance on my part to see that I most certainly am not the only person being affected by this. I want to reach out and touch them, but I can't. My helpless need only adds to all of our arousal though. While my chest pants and a thin sheen of sweat forms along my hairline, my body stiffens at the sight of Carter's hand reaching into his tray before dangling something for Rowan to take. The light catches and reflects off of the shiny white nipple clamps, as if they're winking at me in challenge. As I have expressed to all of them before, both during the contract signing and after Caitlin and Dominic's scene, nipple clamps honestly terrify me. I don't know why, and I'm sure these men have inflicted worse pain by using their fingers, but I'm still scared of the tightening, consistent pinch of them. Dipping back into the tray, I see that Carter has next retrieved a small vibrator for his own hands to use. I can tell all three of them sense my hesitation, and it's shown in the subtle touches they're now giving me. Carter's hands slowly run up and down the insides of my thighs, Rowan's gently tracing over the outline of my breasts, while Dominic's fingers twirl the strands of my hair beside him, playing with it and giving me the time to bring my heart rate down yet again. Even in punishment, they're still so good to me. A part of me wonders if I spoke too soon though when Carter gives the order to restart the timer, none of them wasting a single second before resuming their teasing touches. My breath hitches as Dominic's head dips down, though this time, his hand also curls around my throat, his thumb dragging over my pulse point. He angles my head slightly away and down, adjusting me to the exact way he wants me before licking a long path up the length of my neck. I feel his fingers flex as they move out of his way, just enough for Dominic to move up and nip my earlobe between his teeth. The sharp sensation causes my mouth to fall open, but I suppress any noise that would've dared to escape under other circumstances. Right now, my attention was only noting Dominic's skin against mine, but soon the gift of a gradual build up came to an end. My body shuddered as Rowan's fingers resumed tugging and pulling at both of my nipples, rolling the buds between his fingertips until a gasp was forced from me. Thankfully, they didn't count those moments of sharp breaths against me. The chain connecting the white clamps was currently resting around Rowan's wrist, but it seems he was going to make me wait just a little longer in both anticipation and fear.

In its placement, I suddenly felt a low buzzing feeling against my hip, my eyes flashing down to Carter who's still situated between my thighs. This had to be the quietest vibrator I've ever seen before, because I can't hear a damn thing, only adding to the allure of it. My mouth felt a little dry as the toy was ever so slowly brought down to the apex of my thighs, though never once did Carter travel so that the vibrations could come in contact with my clit. Skipping it entirely, the round head of the buzzing toy dragged down the soaked middle of my slit, my arousal wetting it as my body jerked in desperation. Up and down, over and over, my folds happily parted under the pressure of the vibrator, in turn causing the sensations to intensify until my body was left silently screaming. I couldn't cave into their touch, though. I wasn't going to do this again. With Rowan's hand so close to my body now, I can see that his watch has passed the three minute mark, leaving just under seven minutes left to go. I never realized just how much my body relied on noises as a form of release until just now, but it turns out to be a lot. It was hard enough just focusing on one person, but with three touching me all at once, the overwhelming combination of their hands on me made even the simplest things hard to maintain. My breathing, for example, has now become one of them. My head swirls as Dominic continues to plant dizzying kisses and nips along the column of my neck, his hand adding pressure to either side, but never once pressing down on my windpipe from the front. He seems to be more than in control with what he's doing, and I can't help but slightly admire his ability to know my body so well. Whenever he notices I'm on the verge of breaking and allowing a moan through, his grip tightens just enough to cut it off into nothing more than a pleasurable rush to my head. Mentally, my body is squirming and trembling beneath them, but right now, even my neck movements are controlled by Dominic. He tilts my head down slightly, and my eyes follow path, seeing a split second of Carter's vibrator torture before the sight of Rowan's hands come into main focus. The clamps once hanging over his wrist aimlessly now seem to have purpose and intent as one is held between Rowan's fingers, the clasp being spun until the clamp slowly opened. This time, Dominic doesn't help to cut off my groans, forcing me to bite my tongue as Carter increases the settings on the vibrator by two clicks. My first instinct is to move away from everyone and everything, but not only can I physically not escape, but I realize that I don't have to. Trust is much easier spoken than truly given, but I know that to these three men, it has been given. Rowan must have noticed the slight sigh and acceptance in my body, because I see the smallest of smiles tug at his mouth.

I simply watch and fight down my noises as Rowan's thumb flicks over my right nipple, rolling and pinching the nub with his fingers until he seems satisfied. Tracing his finger in a circle, my heart races as the clamp is brought to my body and placed directly onto my nipple. The expected bite of pain never came right away, my eyes flicking up in confusion to Rowan, but then I felt the pinch of it. It's light at first, but as Rowan's fingers begin to twist the same knob that opened it, it tightened around me with no relent. Soon, the pain I had been expecting came, tears pricking my eyes as my core clenched. While Rowan's hand soon pulls away, my eyes remain fixed on the white piece now attached to me, savoring the aching throb that it brings. I knew I liked pain— loved it even— but I forgot until now just how much more sensitive it made everything. The pinch combined with Dominic's mouth and Carter's controlling of the toy between my thighs, I deeply feared I wasn't going to be able to remain quiet for much longer. "The right nipple clamp was set to setting three of seven." Rowan stated, maintaining the act for this scene. Dominic's grip on my neck resumed once again, and I could feel him smile against me as he continued to mark and beautifully play the sensitive skin there. I have to admit that out of all the men here, Dominic was the best at neck kissing, and right now is no different. The chair I was once wary of has now become my greatest asset because without it, I would be nothing more than a trembling mess on the floor. "Increase it to setting four and apply the second clamp." Carter says to Rowan, causing me to look down at him. I soon realized that was exactly what he wanted though, his eyes not allowing mine to leave him as he shifted closer to my body. My stomach knots as I feel Rowan twist the current clamp tighter before beginning to prepare my body for the second. Only this time, I wasn't allowed to look. Carter demanded that I watch him as he adjusted the vibrator and brought it up to my clit at last, my hips trying to jerk but only being met with the belt and the cushion. No, no, no. The force of my impending orgasm hit me like a train as I suddenly felt that all too familiar urge to let go and lose myself in the waves of pleasure. I couldn't do that though, because not only am I unable to ask for permission to do so, but there's also no way in hell I could keep silent if I climaxed before the ten minutes.

Carter wasn't very doctorly as a smirk drew across his face, the vibrator circling my clit in a medium paced tempo. "I'm going to increase the intensity of sensations by performing factor three." Carter says, no doubt choosing his words in a way that left me confused and wanting. What's factor three? My chest pressed forward at the feeling of the second nipple clamp being tightened to the fourth setting, but I only absently heard Rowan's voice say that it's been applied before Carter reaches back into his tray. Holding it up in the air, my eyes shut in defeat as a steel insertable was shown to me, the end of the tool curved and multiple spherical bumps lining the toy. I sighed and tilted my head back against the headrest, giving in entirely to the restraints and Dominic's tight grip around my throat. At the sight of the object, I knew I could only pray that I'd somehow be able to last. Bringing the metallic toy down between my thighs, I gasped at the cold nip it brought, tingles shooting up my body and down my legs. "What was that?" Carter cocked his head at me with a mean grin, "Something you wanted to say, patient?" Holy fuck. He was treating me like I wasn't even important to him at this point, and as fucked up as this makes me, it was fucking hot and I couldn't deny it. I simply bit down on my tongue and forced myself to focus on my breathing. Dominic was still at my neck, but when Rowan announced that I only had two minutes to go, he began to refine his movements by a lot, putting his previous ones to shame. There wasn't a single nerve ending along my throat that wasn't sparking with pleasure right now, the control of my breaths still lying in Dominic's large hand. His grip was merely to angle my head right now, but as if sensing his friend's intentions, just as Carter pushed the entire beaded insertable inside of me, his hand squeezed, sending a rush of endorphins straight to my head. It was dizzying, and when Rowan pulled at the chains connecting my nipples together, Dominic's grip lessened, forcing me to choke down my scream all on my own. "Good girl." He murmured right below my ear, causing me to clamp down hard on the freezing toy inside of me. I felt myself end up right on the edge of breaking, but somehow I managed to push myself, my eyes clamping shut. It wasn't until Rowan called the ten minute mark that a forced sob escaped me, allowing myself to use my voice again. Seemingly all at once, Dominic bit down on my neck, Rowan painfully ripped the clamps off, and Carter tore the vibrator and insert away in the same movement. I was left dangling just before the peak of my climax, never granted the opportunity to come after minutes of fighting every instinct inside of me down. My head spins as Dominic drags his teeth against the sore spot on my neck before lapping his tongue over the sensitive area. I want to cry from the denial, but I'm not quite there yet, despite my body currently screaming in protest and immense displeasure. "She lasted ten minutes and two seconds on attempt two." Rowan read off of his watch, the nipple clamps now dangling between his fingertips. I finally allow myself to whimper and squirm at the uncomfortable feeling, needing the soothing touch of a mouth or tongue to take away the sore. It was a need that was not granted to me. Instead, my racing heart was never given the chance to steady before Dominic's mouth lifted from my body, his eyes capturing mine in deep thought. Then, he flashed me a smirk that told me who's turn it was with me next.

Hazel

The sight of Dominic rising from his position beside me has my core clenching all over again. Dark brown curls cut along the edges of his face, tempting me to touch them—that is, if I could move. I couldn't even be too upset about my denied orgasm, not when he and his two best friends look as attractive as they do now. "For test two, we'll be observing the patient's pain tolerance to impacts inflicted by a riding crop." Dominic smirks, stepping away and creating a slight pause as he selects the instrument of his choice. "I say she'll be crying by thirty hits." Carter says, holding my gaze as he speaks. Rowan raises an eyebrow in amusement as Dominic lets out a breath in disagreement. "Considering what a pain slut she is, I'll have her cheeks tear stained within twenty." He concludes, walking back to my side with the crop in hand. It brought the promise of pain with it, the ache of my abused nipples and clit sparking to life. "Would you like the gag, or no?" Rowan asks, his eyes flicking to my mouth in thought. "Not this time." Dominic smirks, seeming to have a different plan in mind, "No, I want to hear her as she screams and whimpers under my touch." "She does make the prettiest of noises." Carter agrees, shooting me a look that makes my stomach clench, "Though a blindfold might be a nice addition." Those few words had my heart pounding just a few beats faster, the mentioning of sight deprivation bringing memories of the times before. The thrill of never knowing when or where something's going to happen always leaves me wanting, and Dominic, Rowan, and Carter all seem to agree on this. The latter of the three tosses up a strip of black satin material, one in which Rowan happily accepts as he silently motions for me to lift my head. Doing so, the last thing I saw was the coolness of his eyes before everything went dark, the soft blindfold caressing my skin. The next second, I felt the drag of the leather loop across my stomach, tracing a line up the length of my body before curving to my neck and along the edge of my jaw. I couldn't see any of them, but that left all of my other senses heightened and sensitive. As a finger began to stroke the palm of my clenched hand, Dominic brought the riding crop over the painful ache of my nipple. I can practically picture the smile that would appear by my hiss. "Sore?" He coos, and with a nod of my head, he brings down the leather on my skin.

My nipples were already sensitive from Rowan's clamps, and the sharp jolt of pain from the crop only intensified it. "Count." Carter commands me, and with a shaky breath, I manage. "One, Sir." The second the last word fell from my mouth, Dominic hit again, this time on the opposite nipple. "Two, Sir." This was no longer me numbering the hits, it was a countdown to how long I could last before they broke me. On the seventh impact, I screamed, my body shaking as Dominic sought out the most painful places he could find. My body soon turned to fire, burning up in the heat of their flames. When Dominic hit my inner thigh for the first time, I'll admit, I nearly broke down into a sob right then and there. It hurt worse than any impact before, but my scream melted into a moan as Carter's mouth came down on the sore spot, his mouth and tongue stroking the fiery touch of my skin. He and Rowan did this every time the crop came down on my trembling body, kissing away the hurt and transforming it into pleasure. "F-fuck!" I cursed just before counting out the fourteenth strike. "Aw, don't tell me you're breaking already." Rowan's voice came in my ear, false empathy lacing his tone. My intended words in response were drowned out by my scream, Rowan's mouth capturing mine within the same second. He moaned against my lips as he took my head into his hands, swallowing my noises as Dominic continued to inflict pain and Carter teasingly stroked it away. "Fifteen, Sir." I gasped against Rowan's mouth as Dominic refocused his attention from my stomach to my nipples suddenly. Carter must have moved because his mouth soon enclosed around the bud, sucking it into his mouth and dragging his teeth over it. Tears pricked the corners of my eyes from the action, but I refused to let them fall. My body braced itself for the sixteenth impact, but it was one that never came. I could hear their breathing and feel Rowan and Carter's hands touching my body, but the feel of the riding crop disappeared entirely. It was like Dominic was waiting for my muscles to relax before I felt the leather return, but the whimper that left my mouth this time wasn't from pain, but fear. My mouth opened to say no, but Carter hushed me with an amused chuckle. "What a pathetic mess you've become," He muses, his thumb stroking my jaw, "Don't fight it." Carter's last three words were spoken as a demand, forcing me to loosen as Dominic drags the crop up my slit, and over my swollen clit.

I can't even begin to imagine what it would feel like for the smooth leather to come down somewhere so sensitive, and I'm not sure I want to know either. I'm not exactly in a position to protest though. "Count, princess." Dominic says, and then, the crop hits my upper thigh hard. I cry out, but rein my tears in, my legs fully shaking now from the pain of this all. I can still feel the burning imprint of the leather against my skin, even if it's no longer there. "Sixteen, Sir." My voice is no more than a whisper this time. That's all I can manage. Once again, Dominic drags the crop up my slit, but this time, he doesn't stop. He continues to bring the tool up and up until I can feel it resting against my lips. "Be a good girl and clean this for us, will you." Rowan says, and when I dart my tongue out just slightly past parted lips, the taste of my arousal and the earthy flavour of leather fills my senses. Having the crop so close to my mouth scares me a little, but I lick up every last trace of my wet-ness, memorizing and feeling the crop on my tongue. By the time It's pulled away, I'm hearing soft groans from all three men, likely by the sight of me cleaning the very tool that has me on the verge of tears. Before I can even brace myself, the crop comes down on my other thigh, sending me screaming and shaking all over again. "E-Eighteen, Sir." I whimper, my eyes remaining closed, even as I feel either Carter or Rowan begin to untie the knot securing the blindfold around my head. "I want to see you when you break." Carter says so quietly in my ear, I know I was the only one intended to hear it. His words had my walls clamping down on nothing but air, and just from getting to see his eyes again, I had no doubt that's what they were going to do by the end of this. The next swing was against my lower stomach, but before I even got the chance to scream or cry, Dominic brought the riding crop down directly on my clit. It had been twenty hits and no tears had been spilt, but that single hit shattered every bit of defiance, control, and resistance I may have had before.

I didn't even care if they won these challenges anymore, because at the end of the day, I was theirs and they were mine. "That's it. Cry for us, darling." I didn't even recognize the hot tears now streaming down my face until Rowan pointed it out, my body trembling and crying out as Dominic continued to tap my clit repeatedly with the crop. "Come, Hazel. Just let go." Dominic said, and my body obeyed before my mind could even process his command. Breaking entirely, my mind was an absolute mess as my orgasm crashed through me, consuming every inch of my being. My eyes rolled into the back of my head and my body thrashed against the restraints, even though I wouldn't wish to be anywhere but here. "No, no! It's too m-much." I sobbed as Dominic continued to send shocks of pain and pleasure through me until my head went foggy and my vision blurred from the tears. Though it wasn't a safeword, Dominic still respected my wishes as he pulled back, dropping to his knees and kissing every inch of my skin, alternating between thighs. Even after my orgasm subdued, the tears continued, my body shaking and practically begging to be able to touch them. They either understood the words I couldn't say or felt the same way. Whatever it was, my body practically sagged in relief as all three men got to work, Dominic undoing my feet, Rowan my arms, and Carter my hips and chest. They worked so quick, it only took seconds before I was free from the chair, my mind still spinning with lust. "Come here. I've got you." Rowan says, picking me up from the examining chair and walking over to the bed. I can't hear them, but I know Dominic and Carter followed, all three of them joining me as Rowan laid me down on the mattress. My body was still shaking as my head hit the pillow, my tears slowing and my mind beginning to feel warm once again. It wasn't from the covers though, it was from the tingling on my skin that was heating my blood and allowing my thoughts to clear. I could tell I wasn't in subspace, but I did know that warm, fuzzy feeling it typically brought was beginning to spread throughout my body. "How are you feeling?" Dominic asks from my front, his hand reaching up and stroking some stray hairs out of my face. Rowan and Carter were both sitting behind me, but I was still too shaky to be upright. "I'm good." I gave him a small smile to show my honesty, "I can't stop shaking though." "I can see that," He chuckles, taking my hand into his and planting a small kiss upon it. "We'll wait until you're ready again before beginning round three."

All I can do is nod in thanks, appreciating their calming touches and words of approval. They weren't my "doctors" or dominants right now, they were my boyfriends keeping me steady and grounded. "You've been so good, you know?" Carter says as he rubs my back, his praise making me blush from the approval to be heard in his tone, "I think that warrants you a reward." I had forgotten about that part until now, but it definitely pricked my attention. "Yeah?" I smile, turning over in the bed and angling my head up to Carter and then to Rowan. "Oh, most certainly." The former smirked, watching as Dominic pulled me back with a hand around my waist. "In fact," Rowan started, "I think we'll give you a choice of what we do for the next round." A choice? A choice between what? His voice had become huskier as he spoke to me, and the knowing glint in his eye seemed as if he could see the thoughts swirling in my mind. "Would you like that, princess?" Dominic asks, tugging my earlobe between his teeth afterwards, "Would you like to choose what method we use to break you?" My cheeks warmed at his words, my mouth parting ever so slightly as my leg was lifted up and over Dominic's hip. The position left me spread wide for their view, the faint breeze from the air conditioning cooling the wetness between my thighs. The challenging raise of Carter's eyebrow had me speaking. "Yes, Sir." My response elicited a deep hum from his chest, one that vibrated through my body and sent tingles down the spine of my back. "Mm." Rowan smiled, no doubt noticing the familiar heat of arousal pooling in my lower abdomen once again. "You see, darling, our initial plan was to see how many times we could deny you of your orgasm until you couldn't handle it anymore, but we'll give you an alternative." Rowan's words drew a shiver from my body, any other option already seeming more appealing to me. The tremble in my muscles has now reduced to a minimum, my breath hitching as Dominic's fingertips drew wide circles on the thigh resting over his body. "If you'd prefer, we'll see how many times you can orgasm in a row instead." Rowan offers, presenting me with two options. "And afterwards, we'll go downstairs, eat dinner, and I'll even let you pick the movie this time if you want to stay the night." I can't help but smile at the memory of that horrid film Rowan picked last time for us to watch. I meant it when I said he would never get control over the remote again, but the image he put in my head had a small smile spreading across my face. "I want the second choice." I decide, my head spinning from how exposed I suddenly felt. The cool smiles that appeared on their faces showed they had expected me to choose that option— had hoped for it even.

Despite the warm reassurance spoken only seconds ago, I knew that I was now completely at their mercy, leaving me open, vulnerable, and more than wanting of anything they're willing to give. "Sir," I moaned as Dominic's hand brushed against my inner thigh with a gentleness that was practically overwhelming, nudging me so I was spread even more for them. "Shh," He cooed, placing a warm kiss below my ear, "Do you remember what Rowan said in the car yesterday when you apologized?" Dominic asked, causing my heartbeat to spike. I could only gasp in response as his fingers found my slit, instantly sinking two of them deep inside of me. "You... He said that I wasn't sorry yet, but that I will be." The flashes of memories from yesterday appeared in my head, my muscles clenching involuntarily as I was forced to take a steadying breath. "That's right." I could hear Dominic smirk as he spoke, but my attention mainly snapped to the sight of Rowan moving down on the bed before flipping onto his stomach. My eyes shot up to Carter in confusion, but he merely winked before I felt a mouth latch onto my clit. Rowan had positioned himself right between the gap of my spread legs, his tongue swirling in circles while his best friend finger fucked me at the same time.

"Oh, I—" My words were swallowed by my moan, the light suction and harsh strokes sending my body into immediate overdrive. "I suppose there's still the question of our predicaments." Dominic cut me off, bringing an arm down under my head for it to rest on. "Considering how worked up and sensitive she already is, I'll say she'll break before six orgasms," Rowan lifts his head as he speaks, holding my gaze as he does so. What he didn't have to say, however, was the unspoken promise that they're going to show me just how sorry I can be. Six in a row, though? He can't be serious. The sparks in his eyes tell me just how wrong my hopes are. "Seems to me like she's already about to have her first." Carter teased cruelly, but what I hate most was that he's right. With Rowan and Dominic so close and touching me together, the visual on its own is enough to have me squirming and ready. As my eyes fell shut heavily, my hands blindly grabbed onto whatever they could; Rowan's soft hair and the belt loop of Carter's pants. I just needed to touch them in some way, and when my grip tightened around Rowan, his groan vibrated straight to my clit, sending my hips bucking. The two managed to pin me still though, while Carter shuffled closer until he was kneeling by my head. Opening my eyes, my gaze first shot up to a pair of dark eyes before looking to see his fingers making quick work on the button of his white pants. My hand moved from the loop to his lower stomach, but Dominic ended up gently grabbing my elbow and positioning it so it was pinned between our bodies. It left me utterly helpless and submissive to the man in front of me.

My lips had already previously been parted from the continuous strings of moans Dominic and Rowan were forcing from me, but they fully opened at the sight of Carter's cock being pulled out and stroked in his fist. I panted as he dragged the pierced head over my bottom lip, smearing his precum along it until it mixed with my saliva. My tongue instinctively darted out to lick my lips, brushing against his slit in the process. This was a little new for me, but when his one hand came down to hold onto my head, a gasp replaced my thoughts as his fingers weaved their way into the roots of my hair. In a silent plea for more, I relaxed my jaw and opened my mouth wider, taking in a breath as Carter guided himself ever so slowly into my mouth. While he wasn't as long as the other two, he sure as hell was thicker, and I had to make a conscious effort to remain in touch as he slid further past my lips.

"Fuck, sweetheart. Keep doing that." Carter cursed as my tongue traced the vein on the underside of his cock. I only took him down about halfway, but when he pulled back out nearly to the tip, I swirled and teased his piercing as I explored it for the first time. Carter mostly had control over my actions right now, but Dominic and Rowan had complete control over my body. Working together, they had me moaning and sputtering around Carter's dick until spit was running down my chin and I began to struggle immensely. I didn't even have the chance to see it coming before I fell into orgasm one of allegedly six. Carter groaned along with me, my sounds no doubt shooting straight to his balls as I sucked and stroked him in long, continuous motions. All three seemed to recognize that I was holding myself back, but I soon had no choice but to give in. Like they said, they weren't stopping and Rowan had to use both his hands and his legs to keep me still as I tried to move away. His mouth and Dominic's fingers never left my body, pushing me through my orgasm and continuing until the sensitivity made my head spin. "That's it." Rowan murmured, his fingers replacing his mouth for a short second, "Just let us take over." That's all I could do. "We're going to fuck you limp and you're going to be desperate for more, even as you're screaming and begging for the mercy we won't show you." Tears began to fall down my warm cheeks as a second climax hit, my mouth going lax and my legs shaking around Rowan's head. At the sight of my tears, I swear I felt Carter harden even more against my tongue, his thumbs stroking the sides of my cheeks as he held my head for me. "Shit." He sighed in pleasure, holding my eyes as he used me with no relent. My jaw ached from the force of his thrusts, but I wouldn't expect anything less from him. "Hazel... Fuck, I'm going to come." Grazing my teeth ever so lightly against his cock, I moaned with him as the action drew Carter over the edge. Pulling back and sucking hard on just his tip, I flushed as his head tossed back and his length tensed in my mouth. His arms flexed and his stomach clenched as he came down my throat with a grunt, my mouth remaining around him as I continued to lazily lick and suck every inch of him. I loved seeing him like this, even if I was also being painfully overstimulated at the same time. Still panting in post orgasm bliss, Carter pulled out of my mouth, his hand running through my blonde hair in appreciation before tipping my head up. My mouth is now parted in a silent scream, but he forces me to look at him as tears run down my flushed face. "So pretty." He murmurs, wiping my bottom lip with his thumb. Carter shows false pity as I continue to whimper and tremble in sensitivity, watching as I try to get away, but failing with every half-hearted attempt. "Awe, are you going to come again, sweetheart?" I frantically shake my head no, but in response Carter reaches forward and tugs my nipple hard. The action sends me spiraling to a point of no return. "Good girl." Dominic says, slamming his fingers into me until I began to squirt into the palm of his hand. Rowan made a noise of pleasure as I tried to yank his head away from my clit, but he only groaned from the pain of it. "I—Oh fuck, please!" I cried begging for literally everything and nothing all at once. My juices continued to gush out of me, soaking both of the men fucking me through every last painful second of my orgasm, and never letting me go. My brain soon became on the verge of nonfunctional, my instinct to fight them off fading into the background as complete and total submission took its place.

I think they felt it before I did though, because that's when they switched their positions, moving my shaking body themselves. At some point, Rowan must have taken his shirt off because as I'm placed on top of him, I can feel his warm skin brushing against mine. My head was facing the headboard, but my mouth was left hovering directly overtop of Rowan's hard on straining tightly against his pants. As for myself, my clit was angled perfectly over his own mouth, leaving us in a position that Rowan instantly dove into. His hands reached up to cup my ass, pulling me down and holding me as I tried to get away. My tears had never stopped flowing, and for a second, all I could do was watch as the droplets fell and absorbed into the white material of his pants. With an impatient buck of his hips, I took the hint and somehow managed to get his clothes undone and his cock in my hand within a few seconds. I didn't wait before I was taking him into my mouth, swallowing him down as I moaned and whimpered from his skilled assault on my clit. It already felt like too much, but I soon heard more clothes being discarded in the background and then the feeling of two more bodies surrounding me. Dominic was the person I first saw, his cock being pumped in his fist at the same speed I was stroking Rowan with my mouth. I couldn't see a lot of him, but I did know that my body craved his touch and was desperate for any form of contact with him. Just as my arm extended to do so, I froze and my body tensed as I felt the unusual feel of a piercing being dragged up and down my slit by Rowan's head, the tip of Carter's dick threatening to push forward. With my mouth still working Rowan, I didn't even have time to protest before Carter slammed balls deep inside of me, his hips going flush with my ass. I cried and writhed around the two cocks now inside of me, but no one ever slowed or let up as I began to gag through my tears. "Shit, princess, if only you could see yourself right now." Dominic's low words caused my core to tighten, "You take us so well." I felt his hand brush overtop of mine before he pulled it towards him, guiding my fingers to wrap around his length. I'm too overwhelmed to do it myself, but Dominic doesn't mind as his much larger hand clasps around mine, moving so that both of us are fucking his cock at the same time. Touching him like this is intensely hot, and I feel myself release just slightly around Carter at the feeling. For the most part, Rowan's face was under me enough that Carter wasn't touching him, but just the thought of how close they were together sent detailed images into my head. Every once and a while I pulled up to breathe, but with every hard snap of Carter's hips, he thrusted me back down yet again. I felt their every moan as if it were a part of me, and at this point, it honestly felt like these three men were. They were brutal. And loving. And harsh. And kind. They were everything I could have ever wanted, and even though I feel like I've been stripped bare and exposed in ways that exceed just being physically naked, I've never felt so protected and cared for as I do now. As my climax barreled through me yet another time, my tears were no longer ones of overstimulation and pain, but ones that can only be described as pure affection and happiness. "You're doing so good, princess." Dominic groaned as my fist tightened around him, "Just two more to go. You can do that for us, can't you?" I nodded the best I could with Rowan still in my mouth, but I was suddenly pulled off of him a second later, Carter rocking backwards until I was raised in his lap by my hips. The dark-haired man didn't miss a beat as he began to plow into me just like that. I could feel the slight shake in his legs and the way his thrusts began to grow sloppier, desperation coursing through his muscles. I allowed Carter to use me as I twisted my head back to find his lip caught between his teeth and a look of sheer pleasure lacing his every feature. A look of lust flicked down to meet mine before I moved forward, my lips smashing against Carter's and tugging at his bottom lip as he let me in. I swallowed his moan and smiled against his mouth as his hips jerked and his cock twitched inside of me. A second later, Carter's release spilled out of him, filling my pussy as I milked him for everything he had.

For a long moment, the two of us remained just like that, our bodies still panting and shaking from what had just happened. When he finally let me go, my head turned to find Rowan and Dominic touching themselves to the sight of us, a whimper instantly falling from my mouth. I could feel Carter's come leaking out of me and dripping back down the length of his already hardening cock, the sensation causing me to clamp down around him. I couldn't move or even speak as all three of them looked at me with looks of ad-oration, but I did know right then and there that this is a day we'd never forget. I wanted this more than I've ever wanted anything else, and when both Rowan and Dominic reached out for me at the same time, I happily went to them. Somehow, I lasted three more times as they fucked, kissed, and held me until I was reduced to nothing more than a crying, sweaty mess. "I'm sorry," I managed to gasp as I came for the seventh time, but we all knew this was much more than just punishment. Though it did end with me screaming my safeword, today was all about us. That continued as they imme-diately stopped what they were previously doing, every part of me they'd been touching for my pleasure quickly being replaced with ones of aftercare. "I'm going to pick you up. Is that okay?" Carter asked, and with a nod of my head, he scooped up my shaking body and cradled me close to his chest. Dominic had left to the wash-room about two minutes ago, and when Carter led me inside, I was welcomed by the sight of a freshly drawn bubble bath and the faint scent of lilac filling the air. At first I hissed at the feeling of the hot water meeting the places the riding crop had hit, but then I relaxed completely into it, Carter stepping in with me. I sighed as he laid me back against his body, encouraging me to relax and allow him to do all of the work. I didn't protest a single moment of it, Dominic sitting beside the tub and rubbing my hand as he told me how good I did and how proud he was of me. Rowan soon returned with squares of chocolate, a fuzzy robe, and a bottle of vitamin water, all three meant for me. My tears at last began to stop, replacing all of my trembling and sensitivity with their proud smiles and gentle touches. "You're smiling." Carter said in my ear, kissing my cheek as I leaned deeper into his touch. I hadn't even noticed. "I'm happy." I respond, surprising myself a little. I'm happy. Those two simple words may seem like nothing, but they're everything I've lacked for far too long. I blushed at my admission because I knew Rowan, Dominic, and Carter understood. They understood me. "You wanna know a secret, darling?" Rowan asked, placing the chocolates on the counter before coming to kneel beside me. My eyes held onto his blue ones, my heart squeezing in my chest at his next words. "I think we're happy too."

~ Four ~

Hazel

I feel warm, both on the inside and the outside. After Carter cleaned every square inch of my body with the soap and water that felt like silk, Rowan dried me off with a heated towel before helping me into the fluffy grey-ish purple robe. Even though I was more than capable of doing things on my own, I think aftercare was one of my favourite parts about doing scenes. After going for so long where I had to do everything for myself, it was kind of nice being able to have others to care for you. Over the years, I've had multiple partners and one night stands, but while I've been undressed countless times, never once have I been redressed and cared for in the ways I am now. I'll admit today's scene took a lot out of me, but I loved every single moment of it, even when my head spun to the point of calling my safeword. And what they did afterwards— what they're doing now... it makes me feel warm. I ended up dressed in a pair of loose ripped jeans and a tan coloured hoodie that bagged on me. It was fleece lined and perfect for the weather considering that when Rowan, Dominic, and I walked downstairs, the many glass walls of their house were spotted with rain droplets, the sound of thunder echoing through the space. Letting go of Rowan's hand, I walked over to the glassed-in patio, looking up and watching as the water splashed and bounced off of the transparent roof. I never know why, but there's just something about thunderstorms that I always find calming. The dark sky painted with streaks of lightning is beautiful, and I soon find myself sitting down in the glass dome, staring upwards and letting myself relax. No one bothered me as I curled up on the patio couch, allowing my mind to clear and my thoughts to be consumed by the sound of every fallen raindrop. "Hey." Rowan greeted, drawing my attention to him. I had been so out of it, I hadn't even known he was here. "Hi." I smile, sitting up slightly so he can sit down beside me. "How are you feeling?" His voice sounds gentle as he speaks, moving my attention to the fact his hands were full. Rowan draped a weighted blanket over my body, as he offered a bowl of salted pretzels for us to share. "I feel... I'm a little tired I think." I feel a little out of it right now, but there isn't exactly anything wrong. I'm probably just drained.

"That's normal to feel." Rowan said, placing my legs over his thighs so I can spread out a little more, "How about emotionally? It's okay if things feel a little off." How did he know? I remain silent though because I really don't know how to describe how I'm feeling right now. I subconsciously see Rowan type something on his phone, but I'm more focused on the bowl of pretzels in front of me. Grabbing a handful and keeping them in the palm of my hand, I offer the bowl back to Rowan, but he declines with a small shake of his head. "Keep it." He smiles, "Dinner will be ready soon anyways." I nodded and returned his expression, my focus once again moving to the sound of rain falling around us. I sighed in contentment as I felt Rowan's hands rub up and down the sides of my legs, his touch making my head a little more clear. "Rowan?" I murmured, twisting to look at him ever so slightly. "Yeah?" He said, his blue eyes moving down to meet mine. "Did Dominic kick you out of the kitchen just now?" The grin that appeared on his face showed I was right. "Apparently I wasn't cutting the onion in the right direction." He grumbled, his eyes bright as he took in my smile, "Your company is much better anyways." Rowan added with a wink. "Yeah? Why's that?" I raised an eyebrow in amusement. "Well for one, your tits are nicer to look at, and two, you don't threaten to kick my ass every time I give them pointers." A surprised laugh left my mouth at that, nearly choking on the pretzel I was eating. "Do I even want to know what you give them pointers on?" I ask, sitting up slightly to see him easier. "No, you really don't." Dominic smiled, walking onto the patio with a hot cup of coffee in his hand. My mouth watered at the smell of it, silently praying it was for me. I all but threw myself upwards, gratefully accepting the mug from Dominic as it's offered to me. "Easy, you're going to burn your tongue." Rowan says as I don't waste a second before taking a large sip of the hot drink. "It's worth it if I can clear my headache sooner." I respond, sighing as the caffeine works its way into my system. "I thought you said you were feeling okay." Rowan says, shifting slightly and tugging a stray piece of hair behind my ear. "I am, the Advil just hasn't kicked in yet." I was surprised that I felt a little agitated when he was only checking in on me, but I tried to push it off to the side. "Whatever you're making smells great." I shift the focus to Dominic, inhaling a breath of a combination of flavours. "Carter's just prepping some final things in the kitchen. It's the chicken parmigiana you're smelling right now." My stomach quietly grumbled in interest, whatever I was feeling before promptly fading away entirely. "We'll thanks again for the coffee." I smile, taking another large sip, "I feel a little spoiled from how well you all treat me." "It's no big deal, but you're welcome." I just gave a small nod in response, lifting myself slightly to give Dominic a kiss on the cheek. I smiled as the slight layer of stubble on his face grazed my cheek before pulling back and doing the same to Rowan. His hair was still slightly damp from the shower he himself took not too long ago, and I had to brush away a small droplet of water as I moved back in my seat. I could hear the faint sound of Carter working away in the kitchen, but my eyes snapped to the small layer of pink that had formed on both men's cheeks. Oh my god, are they blushing?

I couldn't believe it, but when they tried to brush it off, it only made my smile grow larger. Who would've thought I could find these men... cute? Just as I moved to call them on their bullshit, Carter's voice came from the kitchen, announcing that dinner was ready and on the table. None of us seemed to be in the mood to wait, our hunger guiding us to the dining room in under thirty seconds. "Are you two blushing?" Carter asked, already seated at the table and pulling out a chair for me to sit on beside him. I couldn't stifle my small laugh as both Dominic and Rowan simultaneously told their friend to shut up. I just smiled as I sat down with Carter, the remaining two ending up right across from us with just as delicious plates of food steaming on a place mat. "I'm in love with whoever taught you both to cook." I said, instantly reaching out for the cutlery while eyeing the chicken breast in front of me. Rowan quietly hummed in agreement as Carter placed a napkin under his glass of water. "When I was a boy and my father was away for work, my mother used to sneak me into the kitchens every day after school to teach me new recipes." Carter shared, surprising me that he mentioned something about his childhood, "It started with simple things like brownies, but by the time I was thirteen I was a better cook than half the hired chefs in our household." I smiled at the image of Carter as a young boy, running around with food on his hands as he tried to prepare something new. "That's amazing." I say, as I cut into a piece of my chicken covered in tomato sauce and cheese, "Even as an adult I'm a lousy cook and an even worse baker." I wasn't surprised at all when hundreds of different flavours burst along my tongue as I raised my fork to my mouth, Carter proving just how skilled he was in the kitchen. "At least I'm not the only one," Rowan chuckled, the corners of his eyes crinkling in amusement, "I can't even imagine how disastrous it would be if you put my ten year old self anywhere near a stove." This conversation is making me realize just how little I truly know about these men, but I like getting to learn these little parts of them growing up. I just know Dominic probably outsmarted everyone in school, Rowan likely got into a lot of trouble but could always charm his way out of it, though Carter, I really don't know what to think about him. "I know we've never really spoken about it before, but is family discussion off limits or...?" It doesn't even have to be family, but I feel like I know everything and nothing about them. "You're always welcome to ask us anything, princess," Dominic answers, giving me a small smile, "We might not always have an answer, but how about you tell us what's on your mind as a start." I knew I would likely have to offer things in return, but unlike most people in my life, I surprisingly felt comfortable with the idea of sharing personal parts of me with my men. "I just figured that since things are feeling a little more serious, it would make sense to know more other than the fact that you're all successful, fairly stubborn men with a soft spot for dark chocolate." I grinned and took another bite as they all looked at me. "How'd you know about the chocolate?" Carter asked, poking my side under the table teasingly. "Because every time you bring some for me after a scene, I find all of you taking a piece as well and moaning as if it's the best thing you've ever tasted." I giggle at their horribly strewn denial. "We do not." Rowan says in mock offense, cutting into his chicken, "I think we all know that only one taste has us moaning and it sure as hell isn't chocolate." It didn't take me long at all before I flushed at his innuendo, though I suppose I did kind of set him up for it. For once, I couldn't think of any quip remarks so I decided to redirect back to my original thoughts. "Well what else do you like?" I ask, "I'm sure you have hobbies." There's a small pause before Rowan says, "Well when I'm not working, or hanging out with anyone, I like to read." I never thought about it until now, but I have seen Rowan around with books multiple times already, and yes, ones other than "How to Get Away with Murder" like when I first slept here.

God, that feels like forever ago when in reality it's been less than a month. "And what about you two?" I ask Dominic and Carter, "That is other than your shared talent of cooking of course." Learning these small things was only the tip of getting to know them, but while they have all spent years together already, I'm trying to learn about three relationships all at once. "I like my bikes," Carter answered with a small smile that made it seem like some sort of inside joke for him. I can't help but think of our first kiss that happened against that motorcycle. I still get butterflies thinking about that day. "I built the Harley I took you on too." He adds, surprising me, "Though growing up, I spent the majority of my time doing weapons training and other things like it." Flicking my gaze down to his calloused, scar painted hands, I didn't find myself surprised in the least. "Dare I ask what your preferred poison is?" I question, thinking back to my childhood and those endless nights my father and I would spend in that abandoned shed down the road. I still remember every moment that we practiced until my knees would wobble and no amount of will could keep my eyes open. A small pang in my heart appeared at the reminder of how much I missed him, but I shoved it down and told myself that it was okay to let myself be a little happy. "While I find guns the easiest to make use of, I remember how much I liked screwing around with swords for a while." "Screwing around?" Dominic let out a puff of air, "I remember the first time you had a sword around me, you knocked me on my ass before I could even retaliate." As if forgetting I was there, Dominic's gaze suddenly shifted to me as if they were all now holding their breaths. They didn't really think I thought they were untrained, did they? I could tell the second I met them, even as masked figures, they carried themselves in a way that showed they were more than capable of holding their own. Knowing the pause in the air was due to my presence, I decided to break it. "Daggers." I said, taking one last bite of my food before growing a slight smirk at their silence, "A dagger was the first weapon I learned to use, and after that, I never found something quite as enjoyable to wield." The remaining food on our plates has now gone long cold, though the glass in my hand has been refilled about three times now with a sweet sparkling drink I can't remember the name of. I don't quite remember when we made our way over to the living room, but I was now happily situated between Rowan's legs on the couch, my own draped over Carter's thighs. Dominic chose to sit on the floor right beside me, even though there was more than enough room on the couch beside both men on my sides. For such hard muscle, I was surprisingly quite comfortable and content being held against their bodies. Our conversation from dinner continued on until even now. As one question appeared, three more sprouted in their wake, ones coming from all four of us in interest and curiosity. While I had my suspicions, it turns out Rowan indeed grew up on the streets fending for himself. He surprisingly came from a rich family of five, though when he was sixteen, Rowan left and never came back. What shocked me more was that no one ever looked for him. I can't imagine how anyone could be so blind to allow someone as easy-going and amazing as Rowan Harris to just leave, but I was both sad and even more angry for the man who deserved so much better. He said it wasn't all bad though. Apparently a good part about being a nobody is that he managed to sneak in everywhere as a teenager, knowing that if he got caught he could just run and relocate once again. I still didn't view it as a good part, but I also wasn't in any position to judge or decide what was good or bad for him at the time. Some of our conversations were sadder, but a lot were happy and amusing as well. It turns out Dominic has a little sister named Nina, Carter's first tattoo— now removed— was of Pac-Man, and Rowan got his left ear pierced at seventeen by a friend. I had turned around when he told me that, and I surprisingly could still see a small scar on his ear where his idiot friend not so expertly poked the hole. I, of course, shared some things about me too, and it was almost overwhelming how intently all three men listened to me as I spoke. It's kind of a sad thing to be surprised about, but these last two hours felt like one of the very few times where I felt genuinely heard. I told them briefly about my family, skipping over the parts about the alcoholism and countless other things that still give me nightmares. I did however share that I could play the piano— loved to even. Though it's been multiple years since I've even been near one, I somehow ended up agreeing to play for them sometime despite none of us actually owning one.

It felt like I couldn't learn, or share enough, myself admitting things that I've never uttered to another soul. I guess things just felt easy with them. As much as I tried to fight it, I felt myself yawn for the sixth time in the last few minutes, my lack of sleep and over-exertion seeming to catch up to me. "Hey Hazel?" Rowan says in my ear, planting a small kiss to my cheek right afterwards. "Mm?" I hum tiredly before lazily lifting my glass up to my lips again. "As much as I'm loving our discussion, I think we should probably call it a night pretty soon." I hated that he was right. "Yeah." I agreed, but made no move to get off of him, my eyes flicking up to Carter and offering him a lazy smile, one in which he returned. I felt Rowan hug his arms around me just a little tighter at my lack of movement, as if he too was perfectly content with how cuddled up we are now. If Dominic found the pillow on the floor he was seated on uncomfortable, he didn't show it. "Are you still feeling good?" Dominic asks, bringing my eyes down to him. "I feel normal." I answer for the third time tonight. It wasn't unusual for them to check in on me after a scene, but they seemed to be coddling me more than typical tonight. "Why do you all keep asking?" I say, no bite in my tone, just genuine curiosity. "It's just that earlier on the patio, we think you were experiencing some minor signs of a subdrop." Rowan answers for him, keeping his tone soft and honest as he speaks. "I was?" I didn't bother to keep the surprise out of my voice in my response. I got a nod from Carter when my eyes fell on him. "The coffee, Advil, and small touches like this were all meant to help with it." He said, drawing my attention to the gentle drag of his hand up and down my calf. Carter had been doing that for the last hour since we sat here, just as Dominic did with my hand, and Rowan did as he held me. "Don't get us wrong, we'd probably still do this whether or not things seemed a little off, but it never hurts as a precaution." Dominic says, smiling up at me. I hadn't even realized, but based on what I already know about subdrop, my uncalled for irritation earlier would make sense. "I think I'm fine now." I say, not feeling any indifference with anything. "You seem fine to me as well." Rowan says in agreement, "But if you do begin to feel even the slightest bit off again tonight or even tomorrow, it's important you tell us. It's nothing to be scared or ashamed of, but we want to be able to help you whether it's as minor as a small headache or as big as breaking down." Taking in this information, I find myself promising to tell them. I was extremely appreciative that I now felt a little more aware with why I felt so off earlier, but mostly, I was just appreciative to have them. For the most part that was the end of our conversation and I was soon able to let my mind drift off to sleep as Rowan scooped me into his arms and carried me up to the playroom's bed now adorned with fresh sheets and blankets. When my eyes fluttered open hours later in bed, the first thing I noticed was that I was encased in a heavy sheet of darkness. The soft material of my hoodie wrapped around me just as much as the two men on either side of my body.

At some point one of them must have taken my jeans off for me, but I couldn't be more thankful now as my legs intertwine with theirs. I have absolutely no clue what time it is, but I know it must either be really late or really early considering how low the lighting was in here. I sighed into Rowan and Dominic's warm bodies, feeling every soft rise and fall of their chests as if it were my own. Currently facing Rowan, I couldn't help but smile to myself at the outline of the messy blond strands of his hair tangling and falling in uneven waves across the edges of his forehead. He looked so much younger in this state, and I was willing to bet I would see the same calmness in Dominic's features if I were able to flip over. Though, as happy as I was to stay here, Carter's absence hung over me and weighed me down as much as it encouraged me to get up. I wasn't sure how he'd react if I asked why he never stays to sleep with me, but I haven't quite worked up the courage to say that question yet. If I at least knew he was okay and in his room, I feel like it would help, but memories of the shattered glass and vulnerability of last time allowed me no rest as my mind began to whorl. Like last time, after a few minutes I managed to unweave myself of the tangle of limbs holding me, though thankfully I was more clothed as I took near silent footsteps over to the door. I felt the brush of my hoodie against my mid-thigh as I walked, making sure to leave the door open behind me so the noise of the padlock wouldn't wake the two men still in bed. I instantly noticed the shut door to Carter's bedroom down the hall, and I let out a relieved breath when I was greeted by nothing but silence. He was okay. I try not to let myself think about how much I clearly care about him to the extent that I feel the need to check in, but I can't help but admit that my feelings for all three of them continue to grow with every passing second. Whether I'm with them or not, I think about Rowan's teasing comments, Dominic's random displays of affection, and the little things Carter portrays in actions when words seem to fail him. I think I like them a lot more than I'm ready to admit, but for now, I just want to enjoy things as they are. Thoughts of turning back to the playroom cross my mind, but now that I know Carter's okay, I'm becoming increasingly aware of how parched my throat is, likely from all of the screaming I did earlier under their touch. Once again, I find myself smiling at the memory, biting my cheek slightly as I do so. Thankfully, the kitchen wasn't hard to find at all, even in the dark. I didn't hear a single stair creek beneath my foot in the oddly echoey house as I moved down to the first floor and over past the counter tops. Truthfully, I hadn't a clue where they kept their glasses, and it took me multiple attempts at opening cabinets before coming across one filled with an assortment of different sizes. Grabbing the one closest to my reach, I quietly closed the wooden door behind me as I walked over to their fridge. I held the glass under the dispenser, watching as a small blue light came on overtop to show just how full the cup was. When I was satisfied, I pulled it away and instantly lifted the water to my lips, grateful for the cool path it brought as it slipped past my throat. Before I knew it, I brought the glass back to the dispenser, but this time, my hand shook and things began to feel off.

Switches to third person POV

Hazel jumped back startled as her hand pulled away from the fridge. She couldn't understand why her chest now ached and even the smallest of things became overwhelming, but she barely even registered the loud smash that woke the three men upstairs. Hazel blinked, the glass of water once in her hand now nothing more than shattered shards scattered and soaked across the hard floor. Was it always this cold? Hazel couldn't seem to remember how she ended up on the floor, but when Rowan was surprisingly the first downstairs, his heart raced as he noticed every detail of the sight before him. Dominic and Carter followed almost instantly behind him, but all Rowan could think about was the sight of his lover on the ground, her knees hugged tight to her chest as her eyes stared forward with a glossy, distant look in them. "Hazel?" Rowan said with a soft voice, trying to not reveal the concern and fear he'd felt when he'd heard her cup smash. He didn't waste a second before rushing to the floor beside and pulling her into his lap, brushing away the hair that had stuck to her face from sweat. Rowan's heart tightened as Hazel jumped slightly from his touch, and it was an action that both his best friends also noticed as they too kneeled on the wet, glass covered tile. They would happily take a few cuts if they could ease away the obvious symptoms of subdrop Hazel was clearly experiencing. "Hey, you're okay." Dominic said, taking Hazel's hand into his lap despite her lack of reaction, "You're safe, I promise." Hazel was highly aware of Carter's every touch as he gently ran his fingers through her hair, but despite his gentleness, Rowan's tight hold grounding her, and Dominic's calming words, she couldn't stop the sudden waves of emotion that passed over her again and again. Carter hated that Hazel was so overwhelmed she'd collapsed to the floor, and this too was his first time ever aiding someone out of a drop. All three men just wished that they could kiss away every inch of their girl's distress, but when Dominic touched her hand again, Hazel this time didn't jump, but instead turned her head to face him. Her eyes were still glossy, and she wore a blank expression across her face, but this time as she blinked, tears came out with it. Hazel felt as if she were in a dreamlike state as many more followed, though she couldn't pin what was making her feel this way. She wasn't in any danger, and she couldn't coherently think of any reason as to why she needed to cry, but that didn't stop the hot tears from dripping down her now pink cheeks. "Can you tell us how you're feeling, sweetheart? Carter asked, still combing his fingers through Hazel's hair and helping to keep her head upright. Tears continued to fall at his question, though Hazel only shook her head no as she reached up to Dominic's face. Her small fingertips curiously brushed against his short stubble of facial hair, finding the texture and smell of the three men near her oddly comforting. After that, Hazel showed no sign of hearing the question, as if lost in her own personal bubble. The men's hearts were still racing as they tried to help their girl in every way they could, urging their initial worries that someone had broken in to go away. "What's going on in your head, princess?" Dominic's mouth dropped down and planted a single kiss along Hazel's wrist when it was brought close enough before pulling her hand away and taking it gently into his hold. "I don't know," Hazel's voice was no more than a whisper as she spoke. She didn't know why she was crying, but it felt so easy to just let it all out. "Rowan?" She says, turning her head to look at him through blurry vision. "Mhm? You're okay." He says, taking her hand from Dominic and placing her palm on his chest, his hand remaining on top of hers and allowing her to feel his heart- beat. "I-I... I just don't know." Hazel stuttered, understanding she's having a subdrop but not knowing how to get out of it. "It's okay, just breathe with me, alright?" Rowan says, "We can calm down together." Hazel only nods in response, noticing every small touch Carter and Dominic are doing.

"Inhale," Rowan said, encouraging the person in his lap to do the same as they both breathed in, "Exhale." All three men do every- thing they can as they try to calm her uneven breathing patterns. Dominic begins to rub comforting circles on Hazel's back, while she tries to focus on their low voices. Trying to regain control over herself, Hazel redirects her mind into the feeling of Rowan's heart- beat beneath the palm of her hand. While the intense emotions and slight dizziness continues, after multiple minutes, Hazel feels her breathing begin to slow. She can't stop the tears, but she at least feels as though oxygen is actually getting to her brain now with every inhale. "That's good, you're doing so good." Carter praised, kissing the back of her head as he felt her breaths steady out a little more, "It's okay to cry if you need to let it all out. I promise we won't leave you." The soothing tone in his voice gave Hazel the permission she felt she needed to just give in and trust that they can handle it. Every single confusing emotion pulsing through her bones was pushed out, dissolving away until she began to feel a little more like herself. And her men, they held her through every single second of it, never letting her feel alone, or abandoned or uncared for. Hazel was able to focus on that until those previous overwhelming convulsions were replaced with the heavy weight of exhaustion. "I'm sorry." She mumbled, still feeling a little dizzy, "I d-don't even know why that happened. I thought I was fine, but... oh god the floor." Hazel became frantic in a whole other way, panicking about the shattered glass and the mess she made. "I'm sor—" "Hazel, it's okay. You have nothing to apologize for at all." Dominic insisted, his hand reaching up to cup the side of her face and encouraging her to look at him. Through teary eyes, she did. Rowan let Hazel go, transferring her into Dominic's lap as his friend held her face in his hands. "I know this is a little scary and that you don't know how to handle it, but I promise we've got you. We're not going anywhere." Hazel didn't know what it was he said, she soon found herself easing down once again. At his words, all three men felt a sharp pang of relief inside of them when a small smile appeared on their girl's face. A very very small laugh followed as Dominic continued to rock her back and forth a little. "That's it." Rowan encouraged, holding her hand as he could both physically and emotionally feel as Hazel began to steady. Dominic moved his hands and guided her head to rest on his shoulder, both of his arms wrapping around her and hoping to take away the slight tremble that remained in her body. That's what all three men did for as long as it took. Sitting on a ground shattered with glass, the last emotion that passed through Hazel's head felt a lot like that one word she wasn't ready to face yet.

I can't deny that I felt like absolute shit when I woke up. My eyes are sore from the endless stream of tears they cried, and my head pounded against my skull as I regained consciousness. On the soft mattress of a bed and cradled between two bodies, I was honestly surprised to find an awake Carter on his side, facing me and running his fingers through the strands of my hair. He doesn't say anything for a moment when our eyes connect, but then he murmurs a single word. "Hey." Carter whispered, a small smile appearing on his face as his eyes trailed over mine as if to make sure I was alright. This morning I was, but last night was something I hopefully won't have to relive. I can understand the science and logic behind subspace, but experiencing it was an entirely other thing. What I didn't expect, however, was how good I would feel the next morning. It could of course just be a coincidence, or maybe just the fact that Carter was laying here as well, but things just felt right. "Hi." I smile back, nuzzling slightly closer to Carter's bare chest. Rowan and Dominic were both on my other side, but I could tell they were still asleep based on the steady patterns of their breathing. "Are you okay?" Carter asks, his thumb grazing the side of my cheek in thought. "Back to normal I think." I respond, leaning in and placing a small kiss to his chiseled jaw, "Thank you for how good you were last night, Carter." His eyes searched mine as if he were looking for something, but with a swallow, he simply nodded. "Always, right?" He flashed a true smile that made my stomach flutter and my heart squeeze. Instead of repeating that word in agreement, I leaned in and kissed him both soft and hard all at once. I used my touch to say the things even words couldn't express properly for me and when I eventually pulled back, I knew Carter understood. "You're awake?" Rowan's voice pulled my attention to him as he pressed me closer to his body. "Morning." I said softly, noticing how Dominic also began to stir in bed, all of us slowly waking up together. "How are you feeling?" Rowan asked, causing me to smile at how many times I've been asked that and how caring they are of me. "I'm really good." I say, answering Rowan knowing that Dominic is also intently listening, "Though... I am kind of starving if I'm being honest." As if on cue, my stomach let out a low growl to prove my point, despite the massive dinner I had seconds of last night. "That's to be expected." Dominic said, sitting up enough that my eyes were able to catch a glimpse of dark brown curls in a perfect mess atop his head. A boyish grin appeared on his face as I turned slightly to look at him, my eyes also dropping to the tattooed designs inked across his chest and further onto his arms. I looked at Rowan next, seeing as he was watching me with an amused look on his face. Before I felt a lot more shy with them, but they were mine just as much as I was theirs. Only an idiot would pass up the opportunity to take in the three men with me, and I'm very clearly taking advantage of my girlfriend status. "You better watch yourself, sweetheart." Carter murmured in my ear, his breath tickling my neck, "Keep looking at us like that and your roommate won't be seeing much of you for yet another day." Jade had only teased me when I told her I was staying here for yet another night, though I'll admit I do miss her and needed to go home sooner rather than later. "Or you could bring me downstairs so I can actually get some food into me." I answered, forcing down my butterflies, "Not everyone are super humans like you who seem to have unwavering stamina." "I didn't hear you complaining about our stamina much a few nights ago." Rowan teased, causing me to sit up before I very well just choose to stay here in bed all day with them.

"What? You're meaning to say you're choosing food over our irreplaceable company?" Dominic smiled in mock offense, swinging his legs over the bed and making a move to crawl where my feet are. Moving over Carter before Dominic even had the chance, I tilt my head as I say, "Yes," in a deadpan tone. He looks like he wants to pounce on me right now, but Rowan is moving too, placing a hand on my lower back and guiding me to the door. "I'm hungry as well." Is all he says as he winks, wrapping his arm around me until the fabric of my hoodie bunches in his hand. Despite the warmth of my top and tight shorts, Rowan's touch sends a tingle down my spine as Carter and Dominic both move in beside us. I hear the soft click of the door close behind just as we begin our descent down the large staircase to the first floor. I shiver the second my bare feet touch the cold hardwood beneath me, but the sound of the elevator dinging causes that thought to fade away as all four of our gazes move to the metal doors now sliding open. Before I even had time to blink, Rowan moved me behind him, his hand tightening around my waist at the sight of four armed men stepping out of the elevator, bags in tow. The one who stepped forward first looked insanely like an older version of Carter, only this man was dressed from head to toe in dark red, his dark hair shaved close to his head. "Ah, you must be Hazel," The man says, stepping into the house as authority dripped off of his presence alone, "It's so nice to finally meet the woman my son has told me so much about."

~ Five ~

Dominic

Vincent MacGuire is currently standing in my living room, no less than four meters away from the one person I hoped he'd never get to meet. Hazel was the first thought on his mind at the sight of Carter's father, but the next one was how Vincent even knew of her in the first place.

My friend is the obvious right answer, but no matter how smart and calculative I consider myself to be, I'm drawing up no conclusions considering Carter himself never wanted Hazel to be known.

"It's nice to meet you too," Our girl politely responds, though there is obvious question in her eyes as she glances first at Carter, then Rowan, then me. Hazel tries to step to stand at our side, but narrows her eyes in confusion when both Rowan and I gently stop her.

"I didn't know you were coming." Carter was the first to speak, tension clear in his voice as he spoke. Vincent only frowned as he gestured for his men to move off to the side slightly.

"You didn't really think I'd miss my only child's thirty-fourth birthday, now did you?" Carter's father rhetorically asked, tilting his head to the side slightly to get a better look at Hazel.

The smugness radiating off of him made me murderous, and I know I was not the only person who shared that exact same feeling.

"Your birthday's today?" Hazel asks in surprise, turning to Carter and pushing past until she stood by our side. Unfortunately, the damage has very much already been done. Vincent knows, and Carter spoke to him about her. I can see as some of the hardness from Carter's expression softened when he met Hazel's gaze, but what he didn't realize was that his father also noticed.

"It's tomorrow." He simply says, before that layer returned before his eyes, "You need to leave." Carter insists, though he was only met with a mere shrug off from Vincent.

"I'll stay for dinner." His father says, not allowing any room for argument, "We have many things of importance to discuss, thought it seems as though you do as well." Yes, Vincent knew everything.

"Not here, you don't." I cut in, raising my chin ever so slightly and forcing to appear relaxed as one grey eyebrow lifts on the man's face. I can feel how barely contained Carter's anger is, and Rowan can't speak out unless spoken to. While Carter and I are both heirs to the crime families that compose of the Italian-American Mafia, Rowan is merely an associate, not a single drop of Italian blood in his bones.

His friendship to us means nothing to Vincent, and we all know that if my friend even dared to speak in discordance, he'd been dead quicker than one could blink.

"Nice to see you again in person, Dominic." Carter's father greets me, my tone with him earlier showing no effect on him whatsoever, "The last time I saw you was what? Right before your engagement I believe." That was a low blow, yet the entire time,

Vincent maintained a controlled, neutral expression. I wanted to punch his face in.

"What's with the cold welcoming?" Vincent questioned, seeming to grow annoyed by our frozen positions at the bottom of the stairs still.

"You have nothing to say? It's not like your little pet doesn't know everything already, so I don't understand this awkward silence." I think I feel a piece of me break from his words, physically feeling Hazel stiffen from beside me at Vincent's words. We all do.

"She's not our pet, nor is Hazel a kept woman." Carter says, shaking slightly from the anger we all share.

The only difference is that when Rowan and I's eyes meet before turning down to Hazel, our hatred is partially towards our best friend as well. Yet another mistake we made in the last five minutes was our silence. I watch as Vincent's face goes from one of confusion to one of pure and utter amusement.

"Cazzo, lei non lo sa?" He laughed out loud, swearing in Italian as he seems to find this comical to him. While neither Hazel nor Rowan could understand what he said, Carter and I most certainly did. Fuck, she doesn't know, was what Vincent said, his voice creating a slight echo in the otherwise silent house. It wasn't supposed to happen like this.

"This trip is going to be even better than I thought." Vincent smiled, looking at Hazel the entire time in a way I couldn't figure out. Intrigue? "Send my bags to the largest guest room on the third floor and then you're dismissed." Carter's father said to the three men with his bags, though I know practically none of them are filled with clothes. "Yes, Don." They all bow their heads before moving back into the elevator. I knew that those two words alone was the bomb that just caused everything to explode. Hazel physically flinched at the name, her head snapping to Carter and staying there. I could tell she knew where the name "Don" came from, and right now I can see betrayment and confusion on Hazel's features. I tried to brush the side of her arm, but she pulled away.

She pulled away.

"Hazel, it really was a pleasure meeting you.

Though I'm sure you won't, you're more than welcome to join us for dinner tonight at seven. I've already hired someone myself to make dinner here and I assure you won't be disappointed." Silence rang through the space, but with a nod from Hazel, Vincent grinned from ear to ear.

The next second, he walked into the house as if he owned the place, brushing right past us and walking down the hall where our library, gym, and entertainment room is.

With him gone, I could tell Hazel was slowly breaking apart, us doing the same because of it. I could see the gears spinning in her head right now, but what was worse was that she wouldn't even look at us.

She was pushing us away.

With a shaky inhale through her nose, Hazel didn't say a word as she walked over to the elevator, pressing a button and waiting until the doors opened a couple of seconds later.

We all watched with pained eyes as she walked onto the platform, but then, she held her hand out. Hazel held the door open and stepped to the side, a silent indication to join her.

Swallowing, we did. Vincent seemed to have somehow gotten past our codes to gain access, so all Hazel had to do was press the button that would take us to the parking garage.

In previous times being in an elevator with us, Hazel was happily distracted by at least one of us, a conscious effort we made because of her claustrophobia.

This time, even if we tried, Hazel wouldn't let us give her small touches or talk about things that embarrassed her but proved as effective in distracting.

I watched as Hazel bit the inside of her cheek, shifted her weight between feet and began to pick at her thumbnail unconsciously. I wanted to reach for her.

Hug her and tell her she didn't have to be afraid and that we would do anything we could to fix this. Anything. I felt as though we were all holding.

We let Hazel lead, but we barely got out of the elevator before she spun to face us, taking a few steps back to create some clear distance between our bodies.

"You're in the fucking mafia?" Everything around us stopped as those five words fell from her mouth. Her voice was so low it was nearly a whisper, but it rang painfully loud in my head.

I knew this conversation would come eventually. I knew it the second I realized I would never let her go, but she didn't deserve to be caught off guard and told like that. We were supposed to have time.

Our silence answered her question, and with that, Hazel drew in a trembling breath, her arms wrapping around her body as if she needed to be held.

"Give us a chance to explain." Rowan's words bordered as a plead as he spoke, "Come back inside... we'll answer whatever it is you want to know, and we can talk." What he was really saying was don't leave us. Hazel's head dropped slightly, shaking it as she tried to make sense of this all.

"I want to go." She said, still not looking any of us in the eyes. It broke my heart. We couldn't let her do that, but we would never be able to forcefully keep her here either. "Talk to us." Carter said, not bothering to hide the desperation in his voice, "Please... don't leave. We can—"

No." Hazel's single word cut through the air, her head finally looking up, not to me, but to Rowan. Her eyes glistened with unsplit tears, but she refused to let a single one fall.

"I'm going home, and you have no right to keep me here." She was scared of us. The realization hit me so hard my left foot took a step back, hating myself for being the cause of this all. Hazel's been through enough and she never should have to feel scared or sad ever again.

"Stay." Rowan's voice broke, but in that moment, I knew we lost and nothing apart from sheer force could keep her here. "Give me the keys to any car here." Hazel said to Rowan, not even responding to his plea.

"Hazel, I—"

"You owe me that debt from the club." Her hand shook as she spoke, but something on her features had hardened.

"I won the bet about Carter, and you said that you would do any one thing I asked of you at any time." Rowan looked like he'd been physically slapped by her words, but he didn't fight what she was asking of him. We had no right to fight with her or yell or demand to be listened to.

Hazel doesn't owe us a single thing, but we owe her the world.

Once again, she's no longer looking at us, and even when Rowan walks away to retrieve a set of keys from the rings on the side of the elevator, her eyes remain down.

The entire time, I just stay silent, wishing with everything I have her eyes would meet mine, but they never do.

Carter and I simply watch in silence as Rowan walks up to Hazel, looking at her even if she doesn't do the same. While Rowan now has a set of keys, when he gets to her he grabs both of her shaking hands, clasping them in his. His thumb brushes against the top of her fingers, willing them to steady and wanting to take away every unhappy emotion going through her. Only when her shaking stops does Rowan flip her hand over, studying her palm before placing the keys into her hold.

That single action seems to flip a switch in Hazel, her instantly taking a step back before lifting her head.

She makes a point of looking each of us over individually, starting and ending with our eyes. While Rowan stopped her shaking, it was herself that willed the distant look in her gaze come to life.

It was one that kept me from breathing. Hazel never said goodbye as she pivoted on her heel, pressing the button on the keys in her hands and allowing that to indicate where the car was. I didn't breathe, move, or even blink as my girl—our girl—walked into one of our easier to drive vehicles, backing out and waiting as Rowan reluctantly entered in a code that had the garage door opening. No one dared speak as she left, a part of us all breaking along with the disappearing sight of the car. Only once she was gone and the door closed once again did I allow myself to think.

Only I didn't. Instead, my only thought was on Carter and the way my fist was now hurtling towards his face. The familiar pain of the impact shocked across my knuckles, but I paid no attention to it as my friend didn't even fight back. Rowan ran over from the garage door to stop me, but he didn't have to.

While I was partially responsible for Hazel's now noticeable absence, Carter told his father about her. While this past week I tried to get him to open up by showing support, I was done with that. Grabbing Carter by his shoulders, I watched as he wiped away the trickle of his blood smeared across his bottom lip before looking at me with watery eyes. It wasn't from the pain of his mouth, though.

He knew what I was asking.

He knew that Rowan was just as angry and insistent to know as I was, but Carter stayed quiet as his muscles shook. I knew my friend well enough to know he needed to either punch or kill somebody right now, but I've been too nice for too long. "Why?" Is the only word I was able to force through the raging shield of my anger, though his answer was something I never wanted to hear. Something I never wanted to believe.

"Hazel's father is Marcus Caddel."

~ Six ~

Carter

The truth is out, and now I must face the consequences of my actions.

I deserve everything I'm getting, but I was well aware of the repercussions that came along with my choices. I will never apologize for them, though.

My lies are the only reason my Hazel is breathing right now, even if she's using her breaths to run as far away from me as possible.

The emotion in my friends' eyes looks as though they wish to do the same, but I know they won't. I hold the answers to all of this, but at the same time, I don't know a god damned thing.

"What?" Rowan flinched, taking a step back from me.

I didn't repeat myself because I knew he'd heard me just fine, and they were words I didn't wish to say again. None of us wanted to accept the fact that the man who killed my mother and threatened to take everything away from us was the same person who raised our girl, but it was the harsh reality.

Is she still ours, though? It was a thought I couldn't bear, so I simply refused to think about it. I could feel my lip throb from the split cutting through the bottom, but I knew I earned it.

As I looked into the eyes of my two best friends, the second blow, this time from Rowan, displayed anger, but I knew on the inside they were mostly scared and confused.

Scared seems to be the only thing I'm capable of feeling right now, and it's a feeling that makes it hard to breathe. I barely even winced as Rowan's fist connected with my stomach, but I took it.

When I forced myself to stop being a coward, I looked up to see the tears in their eyes matching mine, but we never let them fall.

For a moment, all we did was stand there, taking in the harsh truth none of us wanted to accept. It was silent, but the words in their questioning eyes said everything.

"On the night we signed the contract with Hazel, I got a phone call." I started. My heart pounded against my chest as if trying to break free to avoid the truth that was about to come out.

But I couldn't.

"I waited for her to fall asleep before leaving back to my room to take care of some things." I swallowed nervously, but forced myself to continue, "About an hour later, I received a phone call from Vincent saying that he'd found Marcus' weakness." It was the idea we ourselves pitched to him the same day we met Hazel.

I didn't have to say what that weakness was, because it was the same one all three of us now shared.

"Vincent told me that he would send some of our men out the next morning to retrieve the girl, unaware that she was already in our bed." I saw the confusion and pain in their eyes as I spoke, but the words spilling out of my mouth wouldn't stop now that they'd started.

"I was given the order to have her drugged, kidnapped, and held hostage back at the base until we could"

"A ransom." Dominic interrupted with an angry whisper, his fists clenching at his sides as the pieces began to connect with one another.

That was always my role after all.

I was the hunter, and I had been told after one of the best moments of my life that everything I loathed in this world was the father of my girlfriend.

"I did what I had to do to keep her safe... I pitched Vincent a new idea." I forced my need to hit something down as that familiar darkness began to bubble deep down inside of me.

"He wanted us to torture and slowly kill Hazel over a one month period; the month we had off. Vincent told us to strip every one of her emotions bare and video tape it so we could send it to Marcus as leverage." Just the thought of doing that made me feel sick, and nauseous, and entirely lethal.

"He believed Marcus' love for his daughter would be enough to trade his life for hers, with the ultimate plan to just kill them both in the end. I couldn't let that happen, so I created a lie that would only feed into my new proposition." Maybe it made me a coward, but my gaze averted to the line of cars behind Rowan and Dominic, not being able to look them in the eyes at my next words.

"I told him I'd make her fall in love with me." I felt like all of the air was punched from my lungs, despite the fact I hadn't been hit.

"I convinced Vincent that Marcus didn't care for his daughter and merely viewed her as a liability along with Hazel's mom his ex-wife. I told him Marcus left his child with her alcoholic mother, abusive stepfather, and the deadbeat town in Detroit she grew up in.

You see, Vincent believed love would drive Marcus into our hands, but I had to weave a new story." I went to breathe before I spoke again, but Rowan, for the first time in minutes, cut in.

"Hazel was abused?" My friend's voice cracked as he said those three words, my own confirming what we all feared since we first met her.

While Rowan could have more than easily pulled up Hazel's hospital records, he was better than to ever invade her privacy like that.

"Her records are filled with monthly hospital visits and the odd call from schools, but nothing ever came from it. Not in a shitty place like that." There was a lot of information Vincent shared with me that night that led to me trashing everything in sight, but the news of her stepfather pained and angered me more than I've ever felt.

I promised myself that night that no matter where our relationship went, Hazel's stepfather would die by my hands and I would spend weeks dragging him to death's doorstep just to yank him back and do it all over again.

"What caused Vincent to change his plans?" Dominic asked, not commenting on this new information. I knew this wouldn't be the last of this discussion, but there were so many conversations to be had and such little time to have them. "Once he agreed the love that wasn't there wouldn't be enough to lure Marcus out of hiding, I convinced him that while Marcus did not care for his daughter, he did for his image." I had no doubt Marcus cared for his daughter with everything he had sometimes it was the villains of the story who loved the deepest.

However, I still used what was most believable to my advantage. Given my father's bone deep hatred for Marcus, it wasn't hard for me to paint the picture of a man who'd abandon his child, only keeping in contact with her because she was his only heir.

I told Dominic and Rowan just this. "You intentionally had our picture taken with her?" Dominic was picking up quickly, putting together this puzzle out loud.

"I knew Hazel barely ever looked at the news or tabloids, but yes, I made it very clear to the world who she was with in hopes of it spreading to Marcus." I have countless people hired to steer the paparazzi far far away from anywhere we ever went, so I simply extended that to Hazel too.

"I took a selfie of me kissing her on the cheek about a week ago and leaked it on social media. I'm sure you've seen the countless articles and interview requests popping up about us." The slight nod of their heads confirmed they saw, but only now understood.

"I knew I had to make news of our relationship spread quick, and relied on the fact that once word got to Marcus and his people that his daughter was dating the very man they stood against, his entire operation would crumble from the inside unless"

"Unless Marcus came for Hazel himself and convinced her to join him." Rowan finished the words I was just about to say. "None of his followers would have faith in a leader whose own daughter chose to be with their enemies over him." Dominic said, mumbling a curse afterwards.

That was it. That was the truth to the lie I can't seem to find a way out of.

"It's only supposed to be a temporary plan until I can figure out a permanent way to keep Hazel out of harm's way, but it worked." Vincent agreed that was the perfect plan to take Marcus down, and for the first time in my life, he said he was proud of me.

I didn't tell Dominic or Rowan about how I destroyed my room after I hung up, or how Hazel was the only thing that kept me from teetering over a very dangerous edge that night.

All I could do was hold my breath as all of our words hung in the air, as well as the fact that we were missing the fourth person that made us feel complete.

God, just thinking about Hazel hurts. I don't know how we're going to get her back or repair every bit of trust that was broken at my hands, but I would give everything I had to do it. She was it for me. "Fuck, Carter." Rowan said, running his fingers tensely through his hair before grabbing it in frustration. I know. When he took a step to me, I prepared myself for another hit, but all I received was his arms wrapping around me tightly. While I would have let both him and Dominic beat me until I grew unconscious, he hugged me instead, Dominic doing the same. "We're in so much shit." He murmured, and I couldn't help but agree.

"I don't know what to do." I say, pulling back and looking at the vacant spot of the car Hazel took. I turned my head back to my friends, both shooting me a tired, yet relentless expression that said all I needed to know. "I'll grab the keys." We were going to get our girl back.

Hazel

The mafia. My boyfriends are in the fucking mafia, and I didn't know.

Ever since I really began to grow comfortable with them, I had joked around and called it their side business, but I don't think I could've been more wrong.

I'm no stranger to weapons, bruised fists, and even death, but the mafia is some next level shit. Throughout my childhood, one of my first lessons was you either grew a backbone in the town I lived in or you didn't get very far in life. But I remember my father used to tell me stories growing up about the mafia ones that kept me awake at night, hoping to never have to face a darkness like that.

His words are currently echoing in my head, information about what kind of people those soldiers became and the morals they lacked.

Drug and human trafficking, prostitution, robberies, murder. That's what those people stand for, and I can't stomach for a single second that the men I've grown so close to are involved in it support it.

I feel my fists grip tighter around the steering wheel, my foot pressing harder on the gas pedal and allowing the wind to whip my hair behind me.

I know I'm going dangerously over the speed limit, but this is all I can think to do right now. No matter what thoughts travel through my mind, I can't stop the tears from spilling down my face in anger, fear, and sadness as I try to piece everything together.

I know I shouldn't jump to conclusions, but how the hell am I supposed to interpret this? Does Jade know? Would I put her in danger by telling her? I don't know what to do, but I know I need to calm myself down before anything else. It's just so hard when countless memories flash through my head.

The first true day I met them; the gun in Carter's hand; the splatter of blood that flew from that man's head as not a single person there showed an inch of remorse. I think about the guns that my men carried everywhere, the training and knowledge they had that was not required of nightclub owners.

The signs were always there, but never once had my theories traveled to this. I could only blink as more tears flowed, trying to keep my focus on the road, even when the truly painful memories flooded in. That night at the club when they first touched me in their office. How for the first time in years, I was able to look at myself scars and all– and feel true beauty and appreciation.

That's what made this so damn hard.

The fact that I can't hate them even if I wanted to, because they were quickly becoming my everything. The rushing emotions were relentless as they continued to hit me in waves, the same motions happening again and again until I found myself parked on the street outside of Jade's house.

No cars had followed me here and with my phone and purse still with Rowan, Dominic and Carter, the drive had been utterly silent with the exception of my sniffles and the hum of the engine.

It was only me and each of my accompanying footsteps as I strode up the steps to the house, wiping away the tears from my eyes as I walked. I didn't even have to search for the spare keys hidden in the flowerpot before Jade opened the door, a worried look painted across her face.

"Hazel." She said, her warm eyes flicking over my features, no doubt seeing the redness from my crying. And that single look, it made me want to break all over again.

"You knew?" I said, disbelief circling me. I was well aware of their years of friendship, but I hoped... as awful as it is, I hoped I wasn't the only one who felt betrayed.

Jolene's a part of it, Jade's a part of it, the three men who finally helped me learn what it felt like to be happy again were a part of it.

But the reality is that Jade should have been at work, but she must have known I was coming here and turned up to greet me to try and feed me the truths I wasn't ready to hear yet. My words were laced with so much unintentional venom, Jade physically flinched at my tone.

I couldn't bring myself to feel too badly about it, though. Not when it turns out everyone who promised me friendship had lies of their own.

I didn't bother to say anything else before I placed Rowan's keys into Jade's hands. I knew they would come here, and I planned to be long gone before that happened.

"It's" Jade began, but I didn't allow myself to listen to whatever she said. It's like my brain didn't physically let me, my only thought being to get the hell away from here.

I could distantly hear Jade calling out my name, but I had moved into my bedroom too quickly for her hand to reach out to my arm. Grabbing my keys from the drawer, I side stepped my friend standing at my doorway before walking down the driveway and into my parked car.

This time, Jade didn't bother running after me, my eyes catching her figure on the porch for a few seconds before backing out and turning onto the street.

Somehow, I managed to hold back my sob as I drove away for the second time today. It had been just under four hours since everything happened, but no one found or bothered me as I continued to sit on the rocky beach off the highway. Maybe driving to the place where Carter kissed me for the first time wasn't the smartest idea for my emotions, but I didn't know where else to go. I still don't.

However, these hours have allowed me to breathe and actually think about everything I've learned today.

I don't know what I'm supposed to do or how I can ever trust them again if I don't have all the answers. The only problem is that in order to get the answers I'm looking for, I'd have to see them again. I fear that encounter not because of what they represent, but because I worry all I'll want to do is go straight back into their arms. But I let myself be pushed around and manipulated for years with Noah and I know I deserve better than to relive that again. I deserve better than that. But yet, I'm now struggling to imagine how I could live a life without them in it.

The worst part is that I wouldn't just be losing my men, or Jade and Jolene. No, I would be losing a part of myself as well, the part that has only grown brighter with every second I'm with them.

A deep sigh falls from my nose, my body shifting under the hard pebbles beneath me. I have to admit, the sound and smell of the waves hitting the rocks was calming, and as I looked out to the seemingly endless body of water, I couldn't help but think of my father.

What would he do if he were me? I already know, and I can practically hear his voice telling me to hold my ground. If my father were here, he'd go to that stupid dinner Vincent invited me to looking like the best dressed person in the room just to spite them.

My dad wouldn't falter as he'd hold his head high, taking a seat like he fucking owned the place and demand the answers he was more than entitled to. A small smile crosses my face at the image, knowing he'd do exactly that and nothing less. Is it insanely suicidal to challenge who I'm assuming to be the leader of whatever mafia they're a part of? Yes. Am I going to do it anyways? ... Using my hands to help me stand, I brush off the small rocks and dust that had clung to the black material of my leggings.

I was insanely hot from the sun combined with my hoodie, but the only thing on my mind right now was giving myself the courage to do what I'm about to do. I was going to get the answers I deserved and then... Well, I'll figure out that part later.

For now, my attention was set on getting into my car, pulling back onto the roadway and heading for Jade's house. I still didn't really want to talk to her, but I know I'll have to eventually. I guess I just didn't expect to see her sitting on the couch nervously, as if waiting for me as I opened the door, walked in, and placed my keys on the kitchen counter.

"I'm sorry." She says, looking up at me with a small smudge of mascara under her eyes, "I'm not an associate or anything, but I do know what they do." That's the only explanation Jade gives me, probably knowing just by looking at me that I didn't want to talk. With a small nod of my head, I leave her where she is as I enter my room. While I'm more relieved than I thought I'd be that Jade wasn't in the Mafia, I can't help but wonder how she could know what they do and still want to be friends with them.

My father's a murdererI've seen him kill first hand even, but I can accept that. I accepted them even though our first encounter was with a bullet shot into another by their own hand.

What I can't accept, however, are things like human trafficking and all the other countless atrocities the mafia is associated with. I'm disgusted to even think of the possibility of them being involved in that, yet another reason that I need to do this. I need answers, and I need Carter's prick of a father to know that I'm neither a pet nor some little girl he can walk all over.

It took everything in me to not lunge for him when he called me that, but it seemed I wasn't the only one either. I don't think I've ever heard Carter's voice go so dark, his eyes following suit. I had gotten goosebumps from his tone then, and even just thinking about it now threatens for them to return.

They don't, though. Instead, my skin warms as the doors to my closet open and I go to unzip the clear vinyl garment bag tucked neatly in the back.

Keeping the hanger but discarding the plastic cover, my fingers brush over the silky material of the floor length dress, the same one Jade got for me when we went shopping together. It was the fanciest piece I owned, and I had a nagging suspicion that nothing about this dinner with Vincent would be anything less than over the top.

My heart raced at the thought of actually wearing this anywhere, but I didn't have much to lose at this point anyways. Though, I still had to force myself to get out of my head as I stripped off my current clothes, replacing them with the red layers of expensive fabric. I never thought I'd ever have an excuse to wear this any- where but combined with the cut and the strings of crisscrosses holding the back together, I knew it looked good and I would not show up under dressed.

My makeup took me practically no time and the waves in my hair already looked mostly consistent and pretty, so even though it was already five past seven, I was now ready to go.

A small frown appeared on my face at the sight of my reflection in the bathroom mirror, though, not from insecurities, but because of the reason I was wearing this beautiful dress.

I guess I just wish I could have worn it under other circum- stances. With a sigh and a final glance in the mirror, I didn't give myself the chance to back out before I exited my room. My heels clicked against the floor with each step, but I noticed I seemed to be the only one here now. Jade was no longer in the living room as

I moved past it, though a voice spoke just as I reached to grab my keys from the counter.

"Hazel?" Jade said, my head turning to find her leaning her arms on the hallway balcony from upstairs. My eyes on her were my only response, waiting for what she had to say.

"They came looking for you, you know?" She said, but I figured as such at the sight of their car being gone when I got back, "You have every right to be mad, I was too, but give them a chance to explain."

I simply nod my head, forcing myself not to cry again. I see Jade's eyes flick over my outfit, realization of where I'm going passing through her mind.

"Vincent is as mean as they get and knows how to manipulate people better than anyone I've ever met." She says, shocking me slightly by the change in topic, "He probably knows things about you he shouldn't be able to know, and he'll use it against you if he gets the opportunity. Don't let him see your surprise or really any emotion whatsoever. Though, as powerful as he is, Carter won't let him hurt you. Use that to your advantage." I listened to her every word carefully, blinking as I took in this information. This wasn't what I'd expected at all from her, but I was thankful for it, even if I was still more than upset.

"Also... you look beautiful." I swallowed, slipping my finger through the ring of my car keys as I took a step away from the counters.

"Thank you." I nod, not just for her compliment but for her warning as well. Despite what I was about to do, I wasn't an idiot. I knew Vincent was a power hungry asshole, but nothing was going to stop me now short of a car crash. I had made up my mind, and sane or not, Vincent MacGuire was going to lose a finger or two the next time he called me someone's pet. Don't overthink it. My car was parked in the driveway of their mansion-like house, my heart racing and mind spinning. The familiar black gates that lined their property loomed over me, the same number of people guarding the entrance as the last few times I've come through this way.

As I stepped out of my very much contrasting vehicle, I forced my back to straighten and my head to remain high as I walked up to the barred metal gates.

As awful as it is, the person who I've come to know as the scary lady flicks her eyes down to my ring, the thing that's gained me entrance here countless times now. Without a word, the doors silently open before me, nothing more than a slight nod coming from one of the people there.

I took a quiet deep breath as I moved to walk, and while I might have been seeing things, I could have sworn a small smile appeared on the female guard's face as I passed.

Though it was likely just a figment of my imagination, it gave me the courage to not back out as I lifted the flowy skirt of my dress and carefully made my way up the stone steps.

I couldn't help but be a little surprised when it was an old woman who answered my soft knock on the door, but I suppose my presence had been expected in previous times so my men were always the ones waiting for me. I thanked the lady as she took my purse for me and hurried off without another word.

For a moment I fiddled with my hands, not knowing where everyone was, but I soon heard an angry shout come from the dining room to my left. It was Carter's voice.

I followed the sound of people all the way until I reached the small stretch of wall that kept the table mostly closed off from the living room and kitchen. Of course, this also hid my presence from everyone there, but I didn't come here to snoop, I came for demands.

Taking one final moment of preparing myself, I righted my posture as I slipped around the corner, revealing myself to the four men at the table. It took no more than a second before all talk went silent at the sight of me walking into the dining room, my head held high and indeed looking like the best dressed person there.

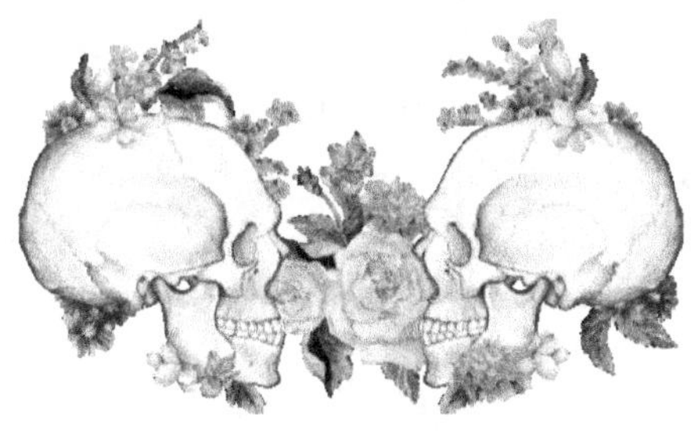

~ Seven ~

Hazel

While I didn't know what to expect when coming here, nothing could have prepared me for the way my heart physically ached at the sight of my men.

Dressed from head to toe in black and dark red, they looked amazing in the perfectly tailored suits I'm assuming Carter's father forced them to wear.

Three gazes hold on me as looks of surprise and sadness are thrown my way. I could feel their eyes as if it were their hands touching my body, but I refused to let any emotion show on my part. I wouldn't give Vincent the satisfaction. Despite his unnervingly luring smile, he's not fooling anybody that he's anything more than a conniving snake.

gnoring the men's pained looks and Vincent's one of amuse-ment, I walked over to the table of untouched food and empty plates, despite it being close to eight o'clock.

"My my," Vincent says with a tone that makes my blood boil, but I force my expression into neutrality, "I hope you didn't dress so nice for our sake, though I'll admit you sure know how to"

"Don't worry, I didn't." I flash him a sickly sweet smile, trying to contain the bile rising in my throat. Asshole. Carter had risen in his seat at his father's words, but I didn't need him to defend me, and I sure as hell didn't need Vincent thinking I couldn't hold my ground. So that's what I did as I held his stare, moving to sit down in the only other place at the table with a plate.

"Pardon you?" He says, his body entirely calm, though I could feel the disbelief radiating off of him.

"I got this dress a few weeks ago for myself is all I mean," I continued to hold his gaze as I pulled out the chair beside him and took a seat, "Though I suppose you did give me an excuse to wear it. I'm assuming your offer of dinner still stands?" It took every ounce of control and sheer will within me to not fold under his stare, and surprisingly, he was the one to break away first.

I knew I was taking a huge gamble talking to him like this, and I saw that in the tense yet prepared states of the three men across from me. It looked as though they were readying to leap across the table in between Vincent and myself as Carter's father remained deadly silent for a moment's breath.

Then, he burst out laughing as if my presence alone was the most entertaining thing he's seen all year. I haven't yet looked directly at any of my men, but I could see the lethal glint in their eyes, even from Rowan who's barely said a word today.

The loud display of amusement echoed throughout the house, similarly to the way it did this morning as well. Nothing stopped the goosebumps from rising on my arms as Vincent turned his head back to me.

For a second, I feared my disgust of him was shown too clearly on my face, but I only found him watching me with a tilted head and a smile formed across his mouth.

"I know why you're here, and for the singular reason you've got the balls to speak to me like that knowing damn well who I am, I'll let you steal these men away early." I picked up on the slight warning in his voice, though, proving that I had indeed offended him and dented his precious male ego.

Good.

I saw through the corner of my eye all three men rise from their seats without another thought, looking at me in a silent plea to follow them.

They were the whole reason I came here, but I also hadn't eaten once today and was absolutely starving. Reaching into the woven basket filled with buns, I grabbed a buttered dinner roll and took it with me as I stood, my dress falling gently against my ankles and ever so slightly across the floor.

Dominic offered his hand out to me as I moved around the table, but I didn't take it, brushing past him and telling myself I shouldn't feel bad about the hurt that crossed his features by my action.

I can't touch any one of them though, because it was either this or crying, and I really didn't want to cry again.

So, instead, I chose to keep my hands busy by pulling off a piece of the bread before lifting it to my watering mouth. Thankfully, not another word from Vincent was spoken as I walked out, following a stone-cold Carter down the hall.

The second that monster of a man was out of sight, I finally felt my muscles loosen up slightly and a steady breath to fall past my lips. This was debatably worse, though, because now I was alone with the very people all I wanted to do was hold but couldn't bring myself to do so.

It soon didn't matter, however.

Before I knew it, Rowan and Dominic had moved to my side, Carter leading us down the hallway and opening the same door to the room we signed our contract in.

I couldn't tell whether or not that was an intentional move on his part, but it still caused my eyes to shut for just a second, pretending that none of this was real and I could go back to the teasing, happy way things were this morning.

Unfortunately, reality soon reared its demanding head, my feet carrying me to the long table and turning so I could sit on it.

My dress neatly tucked beneath my body, my hands wrapping around the edge of the wood and bracing them on either side of my legs.

My heart pounded as the following footsteps sounded.

Rowan was the last inside and was also the one to close the office door, his blue eyes on me the entire time. I finally allowed myself to look at them, but I didn't like what I saw.

Things were very much off between us and the unspoken words hanging in the air left nothing but nervousness and sadness to fill me.

I watched as Dominic moved to take a step towards me, but I instinctively held up a hand. I couldn't let him any of them touch me. Dominic instantly stopped at the gesture, his arms folding around each other as he instead leaned beside the doorway. Rowan ended up on his left, Carter on his right.

"I don't want an apology, I want an explanation." I say with a surprisingly steady voice, but even as a tear threatens to fall against my cheek, all I want is to be held by them.

"Of course," Rowan nods, pain flashing across his features, "Anything." They leave the ball in my court, even though I can tell there are a million things they want to say. But now that we're all here, I don't even know where to begin.

"What does this all mean?" I ask, knowing that doesn't make a lot of sense, but no part of this does, "What are you involved in?" It took everything inside of me to keep from crying as my voice broke slightly at the end. I saw Dominic's eyes ever so quickly shoot to Carter before returning to me. I knew this was a conversation they hoped to never have, but I wasn't leaving here until I got the answers I sought.

"Carter and I are the sons of two of three leaders that make up the Italian-American Mafia." Dominic began with a small sigh, the pounding in my heart increasing, "Rowan was hired as an associate within a few months of meeting us." Rowan didn't grow up in this, then.

"I know... I know we're not in any place to make demands, princess, but we need your word that you're not going to say anything that we're about to tell you. It could put you in more danger than you realize if"

"I won't say anything." I interrupt, my knuckles nearly going white around the table at the use of his pet name for me. Not out of anger, but from sadness.

It was something I had a feeling they noticed, because their moods only seemed to drop even more. "There are so many things we've done we do in this kind of profession, and I don't even know where to start." Dominic continued, loosening his tie around his neck.

My eyes followed the movement, nearly becoming distracted by it.

"Like what? Drug and human trafficking?" I list off two of the first things I could think of, not bothering to hide the snappiness of my tone. At my words, I saw all three men shift in some way as if I had offended them.

"Not people." Carter's dark eyebrows narrowed, distaste clear in his expression, "We would never do that nor allow it to happen under our own roof."

"But you would for drugs?" I say, raising my chin a little as if bracing myself for any reaction to come from them. I didn't miss their careful choice in words.

"It's good money and something we've all grown up around." Dominic answered, his jaw flexing slightly as his arms recross over themselves.

"And what about the police? They just look away?"

"Or we don't get caught." Rowan says, his eyes still focused on me, "Tell me, darling, what exactly bothers you so much about this that has you looking at us this way?" His question caught me off guard, my legs crossing and my back straightening.

"You've been well aware throughout our entire relationship our hands are dirty, and I'm willing to bet yours aren't so clean yourself." I felt Dominic and Carter's gazes on me, but I didn't turn an inch away from Rowan.

"Maybe not, but at least I didn't lie about it." I counter, frustration beginning to bubble up inside of me. All of them seemed to sense it too. It was stupid of me to think they would simply comply for my sake, even if there was partial truth to his words.

"You knew we were involved in something more than just nightclubs and hotel strains." Dominic said, my head snapping to him, "You even witnessed some of our darkness firsthand, yet only a few weeks later I had you under me, more than willing and even more wanting."

"If memory serves right, it was you who were under me, Dominic." I snapped, surprising myself and fighting down a flush at my own words. The smirk that appeared caused me to see red as I hopped off of the table, my heels clicking against the floor when I stood.

"I came for answers, and you're just dancing around them." I say, walking to the door where Carter was currently leaned against.

"Move, I'm leaving." I watched as a dark pair of eyes glanced down at me, a hint of amusement, anger and regret swirling within them. "No." He simply says, clearly trying to spark this frustration pooling within me, though I can't figure out why. "Move." I repeat, taking another tentative step towards him. A ghost of a smile passes across his features, but he only shrugs, bending slowly at the waist as black locks of hair fall alongside his face. My heartbeat stutters as Carter moves until he's eye to eye with me, his warm breath fanning across my cheeks.

"Make me."

I internally falter at two simple words, because I realize what these three infuriating men are trying to achieve by poking me when they should be answering my questions. This entire day has caused me to show a different version of myself, one I didn't even know I still had in me until Vincent and his stupid, self-righteous personality walked out of that elevator. They wanted to awaken it.

"Answer my questions." I demanded, speaking so close my lips nearly brushed Carter's as I spoke. The corners of his mouth tugged upwards slightly, and I snapped. My hand raised, aiming for Carter's cheek as the last shred of my patience broke. I had mentally braced myself for the expected sting of his hard jaw, but it never came, only a strong hand wrapping around my wrist and tugging me backwards into a hard chest. Carter hadn't even flinched, though I knew he saw my strike coming. I couldn't even stop to care about that as I was suddenly in Rowan's grasp, the long skirt of my dress providing no help in keeping me steady on my own. Soon, two large arms curled around my body, one on my waist and the other holding my neck still with sure fingers.

"What are you" "What about we do question for a question again like at the wedding?" Dominic says, moving off of the wall and going to sit down on the table, right where I was only seconds ago. Carter follows, pinning me with his dark eyes. "You're the lying assholes." I argue, willing my core not to tighten as Rowan's thumb traces the side of my throat, "Either talk or let me go, but you're the ones who kept things from me." Fuck, it was hard to remain cold when they were looking at me like this.

"And you haven't kept anything from us, princess?" Dominic challenged, causing my eyes to narrow in confusion.

"What, you really didn't think I'd notice the $, donation sent to Rush just a week after you'd received and protested keeping the exact same amount we gave you?" I stilled at his words. Shit.

"Let me give you a hint, darling. Nobody donates to us anonymously, not when it's well known they could get people like us with power on their good side."

"You don't know what you're talking about." I deny, even though it's a transparent lie, "I just view this as you trying to change the subject from talking about who you really are." The second part was more than truthful.

"In case you're wondering and remember what we told you would happen if you sent it back, we've already set aside $, into a separate account for you. But yes, let's change the topic." I don't even get the chance to protest before they're moving on to something else. To my surprise, however, Rowan lets me go in the process, my body instantly missing his touch as he steps away. Not that I'd ever admit it, though. Carter notices my confusion as he says, "You're free to leave if you wish, but I think we all know you have questions that only we can answer." Things suddenly fell quiet as I remembered why I came here. I can't believe that for a second I felt good again being held and teasing with them.

Could things ever go back to normal with us after learning this? I was surprisingly thankful for their distraction only a moment ago, because now, that returning feeling of wanting to cry and break down washes over me all over again.

"I don't even know where to start," I admit, having so many questions yet I'm left speechless at the same time. Rowan ends up choosing just to start talking.

"I was nineteen when I joined the mafia." He began, moving around my body so he could pull out a chair for me to sit on, himself taking a seat right beside me, "I got in trouble with the wrong crowd and ended up owing them more money than I could ever imagine being able to make at the time." I stayed silent and listened, even though my thoughts instantly traveled to the fact of how young he was.

"I know you're aware that it was Jolene who took me in, but what you don't know is that when she found me, it was because I had collapsed right outside of her Cafe from not eating for the previous three days in a row." My heart squeezed and tears pricked my eyes as Rowan looked down at his hands.

"Jolene took care of me

offered me a place to sleep and made sure I was well fed. She never charged me a penny for her kindness, only asking for a strong set of hands around the Horizon when assistance was needed." A small smile appeared on my face at that, because it sounded exactly like something she'd both do and say.

"It took me more than three weeks before I started to feel like an actual human again, but that day I had feared was impossible eventually came. And then, exactly a month after Jolene took me in, I was visited by two men."

I knew Carter and Dominic were hurting just as much for their friend as I was, remaining still and allowing him the time to gather his words.

"Dominic and his father had come to make me an offer on Jo-lene's behalf, saying they would take care of my money problem if I agreed to take on a single project for them. To this day, neither of us know how Dominic's father learned just how advanced my skills with computers exceeded, but it was an opportunity and it was one I took." My eyes glanced at Dominic for only a split second, catching the undoubtedly strong emotions whirling through his head.

"I took the job, disabling every single camera and audio scanner in a building fit to hold thousands of people that day. I didn't ask why they needed it done and they never offered an explanation. The day after my work had succeeded, the men demanding money from me suddenly went silent as Dominic was sent that night to deal with them." There was a small, hesitant pause before Rowan continued, "They were dead before they even knew he was there." I stiffened at those final words, Dominic showing no denial or shame as Carter's returning stare only confirmed it.

I couldn't bring myself to do anything but breathe as all of this new information sunk in with me, causing an uneasy discomfort in my stomach to brew.

"Truthfully, I thought the deal meant they'd pay off my debts. I was utterly horrified when I learned just how wrong I was, but even when I ran, they found me within the hour. A lot of things happened in between, but one thing soon led to another which led to me being recruited under Carter's branch of command." There was nothing I could think of to say, my words failing me entirely as I struggled on how to react to this information.

I ached for what Rowan must have gone through to get to the point of being desperate enough to knowingly sell himself to the Mafia. I raged at how things couldn't just be simple for him for us. But mostly, I just wanted to hug him. "I'm really sorry you had to go through all of that alone," I said sincerely, but I only got an appreciative nod and small smile from Rowan. I wished there was more I could offer to ease the clear pain in his eyes, but I know first hand that sometimes even the prettiest of words can't heal the unrelenting scars of the past.

"My story was very different, but I too had my own experiences that brought me to this point." Dominic then said, drawing my thumping heart to him, "We all did." Unlike Rowan, Dominic looked right in my eyes as he spoke, remaining completely still on the table.

"I grew up in this lifestyle was born into it even, but the rules and laws in our line of business were very different back when I was a child. I attended some preppy private school until I was sixteen, spending every moment training and fighting to prepare for the unforgiving promise of that birthday." I hadn't even noticed I'd bit my cheek until the soft pain shot signals to my head.

"You see, sixteen is the age of initiation where future recruits are tested in an arena full of onlookers, each person even more curious than the last to see a good show put on as if we're nothing more than entertainment." I didn't miss the sharp bite of hatred lacing his tone as he spoke.

"Each year is different; Carter's was combat and survival skills, though mine was a test of the mind. I had gotten ten minutes to solve ten riddles, each one harder than the last. If the time was up and you still hadn't submitted all your answers, you were shot on sight." A slight wince must have made its way onto my face because I saw Dominic's expression soften afterwards, still looking at me and likely trying to gauge my reactions as he gave whatever comfort I would allow. It wasn't much.

"I was one of three people left standing out of just under two hundred. Carter was one of seven." I was shaking at this point, and I had to sit on my hands to stop them from drawing too much attention. They were sixteen. They were fucking sixteen and sent into an arena to be slaughtered for what... Entertainment? "That was only the mark of the beginning for us. The same day we'd been covered in the blood of our competition, we returned home to parties and congratulations on our successes." Dominic practically spat out that last word.

"For most it would end there, but Carter and I weren't just any new recruits. We were sons of the Composing Three and were expected nothing less than the uttermost cruelty and calculation. And we did our role in exceeding all of those expectations as if it were as easy as breathing." A chill made its way down my spine, leaving more questions and thoughts in its path. They were no longer hiding who they were, and I didn't know what to think about it. They were indeed cruel and ruthless and hard, but whether they know it or not, they were also traumatized, and hurting, and simply them.

"We're not good people, sweetheart, but we are yours." I watched as Carter rose from the table, his whole height towering over me now, even though he was still a short distance away from me. He walked over to my side and smoothly crouched down, holding his palms face up in front of me.

"Give me your hands, Hazel." Swallowing, I couldn't say no at his request. Moving them out from under me, I hated the way they shook still, even as Carter took them into his calloused hands and held them tight.

"Are you scared of us?" He looked up at me, his fingers brushing against mine. With a deep inhale, I said, "Yes." I could only sit there as he stared up, Dominic and Rowan watching me intently from the side as well. I didn't want to see what was passing through their eyes, though, at my words.

"Do you think we'd ever hurt you?" Carter then asked, but I immediately shook my head no. "I'm scared of what you're capable of and the power you hold," I admit, closing my eyes as my thoughts become dizzying. Everything hurts, but I know I need to say this, if not for them, then for myself.

"But most of all, Carter, I'm scared that this is going to leave me damaged in a way that cuts deeper than any physical wound ever could." My eyes flicked to the deep scar slicing through his own forehead and eyebrow, knowing the mark of it wasn't one that only showed across his skin.

"Tell us how we can make this work." He said with the same hint of pleading I'd heard earlier this morning in their parking garage. I could only drop my eyes to my lap, though, pathetically shrugging my shoulders in defeat. I couldn't think of an answer of what the future holds, so instead, I asked, "What happened to your mouth?" A small cut and the slight swell of his bottom lip was something I only noticed with him this close, but the matching marks on Dominic's fists soon answered the question for me.

"I deserved it." Carter brushed it off, his tongue tracing the hurt skin. It needed to be cleaned, but I couldn't stop myself as my attention was suddenly captured by a memory from this morning.

"Are you engaged?" My head turned to Dominic, silently cursing myself for not remembering this.

So much had been going through my mind today that I hadn't even stopped to think about Vincent's words until now. Hurt flashed in Dominic's eyes as he said, "No, princess, I'm not. I wouldn't do that to you." As relieved as I was, I was still angry about this whole thing.

"Oh, so you think dating behind my back is a line that shouldn't be crossed, but you're fine with lying about something as major as being in the Mafia?" He couldn't blame me for asking.

"We never should have lied to you, but in our defense it's not just something you go around telling people you've just met." Rowan says from my front, looking at me for the first time since he shared that small part of his history. I understood that, but it didn't prevent the sadness and confusion I was feeling now.

"That's a weak defense and it's one that doesn't make a difference for me. I gave you every ounce of my trust, but yet this entire time you never gave me the same in return." I removed my hands from Carter's, missing the warmth, but needing that numbing coldness to return.

"That's not true," Carter furrowed his eyebrows in a way that told me he did, in fact, trust me. Did it matter now, though? "Isn't it?" I challenge, "The truth is that I know practically nothing about any of you, even less after today. I didn't even know it was your birthday until your own prick of a father told me, Carter." I saw him move to speak, but I couldn't stop the words from pouring out of my mouth now. "I mean, what exactly did you plan to gain from all of this? Why would you choose me when two out of three of you are heirs to leading this entire thing? Did you plan for me to be a part of that one day or did you just think I was temporary?"

"No, Hazel... No." Carter said, remaining crouched at my feet, "You were never temporary. Ever. We don't know what's going to come of this, but what we do know is that you're everything to us. You have been for a very long time, and soon it wasn't lack of trust that kept us from telling you, but our selfishness." My breath hitched in my throat at his words.

"Because if we're on the subject of truth, the fact that we're self-ish is as candor as statements come. We can't lose you, Hazel, we can't. I know you're hurt, and understandably so, but our actions had nothing to do with the fact of who you are as a person and everything to do with the fact that we're selfish bastards who are never going to let you go." I had to raise my hand to my mouth to muffle my sob as I shattered.

It wasn't pretty, but it was real. I broke, and nothing at that point could have stopped the heavy tears that escaped me, rushing down my face and dripping onto the hands that now held it.

"I'm sorry, Hazel." Carter said as he stood, moving his body in between the spread gap of my thighs, "I'm so fucking sorry." I could barely breathe as he angled me to look at him— forced me to see the pain and remorse and uttermost tenderness in his eyes.

"I'm sorry." He repeated, kissing away a tear as I let him keep me in his embrace. The two words soon became a quiet, devoting chant on his lips, Dominic and Rowan soon walking to my side and holding me in their own way.

I still didn't know where we stood or where my mind was at, but for now, all I wanted to do was let them touch me. I just needed them. I don't know how long we stayed in that large meeting room like this, but it came to a point where I simply had no tears left to cry

. For a little while, it was just us, the rest of the world and the issues that came with it fading away into nothingness. Things had long gone quiet, but it was Carter who later broke that quiet.

"I've never celebrated my birthday before, so I never saw a point in saying anything," There was a very long pause before he continued, "I always wanted one as a child, but when my mother passed away, I think my dream of candles and presents died with her." Even though I was still really mad at him at all of them, I reached out my hand and let my fingertips brush against his in silent comfort.

"Thank you for telling me." I say quietly, my eyes sore from all of the tears I've cried today.

Those two words are all I can offer, my head pounding and my throat dry. I was sad and angry and conflicted, but most of all, I was soon tired above all else.

There was still a lot for me to think about and even more things I needed to decide, but there was still a friend at home for me I needed to speak with first.

Rowan's breathing was steady beside me as he held my hand, but I think he could sense that I was just about ready to leave. I didn't entirely want to, but I needed to. Sitting here with them and pretending we had all the answers could only last for so long. Though, it only made things even harder as I moved off of the table, all three men remaining there and looking at me in ways that made it near impossible to leave.

"Text me when he's gone, okay?" I say, referring to Carter's father, "I don't know when I'll be ready to speak again, but I need some time and I'm going to take it." Something a lot like disappointment flashed through their eyes, but I also saw understanding mixing with it.

"Take however long you need, princess." Dominic nodded, his cut knuckles turning slightly white as he restrained himself from moving towards me, "We'll be here."

"Always." Carter added, promise lacing that single word and causing goosebumps to pepper my skin. I wish he hadn't of said that, and though I didn't repeat it out loud, my response must have been clear on my face.

Always.

I didn't say anything else as I walked backwards and reached out for the handle to this room. My fingers reluctantly wrapped around the metal piece, twisting and opening the silent door as I was left to make the choice I didn't want to. Slipping outside, I left the three men behind as the latch clicked shut, driving so much more than just a physical wall between us.

The second that door closed, I felt myself tense once again, remembering that there was much greater evil roaming this house than the destructive secrets of our pasts.

Keeping my footsteps quiet, I walked down the narrow hallway and absently grabbed my purse hanging on the hook by the door. This was the one I'd brought over three days ago when I came to see Carter, and all it took was a quick look on my part to see that the men had gathered my belongings and placed them inside. It was only a second later that I realized my waver in attention—no matter how short had given Vincent the opening he'd been secretly waiting for.

"Trouble in paradise, my dear?" He smiled as he moved to lean against the wall by my head, though his expression didn't come close to reaching his eyes. I simply ignored him, grabbing my jacket and shrugging it on. The sooner I could get out of here, the better. I took a step to leave, but Vincent clicked his tongue at me, his head tilting to the side as if trying to understand something.

"Didn't anyone ever tell you it's rude to ignore people?" He asked, making the move to effectively block my path, "Though considering the good-for-nothing parental figures in your life, I don't think I can even hold your ill manners against you." This is what Jade warned me about, I reminded myself as near blinding rage boiled my blood.

I didn't allow any form of reaction show on my face at Vincent's words, even though I wanted to scream and tell him he knew nothing of my parents.

When I tried to step around him, he let me, only to wrap a large, unrelenting hand around my upper arm.

That was the final push for me as I rounded on him, praying that Jade's second promise about protection would remain true.

I couldn't prevent myself as I pulled Vincent's thumb backwards towards his wrist, his tight grip faltering when I didn't stop there. Even when his hand had loosened entirely, it wasn't enough for me.

The mere sight of his face was enough to add fuel to the uncontrollable fire burning within me, my now free arm twisting and snapping his fingers back at an abnormal angle.

The cold bastard didn't even scream as I enjoyed the crack of his bones beneath my fingertips, adding pressure until I knew at least three of his were broken.

I hadn't even realized I was smiling until I stepped away, Vincent clutching his damaged hand in his other fist. My feeling of satisfaction was short-lived, however, when his face copied mine.

"Oh, Hazel." He hummed, purposely messing up my name just to tick me off, "I suppose I should thank you," Vincent's smile grew wider, "You see, you've just given me the perfect excuse for killing you, though I must admit you were good entertainment for today." A chilling tingle made its way down my spine at his words, my body sending off warning signals to my brain that I needed to run.

Where was Carter and his guns when you needed them? I only made it a single step back before Vincent drew a long, sharp knife from the inner pocket of his suit, making the move to lift it to my throat.

Just as the fear of death flickered within me, the sharp click of a revolver being cocked made both of us freeze on the spot. Only once Vincent's head reared to my right did I follow his gaze, my eyes widening at the sight of Rowan standing with a gun in hand, aiming directly at Carter's father.

Based on our conversation and the little information I already knew, I'd gathered that associates weren't even allowed to speak without permission around higher ranks.

This was a very, very big deal. I both saw and felt the pure rage Vincent experienced at Rowan's disobedience, his knife now poised at the blond only a few feet away from us. Carter's father stepped away from me and towards Rowan within the next second. He didn't pause once, even as the remaining two men walked into the room, drawing their own weapons at the sight before them.

"Hazel, go." Dominic's voice was a demand as he spoke, his eyes scanning my body and analyzing from the silence alone what he'd missed.

But I couldn't.

Not with this monster of a man pointing a knife at what's mine.

Vincent never even saw me coming before I raised my elbow, slamming it down on a pressure point on his arm.

He wasn't able to recover quickly enough as his hand spasmed open, the knife cluttering to the ground with a sharp ring. I just barely had time to kick the knife over to my men before Vincent sprung, trying to attack me.

I don't know if it was because I was a woman or because he really just didn't know me as well as he let on, but he let his guard down as he aimed to grab my neck, though his movements were too sloppy to follow through.

All I had to do was turn to the side as he stumbled forward, losing his balance and gaining me just enough to leave. I trusted that the three men standing together were more than capable of taking things from here as I quickly slipped out of their house.

"Quella puttana!" Was the last thing I heard Vincent scream, before I closed the door with a small, yet exhausted smirk on my face. It seems as though Vincent clearly doesn't know shit about my life.

I knew this, because despite him cursing at me in Italian, what he failed to learn during his snooping is that I've been near fluent from the time I was seventeen.

And while he may have just called me a whore, at least I wasn't the one with three damaged fingers and an even more shattered ego.

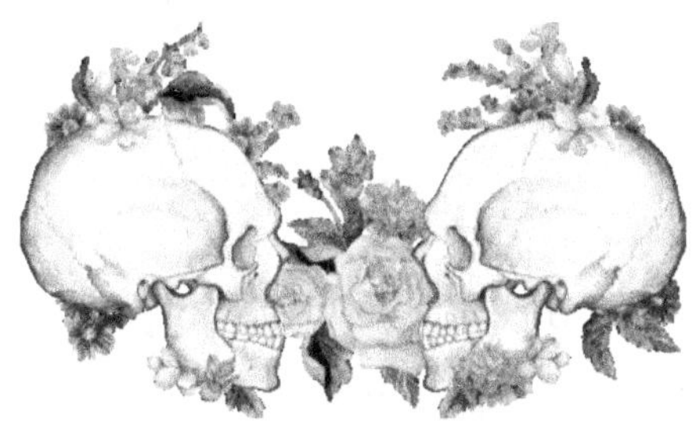

~ Eight ~

Hazel

I'm fine. Or at least I was. I drove home in my own car, this time allowing myself to actually think about my men and everything they told me.

The emotions I'm currently feeling are mixed, but each one seems stronger and more intense than the last.

Maybe it was a longer term effect of subdrop, or maybe it was simply due to all of the stress and sadness I've felt today, but I found myself struggling to get out of my car.

It was small at first, the slight weight on my chest, but as I stepped out of my vehicle and drew my keys from my purse, I began to shake.

I tried to breathe, I really did, but every single part of today soon became too much as I walked up the front steps and to the door of my house.

Lifting my trembling hand to unlock it, I pinched my eyes shut in defeat when I couldn't connect the key to the hole. My chest tightened, my breath quickened, and I suddenly became very very quiet.

I didn't trust myself to speak or call for Jade's help right now. Instead, I just really needed to sit down.

My hand was flat and pressed against my heart, panicking at how fast it was and how I didn't see how I could slow it down again.

I noticed that I began to swallow a lot, but my throat felt dry and scratchy. Absently aware that I was having an anxiety attack, and most certainly not my first, I ended up on the porch with my knees to my chest, breathing rapidly but never getting enough air.

I subconsciously heard the front door open, but I couldn't even care to move and look at the person coming outside. "Hazel?" Jade said my name, surprise and concern clear in her voice. I opened my mouth to say hers, but after many failed attempts of speaking, I simply gave up, shaking even harder. The next second, she was on the ground beside me, taking my hands into hers and squeezing them just to show she was there. I really hate how much of a mess I am right now.

"It's okay, I understand." Jade says at the words I was unable to speak. I had techniques for this, I did, but I was entirely too over-whelmed to remember.

"Is there anything you typically do when this happens?" She asks, and I nod my head, but the action alone was dizzying as the overwhelming urge to pass out came down on me.

When she figured I couldn't respond more than that, she brushed a few pieces of hair out of my eyes as she held me. "What works for me is tensing certain muscles as hard as I can, holding it, then trying to relax my body as much as possible afterwards." Jade offered, and it was a strategy I used as a kid, but had forgotten all about it.

"O-Okay." I managed, even as I just wanted to curl up and stay like that until things passed. I was given a reassuring smile as Jade gently let go of my hand, sliding in right beside me and staying, even when we were given multiple curious glances from others on the street.

"Ignore them." She said, "It's just you and me. Nothing else is important right now." I continued to shake, but I ended up closing my eyes and curling my hands into fists, trying to stop the seemingly never ending tremble in them.

I started by tightening every muscle across my shoulders and upper arms, holding it like that until the mental clock in my brain told me it was time to let go.

I let out a long breath as I relaxed and loosened my muscles, but the nausea and spinning never left.

So, I did it again, this time with the ends of my toes. Again and again, I forced myself to breathe, drowning out everything around me except for my tense limbs and the gentle touch of Jade's hand on my arm. It took me a long time to regain control over my body once again, but even once I could stand on my own, the shaking ended up continuing for hours afterwards. Only this time, I wasn't alone.

I know Jade had many questions, and we had a lot to talk about later, but she put no pressure on me to do anything as she walked me to my room. Somehow, I managed to make sure my now slightly dusty dress was hung up carefully on its hanger, not bothering to put on anything else as I collapsed into bed.

There was a long list of things I'd worry about later, but for now, I let a different kind of darkness consume me, one known as the promising hands of sleep.

This is the third day in a row I haven't seen or spoken to my men. I've worked every single one of those days, but never once did they show at the bar either.

However, even though they made themselves visibly scarce, somehow I could still sense they were close by the entire time. I was for the most part appreciative of it too, because they were doing it for me and respecting my wishes. Only a few hours after I left their house a few days ago, Rowan texted me that Vincent was gone like I asked him to.

I didn't respond. I was surprised at how much I truly missed them, but I wasn't lying when I said I needed a few days to think.

There had been so much on my mind I needed to sort out, as well as determine if I could even continue on with our relationship. I took the time to think about my dad, my mom, and most importantly, my men. After my stream of tears from a few days ago, as awful as it was to endure, it also forced me to realize something. I don't know if I can live without them anymore.

Maybe I'm just in too deep, but as supportive as Jade was, it honestly wasn't my bed I wanted to return to for the night. I've felt cold every single night I've been on my own, and it only got worse with every passing hour that I realized I still wanted them.

They had a lot of making up to do for their lies, and I still had questions I needed to ask, but I wasn't ready to let what we have go anytime soon.

My decision only hit me tonight, and it was one of the realizations that had me laying awake at two in the morning, wishing everything could just fix itself.

I know we will still have things to work through, but that could be a problem for another day.

Right now, I just wanted to see them, even if it was late and the sky was painted black. I honestly didn't care at this point. There were only three thoughts on my mind currently, and with that, nothing was able to stop me as I got into my car and drove straight to the very people I couldn't get out of my head. With a glance at my ring, I walked past the night guards stationed around the gates of their house, and right inside.

I tried to keep quiet as I shut the door, smiling to myself at the sight of the entryway, or more so the memories it holds. Even if he didn't scream, the very fact that Vincent was caught off guard for once in his sorry life brought more pride to myself than it probably should.

Thankfully, there didn't seem to be a trace of him as I walked farther inside, shrugging off the long coat I wore overtop of my nightgown. I hadn't bothered to take the time to change into something better. The house felt dark and large with me being the only one walking around, but I won't be leaving now that I'm here. Though, I'm not exactly sure what to do now that I am. My first instinct is to go straight upstairs, but the glint of the kitchen catches my eye as I walk farther into their house. The first memory that comes to mind is the panic I felt when I dropped into that horrible headspace the last time I was here. It was honestly terrifying, but before I knew it, I wasn't alone anymore. I soon had three amazing, comforting, yet totally lethal men by my side who would give the world for me. I would love nothing more than to go right upstairs and tell them that despite me being angry, I don't want to live a life without them in it.

However, it was also Carter's birthday two days ago, one I missed and didn't bother to even send him a text. I still can't believe I never knew he was turning thirty-four, but ever since he told me he's never celebrated it, I haven't been able to get it out of my head.

So much of his childhood had been stripped away from him before he was ever granted the opportunity to get those excited feelings in your stomach right before getting to open gifts or blow out the candles on a cake. My idea was stupid, and I couldn't bake if my life depended on it, but I wanted Carter to have something. Even if it was this pathetic excuse of a gift I'm already thinking up.

I cringed slightly as I googled the simplest recipe I could find on making a chocolate cake, already fearing this was going to be as disastrous as I feared.

But, I did it anyways.

I dimmed the lights to a manageable setting, tied my hair up, and began silently gathering ingredients from the fridge and pantry.

Their kitchen was practically a maze to navigate and half of the things I needed I couldn't find, but I improvised. My plug-in mixing bowl was replaced by a normal bowl and a whisk in my hand, but so far, I haven't burnt, spilt, or damaged anything. It was a small accomplishment I held onto for now.

I know me doing this was also partially avoiding figuring out what to say when I go upstairs, but I was also content with staying here for now.

Things seemed to be going okay as I slid the circular tray into the oven, setting the timer accordingly to the instructions. I sighed as I turned back to look at the slight mess I had made, but even as a small yawn escaped me, a smile followed with it. At this point, I didn't even care that this was likely going to blow up in my face, because honestly, I just wanted to give Carter something he should have had his entire life... Happiness.

One cake won't make up for all of the trauma I know can consume him, but it was still something he deserved. Hell, he deserved a whole lot better of a cake than the one I pulled out of the oven many minutes later, but this was just going to have to make do. I waited five minutes before my impatience got the best of me, flipping the pan over and allowing the cake to come out after being given a bit of encouragement.

I winced as the edges crumbled depressingly, but I did what I could to press them back on.

Yup, this was disastrous. I couldn't help but bite the inside of my cheek in frustration when the icing didn't spread on nicely either.

Bits of the cake were pulling up with the movements of my blue covered spatula, and soon, the once light coloured icing was mixing into a darker, muddy colour from the chocolate.

It was pathetic, and the top was caving in slightly, but I barely had time to contemplate just throwing it out before someone cleared their throat from behind me. Whipping my head around to the point of slight dizziness, I found Dominic's inked arm resting against the counter across from me, no shirt to cover the muscles scaling his chest. For a moment, I froze up, standing there like a deer in the headlights as my stare met his.

"You're here?" He spoke quietly, as if not seeming to believe I would return at all. I could only nod, suddenly feeling extremely naked with only the thin nightgown to hug my skin. It was stupid because I've been in far less around him before, but things felt a lot more... intimate now.

"Sorry about the mess." I stupidly murmur, suddenly feeling conscious at how horrible the dessert behind me looked, and likely tasted. Dominic only raised an eyebrow as if to say, we both know this is about much more than some failed baking attempt.

"Did I wake you?" I asked, my hands and lower back now leaning against the counter edge. He felt so close, yet so damn far away.

"I smelled food and got curious." Dominic simply replied, though the bags under his eyes suggested he hadn't been sleeping much anyways these last few nights. I hadn't either.

"It doesn't matter much now. I think I'll just go out and buy something"

"You don't realize what this is going to mean to Carter, princess." Dominic began, but the air was sucked from my lungs at the sight of a dark-haired man nearly frozen at the bottom of the stairs. All he wore were his rings and a pair of grey sweatpants, his hair out of place from sleep.

"Hazel." Carter let out a loose breath as he said my name, his eyes glancing everywhere around me and then back over to my face. "Hi." Was all I could think of in response, my heart racing against my chest. I watched as his eyes locked entirely on me, Rowan's tired footsteps sounding down the long staircase, yet also ceasing at the sight before him. They were all here now, though none of us knew what to make of this.

"Although you're always welcome, may I ask what brought you here at three in the morning, darling?" The blond's words were deep from the remains of sleep in his system, his gaze making me tighten up.

For a moment, I looked first at Rowan, then Carter, then Dominic. I let myself actually see them for the first time since I found out they were in the Mafia.

All of the scars, wounds, and tattoos adorning their bodies, they all told a story and it was one I think I was finally ready to learn. I wasn't going to act like I was higher than them, because the reality is that I knew they were capable of killing without a second thought, and I wasn't bothered anywhere near as much as I probably should be.

Right now, with all of their emotions laid bare in front of me, I knew they were the only things I was certain of in my fucked up, messy life.

"I wanted to see you all again," I replied to Rowan's question, taking a breath before continuing, "I forgive you. I'm still angry and I have more questions, but I forgive you... Hence the cake." I added at the end. That sad, crumbling cake—if you could even call it that.

"You forgive us?" Dominic repeated, my words on his tongue sounding as though he never thought they'd be spoken. I nod.

"Though, I do suppose some making up could encourage that forgiveness to stay." I tease, feeling a small weight lift itself from my chest when they all smile back at me in relief. It might take some time, but things can feel right again.

I watched as Carter's eyes focused and held on the dessert behind me, many emotions flickering through his vision. I could tell just by the way he breathed that things were feeling intense for him right now, and when those dark pair of eyes finally reunited with my green ones, I knew he wasn't planning on letting me leave again anytime soon.

I never even had the chance to brace myself before it was surprisingly Dominic who pounced on me first. Taking long, even strides, I was soon in his hold as my hips were pinned to the marble trimming.

"You mean it?" Dominic's eyes look down into mine, his hands shaking slightly in fear that I would change my mind. If I could be certain about anything right now, it would be that I wasn't going anywhere.

"I do." All it took was a blink before I was lifted onto the cold counter top, my nightgown hurriedly being torn straight down the middle and tossed away.

"Dominic!" My eyes widen when he tears my white underwear clean off of my body next. "He'll buy you new ones, darling," Rowan said now from where Dominic used to be, "Just let us take care of you." The next second, Dominic's head dipped until his sinful mouth was within reach of my clit. The suddenness of it all had me gasping, my fingers weaving into his dark curls and gripping until he moaned along with me. He didn't waste any time before two fingers teasingly dragged up and down my slit, angling themselves as he pushed in with no resistance. I could feel Dominic's hands shaking slightly, but his gaze was steady and entirely on me. I was so busy looking down at the man between my legs that I hadn't even noticed that Rowan slid to sit by my side, taking my right leg and hooking it over his. The action left me even more spread and I soon felt the angle of Dominic's strokes change to one that brought me rapidly closer to that blissful high. Rowan's fingers teased my inner thighs, dragging over my lines and stretch marks and then back down again. All of these sensations were dizzying, and when Rowan's free hand began playing with my nipple, I couldn't help but buck my hips up further into Dominic's face. "That's it, Hazel. Take what you need." Carter's voice vibrates through me, making me realize my eyes had fallen shut. I force them back open as my core tightens, blinking a few times before I see that Carter's cut himself a slice of cake, his fork being picked up from the counter.

"Don't—" My words get cut off by a moan when Dominic sucks hard on my clit, his tongue running skilled circles around it, "You shouldn't eat that." My head spun as Rowan began kissing and scraping his teeth against my neck, bending my body and angling me to his will.

He hummed against my throat as he felt my racing heart, whispering quiet words in my ear about how pretty I looked and that he was sorry. All at the same time, Carter's eyes demanded my attention, knowing I couldn't stop him as he lifted a piece of the cake to his mouth. He was looking at me as though I was both his present and entertainment, watching as my lips parted in a pant thanks to his friends' touch and his gaze.

Carter said nothing as he smiled, taking another bite of the dark cake and leaning against the counter to get comfortable. Though it's only been a few days, I forgot how powerful that stare was as he watched my pinned body. He was touching me with his gaze alone and I couldn't stop the tremble in my legs as they locked up, tightening around Dominic's head.

"Sir—" I gasped as his fingers suddenly stroked me deeper, Rowan's teeth grazing a sensitive spot on my neck. Combined with Carter's watchful eyes, it was all I needed as my walls clamped down, my release barreling through me and onto Dominic's long fingers.

"Good girl." Rowan murmured in my ear, nipping right below it in praise as the two of them slowly brought me down, yet still fucking me through my orgasm.

When my eyes finally tore away from the man across from me, I looked down to find Dominic gently resting the thigh that had been around his shoulder back down on the counter.

His tongue continued to lazily lap at my sensitive core until he had licked up every last trace of my arousal, his green eyes watching my every reaction as he did so. By the time he pulled away, I was completely relaxed again, my heart slowly returning to a normal pace. At that, Carter placed down what was left of that god awful slice of cake, his head never turning away from me.

"I'm glad you're back, princess." Dominic said as he placed a final kiss to my thigh before rising, Rowan unhooking my thigh from his leg and hopping off of the counter. I was confused as the two of them both moved to leave, but when Carter's large form snagged my attention, I knew why just by one look at his predatory gaze. I suddenly felt extremely exposed under his eyes, my reflex of covering up becoming greater by the second. Reaching out to my left to grab my coat, I didn't get far before the roughness of Carter's voice caused me to freeze.

"Oh, you won't be needing that, sweetheart." He said, taking a slow step towards me. I shifted and crossed my legs as Carter walked to where I was sitting, not stopping until his hands gripped the counter on either side of my body. His muscles naturally flexed at the action, his mouth so close to mine I could feel his exhales.

"You baked me a cake." He gave me a small smile, his head dipping slightly so his nose could trace a line along my jaw.

"I did." I shivered as Carter trailed down the stretch of my throat, planting a small kiss along my collarbone. For a few seconds, the only sound between us was our breaths. I didn't move an inch as Carter continued to explore my body as if he were doing it for the first time again.

Then, after a long stretch of time, he whispered against my throat, "Thank you." I crumbled beneath his fingertips after that. I'm not even exactly sure how I ended up in his arms, but my body was soon wrapped around Carter's, his two strong arms looping around my waist and holding me tight.

I didn't protest as I let him carry me up the stairs, even though it would have been easier for him to take the elevator. With every breath, I inhaled his familiar scent of leather and pine, happily warming up as his bare skin brushed against mine. When I woke up this morning, I never would have thought my night would end with me here, but I knew in this moment that this was the only place that felt right. In his arms, in his bed, with him. It didn't matter the physical location; I just needed to continue being held just as much as I was holding Carter.

With unhurried steps I was brought into his bedroom, though this time it was cleared of shattered glass and splintered wood.

A new, untouched bed stood in place of the previous one, not a single crinkle to be seen in its dark sheets. From that, I knew he hadn't slept at all today, but Carter didn't seem to have any issue disturbing the neat mattress as he laid the two of us down on our sides.

Our legs instantly wound up intertwined, my fingers finding their way to the dark strands of his soft hair. His own combed through mine, relaxing me and causing a content sigh to fall from my lips. Never once did Carter's eyes leave my face, and somehow I could just tell something was bothering him.

"Do you want to talk?" I ask, my voice quiet as I scan over his uncertain features. He seems to be contemplating my words, as though he was torn by those as well.

"I just... I want to try something, but I've never done it before." Carter answers, causing more questions to form in my mind. My eyes search his, my head shifting on the pillow we're currently sharing.

"What do you want to try?" There's not much I wouldn't give him at this point if I was able to offer it. For another second he didn't say anything, simply looking at me as his hand moved to stroke the side of my cheek.

I leaned into his touch as he held my face, not rushing him or the gears I can practically see spinning in his head.

Staying still as he slowly lifted his neck up, Carter's body shifted closer until he was able to bring his lips to mine with ease.

I blinked in slight surprise at the action before my eyes fluttered shut, exhaling through my nose as Carter gently kissed me.

He took his time exploring my mouth just like that, encouraging my lips to part for him until our tongues danced against each other.

Carter groaned as my one hand held him at the base of his neck, tugging at his hair until he moved his body overtop of mine. Never once did he pull away from me as his hips straddled my waist, rocking against my clit until small bursts of pleasure brushed through me.

"Daddy," I quietly whimpered against his mouth as his tongue licked a stripe across my bottom lip. Carter hummed in slight correction, as if that wasn't what he was wanting to hear. It didn't take me any time to pick up on his hints as my one hand dropped to the waist of his sweatpants.

"I want you, Carter." I panted as my body squirmed beneath him.

He pulled back at that, his eyes connecting with mine and showing me the lust and emotion swirling within them. He helped me as I tugged his clothing down and off of him, Carter's feet kicking his pants and boxers off of the bed.

"Say that again." He growled, spreading my legs and happily resting his body in between them.

My legs instinctively wrapped around his waist, my hips trying to lift and gain any form of relief.

"I want you, Carter." I repeat, moaning as the head of his cock rubbed against my clit, "Please, I need you so bad." That was all he needed to hear as a satisfied smirk formed across his face.

"Ask and you shall receive, sweetheart." He said, pressing his throbbing tip to my entrance, but still teasingly dragging it up and down until my arousal covered him, "Look." Carter demanded, watching me as my eyes dropped down to the little space between us. I instantly clamped down at the sight of his piercing slowly pressing forward inside of me.

That was all it took before he smoothly rocked into me, both of us letting out soft gasps at that initial feeling of each other.

I felt my body stretch to accommodate him as my hips pressed upwards, taking that extra inch of him deeper. His fingers deftly found their way around my neck, though he didn't tighten his grip at all. It was merely to hold me close as he pulled out, just to slide right back in.

My lips parted in a breathless gasp as his own hovered over mine, the both of us moving as one unit.

"Carter," I moaned softly in his ear as his head dipped to nibble on mine. He hummed against my skin before his tongue traced a line along my jaw, his hips once again moving to roll against my own.

"So pretty." Carter murmured as my back arched in bliss, only for his hand to gently press me back down, "I really like you like this, you know. I'm going to savor every inch of you until my lips are permanently memorized by your body." He groaned against my heated skin as I tightened around him, before bringing his head back up to look at me.

The entire time, his thumb ran gentle strokes along my throat.

"It's so much easier to watch you like this, whimpering and clenching around my cock when you know only I can give you more." Unintentionally proving his point, a string of desperate noises left me as he began to brush my clit with his body with each thrust forward.

"I can't ever get enough of you, Hazel." Carter moaned, his lips stroking teasingly against mine, "I'm never going to let you go." Not even a full second could tick by before our mouths reconnected with an intimacy that left me undeniably and entirely consumed.

I knew after tonight nothing would ever be the same, but I think a part of me was okay with that. I never expected to ever feel the way I do now about not one, but three incredible men, yet here I am falling head first into a pool of uttermost affection and devotion. There was no coming back from this, but I embraced it, just as I embraced everything Carter had to give to me. His tongue caressing mine could only be described as pure ecstasy as he filled my senses, gently coaxing my orgasm to that familiar edge.

"I want you to come with me." Carter said against my mouth, pulling back to watch as he continued to touch me in gentle strokes, "Can you do that, sweetheart? Will you let me feel you?" I could only nod my head at him in response, barely being able to contain the writhing pleasure coursing through my veins.

"Please, I'm so close." I whimper as his body drags against my clit yet again, my legs tightening around him desperately. The small smile I receive makes everything inside of me warm, my eyes locking on Carter's and remaining there.

"Whenever you're ready, Hazel." He says, his arm trembling slightly beside me as he holds my head in his hands.

Those final words were all I needed as I gave in completely to the sensations.

I felt my eyes widen slightly as my mouth parted in a silent moan, Carter looking like a god as he towered over my body. In near synchronization, the two of us reached our highs together, gripping each other tight at the feeling of our orgasms blending as one.

My climax has never felt like that before, but it was a feeling I refused to let go of, even as the small sparks of pleasure slowly began to come down.

Even then, however, neither of us felt inclined to release the other. Things simply felt really good like this, a rush of happiness washing over me as Carter continued to gaze down at me.

In that moment as I stared up at him, I saw something was different in his eyes than when we were last this close.

Something had changed a little bit in all of us over the course of these last three days, and while I may be too much of a coward to read his expression, I'm willing to bet my own eyes are currently reflecting the exact same emotion.

~ Nine ~

Rowan

Hazel Walsh—Hazel Caddel—is Marcus's daughter.

Daughter, daughter, daughter.

That single word has been echoing through my head over and over again during the last week we've spent with her. Finding Hazel in our kitchen on Monday was one of the biggest reliefs of my life, but despite that, I don't know how nobody else is expressing how worrisome this entire situation is.

Seeing her back in our home brought a sense of happiness to me I didn't know was possible, but that doesn't change the fact that her father is the same person I've dedicated the last multiple years of my life to killing.

What's worse is that I don't plan to shoot down that dedication either.

None of us do. Where that leaves us now, however, I have no clue.

All I know at this point is that Carter's plan with his father fucked us all over, even if it was his only option at the time.

At the end of the day, that doesn't change the fact that Hazel is going to hate us when she finds out the very person we've spoken so lowly about is the man who also raised her.

Throughout my entire friendship with Dominic and Carter, I've always been the logical one; it is my job after all. And between the smiles and words Hazel and I have exchanged these last few days, I couldn't help it as a daunting thought crossed my mind.

Is it possible this is all a trap? As horrible as it is, it wouldn't be the first time someone has tried to get close with us for information. I had wondered if Hazel was sent by her father to gain intel, because I know Hazel is more than smart enough to do something like that.

That was where my mind branched to when I first found out her relation to Marcus, but then, I thought of every single moment we've shared together as well.

I can still see the fear in her eyes when Carter shot that man all those weeks ago. And the lust she experienced when I teased her under the table at Jolene's.

When she watched Dominic and I take that girl together at the wedding, and the first time she submitted completely to us, just as we've been slowly giving ourselves to her in return.

I would like to think the emotion she feels for us now is and has only ever been real, because the alternative would be a loss I could never recover from. I knew that much for certain.

Then again, this role I'm supposed to play means I've also always been the one to find solutions to impossible problems. That ability was the reason I was permanently hired on with the Mafia, but I can't find a way to get us out of Carter's decoy plan while protecting our relationship simultaneously.

The weight of this situation has been keeping me up for nights, but no matter every possible angle I look from, no outcome is desirable. The reality is that Carter and Dominic are forever going to be in the Mafia.

With the two as current underbosses, both are also destined to become Dons after their fathers either pass away or are forced to step down from their positions in another manner.

Whatever the case, I don't know what we were thinking when forming this relationship with Hazel.

How did we think we could make this work without falling for this beautiful person in the process? I'm just expected to feel fine about this all, but I can't. We're going to lose her at some point; that's the only way we can keep her safe, and it's tearing me apart.

"Rowan." Dominic's voice comes from my office door, causing me to turn and look at him. I watch as his eyes flick over my appearance, no doubt knowing what's going through my head.

"She's back." He says, even though he's well aware I know that.

"But for how long?" I'm happy that Hazel's currently here, I really am, but I don't understand how everyone's just walking around like everything is perfectly okay.

Like Vincent hadn't sent out an order to have Hazel and I both executed for our crimes against him. If it weren't for Carter agreeing to now owe his father two Favours at his leisure, I have no doubt I already would have been a dead man.

"We're not letting her go, Cal." Dominic says instead, only making me more frustrated and honestly scared. We screwed up, and I don't know how to undo it.

Shooting Dominic a pointed look, that was as far as my acknowledgement extended as I walked past him and out of my office. My head was so damn loud as my feet carried me down the hallway and to the kitchen. I would have continued until I was out of this house, but the sound of Hazel laughing from the balcony caused me to freeze. Just one sound and I felt my body calming slightly.

"I'm honestly fine." She says into her phone, not seeing me as I moved towards her, leaning against the door frame outside.

A muffled voice comes from the other line, but I can't tell what they're saying or who it is.

"No, I'm working tonight." Hazel speaks, taking a small pause as if trying to find her words, "If you're still awake when I'm done..." I shouldn't be listening to her conversation, even if the soft sound of her voice helped to tame the restlessness inside of me.

Walking away, I didn't even notice that I had stopped breathing for a moment before I felt my chest tighten and my lungs demand for air. No matter what, though, I couldn't bring myself to breathe in.

I was so angry and worked up that only when I felt a pair of small hands brush against my back did I inhale.

My fists shook slightly as they balled up, my mind not understanding why I couldn't seem to focus right now.

"Rowan," Hazel's voice was laced with concern as she rounded my body, her hands coming up to hold the sides of my face. Her eyes studied mine as I touched my fingers to hers, relishing in the feeling of her simply being by my side.

"Do you want to go out somewhere with me?" I suddenly ask, having no plan whatsoever, but just wanting to get out of this house. Hazel's always been someone who grounds me, whether she realizes it or not.

I just need to go somewhere quiet and preferably get some alone time just the two of us. As much as I love hanging out as a group, while unintentional, Hazel and I haven't ever really gotten to be together much on our own yet. And right now, I really just needed her.

"Where to?" Hazel smiles with a tilt of her head, her little touches to my body no doubt trying to give me silent comfort. "Do you like picnics?" I ask, memory of a secluded park nearby coming to mind. Her confirming grin was all I needed to know. "You're really not going to let me look?" Hazel laughs, blindly walking in step with my body.

"We're almost there," I whisper in her ear, kissing the side of her cheek that isn't being covered by my hands over her eyes. "I can tell we're on grass... Are we on a field?" She guesses, causing me to snicker.

"Nothing gets past you, darling." I smile, finally letting her go and allowing Hazel to see the grassy hills and swarm of trees around us. I may have discovered this place a while ago when gathering information for an assassination attempt, but it's working out to my advantage now anyways.

"Where are we?" She looked around in awe, clearly loving the scenery surrounding us, "It's beautiful." "It's just a few minutes away from your place actually," I say, tossing down the thin blanket I brought for us to sit on. The box of chocolate covered strawberries we decided to bring were entirely melted under the heat of the sun, so I set those down too in dismissal. "Does this work for you here?" I ask, spreading out the fabric until it's wide enough for the two of us to lay down on should we please. Hazel turning and sitting down next to me was words enough.

I had us positioned under a large tree to provide some refuge from the sun, and I was thankful for it when I no longer had to squint when looking at the beautiful woman by my side.

I watched as she too visibly relaxed, moving over until the one side of our legs were flush together, her head moving to rest on my shoulder.

I breathed in under her touch, wrapping my arm around her and ensuring we could stay just like this. Just from a few seconds of having Hazel in my hold, I knew this was everything I needed.

It was clear she could sense I wasn't in the best mood today, but I didn't feel the need to pretend with her either. Hazel has never rushed or pressured me into talking, and it was a courtesy I gave her in return. There were so many things I wanted to say—to ask and to share, but none were pleasant and I didn't want to ruin her day from my own problems. But, she could tell things were off whether I had to say it or not.

I sensed her understanding when she planted a kiss on my shoulder, and again when she slipped her hand into mine, allowing our joined fingers to rest on her thigh.

That in itself told me everything I needed to know I wasn't a burden by needing to talk. A part of me has always naturally felt like that, but Hazel also didn't seem like the type to run away when she finds out my mask of smiles and cocky remarks is often worn to hide what I'm truly feeling at times. I let out a deep sigh as her head rests against my neck, holding her closer when I ask the question I've been wondering most lately, even if it's one that's probably best left unsaid.

"How can you forgive us so easily?" I murmured, trying not to tense or break down or really feel anything right now. I felt Hazel shift slightly in surprise, but in response, she only let out a soft puff of air as if unsure herself. For a moment, we remained in complete silence to the point where I thought she just wasn't going to answer.

"Can I tell you a story, Rowan?" Hazel answers instead, her hand gripping noticeably tighter to my arm.

Furrowing my eyebrows slightly, I angle my head down so I can see the blonde waves of her hair, but otherwise, Hazel has turned away.

"Of course," I say, stroking a few of my fingers down her arm and catching the feeling of the small goosebumps forming, despite the hot weather. I could somehow tell this was something I was to listen to and not interrupt.

"Promise me... please promise me you won't get mad," Hazel hummed against my shoulder, still not meeting my eyes but never pulling away at the same time. I gave her my word without a second thought, even though I worried for her and didn't know how to help the essence of sadness now releasing from her.

In the end, I only pulled Hazel closer, giving her gentle touches in encouragement.

I feel as though that's the best thing I could offer her right now.

"I was eleven years old the first time my mother brought home Andrew, my step-father." She began, picking her nails from the obvious discomfort she was feeling. I don't even think she knew she was doing it, but either way, I took both of Hazel's hands into my one, holding them together on my thigh.

"She had just been through her divorce with my dad, but on the same day, she brought Andrew home and insisted that he was my new father and I was to address him as such. I guess that part doesn't really matter as much as it used to, but I remember that that day was the first time I'd ever felt true fear." I felt her swallow and try to clamp down on her nerves, but she didn't have to pretend with me. She didn't seem to try anyways.

"He wasn't a very good man..." Hazel's hands tried to fidget in mine, so I simply interlaced our fingers together, causing her to pull back and look up at me.

Understanding flicked over her face in appreciation as I brought her hand up and planted a kiss on the soft skin, my thumb rubbing in wide circles. I didn't miss the water building up around the shell of her eyes, and while all I wanted was to kiss her and try to take away the pain she was sharing, I knew the thing that would best help is for me to simply listen.

So that's what I did.

"He umm... He was actually pretty great at first." Hazel continued, pulling in her knees to her chest, "There was even a couple of times my father had come over for dinner with Andrew there and we were able to act like a civilized family." The memory of it flicks over her features, longing for that to have remained clear in her eyes.

"But, of course, that was too good to be true." After that, Hazel paused for a long while, as if contemplating something hard in her head.

"You swear you're not going to go?" She asked after a period of time, looking straight at me as she said it. It broke my heart, because I knew her words were caused by previous experience where people likely ended up reacting in horribly wrong ways. Squeezing her hands for a second, I say, "I promise you with everything I have to give, I am not going to be mad at you, or leave you, or pressure you to say something you don't want to." Hazel goes still for a moment as if those words seemed so foreign to her.

"But..." I continued, "At the same time, I don't want you to feel like you need to tell me this story if you're not ready to. You have control over this; I'll just be here when you need me, Hazel." A tear falls down her cheek at that, but my hand is lifting and brushing it away before it can even fall.

"I just feel like you have the right to know about some of my scars, but I don't want you to hate me for them either." A part of my heart definitely shattered for Hazel at that point, but I didn't let her see it.

Pulling her close to me until she was between my legs, I let her back rest against my front as my one arm wrapped around her waist, the other moving to play with a few strands of her hair.

From her most recent words, I had a feeling I knew where this was going. I also knew during previous discussions together she always seemed the most comfortable when she was physically being held tight.

"You will never be obligated to tell me about that if you're not completely doing it for yourself, darling," I say into her ear, needing Hazel to hear and understand this.

"I could never hate you, no matter what you tell me, and I swear to you there is nothing you could say that would ever make me feel less of you. I'm sorry there's been people who have." I kept her taunt to me, refusing to make her think even for a second I spoke anything but the truth.

"You don't owe me anything," I promise, hugging her from behind, "If you're going to talk, make sure you're doing it for you and no one else. And if you decide you want to leave out certain parts or just stop speaking entirely, that's okay too." I was glad when she seemed to relax into my touch, my words appearing to have relieved some of her distress.

Things soon grew quiet again between the two of us, and I just let it stay that way. If and when she was ready to continue, I knew Hazel would tell me. However, the words that came next caused a stutter to occur in my heart.

"I tried to kill myself when I was sixteen." The sound of Hazel's voice and the feeling of sudden tears against my hands broke the silence between us. It wasn't until many seconds later that I realized a single tear had fallen from my eye as well. "There were always random pills in my house thanks to my mom, and when Andrew..." Hazel's bottom lip quivered and her increasingly uneven breaths soon forced her to pause her words.

Warm tears kept falling from her face, and even though this new information pained me to hear, I only held her tighter, placing a kiss to the top of her head. "Andrew came home from the bar one Friday, and with my mom passed out on the couch, he decided he wanted to see me instead." I closed my eyes when I felt her body begin to shake, trying to comfort her in any way I could while reigning in my own emotions.

"I was asleep in my bed, but I woke up to him...

he was...

he was doing things to me over top of my sheets, saying things in my ear that I wish I could forget, but can't.

I tried to stop him with my words first, but he never did." I could hear my heartbeat in my ears with every thump, the rage and sadness and pain I felt all mixing until I couldn't tell them apart.

"He may have been drunk sloppy, but he was too heavy and I didn't have the muscle or the training back then to defend myself." When Hazel trailed off to take a deep breath, something about her changed. Her expression seemed to harden, even though her relentless tears refused to stop falling.

"That night, it turned out his alcoholism was both a blessing and a curse. Before he could do anything too much farther, he passed out on top of me, but the damage had already been done." The fury ringing in my ears was nearly deafening, and I knew whether that piece of shit fell unconscious or not, he was going to die by my hand.

I hated Hazel's tears and her words because all of them meant she had to endure something that was unforgivable and there was nothing I could do to take that away. But that never once stopped me from trying.

My hands never once ceased their hopefully soothing motions along Hazel's skin, even though her breathing remained uneven and sniffles sounded from her nose.

With her head angled slightly to the side, I could see the redness circling her glossy eyes and the unhappy flush across her cheeks. I could tell just from the way she fidgeted that she wasn't done speaking yet, though she was struggling to find her words.

"I've never said this out loud, but sometimes I feel as though him blacked out beside me was even worse." Hazel confessed, silent tears dripping off of her cheeks and onto our joined hands, "Even now, sometimes despite it being physically over, it never really ended. I can still feel his hands, and" She wasn't able to continue after that admission, heartbreaking sobs rising to the surface and forcing their way over any words she may have wanted to say.

Hazel had shattered with every part of her laid bare to me, but I didn't waste a second before I held her tight, turning her body entirely until her thighs straddled my waist.

I never let her go as her head buried into the crook of my neck, crying and shaking as she took in every bit of comfort I could give her.

Though, she wasn't the only one whose tears were soaking their face. Before today, I feared talking would be placing a burden on others around me, but it wasn't until now I realized just how wrong I was. I knew at this moment I would never let Hazel feel unable to express everything she was feeling again, no matter how painful and hard it may be. "I know that veered far off from your question,"

She sniffled, sighing into my shoulder in sadness, "But to answer it, I chose to stay because when you three saw my scars that night in Carter's office, you acknowledged them in a way that made me feel safe." Dominic and I had gotten to our knees and kissed every inch of her thighs her scars, saying the words we couldn't say. Carter told her she was beautiful while we took care of her, knowing she was ours before she even realized it herself.

"I never thanked you for that, but thank you, Rowan." Hazel sat up in my lap, looking at me for the first time in a long while. The green in her eyes was brighter in combination with her tears, and the sight could only be described as devastatingly beautiful. Her words had my heart squeezing even tighter, my hands lifting from her back to the sides of her face. Holding her just like that, Hazel leaned into my touch, connecting the two of us in a way of no other. "For years after that night... I guess my arms, stomach, and thighs took the pain my heart couldn't handle." I could hear the anguish in her words, but despite this, a ghost of a smile then appeared across Hazel's lips. "For years, I pretended to be stronger than I was, but then I met a group of men that made me feel like the mask I'd become so highly accustomed to wasn't so necessary anymore. You helped me not only learn how to breathe again, but to truly feel alive." When my thumb caught the next tear, I knew it was one of both agony and happiness.

"So that, Rowan, is why I came back to you." It was at that moment I parted my lips to speak, but I was silenced as Hazel's mouth connected with mine. It was not a kiss of lust, but instead, one of relief and sadness and trust. The saltiness of our tears mixed into our senses, but neither of us cared as we remained bound as one.

"You're so fucking strong, Hazel," I said against her lips, pulling back and making sure my eyes held hers, "You said you weren't, but you are." My body warmed as my words caused a small smile to paint across her lips.

"Telling me this took courage, and I'm so proud of you for it. I can't even begin to imagine how hard that must have been to keep that bottled up for so long, but know that you will never have to feel that way again." I leaned forward until our foreheads rested against each other, breathing in the smell of her lavender and vanilla shampoo.

"I need you to promise me something though," I say, feeling her soft exhale fan across my cheeks, "If you ever feel that way again, no matter how small you might think, I need you to come talk to me or Dominic or Carter." The fact that sheer luck is the only reason I have my girl in my arms right now sends ice cold chills down my spine and fear throughout every inch of my body. I will not be able to live a life without her in it, and I never want her to have to feel that way feel alone again.

I felt Hazel nod her head, the action causing her to brush against me more. When I opened my eyes to find water droplets still on her lashes, I also found her looking at me with an emotion that expressed vulnerability and appreciation.

"I promise," Hazel whispered against my mouth, blinking away the last of her tears, "Can you do something for me as well?" She then asked, her eyes flicking away from mine.

"Anything," I answered, and I meant it too. "If it's not too much to ask, do you think you could tell Carter and Dominic what I told you?" I watched as she bit the inside of her cheek for a few moments before her eyes reconnected with mine, "I don't think I can do this again two more times, but I want them to know."

I could never deny her.

"I can do that, darling." I promise, honored that she trusts all of us enough to share this part of her life. I could tell, at last, her heart began to pace itself once again down to a steady beat, her body seemingly shaking less as well. I would hold her for as long as it took and then some.

"While it'll never be enough of a retribution, I want you to know that he's going to pay with his life for this." I swear to her. Her step-father will be paid a visit by the end of the night, whether it's me on my own or with Carter and Dominic by my side.

"No you're not," Hazel says, her voice no louder than a whisper as she forces me to look at her. Just as I opened my mouth to tell her this wasn't up for debate, Hazel stole my attention again, her finger touching to my lip.

"You're not killing him, because I'm going to." The coldness that washed over her was numbing, no lie or uncertainty to be heard in her tone, "And then, I'm going to burn that fucking house to the ground." I didn't have to be Dominic to know she meant her every word, not as a threat, but as a promise.

For a pause, we only looked at each other, neither of us wanting to back down and neither of us speaking until I nodded in understanding.

This was Hazel's choice, and it was one I needed to respect. At my silent action, she relaxed once again, resting her arms around my neck and moving forward until I was laid on my back with her on top of me.

This she was everything I needed.

So there we remained, alone under a new blanket of warmth. It was one that brought the promise of a better future with not just the two of us, but the four that made up our puzzle of shattered hearts.

While we're all a mix of scars and pain and anger, these combinations also blossomed a hope that maybe something good could come out of this.

That maybe, just maybe, we could find a way to heal, not as individuals, but together as one.

~ Ten ~

Hazel

From Rowan: I just wanted to say thank you again for trusting me with all of that yesterday. I spoke with Dominic and Carter like you asked and they said that if you ever need to talk, no matter the time, you can come to any of us. I promise no one is mad, only grateful you were willing to share so much with us. I meant it when I told you are our everything, and I just wanted to make sure you know that.

I woke up to this notification on my phone screen this morning, and I've been crying for the last ten minutes because of it.

Only this time, they weren't tears of sadness.

This entire last week has been a true roller coaster of emotions for me, and yesterday was not something I took lightly. The day with Rowan was everything to me, and even though I still have a lot of my mind because of the Mafia and all, I will never forget those few simple hours we spent in the park.

A lot of the things I told him were things I've never said out loud, and it was a massive step for me to overcome. I was proud of myself for opening up about the thing I've intentionally spent years keeping inside, and when I woke up this morning, I felt different.

It's stupid because I know I'm physically the same, but my steps feel lighter and I feel like I can breathe a little easier. Rowan's response to me was amazing in every way possible, and it solidified the fact for me that he was every part of life I've been want-ing. In combination with Carter and Dominic, these three men are making me feel things I don't even know how to comprehend, but I live for it.

I suppose that's the reality of this all. Even if it absolutely terrifies me, at this point I don't know how I've gone my entire life without them.

Now that I do, I don't plan on ever letting them go. I spent a lot of time last night really thinking about our relationship, and the intense feelings that have evolved in such little time.

I knew my anger with them for lying wouldn't just go away in the span of a few days, but I meant it when I said I forgave them and wanted to move on. I wanted to enjoy every moment of this week, because I knew it was one that I was already looking forward to.

Not too long after Rowan's first text was delivered, he also sent a schedule for this week and what nights I would be seeing the three of them.

Today I'm working, but I'm to see Dominic tomorrow, Carter the day after, and Rowan on Thursday. Saturday is the group scene, all days in which I'm now specifically looking forward to.

The excitement of seeing them again fills my body, and it's sur-prisingly getting to the point where these three days each week I don't see them is only making me wish we could have everyday.

Don't get me wrong, I need my own space and time as much as anyone else does, but I wouldn't exactly hate getting to wake up next to one or all of them regularly.

These men have me hooked so deep and I'm not sure if they even realize it.

Today will be good for me though. I plan to do absolutely nothing at all until my shift, and that's the beauty of it. I slept in pretty late considering I had no plans, but I haven't seen Jolene much recently, and honestly, I think a visit might be nice. She truly has become a second mother to me, and plus, she makes the best damn coffee I've ever had.

I hadn't realized how much I missed her until now, so even as my stomach rumbles for food, I end up getting dressed and leaving anyways.

With a clear head and relaxed muscles, I end up making my way slowly over to the Horizon in my piece of junk car.

I should start saving up to get a new one because I don't trust this thing to get me far without the risk of crapping out on me anymore.

I put that in the back of my mind for now, soon pulling up to the cafe until I realize how little parking there is today. Looks like there's going to be a long walk for me. I ended up parking quite a ways up the street before getting out of my car in dismissal and locking it.

Just seeing the entrance to the small coffee shop down the street has me beyond happy, and after a few minutes, I'm pushing open the glass door and breathing in a deep breath of the fresh smells.

I missed this place for sure. It was beyond busy today and the line was long, but I managed to squeeze my way inside, adding myself to the end of the very long line.

So there I waited, my attention being snagged shortly after I heard Jolene's familiar accent to my left. With a fake smile on her face, I listened as she cursed someone out in Italian for spilling their drink all over the floor and not bothering to say anything until she damn near slipped in it.

She shouted a few muffled words I couldn't make out from here, and seconds later, the man I recognized as Pablo was sweeping up the broken cup with a dust pan while Jolene fetched a mop for herself.

Smiling at the usual chaos here, it was like I had never stopped my daily visits for the last week. I was getting closer to my turn in the line, but when Jolene came back from the storage closet, her eyes caught on me and instantly crinkled at the corners.

I didn't have to think twice as I left the column of people, moving to say hi, but unable to as Jolene was already moving around the counter.

By the time I was there, she already had a bag of pastries in her hand and a steaming cup of coffee made to my liking. "Let's head upstairs where we can talk in quiet." She says, putting a hand on my arm as she guides us away from the till and over to a narrow hallway.

I knew Jolene lived upstairs, but never once since meeting her have I been up there.

Come to think of it, it never really dawned on me that she actually lived here until now.

The floorboards creaked as it took the weight of each of our steps, small lights turning on as it sensed our motions moving upwards. Before I knew it, Jolene was unlocking a door with her keys, and pushing until it swung open to a small space really meant to fit no more than two people.

I knew Jolene has been widowed for over two decades now, but when my eyes caught on a small cot in the corner of the room, I couldn't help but think of Rowan.

Was this where he stayed when Jolene was the only refuge in his life? I was so thankful she found him that day, because I don't even want to think about what else might have happened if she hadn't.

"Don't mind the clutter, dear. Let's sit over here, because I can see we have much to discuss."

"How did you know?" I blinked, sensing that she's a lot more like Dominic than I thought.

"You have that look about you. And you haven't come here in a few days, so I'm assuming things have been... a bit much?" A bit was quite the understatement, but she was right.

"I guess I've just been a bit preoccupied lately," I say, smiling in thanks when she passed me my coffee and opened the bag of sweets on the table between us. Sitting down where her hand gestures, I lean back on the small but surprisingly really comfortable armchair now beneath me. Jolene takes a seat on her own right across from me.

"Well that I know," She grins with a knowing look that makes me flush, "They're treating you well, I hope?" There was a slight warning in her voice that she would go after any one of them if they were doing anything otherwise. I allowed my amusement to show on my face as I said, "They're everything I could have ever wanted." Jolene relaxed at that, leaning back in her chair, but not before grabbing a small cookie out of the paper bag.

"Good." She settles, "If that ever changes, you be sure to let me know." I think we both knew damn well none of them would ever intentionally hurt me. In fact, half the time they act like they're willing to jump in front of a bullet for me. I nodded and took a sip of my coffee, sighing as the hot liquid coursed down my throat and warmed every inch of my body. "Did Dominic tell you about what happened this last week?" I ask, resting my cup on my thigh and keeping my hands wrapped around it. Jolene lets out a small chuckle.

"That boy doesn't talk to me much anymore, but yes, I know." I met her gaze as she looked over my face, trying to find any indication of fear in my mind. Believe me when I say it's most definitely there.

"How are you feeling about it all?" Jolene questions, brushing some crumbs off of her fingertips. Never once does her eyes leave mine. "I don't like it," I admit honestly, crossing my leg over my other, "I don't like that so many people I care about are in constant danger, and no offense to you, but I hate that the men I'm in a relationship with have to answer to Vincent." I had to make a valiant effort to suppress the goosebumps threatening to arise just at the thought of that horrible, malicious man.

"I hate that Dominic and Carter are both going to lead this entire thing one day too, because selfishly, I don't know where that leaves me." These are a lot of things I wasn't yet wanting to admit to my men, but Jolene showed no hostility or indifference towards me.

"It's not selfish, dear, to want to have some normalcy in your life. God knows you more than anyone deserves some."

I took in her words, but ultimately knew nothing would be simple anymore in pursuing a relationship with these men. It was worth it, though. Sometimes simple wasn't meant to be, but even before I knew they were in the Mafia, our lack of simplicity was what kept things so intense and exhilarating all the time.

"I know there's still so much I need to figure out, but I do know that Rowan, Carter, and Dominic are what I want." I say with uttermost conviction. Jolene knew it too.

"That's good," She nods, truly knowing that they were what made me happy, "But you don't have to take this all on your own, you know? I'm willing to bet this whole thing has them just as uneasy about what the future holds." Unbelievably, I'd never even stopped to think about how this might be stressing them out as well.

I figured considering they already knew about these complications for so much longer than I have, they would've already had the time to come to terms with it.

Never once did I consider that the stress of this could be the cause for the dark circles under Rowan's eyes yesterday or why Carter would sometimes randomly hold me in the middle of the night when he thought I was sleeping. Jolene was right. I wasn't the only one worried about how the Mafia plays a role in our relationship now that things are getting serious. God, I love this woman.

"Thank you," I say, reaching over and squeezing her hand, "I think I really needed to hear that." She smiled as she returned my gesture, before grabbing the chair for stability as she stood up.

"I have a gift for you." Jolene waved for me to follow her as she walked to the dresser by her bed, opening the bottom drawer and pulling out a box about the length of my wrist to elbow. It was a plain brown colour, the lid taped to the bottom as she rose and grabbed both of my hands with her one. Placing down the box, her silent nod towards it told me she wanted me to open it. Helping her sit back down in her chair, even though she insisted she wasn't that old, I resumed my previous position as I peeled away the sealing, wiggling the lid until it pulled loose. Inside I found white paper packaging in which I gently removed, my eyes widening as I saw the object inside.

"Jolene, I"

"I have a feeling you're going to need it one day, and even if you don't, I'm not taking any chances." She interrupted. Delicately wrapping my fingers around the hilt of the intricately designed dagger, I removed it from the box as well as the scabbard around the blade.

This weapon was a true piece of artwork, and left me in a state of absolute shock and admiration.

"This is beautiful," I say, lifting my eyes from the blade to Jolene, "This must have cost you a fortune"

"I'm not taking it back." Jolene cuts me off yet again, smiling because she somehow discovered this was my favourite weapon to train with growing up and still is, "The blade is pre-sharpened and already ready to be made use of."

I swallowed, glancing back down to the dagger.

"Do you really think I'm going to have to use it?" I ask, my eyes trailing over every refined detail.

"I think only a fool would walk around unarmed now that some-one like Vincent MacGuire has their eyes set on you." My heart skipped a beat, "He's watching me?" I asked, feeling my palms go cold in fear. "He watches everybody, but especially you. He's killed people for simply blinking at him the wrong way, yet you're still breathing and unharmed. Ask yourself, what does Vincent have to gain by keeping a near stranger alive after doing things that are considered criminal offenses against the Don?" An ice cold chill trickled down my spine at her words, hundreds of questions popping into my head.

"Do you know the answer to that?" I ask, brushing my finger along the sharp edge of the blade and tracing it with my mind.

"Not yet." Jolene etches a small frown onto her face, "I fear it's something only you will be able to figure out." So many questions and such little answers.

"I don't know what to do," I admit, even as I feel a sense of empowerment just by the thought of using this against someone like Vincent. I'm glad Jolene thinks just as lowly of him as I.

"Coffee helps," Jolene gestures to the slowly cooling cup beside me, "My advice to you is to keep your head sharp and think care-fully about who you can trust. Everything will become clear soon, but remember that even the strongest of forces can wield the larg-est vulnerabilities." Her words struck me hard, the truth in them sinking deep and telling me more or less to keep my enemies closer. I needed to keep three steps ahead of Vincent and be wary of who I let into my life.

Easy for me, apart from Jade, Jolene, and my men, there were very few people I opened up to anymore.

"I will." I promise her, knowing this entire conversation is not something I'm going to forget anytime soon, if ever.

I had a strong feeling that last week would not be my last encounter with Vincent MacGuire, but I've learned something re-cently that he doesn't know.

I'm going to gain the upper hand, because his sexist ass won't even see it coming until it's too late to reverse my actions. I smiled to myself as I heard Jolene call after me as I exited the cafe.

She no doubt saw the cash I'd left on the counter for the coffee and snacks, and was now on her way to hound me about my stubbornness.

I feel like so much of my life has been altered in the last seven days, but not this.

This was the same. By the time Jolene's much shorter legs had carried her to the door, I was already down the sidewalk and unlocking my car. With my dagger hidden and tucked up the long sleeve of my shirt, I pulled on the door handle and slid into the driver's seat, gently tossing the knife into the small black console.

Sighing to myself, I forced all of the questions from my brain temporarily, turning on the radio and starting up the engine. Honestly, all I wanted to do right now was go home and watch Netflix for a few hours until I had to return to work and walk around in heels for the night.

Using my right hand, I twist and grab my seat belt, securing it over my body and listening as it clicked in place.

Not wasting another second, I checked to make sure the road was clear before pulling away from the curb and beginning a steady acceleration down the street.

Only ten minutes and I could get back into my sweats for the day. That thought made for a fairly peaceful drive back, but when I heard the familiar sound of my phone ringing, I sighed as it interrupted the song I was listening to and reached back in search of my purse. Making sure to keep my eyes on the road, my hand blindly sought out my phone in the backseat, but I tensed as my fingertips brushed against something that was neither the material of my purse nor the seats. Flicking my eyes to the rear view mirror, my scream was stifled as a large black figure appeared in the backseat, revealing that I was anything but alone in this car. Doing the only thing I could think to do, I slammed hard on the brake, silently praying the driver behind me wasn't on their phone and hopefully paying attention. My seat belt snapped tight to my body, keeping me in place for the most part, but the same couldn't be said for whoever was in the back. The hand that had previously moved to wrap around my mouth was jolted forwards, along with the rest of the masked person's body. My heart fumbled as I heard a series of loud honks come from those behind me, but their vehicles simply veered around me angrily. That beats getting hit, at least. Already finding myself prepared, as the body from the backseat flew forward through the gap between the two front seats, I took my hand and grabbed the neck of who is very clearly a man at closer glance. Before he could recover from his shock, I pinned his head down and kept him still as I pulled off the thin black mask from his face. But before the fabric was even all the way off, I stilled and tensed as the smell of cologne hit me. That break was all he needed as he pushed himself up, slipping the rest of the cover off for me. I could barely breathe as a pair of eyes so similar to mine stared back at me, brushing away the messy blonde strands that had fallen over my face. "Dad?" He's here. After six months of hearing nothing from him, he's actually here, in my car. I'm stunned at how entirely different he looks from when I last saw him, but it's those eyes. Only someone who knew him well would be able to recognize those eyes. "Hey, kiddo." He panted, no doubt slightly winded by the harsh impact of my brakes. Releasing my hold on his neck in shock, I watch as my father sits up with a groan, painfully moving himself to the passenger's seat beside me. My mouth is practically agape in disbelief, but yet another honk draws me out of my daze. I don't take my eyes off of him as I begin to drive again, only stealing quick glances on the road to ensure I wasn't going to crash into anything. This was the first time I've heard his voice in months, and I can barely keep it together as I try to find a place to pull over but finding none. "You're here?" I bit back my sob of relief and anger and confusion. He's been gone for half a year, and now he's back looking nearly unrecognizable and scaring the shit out of me in my own car. Seems just like my father. "I can't stay for long, I'm afraid, but we need to talk." My dad said, leaning down in his seat and keeping his eyes hidden from anyone around. "What's going on? You just left without even a note, and now—" "I know, I know." He said, sounding truly apologetic, but in a hurry, "I'm sorry for that, and I promise I'll be able to explain everything soon, but I really need you to listen to what I'm about to tell you." I was admittedly a little scared right now, but I didn't show it, or challenge what my father was asking right now. With a nod, he continued. "I need you to promise me you won't tell a soul what I'm about to say, Hazel. Not even those men you're seeing." My grip tightens around the steering wheel in surprise he knows about them, but I shouldn't be. Vincent has his resources, my father has his own. "Why not?" I ask, turning off of one road and onto another. "Because there are some really bad people after me right now, and so many things can go wrong from me even risking to speak with you. The less people who know, the better."

I knew I didn't have time on my side right now, so instead of protesting or asking more questions, I simply gave a quick nod. "Thank you," He says, shifting his gloved hand and wincing slightly, ignoring my narrowing eyes at the action, "I've had a feud with an extremely powerful man dating all the way back to before you were even born. When I moved to Detroit with your mother, it was to keep under the radar and not because we were low on money. We had just barely gotten away from him and knew we had to stay as hidden as possible, especially with your mother so far along in her pregnancy with you." It has been years since my father has even acknowledged that my mother existed, let alone speak about her so many times. This was very serious, but all I could do was sit and soak up everything I could. "For years as this man grew stronger in public, I made sure we overpowered him every step of the way in silence. If anything bad ever happens to me, know that I have accounts set up for you with enough money to buy you a new life should you please." A new life? Before I could open my mouth to speak, my father was pulling out a business card and pushing it into my hand. "This is the number of someone who can help you with your finances should you feel the need to access what is both your birthright and what you deserve. I know I wasn't the best parental figure, but you will always be taken care of, that much I can promise you." "What is—" "Turn left up here," My father said, indicating a narrow alleyway that most certainly didn't look safe. "I don't understand—" "I know, kiddo. I'm so sorry that I can't stay for longer, but everything will make sense soon." "Dad?" I turn to him as I roll to a stop, panic pushing its way through my bones, "Stay. Talk to me, and we can figure this out together." I watched as my father leaned towards me, his hand moving to my cheek and brushing away the tear I didn't know I'd shed. "You've gotten so much stronger." He says instead, his eyes flicking over my face as if trying to memorize it while he still could, "Stay with those men of yours. They love you, and they'll be able to keep you safe when I can't." I blinked in confusion and moved to undo my seat belt, but I wasn't fast enough to stop him as my dad's fingers slipped away from my cheek. By the time my head snapped up in regret, he was already gone, blending into the darkness and off to somewhere unknown.

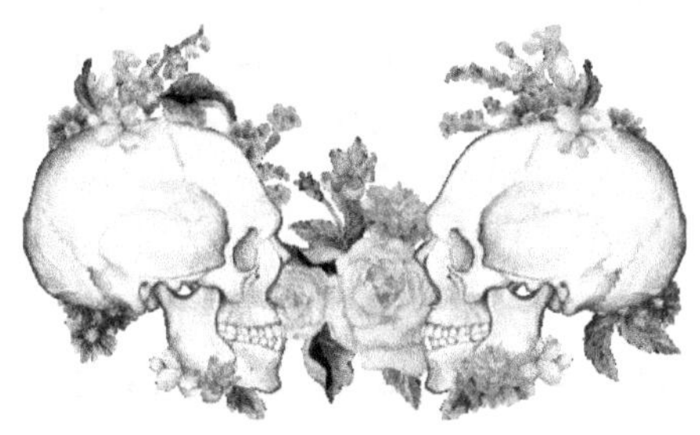

~ Eleven ~

Marcus

I watch as my daughter drives off in the same car she had months ago before I left her behind. With the exception of that, however, a lot has changed about her in the many weeks of my absence.

She looks stronger, healthier.

I can only imagine those who she's been associating herself with were a major role in that. In the six months I've been gone, I made sure to keep an eye out on Hazel the entire time in secret, seeing her in pain, slowly recovering from it, and finding the kind of love I've always hoped for her to find. Hazel was still hurting a lot I knew I was partially responsible for that—but I had to make sure she never found me.

It was the only way to keep her safe and ensure I will one day be able to be a part of her life again. But Hazel, being the well trained person I raised her to be, made my life in hiding extremely difficult for me. Her private investigator, for example, found me within a month of being hired. Well, that's a lie.

I found Callum shortly after she hired him, and then proceeded to pay him off for both his silence and expertise. With some persuasion, he did. Not only did he keep quiet about my location, but I also got him to feed Hazel fake leads that intentionally brought her to New York.

I knew I needed her here for yet another step of my big plan, and even if doing so unknowingly, with my daughter's help the two of us are going to bring my entire organization up to power and obliterate the man who started this all. In exchange for Callum's assistance in this, it wasn't hard at all to make the investigator cave after I offered him triple of what Hazel was giving, as well as taking her money and placing it into the same account I had set up for her.

My little girl has no clue just how many riches she has in her name, but I reckon it's best to keep things that way for now. You see, this entire thing has just been small pieces to a much larger puzzle I've been creating for the last multiple years of my life. And the man who is responsible for all of this chaos is none other than Vincent MacGuire.

Don't get me wrong, I've done way too many things at this point to be deemed as innocent in this ever-growing rivalry between us, but he and his son were the beginning of it all.

The Order is a group I formed the first time I ever crossed paths with the mafia. It was first merely a small gathering of people who too had been harshly impacted by the four crime families, but it turns out I wasn't even close to being the only one who had scores that needed to be settled.

There were thousands of people sick of rolling over to their forces, and most of us didn't have anything to lose anymore. My experience was only one of many, but I've had to spend years in hiding with my entire family hidden under an umbrella of fake identities all because my brother was murdered in cold blood by a father trying to teach his son a lesson.

"You need to learn that this man does not matter, Carter. He's not important and you most certainly should not be crying over him." Those words, along with many others from that day have been permanently etched into my memory, only fueling the burning need for revenge with every passing second.

Vincent forced a gun into his own child's hand and punished him when he refused to obey his order to eliminate his target. The word tasted like ash on my tongue, but that was the reality.

My dear brother, Keith, was murdered at the age of sixteen, and died being told his life was worth nothing more than a lesson in obedience. It didn't matter to me that he owed a huge sum of debt to the Mafia and was unable to pay it back; he didn't deserve to die like that.

I most certainly didn't deserve to see the videotape of his death in warning of what happens to those who think to cross Vincent MacGuire.

I know that evil man's intentions were to break down any form of resiliency he suspected to remain within me, but the effect of his actions were quite the opposite actually.

Here I am now, years later as the head of my own army, having the perfect plan in order. By the end of this all, Vincent is going to watch as I take down his entire empire, killing every single person he cares about along the way, just like I had to watch as my brother died.

Slipping off the black gloves from my hands, I flex my fingers and inspect the fresh cuts adorning my knuckles. Hazel wasn't the only person I came to New York to visit, but a cheating ex-boyfriend who appeared to have already come into contact with three other men.

"Marcus." The voice of my second in command, and newly wed wife called from behind me as she stepped out of the shadows. Turning, I glance over Ivy as she holds her hand out to me. "It's time." She says, raising her chin slightly as I take a step towards her.

"That it is, my love." That it is.

Dominic

Hazel makes me feel like a nervous teenage boy all over again, yet I can't help but like it a little.

Ever since she came back those few days ago, I knew I would never let her go better yet, I would never give her a reason to leave again.

She deserves to know about who her dad really is, but I know the second Hazel does, things are going to get bad quick. That alone scares me, but we're only digging our graves deeper the longer we wait.

I've decided I'm going to run it by Rowan and Carter first for their support, and while I know it's going to be a harsh conversation to have, I swore to Hazel she had all of me.

That includes even the fucked up parts that are hard to admit.

I needed a little time to sort through things though, because I know Carter will be the most opposed to opening up, especially about the whole reason why we've dedicated so much time to killing Marcus in the first place.

Though, I do have something in the works that should motivate him to talk to Hazel, but if my theory is true, that means a lot of pain for Carter.

I just need concrete evidence first otherwise he'll believe my thoughts to be an act of denial for our girl, and not one based on truth and logic.

Either way, things are getting a lot more serious with Hazel, and while it's intense, I'm living for it at this point.

That's mainly why I've chosen to put the entire thought of Marcus away for now, because this is our night. It may make me selfish to stand here at her door, even though I'm sure she's better off with someone else, but when my girl walks out and flashes me a bright smile, I couldn't care less what it made me. I'm here and she is mine.

"Hey handsome," Hazel grinned, walking up and rising on her tiptoes to kiss my cheek. Her lips are soft against my rough skin, and I couldn't help but find myself intoxicated already just by her presence.

Bringing down and turning my head, I brushed my lips against hers, savoring her taste and smell and simply just her.

"Hey, princess," I murmured back, already feeling myself relax into her touch. Looping my arm around her waist, I end up pulling Hazel's body flush against mine, my other hand toying with the strands of her hair as though it had a mind of its own.

"Did you do what I requested?" I asked lowly in her ear, enjoying the small blush on her face before I was met with mischievousness.

"Oh yes." She smiled, her voice as luring as a siren, "I even brought you a present, Sir."

I clenched my jaw as Hazel slowly pulled out a lingerie piece of light pink lace from her purse, slipping the underwear into my hand and closing my fingers around it. When I had told her one of the conditions of tonight was her not wearing anything beneath the silver dress she now wore, I didn't expect this kind of reaction. But she listened, and now I also had one of her pretty little undergarments around my knuckles.

"Hm," I gave her a sinful smile, enjoying this teasing game we had going on, "Just to be sure though." I crouched down as though I had dropped something, my hand instantly finding its way to the smooth skin of her ankle before slowly trailing up the inside of her leg as I stood.

The shining material of her dress bunched up as I got higher, Hazel's breaths going unsteady as I continued to lift the material in the very much public area.

I made sure to shield her with my large body, certain no one walking by would notice anything, but Hazel didn't know that and I wasn't about to tell her.

I continued my path until I got all the way to the apex of her thighs, my single finger brushing up and coming in contact with a completely bare, soaked cunt.

Smirking to myself at the little gasp that came from Hazel's mouth at the action, I only winked as I brought my hand away, more than satisfied with her reaction.

"Ready to go then?" I smirk in amusement at the clear daze Hazel only now just snapped out of by the subject change. It took no time, though, before she regained herself, my heart beating a little quicker as her hand slipped into mine.

"And where are we going again?" She tries, knowing I've purposely kept my mouth shut about our location. What she doesn't know is that I actually plan to take her to two places tonight; a scene and a date.

"Nice try." I kiss her temple before opening the door to my car for her. Her hand slips from mine as she gets in, but it's not long before I'm rounding the vehicle, moving into the driver's seat and resuming our little touches.

Even though I began driving shortly after, I took the time to really take in her dress and how perfectly she obeyed my orders. Wearing the gift I sent her, Hazel's body shimmered along with the silver material that hugged tight to her skin. It was out of her comfort zone, and I was proud of her for trusting me enough to still wear it tonight.

With her hair set in loose curls, she looked beautiful, the black wedges I'm sure she borrowed from Jade setting her a few inches taller.

Hazel was currently looking out the window, though I had a feeling she was well aware of my wandering gaze over her body. Everything was perfect for tonight, and I was already wanting to pull over and take her right here in the car. But, with the little self control I had left in me, I instead settled on placing my hand on her thigh, wrapping around where her legs were pressed tight together.

I smiled as she shifted, and I soon had a feeling my teasing already had her all warmed up for later.

Turning her head back to me, the flush across Hazel's cheeks confirmed what I already knew, and neither of us were complaining in the least.

It was just past ten o'clock now, and under the faint red illumination of my car's interior lights, Hazel looked absolutely stunning in combination with her dark eye makeup.

We may not have been speaking, but our continuous glances at each other made for a lot of sexual tension with still a fifteen minute drive to Rush.

"I—" Hazel had just begun speaking when a call came in on my phone, interrupting what she was just about to say. I instantly moved to turn the device on silent, but the number from my mother's home office had me reaching for the answer button.

My mom hasn't called me in years, and the only reason she would be now is if someone was dead or something else important enough happened to set her pride aside and make the first move.

"Sorry," I apologize as I answer the call through my car's Bluetooth system. The looks Hazel sends me told me it really wasn't a big deal which I nodded to in genuine thanks.

"Hello," I say, already tense for the conversation that's to come.

"Dominic," A small voice cries through the speaker, my little sister's sobs filling the car.

"Nina?" I startle, but force my voice into calmness, "What's the matter, angel?" If my mother knew Nina was in her office, using her phone... I don't even want to finish that thought.

"Ca-can you p-put me to bed?" She asks through her over-whelmed breaths, stuttering as she tries to keep quiet over the phone.

"Where's mamma and papa?" I question, not noticing how tense I had grown until Hazel placed her hand overtop of my own on her thigh.

"They left for a-a party." Which means they left her with the housekeepers for the night again. Nina has never managed well with them, and I don't blame her either.

She deserves her parents to put her to bed, and I know she can't sleep without somebody more than just hired help there.

Looking at Hazel, she whispers to me, "Go to your parent's place. Whatever mystery plans you've thought up can wait an hour or two, don't you think?" Her words allow a part of me to relax, giving her thigh a teasing squeeze in appreciation.

"I'm on my way, Nina, okay? You listen to what Miss Daphene asks of you, and then I'll come tuck you to bed in about ten minutes. Can you do that for me, angel?" I don't know why I would have expected anything less than understanding from Hazel, but I'm still grateful for it. I really needed it right now, especially when I was already so angry with my parents. Leaving my baby sister at home with practical strangers was just the cherry on top.

"Okay, bye." Nina's voice suddenly quickened before the line abruptly went dead between us.

This only made me smile and shake my head because her actions likely meant Miss Daphene, the same housekeeper that watched over me as a child as well, was close to catching her in places we all knew she wasn't allowed to be in.

With the silence of the call and the low music on the radio beginning to play once again, Hazel shifted to look at me better.

"That was your sister?" She asked with a small smile, no doubt also picking up on the slight mischievous side Nina too shared.

"Dominic, it really isn't a big deal." She brushes my words off, truly not viewing this as a disruption, "I'm excited to meet her anyways. I always wanted a little sister growing up, but it just never happened." Honestly, Nina wasn't a planned child, but I don't think I could ever go back to not having her in my family anymore.

"I'm sure she'll love you. She has a really hard time with new people though, so don't be sad when she doesn't speak to you. Enjoy it even; once you get her talking, she'll never shut up." Hazel's eyes crinkle at the corners slightly as she laughs at that, easing the last bit of worry from my body. Just this little thing meant the world to me, and she doesn't even realize it. Pulling into the extensively long driveway that leads up to my childhood house, I watch as Hazel's eyes go wide at the sheer size of everything.

My parents did nothing short of grand and made the place I lived in to seem like nothing more than a small apartment. I always hated this mansion that was always too echoey and large to be called home, and now is no different. I've put up with it and come here multiple times over the years to see Nina, but my dislike has never changed.

Though, Hazel makes it easier. Going straight through the gates and nodding in acknowledgement at the guards, I parked as close as I could to the main entrance, sighing as I got out of the car and walked around to open Hazel's door for her.

Just because she was capable of doing it on her own doesn't always mean she should have to.

Plus, I would do it a million more times if I could get to see her cutely blush in thanks again the way she just did now. Slipping her hand into mine, we walked side by side up the patio stairs until I found myself unlocking the doors to this dreaded place and pushing inside.

Gazing around, I hated how similar it looked with the same horrid memories I can't shake even decades later. At least I wasn't so damn alone this time being here. I barely had time to shut the door before the sight of a giggling Nina came racing down the stairs, her hand trying to muffle her laughs to hide the fact that she very much shouldn't be out of her room. "Dominic!" She smiled, so busy caught up in her excitement that she didn't even notice Hazel as she rushed passed and threw herself around my legs.

"Hey, angel," I bend and hug her, her motions clear that she's tired but desperately fighting it, "You remember me telling you that I met someone, right?" I say, turning my head with Nina as she finally realizes we weren't alone in the room, "This is Hazel Walsh, my girlfriend."

"Hi," My girl says, offering a calming smile, "Dominic's told me so many great things about you." As expected, Nina doesn't say a word to her, though we both watch as she looks Hazel up and down slowly.

She typically does this with strangers, and I feel her nuzzle slightly closer to me in shyness before looking up at my eyes. I only give her a wink, silently telling her that she's okay and that she's safe. As if needing to see yet again for herself, Nina looks back to Hazel in seemingly deep thought before leaning up to my ear.

"Is she a princess?" I hear her whisper, though considering she's only six, Nina hasn't exactly mastered the concept of being quiet. I watch as a grin splits wide across Hazel's face at her words, her eyes meeting mine in amusement.

"She's my princess," I say in response to Nina, though I keep my gaze directly on Hazel as I speak, loving the way she smiles for an entirely different reason this time. I feel Nina nod against me before pulling out of my arms, using one of her small hands to indicate that she wanted us to stay put for a minute. Before I could say anything else, my sister ran off, back up the stairs and to where I'm assuming to be her room.

"You're cute." Hazel's voice pulls my attention away from the staircase, my eyebrows raising in question as I stand from my crouched position.

"Cute?" I question with a tilt of my head, that word not being even close to one of the things I'd describe myself as.

"I didn't realize you were so good with kids." She adds, taking a step towards me and slinging her arms over my shoulders, "So yes. That was cute." I grinned as my fingers found their way to her hips, pulling her in close enough that I could feel her body better against mine.

"Only with Nina," I say, tucking a small strand of hair behind her ear, "She's the only kid I'd do this for... well, I'd probably do it for you too if you asked me to tuck you in." I teased as amusement flashed across Hazel's features.

"Last time I checked, I wasn't a kid." She says, emphasizing her point by closing that last little bit of distance between our bodies. "Well you are nine years younger than me." Hazel straightens slightly, her heels putting her much closer than usual at eye level with me. She used it to her advantage too as she looked at me dead serious and said, "If being twenty three makes me a kid, then you're a grandpa at this point." I couldn't help the laugh that fell past my lips, this conversation completely useless, but entirely perfect at the same time.

Just as I opened my mouth to retort another comment one that was nowhere near appropriate for wandering ears, I stopped myself at the sound of Nina beginning her decent back down the stairs.

Hazel pulled away slightly so that we were now side by side as the two of us watched my sister walk with her hands behind her back, clearly hiding something from us. Looking at her feet as she moved, I waited for Nina to come to me, but instead she stood in front of Hazel, gesturing for her to bend down.

I angled my head and kept quiet as Hazel crouched down in slight surprise, making sure her dress stayed down in the process.

From this angle I couldn't see what my sister was being so secretive about, but I swear my heart stopped for a second as Nina's hands came around to her front, her fingers holding a delicate toy crown.

I know Hazel's breath hitched as well as the twisted metals of golds and greens were placed atop her head, my sister effectively shocking us all.

"Now you're a real princess." Nina murmured nervously, not waiting to hear Hazel's response before she was suddenly tugging at my hand.

This was a very huge thing for Nina to do, and I didn't stop her as she silently told me she was finally ready for bed.

With a nod from a nearly teary eyed Hazel, I smiled as I was led away, knowing that in a few minutes, the beautiful woman who I get to call mine will be waiting for me.

~ Twelve ~

Hazel

"The night is still very young, princess." Dominic says to me as we pull up to the entrance of the nightclub he co-owns. Glancing up at the dark sky, I feel my heart racing at the sight of where we are.

Rush, even on Mondays, tends to be packed with people, and as Dominic and I walk hand in hand through one of the back doors, I found that tonight was no exception.

Saying hi to some of the bouncers, I casually pulled down the bottom of my dress when no one was looking, only to be met with a generous amount of more cleavage showing.

Damn Dominic. And damn his no underwear request. I could feel the cool air meeting my core with every step I took, my nipples taunt, but surprisingly well hidden by the material of my dress.

Under the strobe lights, I sparkled, loving the way Dominic looked at me distractingly from the fact that all it would take is a small bend for some part of me to be exposed. The content smirk on his face told me he knew it too, expecting this exact problem of mine to occur. Smug asshole. He's lucky I like him, because I'm super on edge right now, even though we're walking right into the pit of the most exclusive nightclub in New York. Honestly, sometimes I forget how much money my men have until it's thrown right in my face. While I had expected Dominic to bring me straight downstairs, I jolted as he suddenly pulled me into the crowd of dancing people, moving so that his front was pressed close to my back. "Always in such a hurry." He tuts over the loud sound of music and conversation, lifting my arms until they wrap around his neck behind my head. My dress rose with the action, but not yet enough to expose me entirely. "Let me enjoy you for a little," Dominic says, his hands dropping to my waist and guiding our bodies together as one as we danced together. This was a surprise I didn't expect, but I cherished it all the same as I closed my eyes and leaned my head back on his shoulder, swaying my hips without a care in the world.

Allowing Dominic to take control of me, I simply felt as his hands wandered my body, never inching too high or too low. It was the perfect range that both left me desperate and satisfied all at once.

The two soon blurred into one big wave of emotion, one that left me entirely consumed by the man at my back.

As I breathed in his smell, I no longer worried about the confinements of my dress, or better yet, my mind.

Dominic knew my boundaries, so I put my trust in him, letting him direct where this night went.

For a long time, we remained like this, never once pulling off for a break or removing ourselves from each other.

Despite being in a room with thousands of people, things felt as though it were only the two of us here, accompanied by the fast beat of the music that matched our racing hearts. At some point, I think I had nearly fallen into some sort of trance, both created and broken by Dominic's touch.

At the feeling of a large hand brushing over my ass from between where our bodies were still pressed closely together, my eyes opened, adjusting to the plethora of lights and colour.

It remained as nothing more than that for a little while, but when I soon felt Dominic's rough fingertips dragging further down and up my thigh, my breath hitched and I pressed back against him.

"Dominic, what are you doing?" I gasp, turning my head to see if anyone's watching only for his free hand to grip my chin, forcing me to look back at his heated gaze.

"What? Do the people make you nervous?" He asks in a cruel tone, false pity underlying his words. As if to directly counter that, Dominic slid all the way under my short dress, two fingers quickly meeting the wet center between my folds. "You know they do," I say, a frantic blush forming on my face. I knew everyone around was in their own world and barely paying attention to us, but I didn't expect for the fear of getting caught to make me so sensitive. I was suddenly extremely thankful for the music that covered my moan, Dominic's fingers sinking deep inside of me and curling upwards.

"So if I said I had a public scene planned for us downstairs in twenty minutes, you wouldn't be interested?" Dominic said in my ear, his words causing my heart to race and my clit to throb at the idea.

"You what?" I yell over the music, even though we both know I heard him the first time.

The thought of having people watching me had me nervous just as much as it excited me. Was I really ready for that step, though?

"I booked a room for us with you in mind. The crowd won't be as busy today and I picked you up something that I think will help with your confidence." When Dominic's thumb then brushed against my clit, I had to tighten my arms around him as I felt my knees buckle slightly. He was already on it though, dropping his hand from my chin and instead wrapping it around my waist.

The support let me focus entirely on the sensations, all too aware that I was so aroused it had begun to leak onto my inner, upper thighs.

Dominic refused to let me be embarrassed though. His mouth moved down to my neck, nipping the skin and swirling his tongue in the most intoxicating of motions.

I was given no opportunity to worry as my head became consumed by everything Dominic.

"Not here." I barely manage to say, my legs clamping shut around his hand. I know Dominic could have continued if he wanted to, which I'm sure he did, but I sagged in both relief and slight disappointment when he removed his fingers from me. Turning us, I didn't have a chance to protest before he was licking them clean right in the open, silently demanding for me to watch.

That in itself had my legs pressing against each other further, but I couldn't enjoy it for long before I was being guided by the waist towards the VIP doors. I'm not sure I'm ready for this yet. Just as the thought passed my mind, Dominic leaned down and said, "We don't have to do anything if you don't want to, but I want to show you the room whether we stay there or not." He always knows.

"Thank you," I relaxed, no longer worried as he led me past the bouncers and into the small lobby. There, I saw Cassidy who gave me a knowing smile at the fact that Dominic was by my side and this time I wasn't hurriedly rushing away from him. I guess a lot of things have changed since then.

"Have fun," She smiles, and while Dominic simply gives a small nod in thanks, she winks at me as we pass by.

I don't get the chance to say anything before I'm being led down the side hallway and through a large set of swinging doors.

I suppose I'm thankful for it though, considering it takes away any chance of me overthinking things. Just the mere idea of this room has my mind turning in interest, and it doesn't help my curiosity as Dominic steps forward and unlocks the door now in front of us, pushing it open for me to see.

Stepping inside, my eyes take in the dark blue interior, brightly lit by the hidden light strips in various places.

Feeling a hand press on my back, Dominic encouraged me to move further from the doorway so he could close it behind us. "It's just like our playroom," He says in my ear, walking up and wrapping his arms around my body from behind.

It really was, just a different colour and much smaller in size.

Along the one wall was a long wooden counter, racks of equipment mounted right above it to be used at Dominic's disposal. I spotted four items on it, each making me more and more confused in increasing order.

The first two items were a vibrator and a spreader bar, both things I'm now more than familiarized with.

The remaining, however, had me stepping closer. Some sort of folded black material laid in a neat pile beside what looked to be a lot like a cooler you'd keep drinks in.

Both appeared small in size, but the smirk on Dominic's face showed he had been expecting this reaction.

"Interested yet?" He asks, moving from my back and turning me to face the last wall I've somehow failed to notice this entire time.

It looked normal at first glance, but when Dominic reached out and clicked a button on the small panel to our left, my eyes widened as the once black area became transparent, revealing a section of the club to us. The entire wall turned out to be one large window, the size making it seem as though there weren't any barriers between us and the multiple groups of people engaging in varying activities throughout the club.

"This is the same kind of glass in Carter's office," Dominic explains, his hands gathering my hair and brushing it to my back, "No one can see or hear us right now, but they could if you wanted that." Exhibitionism is a major turn on for me, but it is also one that makes me extremely nervous, so many of my insecurities rising to the surface at the consideration alone. I know Dominic senses this, planting a small kiss on my bare shoulder before stepping away from me.

"Would you like to see your gift now, princess?" He asks, walking over to the counter and running his fingertips over the black fabric I was eyeing only minutes ago. With a racing heart, I nodded, turning away from the glass as I savored the way the sensual music of the club spread throughout my body.

"Good," Dominic says, turning his head back to watch me with that usual calculating gaze of his. Leaning back and curling his hands under the lip of the counter, he tilted his head in a relaxed position as excitement flared in his eyes. And then, with only a single word, he had me completely under his control.

"Present."

That word alone had my skin heating and excitement coursing through my body, Dominic's hard gaze remaining on me. Twisting my arm and pulling on the zipper of my skin tight dress, all it took was gravity and a little bit of encouragement as the straps slipped down my arms.

For a moment just the smallest moment, hesitation had me holding up the fabric flush to my chest, my eyes daring to flick over to the window.

I trusted that no one could see us right now, but visually, I was given the illusion that it was just normal glass between the two sections.

That hesitation wasn't given the opportunity to spread, though, when a small noise in warning came from the man at my side. Instead of risking Dominic viewing it as disobedience, I took a breath and allowed the dress to slip over my curves until it was nothing more than a puddle of silver at my feet.

That simple action was all it took to leave me entirely bare, goosebumps of both excitement and fear peppering my skin under the blue light of the room.

Bending at the waist and reaching for the clothing, I faintly smirked at the sound of a pleased groan coming from Dominic's lips.

To get him back for all of his teasing earlier, I subtly arched my back just a little more, making a show of rising slowly before taking my time to fold the dress.

I knew he wouldn't touch me until I was on my knees in front of him, so I decided to take advantage of that. Everything felt so slow and powerful as I placed both my clothes and purse down on the counter, looking around for a hair tie and finding nothing.

"Don't worry about it for now," Dominic said, his voice rough and eyes taking in every bare inch of my skin. I was almost thankful that I didn't have to braid my hair back for today as I slipped off my painful heels, nudging them with my foot until they were completely off to the side. All that was left now was dropping to my knees in submission, and while I planned on doing just that, I moved to stand right in front of Dominic, holding his eyes as I ever so slowly kneeled down.

I made sure to look at him the whole time as I sunk to the floor, sitting back on my heels and spreading my legs wide out. I loved the dark lust that pooled in his heated gaze, his eye contact only breaking off on my account when I tipped my head down and felt my muscles loosen into this vulnerable position.

With my hands resting palm up on my thighs, I can't help but think about how fond I've grown of the few moments I get in this state, my body relaxing and mind dropping into the warm mindset it always brings.

For a long time, I simply stayed just like that, my eyes fluttering closed as Dominic's one hand came down to stroke my hair almost tenderly.

It was amazing the effect this position had on me, but I found myself completely unworried about the thought of doing a scene with an audience in these few moments.

My answer wasn't a solid yes yet, but nothing really mattered right now except for Dominic's soothing touches and the erotic thrum of distant music.

"You may rise now," His deep voice commanded, my body reacting instantly as though I was a puppet on strings. The first thing I noticed wasn't the dark green of his eyes, but rather the black material from earlier now in his hands.

Silently holding my attention, I watched as Dominic crouched all the way down before he unfolded what I now recognize to be intricate patterns of sheer and lace.

Tapping my ankle with his one hand, I took that as my indication to step into a hole in the material, doing the same with my other foot.

I leaned into his touch as Dominic planted a single kiss right above my knee, pulling the piece of clothing all the way onto me.

My lips parted in surprise at the mostly see through shorts that were now wrapping snugly to my hips, ass, and down to about a third of my thighs.

The black lace wove in simplistic floral patterns, but what I very quickly realized was the fact that the shorts were crotchless, leaving the majority of me bare.

My breath hitched as Dominic slowly rose, and it was only then did I realize that this wasn't for decoration, but instead my comfort entirely.

While there was still fairly every single part of me exposed, the intricate fabric helped to cover two of my biggest insecurities things that I don't think I could ever be comfortable showing an entire group of people to.

"Your scars are never something you should be ashamed of or feel the need to cover up, but I just wanted to give you this option. I know you're interested in exhibitionism, but understandably nervous as well. I promise no one would ever judge you here, but I want you to feel as comfortable as possi—" I didn't let Dominic finish before I was moving forward, wrapping my arms around his back and hugging him with everything I had to give. I refused to cry, though I was tempted to. I will forever appreciate this moment, and how repeatedly, Dominic as well as two other men in my life do everything they can to make me feel good. And I do. Right now, I feel really really good.

"It's perfect." I say against his chest, letting out an extremely heavy breath at the feeling of his hands holding me just as tight as I am him.

"I'm glad, princess." He murmurs back, lifting my head with a finger to look at me, only to plant a soft kiss on my forehead. That alone has my heart swelling, a huge weight being lifted off of my chest.

"I want to do it." I say, referring to whatever ideas he has planned for this room as I take a second glance around curiously. But I'm nervous. That feeling doesn't change my answer, though it doesn't help my mind either.

Dominic seemed to recognize this as he pulled away, walking to my back before pulling my hips flush against him.

"You're too tense," He quietly says in my ear, nipping the sensitive skin right below it before deliciously soothing away the pain with his tongue, "What do you need to fix that, hmm?" I shivered as Dominic's finger's stroked against my stomach, his mouth moving down the column of my neck in a way that ignited a flame deep within me.

"My tongue perhaps?" A kiss against my shoulder.

"My fingers?" A teasing brush against my breast.

"Or maybe it's my cock that has your body growing so needy already?" Dominic continues, my breath hitching at his words, "You're always so responsive—so sensitive." As if to prove his point, my body arched into his touch from a mere stroke of his thumb across my nipple.

"Tongue," I whimpered as he suddenly pulled away, walking us over to the back of the small couch by the window. I don't get the chance to even blink before he's pinning me down over the cushion, my hips angling upwards from the folded position.

I couldn't help but squirm as his hand came down on my ass a second before I heard him drop to his knees, his fingers wrapping around my thighs and spreading me to his liking. Only a breath later, I felt his mouth descend on me, his tongue diving right for my clit as he swirled and sucked over the sensitive bundle of nerves.

"Fuck." I swore as I tried to jolt forward, but his strong hands kept me in place, stroking my thighs in the process. I felt Dominic hum against me, only to push himself farther, not even needing his fingers to make me feel on the edge in a matter of minutes.

It was dizzying how intense everything suddenly became, but I relaxed into it as my head fell forward and my hands reached back. Fisting his curls between my fingers, I whimpered as his tongue took that as his cue to slip through my folds, pushing deep inside of me. I couldn't stop myself from rocking backwards, my hips moving at their own accord against his face in something that could only be described as pure need. The action drew a low sound from Dominic, his moan vibrating in his throat and sending shocks straight through my panting body.

"Sir," I gasped as he made good on his promise of giving me what I needed, keeping me spread while my legs trembled beneath his sinful fingertips.

My breaths grew labored as his attention drew upwards once again, his tongue darting out before sucking diligently on clit. I felt his grip tighten around my thighs as a small shake began to take over, every movement of his sending me falling deeper and deeper into a pit of absolute pleasure.

"Look up," He groaned against me, confusing me until I slowly did as he asked and saw a small group of people now gathered in front of the window, some taking a seat and others standing as they played with their partners. I knew they couldn't see me yet, but this gave me a taste of what it would be like.

As if Dominic knew this would happen, my eyes pinched shut and my mouth parted as I came all over his tongue. My orgasm was so sudden I couldn't help it as my knees buckled, a surprised moan pushing past my lips.

"That's it," He murmured, holding my sensitive body still as his tongue continued to lap away every last bit of my release. He had to have known what my reaction would be, and truthfully, my orgasm just now was one that made me feel unsteady to walk, even though it was only his mouth doing the work.

My body's response to the watchers surprised me, but I didn't hate it either. Pulling back and planting a kiss on my ass, I felt as Dominic rose, his hands slowly encouraging me to stand with him.

"How was that?" He whispered in my ear as he turned to look at me, my face flushing at the mess I made on his face. His once neat hair was now completely disheveled, and his lips were still glistening with my arousal. The sinful grin he shot me at my staring only confirmed he knew where my mind just went.

"It was good, Sir." I answered truthfully, my head turning back to where the gathered people were.

My stomach clenched to see that the number had doubled from only seconds ago, my eyes widening slightly at those who I recognized.

"They came as support knowing it's your first time, but have already agreed to leave if their presence makes you more uncomfortable than at ease." Dominic explains the sight of Jade and Mila together at the front, both as equally naked as me.

It felt wrong seeing them like this, and my head instinctively looked away from the couple gently touching each other. "Don't be shy, little one," Dominic says lowly, lightly grabbing my face and forcing me to look at them, "It's okay to watch here; most people love it actually." I looked as Jade was at Mila's back, her hands trailing all over her body and whispering things in her ear.

"She's my friend." I say, squirming under Dominic's hold, hating how I was already insanely turned on.

"She's a friend that would happily fuck you if she got the okay from all of us." I tensed in surprise at that, wanting to look at Dominic but not being able to.

"The only reason we're fine with you living with her is because we know she wouldn't do anything without a conversation first, but I don't quite think you realize how many people want you, princess." My breath hitched as Dominic began to copy Jade's movements, pulling me flush against his front.

"But she's with Mila." I argue, even though I was admittedly attracted to both of them before I started dating Rowan, Dominic, and Carter. "It would be the six of us together and probably just a one time thing." Dominic says, shocking me at the fact that it seems this is something they've all debated doing, "This is a conversation for another time, but know you are more than allowed to look at anybody here, as long as you know that you belong to us." My men.

"I'm yours, Sir." I reassure, even though I know he already knows that. Pushing back against him, Dominic lets go of my face only because he doesn't have to force me to watch anymore. My eyes trailed over every single person now here, a mixture of different people all gathered for one thing: us.

"Are you ready to begin?" Dominic asks, kissing the back of my head at my most recent words. My heart was racing and my palms felt clammy, but at the same time, my core clenched in excitement at his question.

With only a slight pause, I took a deep breath and said, "Yes, Sir." With only two simple words, I knew things were about to get intense fast. I could feel as Dominic smiled against me, and in the next second, the heat of his body disappeared. With steady and sure movements, Dominic walked over to where the panel to the window was and turned to face me in the same moment he raised his hand.

The look he gave me was primal and more than ready to show this entire club just exactly who owned me. Little did he know I wanted the exact same thing, only the other way around. A wink was all I got before his finger pressed down on a button, the blue light that came on beside it confirming the glass was now entirely transparent.

"Hazel, I want you to present for me in the middle of the room, facing the window." Dominic commanded, and I didn't waste a second following orders.

Somehow, it was only just now that I remembered a lot of these people here already knew Dominic and were probably extremely curious to see the person who he now calls his girlfriend.

Not only did I not want to make him look bad, but I also don't know if I could handle the humiliation of being punished in front of others. At this point, my body simply reacted, wanting to do anything and everything to make him feel satisfied. Already naked and knowing my hair was fine down, all I had to do was kneel as I walked to where he asked, lowering myself to the ground and reluctantly spreading my legs out.

At first, I was nervous panicked at how many people were watching me and the fact I was completely vulnerable in this position. At first, I second guessed my decision to do this.

But as that familiar stretch burned through me and my head hung down, I felt a warming tingle spread throughout my body, slowly bringing me back into that content headspace I've come to love.

With my eyes closed, I urged my body to not only relax, but embrace the things I hate most about myself. For years, I've hated the parts about me that weren't thin or unmarked by stretch marks and cellulite, but these men have helped me day by day to relearn how to love myself. I think I only realized that now, but it's true.

Right now, despite there being at least thirty or so people watching me, I couldn't find any of those things unattractive about myself. I simply felt... calm.

"Do me a favour and pick a number between one and three for me, princess," Dominic's voice came from somewhere to my left, but his words carried far enough for both me and the people outside to hear.

"One, Sir." I responded, forcing myself not to shift or lift my head to see what this was about.

Repeatedly, I willed my mind to go back to that soothing place so I didn't disobey due to my own curiosity.

I could feel eyes on me, bodies near, but my focus soon shifted to the sound of footsteps walking towards me, Dominic intentionally letting me hear where he was. I know damn well he could've been silent if he wanted to.

"I want you to hold this on your clit until I tell you otherwise." He says, crouching down and placing a purple vibrator in my hands. Sucking in a breath, I didn't say anything as I took it from him.

My fingers tingled as Dominic turned the switch to setting three of ten, allowing me to then hold it on my own as he stood.

With my legs already in a spread out position, it took nothing for me to hesitantly bring the toy down between my thighs, pressing the vibrations close to my clit.

I immediately had to bite down on my tongue to avoid any noises falling from my mouth, the sound of the vibrator loud enough on its own. I couldn't look to where Dominic went after that, and even though I knew he was never far, he kept each of his steps lethally silent this time as he moved.

For all I know, he wasn't moving anywhere, simply watching the way I internally struggled against the sensations of the toy.

"Such a good girl," Dominic praises, walking over and crouching down by my side.

My eyes pinched shut as his hand suddenly turned the dial up by two, the sensitivity from my most recent orgasm making me breathe heavily through my nose to keep me still. "Would you like this for tonight?" He then asks, angling my head with a finger over to the black blindfold in his hand. I debated it with a stare, the fabric more than tempting, though I wasn't sure I really wanted it.

"No thank you, Sir." I shook my head in decision, instantly missing the contact as he removed his hand from my face. I knew his offer was to help with my nerves, but there was no mistaking how badly I wanted this. I wanted to see people touching themselves to the sight of Dominic and I together, and more importantly, I wanted to prove to myself that I could do this—that I wouldn't let something like my insecurities hold me back from something I've fantasized about for years. "Hmm," Dominic hums, and I can tell without seeing that he was smiling, pride coursing through him, "Then how about a few more hands perhaps?" Before confusion at his words could settle in, I was suddenly being lifted up, not by Dominic, but fingers covered in dark, engraved rings.

"Hey, sweetheart." Carter says in my ear, just as another set of hands took the vibrator from me.

"You didn't think we'd miss your first show, did you?" Rowan grinned, pressing the toy hard to my clit in my placement. Happiness that they were here spread through me, though it was very clear it was still Dominic in charge.

The other two were only here for additional help, and honestly, probably for support too.

Now that I was standing with Carter's large arms holding my waist, I didn't try to stop the moan that escaped my parted lips.

"So pretty," Dominic murmured as he walked up to my pinned body, simply watching me for a moment as I squirmed in pleasure. I felt my body heat even more under his assessing stare, and as a smile tugged at the corners of his lips, butterflies fluttered in my stomach from that action alone.

Soon, however, watching wasn't enough for him anymore.

When Dominic's hands lifted to my face, holding me close to him, I melted right into his touch as his lips came down on mine.

All it took was that, and he was completely in control of me, his hands wandering even though I was almost too out of it to kiss him back.

This only seemed to make him more turned on, though, his hand reaching up to tug once at my nipple before pulling away and dropping to his knees before me for the third time today.

At first I was confused, but when I looked down to see the spreader bar by my side, Dominic looked up at me with a smile as he slipped each of my feet into a padded cuff.

For a moment my legs remained close together, but I gasped when he suddenly pulled the metal apart, my knees instantly separating and the bar clicking into place.

Now I was completely at his mercy, Rowan turning the vibrator up to the eighth setting now if I could recall correctly.

My knees tried to bow in, but Dominic's hands were quickly there, gently keeping me open and placing light kisses everywhere along my legs.

Everything was just too much, and when the toy clicked up yet again, I tried to move both away and closer to the vibrations.

The brink of my orgasm was coming close, and I knew it would only take a few more seconds of this before it would be too much.

"Can I come, Sir?" I whimpered as my ass wiggled backwards, Carter groaning lowly in my ear. That really didn't help. For a little while, Dominic only gazed up at me, smirking because he knew how desperate he was making me.

"Look at them." Is his only response, clearly referring to the people behind him, "Look at the effect you're having on all of these people, and I'll give you your release." He knew I was close, and he also knew I was trying to tune the eyes of others out by focusing on him instead.

I was too scared to see how many people were watching as I trembled beneath my dominants' grasps. However, my need for my rapidly approaching orgasm soon overpowered that fear, and I surprised myself as I did as Dominic asked and looked up.

My hips bucked forward at the sight before me, every single person touching their partners in some way as they watched me.

Some people had cocks between their lips, while others were simply forced to kneel at their partner's feet, not allowed to do anything but squirm as they looked forward.

So many people doing different things, yet all getting off on the same visual. That was all I needed as a choked breath left my mouth, Carter's lips dropping down to my neck as Rowan turned up the vibrator to the tenth and final setting.

As for Dominic, he forced my knees wide as his tongue dipped inside of me, stroking against my spot and effectively triggering my second orgasm of the night.

As waves upon waves of pleasure crashed through me, one re-occurring thought passed through my mind. I did it. Not only that, but it was one of the most enjoyable, liberating moments of my life to be able to let go like this and not feel ashamed in the process.

What was even better was the way I could feel how proud all three of my men were of me, their touches rough, but caring as they slowly brought me down from my high. By the time I was able to stand on my own again, I was a panting, shaking mess in their arms. I let out a breath as Rowan turned off the vibrator, walking to place it back down on the counter.

At the same time, Carter whispered words of both approval and ones that made me wish I could press my legs together more.

"You're doing so good." He says for only me to hear, drawing a small shiver from my body. I have a feeling most around me noticed as well when he hugged me tighter to him in response.

While Dominic moves to stand in front of me, I can't help but look behind him at the group of people still sitting there. Only now I see two new members that have decided to join.

The couple I remember as Caitlin and Dominic are now sitting down together, the former naked and sitting on his lap. At first it seemed innocent enough, but I soon realized just how wrong I was.

During a moment when Caitlin squirmed, I had learned that she was being filled with her husband's dick, though she didn't seem to be allowed to move.

The sight alone had me flushing and looking over to some of the others. Dominic's hands came up to lazily begin playing with my nipples, and I could see his smile out of the corner of my eye.

Even though none of us had said it, we all knew this was progress for me. I couldn't help but be a little happy for myself as I continued to look around.

My gaze ended up on Jade and Mila after a few seconds, though I found they weren't looking at me, but rather to my left. Following suit, my head turned to see why Rowan hadn't returned, only to wish that I hadn't.

The thing that I thought looked to be a cooler earlier turned out to be just that, only the glass dildo that was pulled out from it had me squirming in uncertainty.

Dominic wasn't lying all those weeks ago when he told me temperature play was a turn on for him, because I had no doubt that toy would bring the sensations of ice without the risks of ice itself being placed inside of me.

That was what everyone's eyes were on, but Rowan's were watching me, gauging my reaction as he took out a white cloth from one of the drawers and wiped off the water from what had melted on it.

"Think you can handle two more orgasms, princess?" Dominic smiles, bringing my attention back to him. That would put me at four orgasms within an hour, and honestly, that knowledge had my heart racing in mixed thoughts.

"Yes, Sir." I nod, even as I looked worriedly at the dildo being walked over to my side, Rowan smirking as he brought the toy up to my lips.

"Get this nice and wet for us, will you?" He says, positioning the long toy at the small part of my mouth. Dominic stepped to the side as Carter held me, no doubt to give the audience a better angle as I opened and let my tongue run along the bottom of the glass.

It was unsurprisingly cold against my taste buds, goosebumps rising on my arms as I relaxed my jaw and allowed Rowan to push a little deeper into my mouth.

I never would have expected taking a toy down my throat to be so arousing, but I literally felt myself drip onto my inner thigh as I pretended to be sucking one of their cocks.

I knew the effect it had on all of my men, and when I heard a moan from someone on the other side of the window, I knew they weren't the only ones.

Who knew this would be so... empowering.

A really small part of me has always wondered if I were maybe a switch, and the thought popped back into my head just now at the power I felt knowing I brought that reaction out of someone else.

My mind was very quickly side tracked though when Rowan hit my gag reflex, my lips sputtering around the now efficiently wet dildo.

Seemingly satisfied by that, I watched as Dominic took the long toy from the blond's hand, teasingly running it down my body and along my already soaked slit.

My hips jolted to the side at the freezing contact, not expecting that feeling even though I knew damn well it would be cold.

Dominic only smiled as Carter gripped my hips hard, allowing them no wiggle room for motion.

I quite literally couldn't shift now to gain myself relief, gasping as the head of the glass moved back into place, not quite pushing in but simply moving up and down over and over again.

Even that didn't seem to be enough for them though.

I watched as Rowan crouched down to my feet, choosing to unbuckle the clasps of the spreader bar so he could spread me even wider. His one hand wrapped around the back of my knee as he stood, lifting it up and out so that not only was I only standing on one leg now, but I was completely open for Dominic as he pushed just the tip of the toy inside. "Ah," I gasped, my breathing becoming extremely heavy as I fought against Carter and Rowan's grip. These sensations were like nothing I've ever felt before, and my heart only decided to join the mix as Dominic cast me a smile that countered the cold touch between my legs.

"I wonder how much of this you can take?" He verbally ponders, clear challenge in his eyes as he pulls out only to thrust double the previous length back inside. While there was practically no weight on my right leg thanks to Carter, it didn't stop my entire body from shaking, not from the cold, but from sheer pleasure.

"Sir, please," I begged, squirming in the only ways I still could.

"Please what, my sweet submissive?" Dominic teases cruelly, planting a light kiss on my jaw as my mouth parted open, "What are you asking for?"

"I-I don't know." I stutter, my head tossing back onto Carter's shoulder for support.

"Mhm," He hums, his thumbs running soothing circles on my hips, "I think you want more, whether you know it or not." Dominic took Carter's words with intention, pushing until three-quarters of the dildo was fucking into me with every forward motion. During a small change in angle, it brushed hard against my g-spot, and that was it for me.

I shattered in their arms as I made a sound of a mix between a moan and a choked sob, everything suddenly becoming too much for me to handle. Nothing could've stopped it as a sudden wave of ecstasy crashed over me.

"Can I—"

"Come, Hazel. Just let go and let us take care of you." Dominic gave me the permission I needed as I exploded around him, causing me to cry out as he slammed the last inch of the toy inside of me. It was nearly unbearably cold, but I felt so hot and overwhelmed at the same time that the freezing bite only added to everything. My heart raced as I was so wet I could hear the toy continuing to fuck into me, and my cheeks flushed deeper knowing likely everyone watching could hear it too. However, I soon realized that thought only increased my climax, none of my men ever letting me go or letting me down from my high.

"One more for us, darling." Rowan encouraged, repositioning his grip on my leg, but showing no struggle with it either. All of my thoughts blurred into one at his words, realizing that I had prom- ised two more orgasms by the end of this. I thought they'd give me a break in between, though.

Stupid me. They were doing no such thing right now as Dominic bent down for a better angle, forcing me to take the ice cold toy over and over again with every motion of his wrist.

I pushed into his touch as he kissed a spot right above my knee in affection, but I was almost too out of it when one of Carter's hands came off of my hip, bringing it up to hold my face.

At first, I thought that's all it was, but when his thumb prodded my lips, I couldn't help but part them to take the finger into my mouth. I moaned and closed my lips around it, my tongue swirling and gagging when he suddenly pushed too deep down my throat. The next second he was pulling his thumb from my mouth, covered in my spit as he moved away.

I relaxed into his touch as he slowly brushed a few fingers down the spine of my back, over the curve of my ass, and down between my legs. I didn't even have time to realize what was happening before I felt the finger at my back entrance, slipping smoothly inside as I spasmed around both the dildo and his thumb.

"F-Fuck!" I cursed, whimpering at the intensity of all of these feelings.

"I know." Rowan whispered, moving down to plant a kiss along the arch of my exposed neck, "Feels good, doesn't it?" I could only manage a small nod in response, my body simply reacting now as it took control of my actions on its own. Without that one hand, I now had more movement of my hips, using the freedom to fuck myself forwards then backwards until I was sweating and close to an absolute disaster. I was already overstimulated from my previous orgasms, and I don't know what caused the change, but sparks of a climax soon began to reappear, flickering deep in my core. "Be a good girl and come for us," Dominic demands, looking up at me the entire time, "I want you dripping down my wrist by the time I'm done with you."

Fuck.

Fuck.

Fuck.

"I can't," I cried, trying to pull away but only gaining more sensations from Carter's thumb.

"You can take it." Rowan says, bringing his head down to my chest and pulling a nipple into his mouth. I was already wet, but they had me dripping by now, my moans and cries combined with the sound of my arousal.

"One more, princess." Dominic says to me, the eyes of those behind the glass long forgotten. Right now it was just us and every sensitive nerve in my body. One more. I knew I would have collapsed at this point without them, and I was suddenly extremely thankful for their hold as Dominic's mouth latched onto my clit, the warmth and suction sending me right over the edge.

"Oh god," I cried from the overstimulation, every inch of my soul being absolutely consumed by the men surrounding me. I felt free as the intensity of my orgasm spread through my body, soaking both the toy and Dominic's hand like he said I would. I don't think I could've done it without all three, and as tears began to spill down my pink cheeks and a blissful feeling washed over me, I knew I did it. Despite my fears, I stood here and accomplished something I never thought I could. The knowledge of that had me sinking to the ground with a wet face, Dominic discarding the toy to the side as he followed me down.

"You did so good, Hazel." He whispered as he pulled me into his lap, cradling me as my head nestled into his warm chest. This was home. The realization dawned over me so suddenly I didn't even know what to make of it, but I knew it was true. Nothing could beat what the four of us shared.

Somewhere in the back of my mind, I saw Rowan walk over to the panel to fog the window as Carter moved to the sinks to wash his hands and the equipment we used. Mostly, however, my thoughts were on the way Dominic was currently holding me in a way I've wished to be held my entire life.

The best part about it was that I got to call him and the two other men with me mine.

"I can't believe I just did that," I smiled in shyness as I hid my face in his shirt, my hands wrapping around his neck just to gain that little bit more of contact.

"I can." I heard him mirror my expression, his hands cradling my face and moving me to look at him, "And you're not going to walk away from this embarrassed, because what you failed to see when your eyes were closed was how many people were wishing to be in our place just to be able to touch you." My eyes widened slightly at his words, or more specifically the heat clearly flaring inside of him now. I suddenly became extremely aware of his hard-on beneath me, but more specifically the different kind of pride to be heard in his voice.

"You have such a power kink." I laughed, now seeing that there was more than one motive to today's scene.

"You're only realizing that now?" Rowan chuckled from behind me, crouching down and revealing the seemingly wet cloth in his hands. When he lifted it to wipe away the tears from my face, I sighed as I realized he had soaked it with warm water to help bring me down.

"You're ours, Hazel," Dominic said in my ear, hugging me close as Rowan continued to take care of me, "Now everybody in this club will not only know you belong to us, but yes, we also take pride in the fact that we're the only ones to get to call you ours when every-one now wants you." I blushed at that, but simply shook my head in amusement.

"I may be yours, but not everyone wants me." That wasn't even my insecurities talking, it was just a fact.

"I've already gotten an email from one of our longest members here wondering what the four of our limits are and whether we'd be interested in letting you scene with him while we watch." Carter's voice and obvious smirk carried from across the room, my head twisting in surprise to where he stood.

"You did?" I ask, not even sure what to think of that.

"First of many I'm sure," He smiles, knowing that I'm going to turn down every offer there is. And every time I do, it's only going to feed more and more into their ridiculously large male egos. I'm sure that's just what they need. "Come on, you're seriously going to make me wait for this surprise too?" I tilt my head, watching as an amused smile crossed Dominic's face. Now fully dressed and back in his car, the man refused to tell me why he had no intention of bringing me home until later. 'A small detour' is what he called it.

He had given me a lot of time to regain my energy back at Rush, and for a little while, Rowan, Dominic, Carter, and I all sat and talked for a little about our days. It felt so surprisingly domestic compared to the things we had done at a sex club of all places only minutes before. It was really nice, though. It was something I could happily get used to.

Even with all of Dominic's secrecy about where he was taking the two of us, he made me smile until my face hurt and it was a nice feeling to have.

"What about a small hint?" I prodded further, slapping his hand away as he went to poke me for asking yet again.

"It's the better half of the gift I wanted to give you tonight, and it includes you getting naked again, so it's a win for me." At my raised eyebrow, he caved after laughing at my expression. I was all orgasmed out for the night, thank you very much. "Look in the black bag in the backseat," Was his only response, accompanied by a wink. Doing just that, I reached out for the handles before bring-ing the whole thing to rest on my lap, my fingers curiously pulling out the lavender hoodie and heathered grey sweats to go with it.

I felt the soft brush of the fleece lining against my fingertips, the material no doubt expensive and well made. Looking at him in question, Dominic only gave me a light shrug, offering no meaning as to how this was supposed to hint where we were going. "I prom-ise you'll love it," He squeezed my thigh with his large hand, "And if you ask where we're going again, I'm going to pull over to the side of the road and spank you over the hood of my car." His words were teasing, but I knew he was serious in every way.

"Dominic?" I grinned, waiting until he looked over to me. Where are we going? My eyes flickered over the green in his eyes, his long lashes, and the extremely light dust of freckles across his nose. He was devastatingly beautiful, and he was all mine. "Nothing," I only said, suppressing the brat inside of me tempted to ask that question yet again.

Sinking down slightly in the seat, I simply wrapped my arm around his much larger one, resting my head against him and holding him close.

~ Thirteen ~

Hazel

When Dominic told me a part of my second gift would be getting me naked again, I didn't expect for it to result in him redressing me almost instantly.

For just under half an hour, the two of us drove far under the dark cover of sky, small stars poking out of the gatherings of clouds overhead.

I couldn't explain why things felt so special right now, but they truly did. Whether we were talking, smiling, or simply holding each other's hands, my thoughts were always interlaced with his as the engine hummed in the background. Everything about this drive had relaxed me, just as much as it piqued my curiosity.

I was a little tired and felt myself slowly dozing off a few times, but when I felt Dominic's car eventually come to a gradual slow, my eyes fluttered open to find us parked at the edge of a fairly short pathway.

I straightened my posture at the sight of small lanterns glowing in a line down the path, my eyes looking at Dominic beside me. Is this a date? I was surprised to find a small flicker of shyness in his expression, only for him to grab his keys and move out of the car.

Within a few seconds he was opening my door and motioning for me to hand him my bag of clothes as well as his own from the backseat.

Once I got out, that was when he demanded I turn, his hands gently touching my body while curiosity filled my mind. It left us in a comfortable silence, my muscles relaxing as Dominic's fingers made quick work of my dress, placing it on the roof of the car along with my heels.

Before I could feel shy about my nakedness, I was spun to face him with my arms being guided into the holes of the hoodie he bought me, the sweats following afterwards.

I couldn't believe how soft the material was, and when he tugged on a hoodie of his own, I didn't even get a chance to blink before I was being scooped up bridal style into a pair of strong arms.

"Dominic!" I laughed at the sudden movement, my arms wrapping around his neck for balance, even though I knew he would never let me fall.

A smile was given to me as I was hugged tighter to his body, my eyes directing to the glowing pathway the two of us were now moving down.

My head tilted in interest when I soon heard the faint noise of water, the ground transitioning from stone sidewalk to a wooden dock.

Smiling again, Dominic teasingly nipped my ear in response to my curiosity. This time when I looked over at him, I found that any kind of nervousness from before had long passed.

Now, every expression on his face was one of confidence and affection, still not allowing me any hint of what was happening until he suddenly stopped.

I had been so lost in watching him that I'd failed to notice his move to put me down, hugging me from behind as my eyes took in the sight before me.

For the first time in a long time, I was at a loss for words.

Standing on planks of wood along the edge of a lake, everything from an outdoor mattress to wine and candles were swarming my vision.

The bed alone was large enough for the two of us, fresh sheets and pillows decorating the sides and looking comfy enough that I just wanted to collapse onto it.

Then, of course, there were all the more subtle details such as the coolers, the small lights, and the scented candles that I can only assume are meant to keep the bugs away due to the faint citronella smell.

"What is this for?" I ask with partial tears in my eyes, having never been given a gift as beautiful or as thoughtful as this. "You're mine and I am yours." Dominic says quietly in my ear, "Do I really need a reason other than that?" I shivered when he leaned down to plant a light kiss against my temple, my body sighing into him as butterflies flooded my stomach.

No, I guess he doesn't. The scene before me seemed like things you'd only see in movies; moments many have dreamed of having, but never strayed farther than their imagination.

Who knew Dominic was a romantic? In the past month of being with him, I've learned many sides and versions: the playful one, the dominant one, the loving one, and the saddened one. Never once, however, did I expect to see the one who was in support of candle lit dates and surprise gifts.

"Here, sit." He says, pulling away some of the covers from the bed and gesturing for me to take a seat.

I watched as Dominic then opened the nearest cooler to the mattress, memories of the one from earlier causing my cheeks to flush under the light of the stars.

His small smirk told me he knew just where my thoughts traveled, though he never commented. Instead, Dominic walked over to me with a bottle of what looked to be really fancy champagne and two glasses for it.

"When did you set this all up?" I ask, pleasingly astonished at the unrealness of this all.

Passing me my drink, I gratefully accepted it as I pulled some of the covers over my lap, smiling as Dominic joined me in the bed.

"I did most of it before I picked you up, but Rowan and Carter also stopped by just a few minutes before we parked to make sure everything was still set up the way I wanted it to be".

He really thought about this. It was undoubtedly sweet, though I'll admit it was a gift I never would have expected. Setting my glass down beside me on the dock, I shifted closer to Dominic but let my eyes travel up to the stars above.

"Don't you guys ever get jealous of each other?" I question honestly, something I've wondered countless times before but never thought to ask.

I knew Dominic wasn't offended by it and would answer truthfully as he wrapped an arm around my waist just to hold me a little more.

"You know you're the first girl we've ever shared, right?" Dominic says, planting a kiss on the top of my head. I remember one of them telling me Carter's never stayed to scene with them before me, and I knew I wasn't the only one having to get used to new adjustments for our relationship.

"Mhm," I hummed in response.

"Well, when signing that contract with you, we weren't exactly sure how things were going to play out. We didn't know if what we had was something that would be long term or not, but all it took was that first night with you to know it would be."

My mouth parted ever so slightly as I heard Dominic place his drink down, only to tilt my chin until my eyes met his. Even once I was looking at him, his touch remained.

"We've been with many partners at the club, but none of us have dated in years. All of our relationships never ventured farther than one night stands and repeated public scenes for purposes of training and demonstrations." It was a little weird to hear about his past in that way, but I was surprisingly more interested than jealous. He was mine now, so what did it matter?

"Carter was never even interested in sharing until you, but I'm sure at the start, if he could've kept you for himself he would have." I feel like confusion must have been showing on my features as Dominic's thumb brushed against the side of my cheek, his eyes watching for any reactions I'd offer up.

"So how did we get to this point then?" I ask, a little surprised at his admission. At the same time, at first glance, Carter didn't exactly seem like the type to share to me either.

"Honestly, it came more naturally than any of us expected. We have you, we have each other, and somehow it's just worked." We just worked. Crazy to think it was that simple, but I guess it was.

"Though..." Dominic adds with a smile, "It pains me to know you're thinking about other men on our date." I knew he was teasing, so I teased back, shoving him lightly away to reach out for my champagne glass. Before I could even react, my breath was whooshed past my lips, Dominic pushing me onto my back before moving to hover over my body. My legs instinctively spread, widening for the width of his hips to fit snug against mine.

"Hey!" I laughed, not being able to stop him as Dominic reached over me, grabbing my glass and bringing it to where my head rested.

"No date of mine should have to serve herself." He says, moving the half filled drink to my lips, "Allow me, princess." Dominic left me breathless as the sweet liquid poured into my mouth, slow enough that I could take a steady sip without spilling. I couldn't stop smiling as he eventually pulled the glass away, though his eyes never left mine. Well, that is until his gaze traveled down to my lips, and likely the slight remains of champagne across them.

One second our eyes reunited, the next, they were fluttering shut in pleasure, our mouths lightly brushing against each other. Dominic's touch was more intoxicating than any amount of alcohol I could drink, and right now, I was spinning with lust, happiness, and every little part Dominic had to give.

The contact between the two of us was gentle and brief, but when Dominic eventually pulled back from my lips, the lazy smile he gave me had me offering one in return. I liked this. A lot.

"I know I've already said it, but I really am proud of you for today." Dominic said against my mouth, his warm breath fanning across my cheeks.

My face flushed what I'm assuming to now be a shade of pink at his praise. Biting just the edge of my bottom lip, I ended up leaning to plant a small kiss to his jaw in response, his body rolling to lay next to mine and pulling me with him. Within a second Dominic was tucking me under his one arm, my head fitting into the crook of his neck and resting against his shoulder.

"You put a lot of trust in me—in all of us—by saying yes, princess... and I wanted to thank you for that." Lifting myself slightly to look at him, I found his eyes already trained on me in sincerity.

"You don't have to thank me," I tilt my head to the side, my gaze trailing over the light dust of freckles across his cheeks. My trust in him was earned, not simply given. My heart fluttered at the small chuckle he let out at that, as though he believed otherwise.

"You're the best thing that's ever happened to me, Hazel," Dominic whispers, his hand moving to cup the side of my cheek in affection, "I know those are only words, but I mean it with every part of me." His hold on not only my body, but also my heart, made sure I knew that there was not a bare inch of falsity in the statement spoken like an unspoken promise.

"They're not just words," I say, my fingers brushing past his forehead to run through his brown hair, "I don't know where all of this is coming from, but this means more to me than you know, Dominic." I continued to look up at him, his curls parting beneath my touch and his body seeming to relax from the slow motions.

"All three of you have saved some part of me over this last month," I say, extremely aware of just how true that was after saying it aloud, "You brought back my excitement." Rowan, my humor. Carter, my affection.

There was so much more they've been able to do for me, but the way Dominic was speaking right now was as if he'd never get the chance to say it if it wasn't now. It made me a little nervous. Though, it did amaze me a little how I could visibly see how my touch alone was making him feel a little more grounded.

"I brought back your excitement?" He asked in question, sitting up slightly and brushing a strand of hair behind my ear. "Mhm." I gave him a small nod, "For almost the entirety of my life, I've struggled to be able to piece together what a future for me may look like." I swallowed, but offered a smile to show I was fine. I really truly was, because Dominic was here. "At first, I wondered if I would end up like my mother; an alcoholic married to a man just as abusive and miserable as she was." It sounded horrible, but the truth was very rarely pretty.

"I don't resent my dad for leaving me with her; once he realized how bad things were, he even took me with him as he traveled for a little until I was old enough to take care of myself." I caught the small tightness that appeared in Dominic's jaw at that, but I wasn't sure if it was from the mentioning of my father, or the 'how bad things were' part.

"And how old was that?" Dominic asked, no judgement in his voice, just interest.

"I was almost seventeen, but my dad was never exactly the best guy to be around for social popularity. He had a lot of enemies and made it very complicated for someone simply trying to make it through High School." He didn't like the reality of that answer, I could tell, but Dominic kept quiet.

"Anyways, I guess I worried a lot that nothing would ever end right for me. So many people have left me in my life, I think that's why a huge part of me stayed with Noah for so long and overlooked just how bad he really was." That was hard to admit, but I'd been trained to be a hell of a lot stronger than what I was with him. I suppose, however, abusive relationships never start bad.

"I guess I just can't bring myself to worry as much around you. The unknown used to terrify me, and honestly, there's a lot of that in our relationship... but I'm not alone in it. And instead of stressing, I find myself excited." The faint crease between Dominic's eyebrows had now eased at this point, and I could feel he was now holding me closer, even if there wasn't much more we could do to achieve that.

"Yes, all of you are responsible for making me happy, but whether it's being blindfolded or taking me on surprise dates, you make me excited about a future I never thought would be possible until a few weeks ago." That was the truth, and it was neither pretty nor harsh; it was simply me. For a few seconds I couldn't tell what Dominic was thinking, his only action being the continuous brush of his thumb across my skin. He looked like he wanted to say everything and nothing all at once, but he simply decided on, "Come here." Dominic's hands dropped to my center, lifting me by my waist and sliding me to lay on top of him. There was nothing sexual in the action, it was simply him wanting to hold me.

The weight of his large arms wrapping around my back felt right as I laid down on his chest, the only thing remaining upright being my head. My hands rested softly on the sides of Dominic's neck, my elbows keeping me up propped just enough so I could continue to look at him.

"I know," Dominic starts, his eyes moving up to mine before he continues, "I know I can't do anything to change the past, but I can say that I'm never going to leave you." I leaned into his touch as his hands kept me close, my heart swelling at his words.

"I promise with all my heart I'm not going anywhere, princess." For the hundredth time tonight, I smiled. It was one built off of a hint of sadness and even more one of repose, and while I knew none of my men would leave like everyone else has, it was so different hearing it out loud.

Dominic meant every word he'd said tonight, and it sent an intense combination of emotions straight to my heart and realization to my mind.

"I believe you." I say, not doubting for a second he wouldn't stay. It was an unfamiliar comfort to have, but not even the largest amount of distance would be strong enough to tear apart how I feel for him—how I hope he feels in return.

"I know the Mafia complicates—" Dominic began speaking, but his words died off when I moved to run my one finger across his bottom lip.

"Not tonight," I whispered, sitting up just a little more on my own, "Tonight, I don't want to be the girl scared of her past and you to be the heir of the Mob." I leaned my mouth down to hover right above his, my hand sliding to touch his face in the way he has mine multiple times before.

"I just want to be Hazel and Dominic..." I say, my lips brushing against his as I spoke, "If that's alright." I just want to be us. Us and the stars. My mind traveled back to that day on the balcony all those nights ago, when I had come back from Rush with them and took the first thing I'd ever been sure about. I kissed Dominic right there under the night sky for the first time, and now, whatever this is is happening under its glow as well.

"Of course, Hazel." Dominic whispers against my mouth, his nose brushing the side of mine as he shifts slightly, "I guess the real question is what do you want to do?" The playful smirk spreading across his lips had me returning one of my own, liking the sight of him beneath me. His mouth was too tempting to not kiss, just as his arms were to hold and his torso was to straddle. I wasn't exactly sure where I wanted to take this yet, but I was happy where we were right now as my tongue traced a teasing line across his bottom lip.

I pulled back to smile for a short second as I felt the rise and fall of Dominic's chest grow deeper, but when I leaned back in, I could instantly tell he was done letting me take over.

Though, I wasn't sure I was done trying. Moving down his front, I positioned my hips directly above his before rubbing forward, enjoying the small sounds that came from both of our mouths at the action.

"Fuck, Hazel." Dominic curses under his breath, trying to take control and unknowingly failing as I sat all the way upright. A part of me was tempted to hum at his response, but I knew that would lead to me pinned front down before I could even blink. As much as I'd love that, I wanted to watch him tonight. Not to top him—not yet—but I wanted for every last second of tonight to be as engraved into my memory as possible.

"Can I?" I ask as my hands drop to the V of his hips, stroking the sliver of hard muscle showing just above his belt line. Dominic's body flexed beneath mine as I continued to tease my fingers just under the bottom of his hoodie, and I wondered if it was that or the sultry glance I gave him that had him tossing me to his side.

At first I thought it was an act of dominance, but when he swiftly pulled off my sweats and then positioned me back up on top, I found myself surprised. Only this time, Dominic was almost all the way reclined, his fingers coming up to my throat only to begin a slow southward path over my clothes.

"I've been hard since I first picked you up earlier." He says, his thumb brushing against my nipple before continuing his way down my front, "And I don't know what game you're playing at right now, but I think I'm just curious enough to indulge in it for a while." My heart quickened a little at the permission he just gave me. Dominic was okay with giving me a little bit of freedom. It wasn't all the time I felt this way, but right now, especially after everything he's told me today, I knew I wanted to be on top and show him just how thankful I was for this.

Planting my hands on his chest for balance, I rocked my hips forwards and angled them down, making sure to brush every sensitive nerve of ours against each other.

My face heated a little at the sound Dominic made in response, so I did it again and again.

This was new for both of us, and I was having more than fun exploring both of our bodies in a way neither of us were used to.

"Hazel." Dominic groaned after my fifth pass over him, and I couldn't help but smile at the restrained warning in his voice. I knew he was worked up from not getting any kind of release at Rush, even though I tried to take care of all three of them after I'd come down from my own high. I was told to rest instead, probably figuring that things would lead to exactly this and that I'd need my energy.

The slightly feral expression on Dominic's face right now had me thinking the same thing.

"Yes?" I said innocently at the sound of my name, worrying I'd pushed him too far as his movements stilled for a short moment. But then, the hand that was now at my stomach slipped under my hoodie and up to my breast, pinching one of my nipples harshly between the pads of his fingers. I cried out and rocked forward at that, my body being forced to use his for support.

"I'm not going to last long if you keep on doing that," Dominic bit out, his fingers still working the same spot in punishment, "And believe me, princess, when I say the only place I plan on coming is inside of that soaked cunt of yours." His tone awakened my natural instinct to submit to him, and Dominic saw the opening and took advantage of it. Lifting both myself and his hips, within a quick moment his pants and boxers had been tugged down just enough to free his cock, the hard length of him throbbing and wet with precum.

I almost felt a little bad for teasing him so much, but it was also empowering and had me reaching down to wrap my fist around the base of him. I flushed as Dominic took his lip between his teeth when I slid my hand up, tightening slightly around his tip and running my thumb across his leaking slit. Instantly his hips bucked upwards to have me touching him again, but I countered that by pushing him down and lining his cock up at my entrance. My body rotated to the left slightly to gain better balance, but Dominic didn't care or allow me to take my time with it. I fell onto him as he slammed all the way inside of me, both of his hands now on my hips as he physically kept me pinned flush to him. "Brat." He growled in my ear, and I knew his urge to put me in my place was conflicting his need to take this slow and let me explore him at the same time. I squirmed as Dominic didn't let up, keeping himself buried deep inside of me and smiling at my own sensitivity.

"I took you on this date to show you I'm more than just your dominant, yet you keep testing my patience, little one." I gasped as he rotated his hips, rubbing me in the perfect spots and leaving me tightening around him in pure desire.

"If you're not careful I may just remember how easy it is to overstimulate you and throw away my plans of slowly memorizing every inch of your skin tonight." His words had my lips parting in a breath, and Dominic knew he had me there. Understanding where my mind was at, he gave me back a little bit of my freedom as his still tight grip on my hips became less restrictive, allowing me to guide the movement of my hips as I used my knees to raise my-self back upright. I pulled upwards until I was nearly empty before lowering back onto Dominic's cock, whimpering at how perfectly he fit inside of me and how needy that single motion left me.

"You feel so good." He whispered, only adding more fuel to the fire burning hot in my core, "I could get used to fucking you in the things I buy you." His eyes dropped from my face to the faintly visible peaks of my breasts through the light coloured hoodie.

"Maybe one day I'll even get something to put here," Dominic said, two fingers tracing the center of my bare neck in thought.

Did he mean what I thought he meant? I wasn't able to coherently ask as I was suddenly pulled down to meet one of his thrusts, my mind slowly dissolving into a pool of bliss. Dominic very quickly had me writhing on top of him, my body forming a mind of its own as I took both of his hands into mine and interlaced our fingers with one another. There was no protest as I leaned forward, my breasts brushing against Dominic's hard chest and our hands resting together comfortably on the outdoor bed. The change in position led to a new angle—one that had me dripping and making a mess of the dick I slowly fucked myself onto.

"You're so deep." I whimpered, breathing heavily into Dominic's ear as I fell into a steady pattern that left both of us dizzy with pleasure.

"And you're so wet." He countered, his voice husky from his own arousal and sending shivers down the spine of my back, "I don't think I'll ever get used to how soft you feel against me." Both of our needs for dominance soon faded away into a distant want, the only thing remaining being the way our bodies joined with every deep roll of my hips. I couldn't get enough of this of him. I never wanted this moment to end, yet I couldn't stop myself as I turned my head slightly and pressed my lips to Dominic's neck.

"Sh-shit, Hazel." He cursed at the action, his hands tightening around mine as my toes curled into the sheets. "Mmm." I hummed against him, kissing along the skin and seeking out the places that felt best. It didn't take long to realize the tensing of Dominic's muscles was because he was close, my own orgasm slowly approaching and telling me I was only moments away from being consumed by the man beneath me all over again.

"I can't until you do." Dominic breathed through clenched teeth as I sank all the way down on him, my lips sucking at a spot right below his ear. I was lucky he couldn't see my face right now, or rather the small smile that appeared at his desperation.

He could have removed my hand to touch my clit, but he liked the way we were together right now just as much as I did. "It's okay," I said honestly, lifting my head from his neck to move to the corner of his lips, "Just let go." I don't think I've ever seen anything as erotic as the sight of Dominic mouth parting in conflict, but his body not being able to obey his will to wait for me. Surprisingly, however, I almost preferred it this way at the moment. I was able to see as Dominic's eyes screwed shut in pleasure, a low moan falling from his lips as he swelled inside of me before letting go and giving into the lust that threatened to take over.

"Fuck." He swore as I tightened around his cock, instantly struggling to continue my movements at the feeling of his warm release filling me.

"Dominic." I moaned into his ear as his hips lifted on their own, circling in a way that added a delicious pressure to my clit at the same time as he brushed against my spot.

"I need you to come for me, princess." He groans through heavy breaths, still making little sounds of pleasure as his climax continued to spread through him.

That seemed to be all I needed. Clamping down around him as a small shake took over my legs, Dominic held me close, whispering words of praise and encouragement that sent my orgasm spiraling.

"That's it." He murmured, taking over my previous actions and wringing every last bit of pleasure from my exhausted body. There was no more energy left in me after that, the only thought I was capable of being the person next to me. I may have been tired, and spent, and undeniably sated, but I refused to allow my eyes to shut under the heaviness of the night refused to allow myself to miss a single part of this beautiful moment.

A content sigh left my lips when a light kiss was placed to my forehead, a very strong emotion suddenly coming with it. I was perfectly happy as Dominic righted himself, sliding me so that I was on my side and facing him. Because of that, I couldn't explain why Dominic's fingers came away wet when they lifted to brush at my cheeks.

I think that the weight of everything around me was currently pressing down on my body, but I think the emotion I felt most was relief. For most of my life, a lot of the time I felt as though I was always living through someone else's eyes, nothing ever feeling real and never being able to visualize a future that I could look forward to.

Everyone around me would always leave; whether it was physically or emotionally, things always seemed to end with myself as my only true company. But right now, there wasn't a doubt inside of me that made me believe this was anything but real. Dominic would stay they all would stay, and maybe I wouldn't have to feel so alone anymore.

"I know, princess, I know." Dominic says, wiping my face of the tears he could before pulling me flush to his chest, "I've got you." He always knows. Under the flicker of stars and the embrace of everything else, a realization struck me so hard I was thankful I was being held so tightly right now.

As Dominic wrapped his arms around me, showing me the promise of forever, I knew that I'd fallen.

Fallen into his touch. Fallen into the world around me.

Fallen into the dangerous hands of love for not one, but three people who've quickly become my everything. My men.

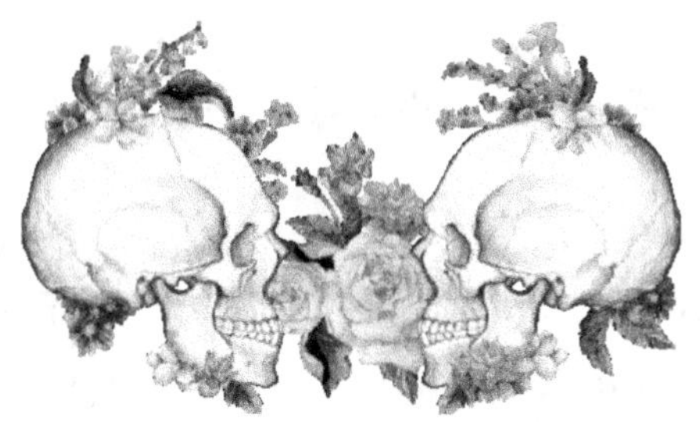

~ Fourteen ~

Hazel

"You honestly didn't have to do this." I insisted as Carter continued his work on making a homemade meal for me. When he said we were doing dinner before our plans tonight, I hadn't expected all of this effort to be put into it, especially when I was currently useless.

"Sit." He gives me a half smile, knowing it was killing me that he wouldn't let me do anything, even simple tasks like setting the table or cleaning up dishes. I always felt weird when it came to people doing things for me when I couldn't offer anything in return.

Only right now I could, yet Carter insists on doing all of the work. Maybe his birthday cake was so awful he didn't want the risk of me setting foot in his kitchen ever again. The thought was mainly a joke, but I'd be horrified if it were true nonetheless.

"Can I at least set the table?" I offer, flicking my eyes over the neatly rolled sleeves of his shirt and the way his hands were currently preparing a light garden salad. It was a side addition to go with the burgers he was grilling on some special stovetop meant for indoor barbecuing.

This time at my words, Carter's gaze met mine. While he placed down the knife that was once chopping a head of lettuce, my heart sped a little quicker as he fully turned towards me.

"I'm trying to cook a nice meal for you so you can relax after what I'm sure was a long day of work, yet you can't sit still." Carter says, amusement filling his tone as he speaks.

"Placing down a few plates isn't going to be the end of me." I argue with a raise of my eyebrow, my one hand resting comfortably on my hip as I leaned my lower back against the counter.

"No?" He asks almost in challenge, instant confusion-fueled regret filling me from a single word. I tilted my head as Carter took a step towards me, then another and another until I learned that he wasn't getting closer for me, but for the staircase behind.

"Fine. If you want to be useful then do me a favour and don't let the house burn down." My mouth parted in disbelief as he shot me a wink, soon turning away from me to go upstairs for some unspoken reason. He was leaving? I wasn't even able to protest before I was left alone in his kitchen, food both on top and inside of the oven.

"No promises." I mumbled under my breath at his exit, looping around the counter and willing my stomach to stop growling at the delicious smell of food. Don't burn down the house, I mentally scoffed to myself, moving to where the cutting boards were and grabbing the handle of a knife with the intent to finish what Carter thinks I can't do.

"I don't think so, sweetheart." His voice sounded from the stairs before I could even lift the blade, my hips twisting to look at him. Whatever Carter grabbed was now well hidden behind his back, his hurry to get back down here almost insulting.

"If you'd like cooking lessons one day all you have to do is ask, but right now what I'm more curious about is if you did as I asked?" His question had me loosening my grip entirely from the knife, my face growing very likely dark red at what he was hinting at. And no, it was not the whole 'don't let the house burn down' command.

"Mhm." I simply hummed, not making eye contact as I stepped away from the cutting boards. Even though the lovely text I received this morning mentally prepared me for what we were going to be doing tonight, anal douching was something I don't ever want to discuss with anybody. I was excited but embarrassed like no other.

"It's nothing to be shy about." Carter says, continuing to walk towards me as though he hadn't just asked an extremely humiliating, yet valid thing. "You try cleaning out your ass, Carter, and tell me just how enthusiastic you are to talk about it." I say teasingly, though I was entirely serious about it too. He only let out a low chuckle, taking that moment to reveal what he had been hiding, or rather his purpose for going upstairs.

"No." I instantly shake my head, and I imagine my eyes are practically out of their sockets right now, "No." I add again for good measure.

My response seemed to be the one Carter was hoping for, amusement clear on his features.

"How do you expect me to fuck you tonight if you can't take a small plug?" He challenges, smiling that he now has me backed up to the counter with nowhere to run.

"That is not fucking small." And neither is he.

"Did you really think I asked you to clean up just for fun?" I gave him a blank stare. Fun? He couldn't be serious. I practically had to beg Carter to let me do as he calls it 'clean up' on my own, and while it took me a while to figure out, douching is something I am not a fan of.

"Well that was before you brought down that thing and a bottle of lube." He was trying not to laugh at me, but I was overthinking this now.

"One, that thing is called a butt plug, and two..." Carter begins, a very clear change beginning to happen in his eyes, "Turn around."

"Maybe you should check on dinner instead?" I suggest, delaying what I already know is going to happen. My body tenses in awareness as Carter steps closer to my body, my head being forced to incline just so I could meet his eyes.

"Trust me when I say this is going to feel good, sweetheart." He says, leaning down until his mouth is right next to my ear, his lips just briefly touching, "And I've been waiting to claim this untouched ass of yours since you first signed your name on our contract." What Carter was really saying was that I needed to trust him, and that I better turn around before I get a punishment on top of the anal toy.

Taking a breath, I meet his eyes one last time before turning to the clean section of countertop, obliging the hand on my back that instantly pushes my front down. The tight material of my dark green shirt barely shifted at the action, but the same couldn't be said for my tan coloured, mid-thigh skirt.

Goosebumps formed on my legs as I felt Carter run his hands slowly up and down the backs of my thighs, working me up in a way that brought me comfort just as much as it did fear.

"So pretty." He murmured so quietly I barely caught it. Keeping my legs tight together, I closed my eyes as the back of my skirt was bunched up to my waist, both of Carter's hands fondling the curves of my ass. I wasn't exactly sure where the plug was now that he was touching me, but I was too nervous to look myself.

"This is no different than before." Carter reassures, his fingers moving to teasingly work along the edges of my underwear and stroke the skin he knows is most sensitive, "We'll go slow, but I can assure you it's not as big as it looks." We'll have to disagree on that, but I was no longer fighting him as he slowly slid the simple fabric down my legs until it pooled at my feet. My heart was racing as I stepped out of it, annoyed at the already tightly forming knot working its way deep into my core. And all it took were a mere few touches.

"Stay just like that." Carter says, planting a kiss to my ass before I felt his body rising. The breeze from his movement had cold air brushing against my clit, my hips shifting in need, yet terrified of what was going to fulfill it. Turning my head to the side, I remained bent over the counter while I watched Carter first flip the burgers over, and then proceed to thoroughly wash his hands in the sink while watching me.

His focus never left my body, and with my eyes now open, I could see that the toy and bottle of lube had been right next to me this entire time. Drying his hands, it wasn't long before Carter was back at my side, though he knocked the breath from me in an instant when he swiftly slipped two fingers inside of my cunt at the same time.

My wrist mostly covered my moan, but there was no mistaking the satisfied smile on Carter's face.

"Seems to me like you like this idea, Hazel." He says, continuously drawing his fingers in and out of me with no resistance, "A lot, actually." I was.

"Shut up." I grumbled, but that only earned me my head being yanked back, forcing me to meet a dark gaze.

"You seem to have forgotten your place with me." Carter tuts, beginning to curl his fingers as intense pleasure awakened deep inside, "Let me remind you." The fullness was gone within no more than a second, my head being let go of only so he could spank me. Hard.

"Fuck!" I cursed as my hips kept me in place, but offered no aid in the stinging burn of Carter's palm. Again, his hand met my ass, this time on the other side.

"You've been getting too comfortable, so let's get you back on that edge, shall we?" I gasped as his middle finger rubbed against my other entrance, but before I could comprehend the wetness was from my arousal, Carter pushed easily past the tight hole.

I couldn't even make a noise this time, my hands clasped into tight fists as he simply remained still, the cold edge of one of his rings just slightly brushing against the rim of my ass. We stayed like that for a short moment, but then I heard the opening of a cap followed by the cold, wet feeling of lubricant being poured onto Carter's finger.

"If I'd known this was all it took to show you your place, I would've done this a long time ago." He smiled, pulling out and instantly moving to add a second digit into me.

"Daddy," I whimpered, my clit genuinely throbbing from these still relatively new sensations. But he never stopped, never giving me any breaks and never letting me move away from his unrelenting touch. I was helpless beneath him with every delicious stroke of his fingers, every shiver and hitched breath only seeming to please Carter more.

"Please." The beg fell from my mouth before I could even stop myself, squirming against the restraint of his hands.

"Oh?" Carter says, his lips no doubt quirking into a smirk, "I thought you were so sure of yourself only minutes ago you wouldn't like this." Well I was wrong. I wasn't about to admit that, but still. His actions sent tiny bursts of pleasure tingling across my skin, but that was not even close to enough of a reaction for the man at my back.

Carter whispered and teased about how responsive I was, continuing to learn my body and seeing what angles and thrusts pulled the most desired noises from me.

"Shit—" I swore, crying out when he found just the right spot that had my fingers and toes curling in desperation.

"Right there?" Carter cooed, stroking that same place again and again in a steady rhythm that left me overwhelmed. I could only nod, still completely unused to this kind of stimulation even though he's been prepping me for almost a month now for this day.

"When you come, sweetheart, I'm going to put this toy inside of you while you're still orgasming." Carter promises, knowing I was close and beginning to lubricate the plug as best as he could with one hand, "I didn't want you to feel caught off guard when it happens." Because it will happen.

Considering how new this all still was, I was equally thankful for this information just as I was wanting to fight off my rapidly approaching climax in fear. Both fortunately and unfortunately for me, I didn't seem to have much of a choice in the matter. I was too far gone, lightheaded and lost in the lust that overpowered my every thought.

"Come." His single word gripped onto my every protest, my will giving out as my orgasm rushed through my tensing and writhing body. I clamped down around Carter's hand hard, but his movements were just as quickly removed from me as promised. My hips jerked as the same two fingers that were just inside of me came around to play with my clit, spurring on my release and leaving me gasping on a choked sound of pleasure.

"Relax your muscles." Carter said in my ear, urging me to loosen the part of me that was tight and spasming from my orgasm. Doing as we've done a few times before, I first intentionally tensed before willing myself to go limp, the action causing the toy pressed at my back entrance to push easily inside of me.

It was cold and wet with lube, and by the time the plug was flush inside, my climax had already ended. Though, I was left throbbing and desperate on the flip side of it all.

"Look at you all stretched out for me." Carter nipped my ear in approval as he pulled me up with him, a gasp falling from my mouth when the shift caused the toy to move, "I can't wait until it's my cock filling you instead."

"Carter." I groaned, pushing back on him and growing frustrated when his hands clasped my hips, not allowing me any relief. I felt so full and turned on, I couldn't even deny the slight shake of my body.

I've thought about this day for weeks, and I can't even begin to process what it's going to feel like after dinner when he takes me upstairs.

"Mmm." He hums in amusement, fixing my skirt casually, "I changed my mind. Since you've been so insistent on helping, why don't you set the table for me?" I stiffened because I knew his words were not ones of request. Angling my head back, Carter flashed me a knowing smile that his command would require a lot of moving.

I could barely even stand without feeling on the brink of yet another orgasm, and I knew this was going to be hard when a slap was landed to my ass in encouragement. Biting back my moan from the pressure inside of me, I give Carter an incredulous look before walking to the cupboards by the fridge and reaching for the doors.

Every single step has me fighting against the shake in my knees, suppressing the urge to swear at the man amusedly watching my every movement. Flashing a fake smile, I grab two forks and two plates, refusing to make eye contact with Carter as I walk past him and in the direction of where I assumed we'd be eating.

"Leave the cutlery on the counter and come back for it." An annoyingly sensual voice sounds at my back, and when I spin around to face him in disbelief, I find him tending to the burger patties as if I didn't have a toy inside of me.

"You're kidding?" I try. When he only spares me a quick glance, I knew he was dead serious.

"Wouldn't want your hands to be too full." Carter smirks, moving over to the cutting boards to finish preparing a series of different vegetables. Oh, he was so doing this on purpose. I racked my brain for a way out of this and came up depressingly empty handed. Short of using my safe word which I had no reason to do I was going to have to endure this.

"Fine." I say, gently placing down the forks on the counter while keeping my eyes on him, "And where will we be eating dinner, Daddy?" Purposefully using that name with him, I felt a little bit of satisfaction at the clench of his jaw that told me all I needed to know.

Carter would get to endure this teasing too. And I wouldn't put it past him at this point to make me move the plates again from setting up in the wrong spot since I was about to assume without asking.

"The balcony right off of my room would be great, sweetheart." He answers after a pause, and this time it's my turn to grind my teeth.

I didn't have access to the elevators which meant I'd have to go up and down those stairs twice at a minimum.

Clever, stupidly attractive bastard. Holding my tongue, as well as my whimper, I walked away with the two plates in hand, well aware of the dark eyes watching my every move. It was bearable until I made it to the stairwell.

Stairs that I could normally climb in thirty seconds took me three minutes, and by the time I made it to the top, it took everything in me to not beg for relief.

Carter spent the next twenty minutes doing this, taking his time with dinner and finding immense entertainment on all of the corrections he's been making. Once I was finally able to place the plates on his balcony table, I came back for the cutlery, refusing to speak to him. My clit was throbbing, and my ass was painfully full, and at this point it was a miracle I made it up the stairs for a second time. A thin line of sweat had formed at my hairline from the never-ending stimulation, but when I came back down to the kitchen, Carter's smile told me I was nowhere near done.

First, he made me take up napkins for each of us, then drinking glasses, and then drinking glasses again when he decided the first ones were too small. Every little movement was torturous and one hundred percent intentional on Carter's part, my knees trembling on my final move to go upstairs. I decided at this moment, I would refuse having to walk back up for a sixth time if he were to command it.

I would take a punishment, because anything would be easier to handle than this. Making it to his room and placing down a large glass jug of water in the center of the table, I did a final glance over my setup before shakily walking down the staircase I've come to despise.

I hated the way I was so turned on, especially because the infuriatingly handsome man standing in the kitchen was the cause of this. I hated how nice his pants made his backside look, and how the neatly rolled sleeves of his button down revealed all of the tattoos I've begun to memorize by heart.

Damn him.

"Are you going to continue to stare at my ass all day, or are you going to come over here and let me take care of you?" Carter's steady voice caught me red handed, but I didn't have it in me right now to feel embarrassment.

"I don't know. You do have a really nice butt." I grin, his head turning my way, but not denying anything.

No, I'm supposed to be mad for his chores, not want to fuck him for it. When Carter fully spun around, now with a plate of burger toppings and a bowl of salad, my heart fluttered as he handed me both items. I took them into my hands, but just as I opened my mouth to protest, I was being scooped up into a pair of muscled arms.

"Yours is better." He whispered in my ear, just as his hand came down to tap the round jewel of the plug. The action had me squirming and pressing my legs tight together, but the plates forced me to keep my attention on steadying them as Carter carried me up the stairs himself. It took everything in me to not drop or spill anything, and it annoyingly took every bit of this man's support too.

"Don't be mad." He whispers lowly in my ear, planting a kiss right below it and sending pleasure induced tingles throughout my body, "You'll be thankful for this when I'm the one filling you up later." Just like that, I was dissolved into a pool of desire in his arms.

Carter knew it too. Opening the door to his bedroom and being cautious of not hitting my head on anything, Carter brought me straight out to the balcony before gently placing me down. Within a second, he was taking the food from my tight grip and organizing it on the table, pulling out my chair for me and smiling as I sat down.

"These smells great." I say, thanking him for the gesture and watching as he took a seat right across from me. Both of our bodies instantly relaxed in each other's presence, small signs of a setting sun causing a golden glow to pass over both of our faces.

"I figured something a little simpler would be good for tonight." Carter says, grabbing the pair of tongs he made me bring up and plating salad for both of us.

Simple or complex, I really didn't care. Carter has yet to make me something I disliked, and anyways, the view of him in the kitchen earlier would make even the most awful food edible. Nodding, I happily take my plate from him before grabbing a burger bun and layering it with mustard, lettuce, tomato, bacon, and then, of course, the burger patty.

My mouth watered at the sight, my mind almost capable of fully straying from the ache in my core.

"Thank you for making this," I hum in appreciation, looking up to find Carter plating his own food. He gives me a small smile and nod in response, his knee brushing just slightly against the side of mine under the table. The contact was nice, and I finally felt myself grow calm as I lifted my sandwich to my mouth and took a bite. As usual, Carter's cooking didn't disappoint.

Something that seemed as simple as a burger had flavors bursting across my taste buds, the taste almost making it worth going up and down those stairs so many damn times. At least I could be well fed if I were going to have to deal with this pain. "How are you feeling?" Carter asks after a bite of his food, his knees brushing mine again and showing me it was intentional.

Squirming at the reminder, I can't help but feel a little embarrassed to talk about this as easily as talking about the weather over dinner.

"I'm good," I nod, taking another large bite of my burger to spare me from conversation. I've actually gotten a lot more confident and relaxed around him, but some things just refused to come naturally to me.

"Be more specific." Carter smiles, knowing it's nearly impossible to ignore the ache in my body by forcing me to acknowledge it. Even though I'm able to take my time eating, I know this conversation is inevitable.

He was patient, though. Frustratingly patient. I knew I'd have to cave and give in, so I placed down my burger, but kept my eyes on my plate.

"It feels good." I flush, clearly picking up on the change here, "I'm sore, and it feels a little uncomfortable to get used to, but I'm mostly just turned on." My heart speeds a little at the brush of his forefinger under my chin, tilting my head up so that I had to look at him. Carter's eyes had gone dark, his thumb tracing a line against my bottom lip.

"Apart from the unusual feeling, are you in pain, sweetheart?" He asks, my face leaning into his touch as he held me a little.

"No, Daddy," I answer, my legs pressing together under the table, "Quite the opposite actually." I watched as Carter's throat moved as he swallowed, faint swirls of ink peeking out of the collar of his shirt. He was sex on legs in every way, and he was making it very hard right now to remember the importance of eating.

"Good," He says, brushing my cheek one last time before retracting his touch, "Then finish your meal so I can have my dessert." As delicious as it was, the rest of dinner was even more torturous than climbing the staircase multiple times.

Carter was always touching me in some way his knee, his hand, his forearm.

I feel like it was almost being done unconsciously, but it was his eyes on me that made things so hard. We still talked as we ate this time about more dinner appropriate things, but it was our glances at each other that kept me on edge the entire thirty minutes it took us to finish.

We were both excited, and though Carter finished eating long before I did, he insisted for me to not rush myself. When I placed my fork down for the final time, I looked up to find him following the movement of my hand before standing from his seat.

I could only blink as Carter's large form towered over me, extending a hand in which I instantly accepted. The man of few words remained that way as his hand transferred to my back, not leading me to the hallway like I expected, but rather to his bathroom.

My curiosity of his choice had me distracted enough that I could walk without collapsing to the ground, understanding and gratefulness crossing my features when he moved to the sinks.

Offering a lilac coloured toothbrush to me from a holder on his counter, I smiled slightly at the sight of him grabbing a black one as his own. He got me a toothbrush? Yes, it may be something stupid to be happy over, but Carter was making a conscious effort to make me feel comfortable here.

It was only then that I noticed he also got me my special toothpaste meant to help with sensitive teeth, while he just used a normal mint.

It was a small gesture in size, but it spoke volumes to me.

Planting a light kiss to his shoulder in appreciation, I left it at that as I prepped my brush before running it under cold water.

Carter mimicked my action before bringing it up to his mouth, a smile to be seen in his eyes as our gazes met in the mirror.

It was weird doing something so domestic with him, but nice all the same. It was that unspoken balance we had together between words and gestures, and today had been full of both that left me with butterflies in my stomach and throbbing between my thighs. Spitting out the blue bubbles from my mouth, I repeated this action a few more times before rinsing the head of my toothbrush and leaning over to put it in its holder. The holder next to Carter's. One second, I was smiling at the sight, the next I was being spun to the side and bent over the freezing countertop that contrasted the heated flooring beneath my feet.

"What are you—" I gasped but was cut off at the cold feeling of my skirt being lifted up.

"I'm getting my dessert." He says, and the next minute my hair was gathered in his hand and being pulled back, our lips instantly connecting in a flurry of passion. My knees threatened to buckle beneath me at the intensity, my body humming as the weight of Carter's much larger one kept me pinned down. My heart raced as his free hand moved to rub my ass, spanking me just so he could swallow my moan with each movement of his tongue.

"Please." I whimpered against him when his palm met my body again, the plug feeling impossibly deeper every time he tapped it with his thumb.

"Is this what you're begging for, sweetheart?" Carter asks cruelly against my lips as his hand moves to hover right over my clit, my arousal making me slick between my legs.

"Yes—" I couldn't even finish my sentence before a finger easily slipped inside of me, the heel of his hand being used to rub me in the best ways. All the while he continued to dominate me with his lips, taking every part of me and leaving me bare for his pleasure. It was almost embarrassing how quickly I started to reach my high, but I couldn't stop my moan as a second finger slipped inside, a third following quickly after.

"Carter," I groaned at how rough he was being with me, my body crying out when he pulled his mouth from mine and turned my head to meet my reflection in the massive, circular mirror. I've never seen myself like this, my skin so flushed and my eyes so full of lust. And all of it was caused by the man at my side, his lips moving to my neck while watching my every reaction.

"I don't think I'll ever be able to get enough of you, Hazel." Carter says in my ear, his erection strained against my back, "You're a fucking addiction." It became hard to breathe at his words, his fingers dripping as he continued to pound into me at a dizzying pace.

"Oh god." I cried out, my legs trying to clamp together but only finding Carter's knee keeping them apart. My head began to lull as he held me up, forcing me to watch as he unraveled me just like that. I tried to push up from the counter in sensitivity, only to be pressed back down, Carter smiling as I screamed out my release.

"There you go." He whispered, his palm still rubbing my clit as I fell apart beneath him, my orgasm dripping down my legs with the combined sensation of the plug still inside of me.

No amount of will was able to keep my eyes open after that, Carter's motions gradually slowing as he brought me down from my high. Gently letting go of my hair and guiding my head to lay against his one hand, I remained limp right there as I panted and tried to regain myself. The entire time, Carter stayed with me, placing a light kiss to my temple and running his fingers through my hair calmingly.

I'll admit, it did take me a little longer than usual before my eyes were able to flutter back open, but it was perfect when the first thing I saw was my messy haired boyfriend.

"Hey, sweetheart." He offered me a small smile, my arousal already clean from his fingers.

"Hi." I murmured, pushing myself up onto my forearms so I could see him more comfortably.

That soon didn't matter as Carter moved me himself, picking me up and turning me so I was sitting upright to face him. A small tremble remained in my legs, and my arms had to reach out to his arms for support, but he held me.

Carter never once made me feel rushed as I looked up at him, and when he brought his lips down to meet mine, I felt the air part from my lungs. In a single touch, I was melting beneath his fingertips, every caress making it feel like the first time all over again.

He tasted like mint and wood, my senses becoming consumed by his kiss and urging my body selfishly for more. Running my hands up and down the planes of hard muscle along Carter's arms, I explored him diligently all while meeting his tongue stroke for stroke.

I felt warm as he cradled my face with his palms, angling my head back to get closer to me—to feel more. His desire was undoubtedly as strong as mine, and when I finally slid off of the counter to my full height, I broke off the kiss to slowly move to my knees on the ground.

"Present just like that, sweetheart." Carter says, his hands still touching my face as I spread my legs outwards and fixed my posture. Once again, the change in position had me shuddering from the plug, and it was horrible now that I couldn't rub my thighs together for relief.

It was me who initiated this, though, and I didn't regret it for a moment. Especially at the feeling of Carter's eyes on me, his one hand dropping to the waistband of his pants and unbuckling his belt.

My mouth watered when he finally drew his cock from his boxers, unable to see him from my eyes being pointed to the ground, even though I knew what awaited me. He would be thick and hard, his tip dripping with precum and running over the shiny piercing that has brought me more pleasure than imaginable.

I could see through my peripheral view the sight of Carter's fist running along his length in deep strokes, close enough that I would only have to lean forward to take him into my mouth.

I hated that I wasn't allowed to look up, but I did know one thing for certain. It was my turn for dessert.

"Is this what you wanted, little one?" His low voice thrums through me, excitement coursing through my veins at the memory of the sounds he made the last time my lips were around him.

"Yes, Daddy." I answer, feeling myself go into that calming headspace as I open my mouth in invitation. It was one Carter gratefully accepted. All it took was a single step forward before my tongue was able to lick a slow line across his slit, a large hand coming to the back of my head and gathering my hair for me.

The realization that I wasn't allowed to move that Carter was going to stand there and use me as I knelt in submission at his feet it was one that turned me on so much it hurt.

"You're such a good girl, Hazel." He praised as he guided himself farther into my mouth, and I heard his smile as I shivered in response to his words.

The urge to please him went from a want to a need, my brain forcing myself into stillness as I relaxed my jaw to encourage him to go deeper.

The only thing I had control of was my tongue, and now that I've learned what Carter likes, I wasted no time tracing the vein that ran along the bottom of his cock, my lips wrapping closed to suck.

I never moved my head, but the groan my actions elicited from him had me tempted, his hips beginning to slowly thrust as I controlled my gag.

Or tried to. He was slow at first, working himself deeper and deeper down my throat until I couldn't stop myself from choking, spit dripping from the corners of my mouth.

The pace allowed me to breathe more easily, but it became a real effort to keep still as Carter began hitting the back of my throat, my nose brushing against his front with each pump of his hips.

For a moment, he just held me like that, restricting my air and enjoying how my throat constricted around him from his size.

My first sign of real struggle was the twitch of my hands still forced against my thighs, tears forming in my eyes but not quite spilling down my cheeks yet. I knew my hand signal was to raise it above my head if I needed to safe word, but when Carter tilted my chin up to meet his gaze, I knew I could take it.

For him.

For myself. For this. When the last of my resistance faded from my eyes, that's when he pulled out and allowed me to breathe once again, coughs instantly falling past my lips.

I could feel what a mess I was as spit and precum glistened on my face, my mouth reopening and silently asking for more.

I never enjoyed giving blowjobs until these men, but I knew if Carter asked, I would remain here on my knees for as long as he wished, begging just to be able to taste him again.

If that didn't show how into this I was, then I don't know what does.

Remaining there and watching as Carter's dark eyes held mine captive in his gaze, I waited for the touch that never came. Instead, I was soon being lifted up to stand, given a few seconds to regain my balance as a thumb was dragged in a single sweep across my chin, wiping away the mess he made.

Taking the hint, I opened and wrapped my mouth around the finger, moaning at the faint taste of him against my tongue as I licked and sucked him clean. I could see the clear hunger in his eyes as I mimicked what I was doing only seconds ago, offering a teasing smile as he pulled his thumb away.

"I want you to take off your clothes and wait for me in my room." Carter says, walking to the counter and grabbing both an elastic and brush from his drawer. I stayed silent as he moved to my back, my scalp tingling as he untangled my hair before braiding it back in sure movements.

Sighing as his mouth came to my ear, his fingers continuing their work on my hair, heat pulsed through me as he whispered, "No playroom tonight. When I fuck you, it's going to be in my own bed." With that, I felt the final pull of my hair, an elastic band securing the strands in place better than I could ever do myself.

Carter didn't need to speak to tell me what was about to happen, his body following in step with mine as I exited his bathroom, pulling off my shirt as I walked. I don't think either of us were eager to wait as I messily folded the material and placed it on his TV stand, stripping off my bra and skirt next.

The action forced me to turn away from Carter, but the second my clothes were set down, he was on me. His lips on my neck, his hands roaming my aching body and pressing me to his now bare chest.

As a matter of fact, not a single item of fabric separated us now as I was turned to Carter, his hands dropping to the backs of my thighs and silently telling me to jump.

Obeying, I wrapped both my arms and legs around his body as our mouths reunited.

Our kiss was wild and passionate, the only two words that were capable of describing our need for each other right now. Even our skin felt like too much of a barrier, but I knew I was about to be connected to Carter in a way I've never experienced before.

~ Fifteen ~

Carter

With Hazel wrapped in my arms, I felt the bed sink slightly under our weight as I pinned her with my hips. I haven't been able to stop thinking about her since the last time we were together—since she made that god awful cake that meant everything to me. My girl has been on my mind for far longer than I'd like to admit, but she was here now and that's all I could ever want.

"Please," Hazel whimpered against my mouth, her hips rolling upwards to gain friction against mine, "I need you inside of me." Those words had an effect on every part of my being, and it took every ounce of my control to restrain myself from fulfilling her pleas right here right now.

This was not something I wanted to hurt her in and wanted to make this as enjoyable as possible.

"Not yet, sweetheart." I murmur, licking along her bottom lip before pulling away to watch her. I couldn't stop myself as my eyes raked across her body, taking in the details I've already memorized by heart. I knew every scar and stretch mark, every dip and curve. I knew every inch of the perfect woman beneath me the same one I was lucky enough to call mine.

"This is not something we're going to rush." I say, dipping my head until my mouth was able to connect to her jaw, planting a kiss there before continuing a path downwards.

I covered the marks that were clearly older from a few days ago, as well as the ones I know Dominic gave her last night. I worshiped the dip of her collar bone and the curve of her breasts, tracing patterns with my tongue down her soft stomach and then along each shape of her hip bones.

By the time I was crawling back up her trembling body, there wasn't a trace I left untouched. As planned, Hazel was now reduced into a beautiful mess, waiting and more than ready for me to take her. I've thought of a million different combinations as to how this could play out, but I knew one thing for certain. She would be looking at me the first time I fill her up.

"Such a sensitive little thing," I tease, brushing my lips down to graze across Hazel's nipples once again. The action had her back arching up to me, only to be met with the large wall of my body. She had no escape as I took extra time memorizing the hardened peaks, loving the sounds I pulled from her lips with every pass. Those fucking noises that threatened to bring me over the edge before even being inside of her.

"I-I can't." Hazel gasped when I took her nipple between my teeth, releasing it with a harsh tug before soothing away the pain with my tongue. I knew the combination of gentle and rough is something she's grown very fond of, and who was I to deny her.

"I've dreamt of this moment for weeks," I admit, my eyes never straying from her own twisting in pleasure. She was ready for me, and what a beautiful realization that was. Finally giving her nipple some relief, I redirected my attention to my hand slowly traveling down her front and down to the base of the toy at her ass.

"I'm going to take this out, okay?" I warn, lifting myself up a little more so I can remove it safely, "It's going to feel weird, but I really need you to relax for me. Can you do that, sweetheart?" I know Hazel is still zoned in more than enough to comply with this, but considering how much larger this plug is, I know it's going to feel a little strange being taken out.

"Yes, Daddy." She nods, propping herself up slightly on her elbows and likely expecting pain. Well... Holding one hand on her lower stomach to keep her from twisting, I slowly began to pull at the base. As expected, Hazel's body tried to shoot up, her hand moving down to hold onto my wrist.

"I promise you it's not what you think it is." I assure, holding her hand and not moving an inch. I already spoke to her about this part before she came here, but it's very different hearing it than feeling it.

"Sorry, fuck, I know." She offers an embarrassed smile to which I stroke her hip in response with my thumb. Something no one talks about when removing anal plugs is that they can feel very similar to pooping. It's not that in the least, but I was well aware her fear stemmed from a very justifiable place.

"Breathe, Hazel. You're good, I swear." Slowly, ever so slowly, I felt her muscles relax, but her hand remained on my wrist. I allowed it, giving her small murmurs in encouragement as I began to pull out once again, seeing her body fight between tensing and loosening. It was a long process, but one I had every intention of taking my time with to make sure Hazel wasn't in pain.

My prepping her and getting her to move around earlier may have been torturous—as expressed in her multiple glares my way but it made things so much easier now.

We went slow, and I offered her everything I could to make her feel comfortable. I could visibly see the tension free itself from her body when we got past the hardest part, the plug easily removing after that.

I didn't give her time to think before I leaned back over her, discarding the toy and making sure Hazel's mind could go back into that calming headspace. Her knees were currently bent, her feet keeping them upright on either side of my body as she spread for me, expectedly squirming and growing increasingly turned on.

After being stretched for so long, I know every part of her is craving the feeling of being filled again. It's another natural response, one that only makes me harder from the sound of her whimpers and pleads.

"Carter," Hazel groans, her hips rolling up to meet mine and her body jerking from the sensitivity. I didn't bother to correct her, rather liking the way my name sounded on her lips.

"Mhm?" I hummed, smirking at the desperation rolling through her. I knew in that moment I'd waited long enough. I was about to claim Hazel in the filthiest way there was and I couldn't wait to see her fall apart around me. Blindly reaching out for the lube I'd left on the nightstand, I felt her pretty green eyes track my movements when my fingers wrapped around the bottle.

"We're going to need to take this really slow, and I need you to be honest with me about how you're feeling." I say as I pop open the lid and apply a more than healthy amount of lube onto two of my fingers, "Anal can feel amazing when done properly, but one of the most important parts is communication."

I watch as this information sinks in before Hazel nods in under-standing. In the next second, I began to probe a lube covered finger at her tight hole, easily being able to push in but having to hold Hazel down to keep her from moving. Once I knew she wouldn't hurt herself, I slipped the whole finger in with ease, mentally groaning at the combination of a whimper and gasp that came from her mouth.

"That's it." I say, pulling out and adding more lube. This time, I slid two inside of her, pleased at the way she naturally stretched around me, "How does that feel, sweetheart?"

"Good, Daddy." Hazel moaned, still trying to roll her hips, "Please, I need more." I know. For a little while, I remained like that, kissing the inside of her knee as I pumped my fingers in and out of her. It was more than clear our weeks of prep paid off, with more lube, a third being able to push inside with only a little resistance. I could see as Hazel's brain slowly drifted into pleasure, her thoughts going foggy as her body welcomed me gratefully.

"Fuck." I murmured under my breath at how tight and warm she was, continuing to curl and scissor my fingers until there wasn't a single second where one of us wasn't letting out heavy breaths in desire.

"Ah—please!" Hazel cried out when I hit a certain spot inside of her, my movements growing rougher as her hips bucked up. I only continued to plant gentle kisses along her propped knee, heat burning through us both with every passing second. Never once did my eyes stray from her's, but when Hazel met mine with an adoring smile, her thighs shaking, I knew it was one of my new favorite sights of her. That and the flushed expression she wore the first time I kissed her by that lake.

"I know, sweetheart." I smile with every pant that leaves her body, tears forming in her big eyes as she stares up at me pleadingly. It was beautiful she was beautiful, and I was about to have her in a way she's never been taken before.

Satisfied and pulling my fingers out of her, I gauged her reactions and encouraged her to watch as I poured much more lube onto the palm of my hand. It never hurt to use too much, but I knew just from stroking my cock with my fist that having to be slow with her would be both hell and heaven all at once.

There was just one last thing I needed. Reaching over with my non slippery hand, I grabbed one of my thicker pillows before encouraging Hazel to lift her hips, sliding the object right below her ass. Her body tilted to the perfect angle at the change, her eyes blown and full of need as her gaze flitted between mine and my cock.

"Ready, Hazel?" I ask, restraint clear in my voice as I shifted forward slightly. Despite her obvious eagerness and anticipation, I could see Hazel couldn't fully quell the nervousness inside of her. It was understandable, which was why I remained still, rubbing my free hand up and down her leg.

"You're in control, sweetheart. You determine the pace and tell me what you like." A nod of her head and a sigh to relax herself was her response, her hands moving to rest on her stomach in a sign of trust.

She showed only desire as I pressed the tip of my cock to her back entrance, moving myself around the tight rim before ever so slowly pushing in. Almost instantly I felt her body tense up, my movements halting as I continued to stroke her skin with my hands.

"You okay?" I check in, my fingers moving to gently play with her nipples and forcing myself to remain still at how good she felt. Yup, this was pure torture yet the most beautiful form of sin.

"Yeah, sorry." Hazel panted, her eyes pinching shut in concentration, "You can move now." I felt the instant her muscles relaxed around me, allowing me to slide just slightly deeper inside. This time, I was able to get a little farther before her body once again restricted me.

"I've got you," I encourage, not allowing her any time to feel bad about freezing up.

This was about her, and I knew just how hard it was to adjust to all of these new sensations. Deciding to pull out all of the way, I applied even more lube to my length before pushing back in, groaning at how her hole all but tried to pull me into her.

It took everything in me to go as slow as possible, despite how desperately I wanted to plunge right into her in a single thrust.

This was a process, no doubt, but I was patient as I waited over and over again for her to relax into my touch.

My hands were shaking slightly once I was about half way inside of her, holding myself still and digging my fingers into her hips to control my instincts.

"Please, Carter." Hazel shook, loosening around me, "Keep going, I'm good." Her lashes were wet with tears, face flushed with arousal. I could only focus on that and the way our bodies melded perfectly together, slowly pressing my hips forward and paying keen attention to every desperate sound that fell from her parted lips.

This time was different, Hazel's body accepting me as I rolled my hips deeper. Both of us were shaking at this point, my grip sure to bruise when I eventually got as close to her as we could be.

My final thrust was sharp as our hips connected, closing the gap between us entirely.

The feeling of her had me stilling my every movement, whimpers leaving Hazel's mouth as we paused to readjust. Nothing has ever felt as good as this as good as her.

There was no going back now, and as I drew my hips back, nothing stopped me as I drove back into her, my pulse quickening immensely from the sounds of our shared pleasure.

"More." Hazel pleaded when I fully began to move, still taking my time so I didn't hurt her.

She begged and begged, slowly breaking apart beneath me as I filled her with my cock, fucking every thought from her mind. There was only one that mattered, and it was us.

"Fuck, you're perfect." I cursed, leaning forward and cupping the side of her face, tears beginning to soak her cheeks and now my hand. I all but forced her down as I continued to stroke her, gradually increasing my speed at a pace I knew would keep this enjoyable for her. Hazel liked the pain, so I brought it, the only thing keeping her from sliding up the bed being my unrelenting grip.

"You feel so good, Hazel. So good." My fingers dug into her side, using her thighs to pull her closer as my thrusts grew more forceful. I meant it earlier when I said Hazel was an addiction, my mind getting high off of the sound of her moans, the soft feeling of her touch, and the lavender scent of her body. I was fucking addicted to this woman, and the taste of that craving was dangerously blissful.

"Oh god. Carter!" Hazel cried my name, knowing our stomachs were tightening with every frantic movement, desperation coiling tighter and tighter within us. With both of our breaths labored, our pleasure threatening to burst from us, my hand came down between our bodies, my thumb finding her swollen clit and circling in time with my thrusts.

That was all it took for her. Hazel screamed, her muscles spasming as she jerked and tensed up before everything rushed out in a single sweep.

Her release messily soaked the two of us, my hands having to hold her down as I pounded into her ass and chased my own pleasure.

My limbs shook and my vision blurred from the feeling of her coming, my forehead resting against her arched chest as I thrust once, twice, thrice, before I followed her over the edge.

Hazel clung to me as I spilled myself into her, tears staining her cheeks as she trembled beneath me. I could barely keep from collapsing onto her, her ass milking every drop of my orgasm from my sensitive body.

"Shit," Hazel let out a small laugh, whimpering as my cock slipped out of her tight hole, "I didn't know it could be like that." That would make two of us. My breaths were still heavy as my release slowly dripped out of her, my dick threatening to harden all over again from the sight alone. It was much too soon for that, though, instead rolling onto my side and guiding Hazel's legs to remain intertwined with my own.

I would not be letting her go for a long, long time.

"Me either," I panted, my hand caressing the side of her face as her green eyes stared up at mine.

They were sated and filled with warmth, stunningly brighter because of her tears. That single look had the power to bring me to ruin, and she didn't even know it. My beautiful destruction.

"How are you feeling?" I ask, noticing her eyes grow heavier with each passing second as I glanced over her flushed skin. "I'm sore," Hazel admits, a soft breath leaving her lips, "And tired. But mostly, I'm really happy." That's all I could ever want. I felt the same in more ways than one, but instead of expressing it in words, I did what I do best, using my actions and pulling my girl into a slow, deep kiss. Hazel relaxed against me as our lips moved languidly together, unhurried and at total ease with each other. Neither of us pulled away for a long time, and even once we eventually did, we never strayed far.

We spent some time fixing both the bed and ourselves, parting for only a few seconds in between, but at the end of the night, the only thoughts that remained were of the other.

Everything felt right as Hazel's small body was tucked close to mine, her dark eyelashes fluttered shut in tiredness.

She was by my side, and while I knew sleep would not find me tonight, I didn't mind staying up.

This day was something I could never forget. So, I remained awake, allowing myself for the first time in years to embrace what true happiness felt like with my only thoughts being about the blonde haired woman passed out in my arms.

Rowan

The rain currently pouring outside was effectively souring my mood, however the knowledge of who was about to be at my door brightened it immensely.

I've painfully waited twenty four days to have Hazel to myself for the night, and while the rain ruined my plans of taking her out, I refused to allow this to be anything less than perfect.

I may not be able to cook and don't know the first thing about dating, but that didn't stop my heart from racing nervously, yet excitedly, at the sound of the doorbell ringing.

Tonight was going to be about me and her. Adjusting the cuffs of my leather jacket, I steadily walked over to the door to find Hazel absolutely soaked on the other side, her hair wet and makeup running under her eyes.

"Hey, darling." I smile at the sight, trying to add some teasing into my tone to lighten her noticeably unhappy state. All I get is a quick hi in response, Hazel walking past me and hastily placing her purse onto the front table.

"Whoa, what's going on?" I ask, reaching out to her with my hand only to just be brushed off with a shrug of her shoulder. Seeing her reflection in the mirror, I notice her eyes are slightly puffy, and I know that's not from the rain.

"Hey," I say again softly, my eyebrows furrowing at the sight of Hazel's obvious mood right now.

"Not everything's your business, you know." She murmurs under her breath, trying to reel away from me. I didn't know what was going on, but something is very very wrong here.

I watch as Hazel pushes off her shoes with her hands, soon standing barefoot on the front hall mat, not wanting to drag water into the house. The way her arms wrapped around her body indicated her trying to close everything off, but that wasn't happening.

Especially not with me. Walking towards her and forcing her to turn to me, I don't allow her to look away as I tilt her head up to meet my gaze.

As I suspected, there was no doubt her messed up makeup wasn't caused by the rain alone. She'd been crying, and I was ready to end the person who was the cause of it.

"Okay. You and I are going to talk about what's the matter, I'm going to pamper you and treat you to a proper date, and then I'm going to remind you who you're speaking to here." I say, holding her and not letting Hazel shut me out. So far this night has gone anything but what I'd planned, but I refused to let anything ruin this for us.

"Do you think I could get a towel first?" Hazel asks, and though I know she's trying to rein it in, I could still hear the bite in her tone.

Either she was mad at me, or something else was up and I simply got the job of being her punching bag. That was not something I planned on allowing to slide either. Not giving her the chance to move away, I picked Hazel up into my arms and began to walk into the house. As expected, it surfaced her usual self, protests of getting me wet causing her mind to stray from whatever it was that was eating away at her.

"I—" She began, but I cut her off with a pointed look. It was taking everything in me to not toss her over my lap and spank her ass raw for using that tone with me, but I could tell something serious was bothering her. The reprimanding would have to come after. Promptly carrying her up the staircase and to the main bathroom on our right, I placed Hazel down on the counter and silently wet a cloth under the sink. Even with mascara smeared across her face, she was breathtakingly beautiful. Though it wasn't hard to tell the mess was bothering her immensely. It was why I focused on taking care of her first, knowing punishment would only cause a fight I never wished to have.

"I'm sorry." Hazel apologizes as my hand raises to her face, my fingers clutched around the damp, warm towel for her eyes. As her gaze fluttered shut, I saw her swallow guiltily as I tilted her head up for better grip. I didn't say anything, instead wiping under her eyes gently, watching as the dark makeup slowly began to transfer onto the cloth. "My mom called me today." She shared, distaste and tenseness clear in her features, "The last time we spoke was about her spending thousands of dollars of my money behind my back, and now she's guilt tripping me about how I never make an effort to be in her life." As displeased as I am about the way she acted when I first answered the door, all of those emotions became channeled into Hazel's admission the second the words came out of her mouth. I knew more than anyone about people related by blood not automatically equating to family. Hazel just hasn't accepted that yet. I see a lot of myself in her at that moment, but instead of revealing how angry I was for her, I simply ask, "What part about that bothers you most?" The question clearly surprised her as her eyes reopened to meet my stare, the one half of her face now clear from not only eye shadow, but also distress. She pauses for a thoughtful second before she grimaces.

"The fact I agreed to visit her next Monday." My movements instantly ceased, Hazel's eyes not meeting mine.

"I'm saying goodbye for good." She quickly adds, trying to blink away her tears of frustration and the ones of the little girl who was never cared for in the way she should have been, "I need to do this for myself, but that doesn't make it any less damn hard." I try to process her words as I go back to wiping her face, understanding filling me along with the worry. I didn't want Hazel within a hundred miles of either her mother or her stepfather, but at the same time, this wasn't about me. I hated that her sadness would be inevitable because of this visit, and I hated even more how deeply I understood. Even though my every instinct tells me to, I won't stop her from gaining the closure she needs. All I can do is support her and hopefully take her mind off of this for now.

"And I look like shit." Hazel finishes with a sigh, "I wanted to-night to be perfect because it's the first...." Hazel trails off, though I know what she's trying to say.

"It's our first time together, and you're excited so you wanted it to be perfect." I nod, knowing because I'm feeling the same way. Her confirming nod and exhale of tension told me all I needed. Finishing with the towel and tossing it into the sink, my fingers dropped down to Hazel's, gently taking them into my hold.

"Who said this isn't just as perfect?" I plant my lips to the back of her hand before returning the gesture to her other, "I've been scrambling for a week to take you out on a date, every bit planned out because I thought that was what would make this a special moment for us." I smile down at Hazel, her hair dark and wet from the rain, the strands curling into little ringlets.

"As nice as that would've been, this night is about us. Who cares where it happens?" The rest of her worry dissolves with my final words, and it's then that I allow an amused smirk to appear across my face, "We both know this is going to end with you in my bed anyways." At the sight of the shy blush forming on Hazel's cheeks, I knew she was back to herself.

I was more than glad too, because I no longer felt guilty at the idea of stripping off the skin tight dress she put on for tonight, nor the soaked lingerie she wore underneath.

The cold rain had her nipples rock hard, and I didn't bother to be discreet as I admired my girl, my eyes inching over her body slowly.

When she shivered, I knew it wasn't from the cool chill of the counter.

Though I had no intentions of taking this any further yet, I loved that even after being with us for four weeks, she's still painfully shy.

It was the reason I took my time unbuttoning my black shirt bit by bit, keeping my eyes trained on Hazel's every reaction and smiling as I pulled the long sleeve onto her.

The fact she was surprised made it even better, rolling the bagging cuffs and securing the material to her body. I knew the shirt would smell like me, and honestly, a very possessive part of me liked the idea of her wearing not only my clothes but my scent as well.

Not minding in the least that I was now topless, my leather jacket forgotten on the counter, I guided Hazel off by her waist before leading her back out to the hallway.

This may not have been anywhere near what we'd planned, but it was almost better. It felt less forced, and it sure as hell made it easier to get her bare beneath my clothing.

"The movie's yours to choose tonight, darling." I say in Hazel's ear, relieved that she not only smiled in response, but also leaned into my touch. I had so many new ideas for tonight, but right now, I wanted her in my lap and cuddled up on top of me.

Scooping her up and carrying her over to the couch, I happily plopped Hazel down, laughing at her squeal and the way a few pieces of her wet hair stuck to her forehead at the movement.

God, she really was beautiful. Moving over to the kitchen, I quickly prepared some cheddar popcorn while grabbing a small container of ice cream as well. My eyes never strayed for long from Hazel who was currently wrapping herself in one of the throw blankets, going through my Netflix account in search of something to select.

I watched as she kept her knees tucked to her chest, a relaxed expression resting on her features until her face lit up at some of the choices she was scrolling through. Good. It was the only thing keeping my possessiveness at bay at the fact her mother stole from her and was going to steal her away from me for a week when she doesn't deserve even a second of her daughter's time. "Oh! Can we watch this one?" Hazel asks as the scroller moves over something I've seen before, not that I was about to tell her that. It didn't matter. I had other plans for her anyways.

"Go ahead and start it. I'll be right over." I answered, pulling the lid off of the ice cream and sticking a spoon hard into it so it was easier to carry.

The bowl of popcorn followed into my grip soon after, walking over to the living room and placing both items down on the table across from where Hazel was. Bending to kiss her temple, I just as smoothly picked her up and placed her onto my lap. "I can move myself y'know?" She squirms, but my hold on her waist very quickly stilled her.

I smirk as I drop my mouth to her neck, planting a slow, teasing kiss to where I could feel her fluttering heartbeat beneath the skin. My hand then looped around her, pulling her back flush to my front, her bare ass sitting directly on top of my very much hardened cock.

"I like moving you more." I whisper in response, pulling the blanket back up over her for warmth before placing the bowl of popcorn in her lap, "But if you don't sit still, Hazel, we're not going to get very far into the movie." Hazel froze at that, mumbling a sheepish apology and leaning back into my touch.

A small, breathy sigh came out of her mouth when we were finally comfortably situated, my hands happily holding her with the distant noise of my new favorite kind of weather pattering against the windows. Oh, this was definitely better than anything planned could have offered us. With Hazel in my arms, the faint smell of lavender and peppermint filling my senses, I was happy.

"He's such an ass." Hazel curses at the screen, myself trying to contain my snicker in amusement.

"You tell him, darling." I murmur in her ear, tossing some popcorn into my mouth and smiling harder at the look she gave me in return. Mock raising my hands in surrender, she turns her focus back to the television, about an hour left of the movie. It's been a lot of this for the last multiple minutes, but what Hazel didn't know was that I've been waiting for the one hour remaining mark, something that just ticked by now.

Gently gathering her now mostly dry hair and pushing it to her back, I tucked a few strands behind her ear before undoing the first button of my shirt on her body.

"Rowan," Hazel says my name at the action, her tongue darting out to lick across her lips as I continued down to the second clasp, then the third. As usual, her body was so responsive to me, her heart rate already picking up while her breaths became heavier.

"As understanding as I am about your behavior earlier, you should know better than to speak to me that way, darling." I smirk, moving southwards and exposing her skin inch by slow inch, "Place your legs on top of mine." She initially does quite the opposite at the sound of my name for her, knees pressing together before moving the popcorn to obey my order. Hesitantly, her thighs eventually spread, leaving her open for me as each one moved to hook around mine, parting wider when I forced them to. Hazel's body instantly reacted to my touch, my fingers undoing the last of the buttons before pushing the material to the sides, still on her body but leaving her curves free for my hands to cup. I do just that, feeling her racing heart against the palm of my hand as I encourage her to keep her eyes on the screen.

"What—" She began, but whatever she was about to say became replaced by a gasp when I took her right nipple between two long fingers. With her leaned against me and spread out, I lowly say, "I don't want to hear a single sound come out of that pretty little mouth of yours. You're going to sit here and watch the movie like a good girl while I play with you, and every time you make a noise, I'm going to slap you here." My one hand drops to between Hazel's thighs, my thumb warningly brushing against her clit in indication.

I grow even harder at her whimper, her mind desperately trying to focus on the screen but slowly failing already.

"I may even be persuaded to let you come after the movie, but right now you're going to stay still and have this needy cunt of yours as a reminder to respect who owns you." I bring my palm down on her inner thigh when she whimpers again, and though I have to hold her body down, I know she understands my command.

And so it began. Hearing the distant words of characters from the movie, every bit of my focus went into Hazel, my hand pulling away from her thigh and up to resume its place around her breast.

I've wanted to explore her here for a painful amount of time, and when my thumbs circle in sync around her areolas, I'm pleased with the way they harden beneath my touch.

"Such a sensitive thing." I smile, beginning her punishment and my torture at the same time. Reacting perfectly, Hazel tries to both lean backwards and forwards, her body conflicted by the pleasure and her moans no doubt catching in her throat. Unfortunately for her, I'm not very intent on watching her succeed in this.

Rolling both of her nipples in my fingers, I came close to eliciting noises from Hazel's slightly parted mouth, but I had no interest in rushing this. I have weeks' worth of time to make up for with her, and I planned to spend every last hour of tonight making Hazel come with my hands, cock, and tongue until she couldn't take another second of it.

Yes, this was only the beginning. Taking my mouth and sucking gently at the pulse of her neck, I was able to feel every uneven heartbeat, every shiver, and every breathy exhale that escaped Hazel's body. She responded to me so well, and when I drew a low moan from her lips, I grinned as I brought my hand down on her clit, locking her body to mine so she couldn't escape.

"I bet I could make you come just like this," I bring my attention back up to her rosy nipples, experimentally applying more pressure before twisting them between torturous fingers, "If only you had manners." Just like that Hazel was under my control.

I could tell by the glossy look of lust in her eyes and the submission pulsing through her veins. That single glance she gave me had me wanting to pin her to this couch and fuck her right here, the urge to feel her stretch around me almost overpowering my need to overstimulate her until she cries.

"Rowan," She groans, earning herself another slap.

This time, I was met with a soaked cunt when my hand retreated.

Her open mouth was too perfect of an invitation, two of my fingers slipping past her lips, knowing she could taste herself on me. I felt her tongue glide over the skin, licking away her arousal and using them to bite back her sounds of pleasure.

Perfect. Hazel was so fucking perfect.

"I can't wait to take you later." I whisper in her ear, keeping my fingers in her mouth and ever so teasing her gag with them, "In my room, darling, I have an entire wall just made of glass." Hazel's eyes closed at that, her ass rubbing painfully on the erection straining in my pants. I knew she was visualizing my words, and I wouldn't have it any other way.

"It faces right onto a park always full of people, distant enough to not be a disturbance yet close enough to get the beautiful scenery." I feel her breath hitch as I take my fingers from her mouth, instantly using them to pinch and roll her nipples beneath my touch.

Goosebumps pimpled her arms, and I could feel every warm breath that passed her body.

Licking a long line up her neck before blowing on it and watching the shivers it brought forth, I continued.

"No matter how warm of a day, by the afternoon the glass goes ice cold, but rarely ever frosts.

It may be raining now, but another time I'm going to fuck you against it." The quietest of noises fall from Hazel's mouth as her head tilts back to rest against my shoulder, but I let it slide because I liked the sight of her like this, the movie long forgotten.

"I would strip you completely bare and press you against the cool glass, front first so I could watch as your frantic breaths fog the window. I wouldn't care how unsteady your legs would be or how badly you'd beg for your release, I would take my time with you, just as I'm going to tonight." Hazel's hips bucked up to try and get some relief, her knees fighting against mine in an attempt to close. It was a pleasure I didn't grant her.

"I would kick your legs far apart, your hips angled perfectly to take the rough pounding I know your body craves. You'd beg for the pain, wouldn't you?" I didn't expect a response as I twisted both nipples between my fingers, not soothing away the hurt, but rather continuing.

"I'd spank you as I'd take you from behind, pulling you flat on your feet so you couldn't escape my brutal motions. You'd be crying by the time I was done with you, and then I'd shatter you on my cock for the whole world to see." When Hazel gasped, I pulled her from the fantasy I'd placed in her mind, lifting her head to look at me.

"I may be yours, darling, but you're sure as hell mine in return." I planted a kiss to her soft lips, forcing her to feel my affection for her, "It's only a matter of time until the rest of the world fucking knows it as well." When Hazel moaned and murmured words in agreement, I was done with the movie. I needed to be inside of her and watch her fall apart over and over again around me, preferably screaming my name as she does so.

"Please, Cal. I need you." With those five words, Hazel snapped every last bit of restraint I had.

~ Sixteen ~

Hazel

One second I was on his lap, the next, I was being abruptly turned to straddle him, the blanket once warming me falling to the ground.

I was soaked and shaking and beyond desperate for his touch, Rowan's hand sliding to cup my face as I leaned forward to kiss him.

He went in gentle, but I wanted it all.

Wrapping my arms around his neck, I pressed my front to his, running my fingers through his hair and angling his head back to meet my lips.

It was pure need that controlled me right now, my hands moving to run across Rowan's chest and my nails leaving trails of scratches in their wake.

The sound of pleasure it drew from his throat had me grinding my hips down, rolling against the hard length of his dick. My mind was spinning with pleasure, my lungs burning with the need for air and only getting it when Rowan yanked my head back, heavy breaths falling from both of our swollen lips.

"Mine." He growled, his mouth latching onto mine once again and repositioning us so that I was straddling his one thigh. "Yours." I gasped as two strong hands gripped my waist, pulling me down onto his leg and forcing my hips to drag back and forth, "Ca—" I couldn't even vocalize my embarrassment as Rowan licked away my words, his tongue fucking my mouth and dissolving every last bit of control I had. As much as my instincts told me to pull away from this, my body sought out the pleasure instead, my clit swollen and begging from the pressure building inside of me. When I began to move on my own, I felt Rowan smile against me.

"Such a good whore." He murmured, lifting his leg slightly to angle me better, "Look at that pathetic cunt of yours getting off from riding my thigh. You're dripping." A tear escaped me when a small dark patch began to form on the material of his pants, my stomach tightening at the sight. Rowan told me a long time ago how he wanted to degrade me, but only now am I realizing just how much he was holding out around the other two. Right now, he made sure I felt humiliated, uncontrollable desire pooling deep in my core.

"That's it, Hazel." Rowan gave me a cruel smile, wiping away my tears just to run the same fingers across my nipples, "Rub against me until your orgasm soaks my jeans." Fuck. I couldn't stop the tremble in my knees as I rocked against him, over and over until I needed him to guide me himself.

Rowan was so much harsher in his movements, though. He knew just the right spots to rub, angling me perfectly so that with every pass over him, shocks were being sent to my clit and fueling the climax coiling tight within me.

"You should take this time to prepare yourself, darling." Rowan warns as he watches me, seeing the way my body's tensing up. My heart races as he leans in, his wet lips brushing ever so slightly at my temple before moving to my ear. "I've waited for weeks to see you like this, and believe me when I say I'm going to enjoy devouring you." Rowan's teeth dragged over my skin, holding me still when I cried out in response, "I even bought you a present so you can see for yourself." Before anything else could happen, every inch of my body tightened and my orgasm struck through me, Rowan keeping me down as whimpers fell past my lips. He didn't care how sensitive everything was.

All I could do was lean forward and hold on for dear life while wave after wave of blinding pleasure consumed me. I was pinned to his thigh until I made good on his promise of making a mess, my release soaking his leg and turning the material dark and wet.

As I stared down at the spot I was still being dragged across, I knew I couldn't go another full week without being touched by this man in some way.

Rowan's hungry expression as he finally let up on his movements told me he was in agreement—an agreement he was planning on proving right now.

Wrapping his arms tight around me, his shirt that did nothing to cover me parted even farther as he stood from the couch, not bothering to turn off the television or put what was left of the ice cream back in the freezer.

It was clear his only thoughts were of me, my legs hooking together at his back for support while Rowan moved us to the stairs.

"Take the elevator," I say against his neck, causing him to freeze in thought. I know it was because of my claustrophobia, but there are very few times where I feel distracted enough to challenge myself.

Now was one of those times. And, I felt guilty making him walk up the stairs while carrying me, even though I'm sure he lifts more weight as a warm up at the gym.

"You sure?" Rowan pulls me back to look at me, and I nod sincerely in response. It took me three years of panic attacks to overcome my fear of small spaces enough to do things like drive and take elevators, and although I don't think I'll ever fully be comfortable, pushing myself is the only way to maintain that progress.

As Rowan respected my wishes and carried me to their main elevator, I felt fine as the doors closed and a button was pushed to take us to the fourth floor. His choice had me looking up at him in confusion, since I had assumed we'd only be going up one level.

"My room's higher up than Dominic and Carter's." He explains, understanding passing through me, "The location worked better for me, and there's more room to keep all of my books." I simply nodded in response, planting a kiss in appreciation to his lips in both thanks and distraction as the door dinged.

The fact his room was three floors up and he still tried to carry me meant a lot more than I could ever say in words.

Though I was fine, I still felt a weight relieve itself from my chest as Rowan walked us out of the elevator and down a hall decorated just like the rest. More rooms, more windows, more money.

"So I'm guessing no playroom tonight?" I say, realizing both he and Carter made the move to take me to their own individual rooms. Honestly, it was kind of nice and I liked it a lot.

"Not right now." Rowan sends me a smirk that results in thousands of butterflies going off in my stomach.

"No, the only place I'm fucking you tonight is in my bed so I can have the memories of you writhing beneath me every time I try to sleep."

Holy.

Shit.

I don't know what I'd expected, but fuck.

I wanted that too. Even though I've never been in Rowan's room before, I found myself excited and curious as he bent to twist the handle, pushing the door open with his foot.

Walking the two of us inside, my eyes widened at the sight, most of the walls a very light grey in contrast to the rest of their house. Shelves upon shelves of books hung across entire sections, enough to fill a small library. Rowan put me down so I could walk around, and he wasn't lying when he told me about the large window that spread the height and width of an entire wall, black casing framing the glass.

"This is..." I begin, spinning back to Rowan, only to find more books on the shelves behind him. Only, my words trailed off because I recognized many of the titles as some of my favorites, as well as new ones I didn't recognize.

"I saw some of these in your room," Rowan says, coming up behind me and wrapping his arms around my body.

"I wanted you to have the options here too if you ever just wanted to hang out for the day." To say I was stunned was an understatement. There had to have been just under a hundred books in front of me, a small percentage compared to the rest, but still.

"You really didn't have to do that." I say, even though pictures of me curling up in bed with Rowan, reading and cuddling on a day when it's raining like this, popped up in my mind. His response was planting a gentle kiss to my neck, my skin tingling from where his lips touched.

My hand wove back to curl my fingers through his hair, his mouth slowly trailing a path downwards and sending warm sparks through my blood.

"Doesn't mean you shouldn't have it." Rowan counters, his hands holding me close as he roamed my body, smoothly pushing off his shirt from my shoulders and letting it drop to the ground. Long fingers instantly replaced the fabric's caress, running over my hardened nipples and circling them teasingly.

"Sir." I groaned, my legs pressing together as I leaned back, molding my sensitive body to his.

"I've waited so long for you, Hazel." Rowan murmurs, his mouth continuing to work along every pleasure spot on my throat. His touch made me feel weak, his arms needing to support my body as I melted under his touch.

My eyes had fallen shut, and I hadn't even known we'd shifted until Rowan's finger was at my chin, tilting my head to the side.

"Look at you. Look at how pretty you look." He says, my hands moving to grab his at the sight of the large mirror at the side of his bed. I'd been so distracted with everything else that I'd missed our reflection.

I couldn't now, though. I couldn't not see the flushed girl staring back at me, my knees pressed together, my eyes bright, and my nipples red and desperate as Rowan rolled them between his fingers.

"A mirror?" I question, even though I'm well aware of the intentions behind it. I both liked and disliked its presence, but overall, it had me tensing in place.

"Mhm," The man at my back hums, his blue eyes meeting mine in the glass as his mouth left marks all along my neck, "I want you to see yourself the first time I fill you up." His words made my core tighten deliciously, but I remained frozen, the woman I'm seeing looking nothing like me.

I could see my arousal glistening from between my thighs, my blonde hair messy and matching Rowan's as my hands remained connected to him.

"What, darling?" He cooed, his nose brushing against my jaw as he continued to play with me.

I knew his tone was meant to be comforting, and it was, but it was also a genuine question that he expected an answer to. "Nothing." I say breathlessly, tilting my head back to the ceiling so I didn't have to look at myself anymore. I felt so vulnerable like this, and I didn't know how to tell him.

My response was not one Rowan accepted though, a punishing slap going straight to my clit like he said it would. "I just don't think I like watching myself, Sir." I corrected, obliging his hold when he made me look at my reflection, but unlike the first time, I wasn't sure I liked what I saw anymore.

My eyes instantly began to glance over every single one of my insecurities, hating the stretch marks on my hips, the scars on my thighs and the way my stomach isn't toned. I hated that was what I saw, knowing the cellulite on my legs didn't offer the perfect skin I wished I had. Mostly, I hated that I felt this way, but nothing could stop me from seeing every one of these things as reminders of how I was never enough for the people around me.

Rowan didn't falter in his movements at my admission, but I saw the conflict in his eyes.

He knew where my mind had selfishly traveled, and when his mouth finally pulled away from my neck, he knew my heart was racing for things other than desire.

"Tell me one part about your body you dislike." He says in my ear, still not allowing me to look away.

"What?" I whispered under my breath, holding his hands in mine just as his eyes held my attention.

"Tell me, darling." Rowan repeats, rounding my body and moving to my front to focus on him. I knew what he was asking, but the question made me feel stripped bare in a sense so much more than the nakedness of my skin.

"My scars." I forced out, hating the admission and the understanding that flickered in Rowan's gaze. The next second, he was dropping to his knees before me, hooking my leg over his shoulder and running his lips across my thighs—across the pain that cut deeper than any physical mark could.

My chest tightened and tears formed in my eyes at the sight, Rowan not missing a single inch of my skin before moving to my other leg. I shook, but he held me, kissing away the parts of me I hated most and replacing them with this beautiful moment of affection, acceptance, and understanding, because that's what things were with us. I was in love with Rowan, not because he introduced me to an entire new world of pleasure, but because he held me together and made me feel safe while he did it.

"What else?" His voice rasped as he spoke, staring up at me.

This time, it was easier to answer, my chest feeling lighter.

"My stomach." My voice broke as I admitted, but my thoughts soon became consumed as Rowan's hands moved up my body, landing on my waist before his mouth began at my hips.

My breath hitched as he kissed the spot on my right side of my body, holding my eyes with every healing touch. That's how everything continued, his mouth dissolving away everything about myself I despised, starting from the bottom and working his way up until he was standing again at full height.

"Rowan—" I whimpered, but he took away the words too, his lips connecting to mine and breaking off the last insecurity to eat away at me: my fear of never finding love.

"I wish you could see yourself the way I do, Hazel," He says against my mouth, curling my hair in his fist and gently pulling my head back to look at him.

"Because if you did, you would never feel insecure again. That much I can promise you." As the final tear ran down my cheek, I knew that nothing else mattered anymore apart from the two of us and this moment. A lot has changed in this last week, and I wasn't the only one who felt it either.

And this... this felt like a shift that I could never come back from.

Rowan, Dominic, Carter. They were it for me, and I was too damn tired to let myself be held back anymore.

"Kiss me." I whisper, and just like that, everything around us snapped. Rowan was on me in an instant, recognizing the change within me and feeding off of it as I was picked up to wrap around his body.

We didn't break off, not once, even as I was laid down onto the edge of his bed so that my front was facing the mirror.

I didn't care, my hands frantically dropping to Rowan's belt and blindly unfastening the buckle, needing his help to push his clothing off of his lean body. "Please," I said against his mouth, that single word leading to me being flipped onto my stomach, my hips being drawn upwards until I was on all fours.

"Look at yourself and don't look away." Rowan's demand controlled my body for me, my head turning and my legs pressing together at the sight of my back naturally arching to his touch.

I watched as my thighs were spread wide apart, the action causing my ass to curve upwards into the air. For a second, the only thing that happened was Rowan's fingers slowly moving up and down my back, my senses attuned to every gentle brush of air parting from his mouth.

There was no doubt he knew the effect he was having on my body, and by the time his touch moved to between my thighs, he had to steady me from how sensitive I was.

"Such a pretty sight." He allowed a small smile to show, watching my reactions in the mirror as my hips squirmed, "I thought I liked you like this before, but it's so much better getting to see your face as I ruin you." After that, Rowan dragged his finger on the underside of my clit, not giving me any time to catch my breath before circling the nub in tight motions.

"F-Fuck!" I cursed, trying to keep still but failing with every second that passed.

The reflection I'd just previously hated now made me consumed with pleasure, the sight of Rowan stroking himself while he played with my clit drawing me taunt.

I ended up leaning forward to rest my head against his pillow when I couldn't hold myself up anymore, still looking into the pair of icy blue eyes as I inhaled his scent from the sheets.

That act of submission was one that had Rowan smirking in satisfaction, seeming to be what he was waiting for as his thumb took over the circling between my thighs, two fingers moving to my entrance before slipping deep inside. I could barely keep my eyes open as I was stroked in just the right spots, my knees threatening to close in together from the overwhelming sensations.

"There you go." His deep voice sounded in my ears, holding my gaze as my body slowly began to crumble beneath him. Rowan never tired and he never let up, his motions only growing harsher and harsher to find which angles drew the most whimpers from me. The answer: everywhere.

There wasn't a single one of my senses that wasn't under Rowan's control right now; my body responding to the sound of his heavy breaths, the sight of him in the mirror, the feeling of his fingers, the fresh smell of his bed sheets, and the taste of mint from the gum he was chewing earlier. I was completely and utterly consumed, rapidly being brought up to my second high of the night.

"Oh god!" I cried out, my fingers curling desperately around the bars of Rowan's headboard for support as he seemed to sense my approaching orgasm as well. I knew, because his hand moved off of his cock to wrap around my waist, keeping my legs spread as he continued to thrust roughly into my soaked cunt.

"Darling, not even god can save you from how hard I'm about to fuck you." Rowan warned, and that was all it took to push me over the edge.

Though I tried, I couldn't get away as my climax crashed through me, my body being pinned down so the two fingers at my entrance could continue to slide into me.

The action alone erupted every single one of my nerves with white-hot pleasure, having me crying out in desire.

With Rowan's name still on my tongue, I collapsed to the bed in a heap of exhaustion, knowing that was only the first of many to come.

As if he'd read my thoughts, I barely had time to catch my breath before I caught a glimpse of his large body moving to hover over mine, the warmth of his chest spreading over my back.

My skin tingled at the contact, my hips angling upwards in a silent plea against my muscles' better judgement.

Rowan's fingers alone had me ready to pass out, but I knew I wouldn't be sated until he was filling me with his release.

My desperation was the real cause of my trembling, and I almost fell apart at the feeling of his tip dragging up and down my entrance, threatening to break me on the length of him.

"Eyes on me, pretty girl." Rowan murmurs in my ear, and when my head turned to meet his eyes in the mirror, I watched as his hand pinned me to the bed by my neck, thrusting inside of me in one smooth, hard motion. It was like all of the air in my lungs had been replaced by the feeling of him, because in the same second, I orgasmed all over again, my face twisting in a kind of pleasure that had me writhing.

The entire time, Rowan remained still, groaning at the feeling of me spasming around him and smiling at the fact all it took was a single stroke to make me come. I couldn't even care, though, too wrapped up in the fact that my climax never stopped, even after multiple seconds passed.

"Rowan," I cried as I shook and squirmed, unsure whether I was currently experiencing multiple small orgasms or simply one long, continuous pitfall of pleasure.

"I know, darling." He says as he holds me still, pulling his cock out entirely and waiting for my release to come down to a gradual cease. It felt like forever before that happened, though.

Never once have I experienced something so intense before, and I hadn't even noticed I was soaked between my legs until my head began to clear again.

I had no idea how long that just lasted for, but I knew it wasn't like any other release I've had before. Rowan's comforting kiss to my shoulder confirmed that this wasn't all in my head.

My orgasm just lasted for at least two minutes straight, and I didn't even know that was physically possible. It damn near wiped me out, and I was surprised I could still manage to speak as I whimpered, "What the hell just happened," my body refusing to stop shaking, even when Rowan encouraged me to lie all the way down.

"That was your first continuous orgasm, Hazel." He says in my ear, kissing my temple and rolling onto his side next to me as I was pulled flush to his body.

At the movement, a gasp left my mouth as his cock re slipped inside of me from behind.

I was facing the mirror with Rowan at my back, and though my eyes were too heavy to open yet, I knew what I would see staring back at me. It was a sight that kept my knees tight together, only making the cock filling me feel all that much bigger.

He didn't move, though.

Rowan simply stayed in place, his fingers dancing along my skin and bringing me down from the emotional side of my orgasm, even though physically I was currently unmoving.

"That was also the first time I've ever made someone experience that." He adds, shocking me but liking that I was his first in something too.

Everything about our relationship has been built on new for me, and that only made this whole thing feel that much more... perfect.

"I didn't even know my body could do that." I admitted with a very quiet laugh, my blood humming with the rumble that tickled from Rowan's throat in response.

Very much aware of the fullness inside of me still, I tried to press back to get him deeper, but the hand on my waist stopped me.

"Not until you've stopped shaking, darling," He says, though honestly, I hadn't even noticed I still was. I felt so good and my head felt so light right now I wondered if I was falling into subspace, but this didn't feel the same as previous times. I think my body was just so damn satisfied from Rowan that my natural response was to be contentedly relaxed.

The cheeky grin on his face told me he was more than happy about that, probably thinking of all the ways he could brag to the other two about this. I make sure to hide my eye roll as I sigh and think men.

"All jokes aside, Hazel, I'm pretty sure your smile is my favorite thing about your body." Rowan says, poking the dimple I didn't know had formed until now. Our eyes met in the mirror and I pointedly raised my brow as if to say I wasn't buying the act. Rowan was sweet, but I knew he was also a lot more kinky than he has yet to let on. I couldn't wait for the day he truly snapped.

"Honest," He smiles, but I see mischievousness in his eyes a second before his hand moves down from my waist, "Though..." He begins, "This pretty ass of yours is a close second." I don't even get time to blink before he's spanked me, not for punishment, but because he simply could.

I wasn't able to tell whether I'd stopped shaking yet or not, though, I didn't really care right now.

I'd love to see him try to stop me as I arched my back and pushed myself deeper onto his dick, groaning in both sensitivity and the need for more.

Little sparks began to go off in my core, meeting Rowan's eyes in the mirror as he watched me slide forward, just to sink back again.

It looked like I had calmed down enough from my last orgasm at this point, and there was no doubt Rowan was in agreement when my leg was lifted up and over his one thigh, leaving me spread wide open for the both of us to see. I figured he would've been done after that, but he wasn't.

No, my heart rate was forced to a fast beat as his free hand looped around my body and found its place wrapped snug around my throat, his long fingers flexing as they tightened.

I've never been in this position before, but it didn't take me long to realize Rowan was in complete control of my body right now. I couldn't move away and was trapped entirely in a puzzle of limbs.

"Play with those pretty nipples of yours." Rowan holds my eyes in the mirror as he gives the command, tracking my movements when I cup my breasts in each of my hands.

They feel so heavy, so sensitive, and the second my fingers began to pinch gently, Rowan started to move. That was when the real pleasure began. I was silently demanded to stay still, so I did, watching as his cock slowly dragged in and out of me, hitting every right spot with each full motion.

I could hear Rowan's breaths in my ear— feel the warmth of them against my skin.

He demanded my attention through every minute of this, making me look at him as my body took him over and over again until his hold on my neck and legs became more restrictive so he could continue to edge me.

I wasn't able to press my knees together now, and every time I tried to give my nipples some much needed relief, Rowan's hand tightened around my throat until I was forced to comply.

He was slow but undeniably rough with each thrust, my face flushing because I could hear how soaked I was between my spread thighs, able to see my arousal glistening on his length every time he pulled out.

What was he waiting for, though? This wasn't him making love, but it most certainly wasn't the hard fucking he promised me either.

Bringing my eyes up from where we were joined and over to his amused, dark expression, that was all it took for me to understand what he wanted. It was something that never failed to humiliate me, and that was exactly what Rowan was asking for.

"Sir," I whimpered, his hand on my throat making it hard to form my words, especially with his cock still stroking my spot with no relent.

"Yes, little one?" He smiles, letting up his grip just enough to allow me to think.

Rowan knew how desperate I was, and there was no chance of me getting what I wanted until I submitted to his desire.

"Please." I begged, even though I was well aware that was nowhere near enough to get me what I wanted. His demeaning grin was confirmation, his fingers stroking the side of my neck and eliciting shivers from my overstimulated body.

"Sir, please fuck me harder. I need you so bad." I pleaded, but Rowan was different from Dominic and Carter in this sense. He got off the most on degrading me, and I knew he would not let up until I was genuine enough in my desperation. I didn't know what to say, though, not that he cared.

The one thing it was clear Rowan had was patience, and I knew he would happily spend the next hour just like this, edging me as many times as he pleased until I broke beneath him.

Unfortunately for me, I couldn't give him what he wanted. It's just never come naturally, but based on his look in the mirror, Rowan liked it this way.

This man has left me both physically and emotionally open multiple times today, and I knew he wanted me to get out of my head. When he stroked me in just the right spot to push me over the edge he was steadily working me up to, I screamed when he pulled out all the way with a smirk, denying me of my orgasm entirely.

"Rowan!" I protested, earning a slap to my thigh as a result.

"You know what you need to do, darling." He smiles cruelly, making me change my mind. I hate him now and so does my clit.

"Come on, please," I say, but it wasn't good enough. With a thrust, Rowan slammed all the way inside of me, his hand tightening around my throat to the point where I couldn't breathe anymore, only able to get out small pleas and whimpers.

"You're such a good girl." He murmurs, fucking me back up to my climax and denying me for a second time. It broke me, and Rowan knew he'd won.

"Sir, please, please, please bring it back. I'm sorry for earlier, but I want to feel you. I don't even care if I don't come, but please, just keep going." My words were all a string of begs slurring together, tears wetting my face at the thought of Rowan stopping again to punish me. This was a test to see if I could take him, I knew it was, and no words could accurately describe the relief I felt when he started moving again.

This time was different, though. His hand on my throat shifted, no longer to control my breathing, but rather to keep me still. Rowan was bracing me, and when his mouth dropped down to my ear, I knew this was only the beginning, not just for tonight, but for us as a whole.

"Unless it's a safe word, Hazel, I'm not fucking stopping." With that, I watched with blurred vision as Rowan's hips reared back, snapping forward to meet my ass just as quickly. The force would have sent me off the bed, but I didn't, forced in place by the hands holding me with ease. Unlike last time, however, there were no breaks.

I was given no reprieve, no time to catch my breath, and most certainly no time to sort my thoughts before he was back inside of me, his face set on mine in focus. Gasping and looking at the mirror, I knew this was Rowan. This was every bit of him he hid under his friendly smiles and sense of humor.

This was the man who promised me that one day he would break me for his pleasure, knowing I would happily oblige every step of the way.

"I—ah, fuck." I couldn't even form proper sentences anymore, but Rowan understood as he whispered dirty words of encouragement, telling me what a good whore I was for taking him and that I felt like I was made for his cock. I could only cry and beg in agreement, feeling like I was both drowning in Rowan's touch, and being set aflame in the most beautifully ruinous way possible.

He'd ignited me, watching me burn in the flames of his lust as he stroked, kissed, and worshiped my body with everything he had to offer. And I was feeding off of every second.

"Shit," I cried, and Rowan knew he had just reduced me into nothing more than a willing hole for him to fuck. That in itself was degrading, but I embraced it, no longer embarrassed or worried about what I looked like.

It was surprisingly erotic to see myself like this, even better that Rowan was at my back as he kept me open for our viewing.

I was able to capture every minute of this, and when he was certain I was conscious enough to watch him, Rowan moved the hand that was on my thigh slowly down to between my legs.

Sure fingers brushed over my clit, my body shivering in response, but what had my body jolting was that he didn't stop there.

I was demanded to watch as two fingers slipped down to the soaked entrance currently being fucked raw by Rowan's harsh movements, the tips teasingly pressing at the spot I was being stretched. A gasp fell past my lips the same second he pushed inside, curling his fingers to stroke my g-spot in time with his cock.

It was too much for me to process all at once, but my body seemed to react on its own, a choked sob leaving my mouth. "Fuck, Hazel. You're so perfect." Rowan groans, kissing my shoulder and taking in every part of my reflection as I did his. I saw tears beginning to pool in his eyes too, and when I turned my head back to kiss him, the second our lips met I shattered in his arms.

Rowan swallowed my moans and continued to tease at my mouth, but I felt his breaths as though they were the ones currently keeping my heart beating. I felt him, and when I tightened and clamped down with my release, I knew it triggered his own.

Rowan and I came together, riding out our orgasms and holding each other like we couldn't survive without the contact. His touch set me on fire, and I happily fell into it, knowing he would never let me go.

~ Seventeen ~

Rowan

I don't think I've ever felt as good as I do now.

This is hands down one of the happiest moments of my life. Only minutes ago I had repositioned Hazel to be facing my front, and I refused to let her go as she snuggled up next to me, her head laying on my chest.

My arms naturally curled around her, breathing in her calming scent as the two of us slowly came down from our highs. Both of our bodies were still shaking in the aftershocks of our pleasure, and I couldn't help but grin as Hazel's flushed face and blown out eyes looked up at me tiredly.

"Rowan," She smiled, not as a question but instead of acknowl-edgement of what just happened. It sent me back all those weeks ago to the first day we officially met, her leaving Jolene's cafe to grab her photography equipment from her ex's house.

So much has happened since then. Who would've thought we'd end up here?

"Darling," I say in response, leaning down and capturing her lips with mine, gently tasting her and savoring the way she feels against me.

Neither of us made the move to deepen it, and after some time, the soft caresses of our touch led to me carrying Hazel to the washroom, even though she insisted she could walk herself.

I smirked when she tried, but couldn't even push herself upright on her own to swing her legs over the side of the bed. That's how I knew I'd fucked her hard enough, and I felt my heart swell when she angrily gave in to my help.

Stubborn to the very end. With Hazel curled around me like a koala bear, I happily drew a bath for the two of us, adding in some bubbles and lavender scented bath salts, not caring that I'd smell like it when I get out.

I could feel my girl growing rapidly tired in my arms, but after care was something I was never willing to skip on, even though there weren't really any BDSM aspects to our night.

Plus, I liked the idea of getting to wash her and take care of her after she gave so much to me tonight.

Planting a kiss to her head, I cautiously placed my foot in the full tub of water, biting back my hiss at how hot it was.

I knew Hazel has always liked her baths and showers at an inhumanly scorching temperature, but it was an effort to get in as I mentally held my tongue. I suppose it was worth it though when I felt the last of her tenseness dissolve with a contented sigh, her body slowly sinking with mine into the freestanding tub.

"Mm." She hummed against my neck, her long hair cascading smoothly down the flat of her back as the tips turned dark from the water.

Hazel was exhausted with her body sagged against mine, but the two of us still talked as I ended up washing her hair for her, growing hard again when I took extra time massaging her scalp and drawing a long string of innocent, yet pleased moans from her.

It was an effort to wash all of the bubbles out, because admittedly, this was yet another new for me tonight. I've never liked someone enough to show such an intimate side of myself, but with Hazel, everything was different. Once I had managed to clear her hair of the shampoo, and then the following conditioner, I reached over to lather my hands for myself, only to be stopped by small fingers.

"Let me." Hazel whispered, her throat too worn to speak any louder than that.

My heart clenched as she took the soap into her own hands, pouring a small amount before reaching up to my wet blond strands.

I stared at her mouth as she took her tongue between her teeth in concentration, looking truthfully adorable as her fingers began to run through my hair, bubbles popping in my ears.

Though very few words were spoken, this was one of the most loving experiences I've ever had, surprised at how good it could feel to be taken care of by another just as much as I liked taking care of her.

"Do you think you can... um." Hazel smiled, gesturing to the small container we've been using to wash the shampoo out with. I did it quickly myself, being sure not to get any bubbles in my eyes as I slicked my hair back. I couldn't help but smirk at the sight of Hazel licking her lips, very clearly liking the position we were in right now.

She wasn't the only one.

In fact, by the time we were stepping out, our fingertips had wrinkled and the bath had finally cooled to a reasonable temperature that Hazel insisted was too cold. All I did was shake my head and smile at the claim.

It wasn't long before I was grabbing a heated towel for her anyways, letting her lean against the counter as I thoroughly dried every inch of her body.

Hazel ended up shakily doing the same for me in return afterwards, and I've never hated having a dick more than I did now as I grew hard again beneath her touch. I received a mischievous glance at that, but I still ended up carrying my girl back to my bed instead of the clear intentions Hazel's mind was traveling to.

Even after the bath, I could feel the small shake in her tired muscles, and the only thing she had in her plans was a long night's rest next to me in my room.

Not that that ruled out any wake up sex, though. I meant it when I said I planned on having her over and over again, but she needed sleep and there were things I still needed to do. Wishing I didn't have to let her go, I gently laid Hazel on my bed while stripping the mattress of its comforter, allowing her to curl up as I walked to my closet for fresh sheets. I had many stacked in a specific space, and it took me no time before I was walking back and tilting my head at the sight of Hazel out cold. Her arms had wrapped around my pillow and her one leg was bent close to her chest, making me smile at how peaceful she looked.

She really was perfect, and better yet, she was mine. I couldn't describe the connection I had with her, but I knew I was in love with Hazel as I fanned out the blankets over her curled up body.

I feel like I have been for a long time, and I was well aware of how much that thought terrified me on its own. When in the Mafia, you're not supposed to fall in love with people as pure and kind hearted as the woman in my bed, but my heart simply doesn't seem to care.

I have no idea how to tell her or even if I should, but I knew it was my feelings for her that had me planting a soft kiss to her forehead in goodbye, knowing I would return before the next time she wakes up. Despite my trust and respect for her decisions, I would not let Hazel spend even a minute in a house as abusive and heartbreaking as the one she described to me as her childhood home.

Never will I hold her back from doing something she wants, but that doesn't change the fact there are two people long over due an inevitable visit.

That's why I was silently dressing and stepping out of my room, dialing in the number I knew was always certain to answer.

"Hello?" Carter says through the speaker, likely from his office at Rush if his plans remained the same as what he'd said this morning. Closing the door and making my way down the hall, I raised my phone to my ear.

"I need you to grab Dominic and have the jet ready to take off in ten.

There's some lessons that need to be taught in Detroit."

Hazel

I woke up this morning to the sight of Rowan between my legs, licking me to orgasm and smiling as I cried out his name. His hair was messy, his eyes were bright, and his damn perfect smile brought butterflies to my still sore body.

I haven't even seen my neck yet, but I've never had so many scratches and bruises and hickeys as I do today.

I looked like I was attacked by an animal when in reality it was really just Rowan, the dopey faced blond who had gone from comforting to dominant to sweet, all in a matter of a few hours.

"You feeling okay?" He asks, slowly crawling up by body and forcing my thighs to part around him. Even that movement made me ache, but it was in the most delicious way.

"Mhm." I hummed sleepily, rubbing my eyes before meeting his gaze, "But I also feel like I just ran a marathon." In reality, it was just spending a night with Rowan.

I was surprised at how happy I was from something as simple as waking up beside him in the morning, but it was a treat I could most definitely get used to.

"Yeah?" He says, kissing my cheek before flipping me onto my stomach, "Let me help with that, darling." I couldn't tell what he was doing when I felt his weight leave the bed, but I was too drained to turn my head to see the cause of the small clinking behind me.

I found out soon enough anyways when I felt him return, his partially dressed body straddling mine. "What did you end up thinking about the mirror?" Rowan's scratchy morning voice spoke by my ear, the next minute the feeling of warm oil being spread onto my back and shoulders.

For a moment, I became so lost in the feeling of strong, steady hands massaging at my tense muscles that I'd forgotten to answer the question.

"I liked being able to watch us." I admitted against his pillow, liking that I could still smell him on it, "It was something I didn't expect to like, but did." I felt Rowan's hum at my back in response, an amused noise coming from him when I groaned from a particularly sore spot currently being kneaded under his fingers.

Fuck.

"Right there, huh?" He murmurs, laughing and grabbing my hand when I bend it behind me to blindly hit him.

To my dismay, though, he didn't give it back, instead pinning my arm to rest against my ass. I made another noise as he continued to work at that one spot, hating how just a few touches made me feel like mush beneath him.

"I might have to do this more often if you're going to keep sounding like that." Rowan says, and though my face is in his pillow, I just knew he was smirking above me.

It was only once he was sure I wasn't going to try and smack him again for his teasing that he let my arm go, skillfully returning to massaging away the tension in my shoulders, back, and legs. He ended with my hands, something I didn't even know could feel good being loosened.

By the time he was done with me, I was as limp as I was last night.

"I really did mark you up, didn't I?" Rowan says more to himself than me, his fingers running up and down the bruises he created only hours ago.

"Have you looked in a mirror recently?" I smile, pushing him off of me so I could sit up to look at him. When I met his eyes, it was clear he hadn't even looked at his body yet, but just his marked chest told me how much we enjoyed last night.

It was interesting watching Rowan look at the mirror still by the bed, and I felt my face flush when a curious smile made its way onto his face.

Running his fingers over the scratches across his front from when I was riding his thigh on the couch, Rowan then looked at his neck covered in the kisses I'd planted both during sex and in the bathtub when he washed me.

It felt like the sight had marked him as my own, and I surprisingly felt both pride and possessiveness fill my chest at his reaction. If last night proved anything, it was that while I was his, he was sure as fuck mine.

"You're so hot." I heard Rowan murmur to himself, and the next second he was on me, pinning my neck to the bed and towering over my body.

I allowed my legs to part for him once again in accommodation, my breathing growing heavy at the sound of his sweats being tugged off and tossed to the side.

By the time we made it downstairs, we had both orgasmed twice more, our bodies finally satisfied and our minds sated. For now, that is. I had a strong feeling that Rowan Harris was as addictive as a drug, and now that I've had a taste of him, there was no going back.

Once again taking the elevator down to the main level, Rowan's subtle attempts at distracting me with his touch didn't go unnoticed. It was something all three of them did, I just don't know if they're aware how much it helps to relax me. I was fine within seconds, though, the doors opening to the sight of two topless, very tattooed men I get to call my boyfriends. "Morning." Dominic says with a small smirk, Carter's expression mimicking the look but not saying anything. It made my face flush and my ears go red, unsure of what the smugness was about.

"Hi." I murmured with a small smile, walking with Rowan to where they were sitting in the living room, only to find the delicious smell of food was coming from the kitchen. The mostly empty plates across from them indicated they'd already eaten a while ago.

"Might be a little cold, but we made enough for you both as well." Carter says, and while I move to get myself some breakfast, Dominic's up and pulling me into his lap before I can take another step.

"I'll grab you a bit of everything, darling." Rowan winked and walked off into the kitchen while Carter pulled my legs to lay over his thighs.

I was more than content with the position, resting my head against Dominic's chest as strong hands slowly ran up and down my legs in a soothing manner. My entire body still felt loose from my massage this morning, so this only made me feel even more calm.

"How was your nights? I ask the two of them, my heart racing as Dominic brushes some of my hair back to look at my neck more closely.

Fuck, that's why they were smirking. Not just me, but Rowan as well, are covered in bruises for their eyes to openly see.

Oh god.

"Quite satisfying actually." Carter answers, the rough pad of his thumb slowly inching its way to brush along my inner thigh. I squirmed, my response being, "Mm, in what way?" I'd forgotten how surrounded I could sometimes feel with the three of them together.

Never in a bad way, but in a way that had my body always responding to their constant dominance.

"Punishing deserving people is always a good reliever for me." He surprises me, my eyes drawing to his knuckles but not seeing any marks of fresh cuts.

I didn't expect this kind of honesty or openness, but I suppose they all meant it when they said they wouldn't lie to me anymore about their other businesses. I asked, they answered.

They made it as simple as that for me.

"You're not hurt, though?" I check, not seeing any bruises along his chest nor the hands still on my body. Carter only shook his head, and that was enough for me.

I was really happy that he'd trusted me enough to share that, even if it wasn't much spoken in words.

It showed progress, and it also told me he was beginning to get more comfortable with opening up. Leaving the conversation at that, my focus shifts to the sight of Rowan walking over, my stomach rumbling impatiently as a warm plate of food was placed into my hands.

"Bon appetit," The blond grins, planting a kiss on my cheek before taking the chair slightly across from us. I don't miss the way his eyes roam the sight of all three of us, my stretched out body more than anything.

"It's not jealousy, princess." Dominic murmurs in my ear as Carter takes the plate from me and begins to poke at a piece of scrambled egg with the cutlery.

Dominic, of course, was right. The emotion flickering in Rowan's eyes wasn't one of anger, it was of desire. Not knowing what to say, I simply hummed in response, smiling thankfully as Carter lifted the fork to my mouth. I happily bit off the food, still not fully used to this kind of care and loving it all the more because of it.

"So what do you guys have planned for the day?" I ask through bites, slowly waking up as my focus at last begins to sharpen. As Dominic picks off a piece of bacon to snack on, it's Rowan who responds, placing his plate on the glass table. "Well that depends." He says, his hand reaching out to toy with the fabric of his shirt I borrowed.

I knew he liked me in his clothes, and I liked that they smelled like him.

"On?" I ask, taking the strawberry Carter offered me into my mouth. It was a genuine accident when my tongue ran over the pads of his fingers, but I knew it was that action that had his eyes darkening.

"Whether you'd like to spend the day with us or not." Dominic answers for Rowan, smiling because he already knows I would miss them.

Don't get me wrong, I need my space just as much as any other person does, but I kind of liked getting to do the whole breakfast thing with them as we slowly woke up together. Our agreement outlines that today is my day for me-time, but the scary truth is that I don't think I want to leave.

"And what would happen if I decided to stay?" I grin, turning my head to look into the green eyes mirroring mine. A smirk tugged at the corners of Dominic's lips in response.

"I know you guys are well known for all of your surprise adventures, but this looks like a place you'd go to bury a body." I tease, gazing around curiously at the entrance to Buttermilk Falls. They purposely parked in some secluded section for the privacy, even though I knew there was plenty of space in the main area where the washrooms and actual gates were.

"Nah," Rowan waves a dismissive hand jokingly, "Too many cameras." His words made me tilt my head confusedly, but when I felt Carter's large body step up behind me, his fingers turned my chin to our left. It took me a second to understand, but in the distance, I could see the sight of a round black security camera on the edge of the park office. My gaze was then turned to the ticket booth and lastly the restrooms.

They had easily noticed all of these things, even though the majority of our surroundings were lined in trees and pathways. It was a slightly chilling reminder of who they are and the reasons they have to be so attentive to something as laid back as a hiking trip. At the same time, however, it was honestly a little admirable about all of the details they must notice that I don't.

Half of the time, my natural instinct is to move so fast every-thing else around me just becomes one big blur. Right now, though, nothing was rushing the four of us and the plans I never could have predicted for the day.

"And how long did you say the walk is?" I ask, gazing at the narrowed pathway breaking off in the distance.

The smirks in amusement I receive tell me all I need to know: it was long enough they knew I'd never agree to it prior to being here.

"Here," Dominic says, walking in front of me and placing a can of bug spray into my hands. With that, I noticed the pair of black hiking boots he brought with him, dropping to a crouch in front of me.

I knew better than to ask how he knew my measurements or why he had women's shoes in my exact size just laying around their house.

Though it bothered me greatly how much money I'm sure they've spent on me without my knowledge, I couldn't stop it, and I knew it was coming from a place of good. Plus, I most certainly couldn't complain about the sight of Dominic kneeled before me, slipping off my current shoes and replacing them with the much more durable ones. As I'd thought, they fitted perfectly.

"Thank you." I blush as he rises, Rowan tossing him a backpack from the car before the noise of it locking sounds from behind me.

"Anytime, princess." He winks, slipping his hand into mine and tugging me forward where Carter's already moving. I applied my bug spray the best I could as we walked, offering it to Rowan who had come up to my side within no time. It was clear Carter planned to lead us to wherever the hell we were going, and though I was confused as to where everybody was, my attention was very quickly pulled to the map of all of the trails.

The one Carter moved down was a just over a six mile hike, and my legs were still slightly shaky from this morning.

Lovely.

Slipping my hand out of Dominic's, I make sure not to drag my feet or trip over any roots from the many trees surrounding us on either side. Admittedly, the trail was really beautiful, the woods secluding us from the rest of the world within minutes.

I followed in step with Carter, Dominic at my back and Rowan behind him. Now, there were no roads, no buildings, and no signs of infrastructure whatsoever.

All there was a dirt path muddled with uneven rocks and broken branches, my men on either side of my body. No one made the move to talk, but I was okay with the silence just as much.

Although, it was never truly quiet.

An endless number of birds sat atop branches all above, remaining hidden from the human eye despite their songs of different pitches and tones revealing their whereabouts.

I could hear the calm flows of distant streams ahead and smell the variety of different scents that made it feel easier to breathe.

The last time I'd done something like this was a week before my father's disappearance, and though I had expected to feel sadness at the realization, the soft burn in my thighs and the fresh blends of colours simply seemed to ground me instead. I think I've finally found myself happy enough to no longer feel despair at the fact he left, knowing he's out there somewhere, hidden, but alive.

And, I have so much more going for me than those seven months ago. I opened a business, broke up with my ex, allowed myself to face hundreds of fears of mine just to come out on top with not only respect for myself, but for the three amazing men in my life.

Nobody can take away from me, and that knowledge allowed me to enjoy this moment.

"You never did say where we're going exactly." I prob at any one of them, keeping up surprisingly well and containing my stumbles to a minimum.

Even if I couldn't see their faces, I knew they were all likely smirking at my curiosity, knowing they had the answers I very clearly wasn't about to receive.

"You'll find out soon enough, Hazel." Carter says back at me, not offering me any hints, "Just enjoy the view and we'll be there in no time."

That confirmed there was indeed a specific place they were taking me to, but I couldn't help but reveal my own smirk at his words.

Shamelessly glancing down at his ass, I knew that I had no problem with the view at all. I wonder what he'd do if I spanked— My thoughts were cut off abruptly as Dominic saved me from my stumble, smiling up at him sheepishly as Carter turned to see what my gasp was for.

I just waved a hand to indicate I was fine, suppressing my guilty grin at being caught, because I know Dominic was well aware of where my thoughts had traveled to.

"Go ahead, princess," He whispers in my ear only minutes later, daring me to find out. Carter had obviously heard his friend's words, but didn't make a move to prevent me from trying.

He probably wouldn't even care because it would give him an excuse to punish me in turn. Maybe another day, but I was already sore and didn't feel like losing my ability to sit comfortably as well.

That didn't stop me from looking, though, contentedly following my men deeper and deeper down the uneven pathways.

"Nope." I shove Dominic's hand away as he makes the move to pick me up like he would a child.

"No offense, princess, but you're slow. We're almost there anyways." He argues, but while I'm keeping an eye on him, Rowan sneaks up and grabs me before I can protest.

My laugh carried throughout the forest, the air damn near being knocked from my lungs at the swiftness in which I was taken into his arms. "I'm not that out of shape." I pant, even though I'm well aware of how lax I'd recently become on my running and strength training. It's been weeks since I've stepped foot inside a gym, but that's besides the point.

"Okay, maybe a little, but I can still walk." Despite my words, Rowan only plants a kiss to my cheek that sends butterflies skyrocketing in my stomach. It was unexpectedly sweet and it kept me distracted enough that by the time we got to our destination, it took five minutes instead of the likely fifteen on my part.

I heard it before I saw it, but as the pathway turned from natural to man-made, all I could do was drop my mouth open in absolute awe at the sight of the well over one hundred foot tall waterfall before us.

The area was absolutely massive with stone staircases and hills in every direction, my hand silently telling Rowan to put me down as I smiled.

Maybe it's stupid, but I've never seen a waterfall before today with my own eyes. It was so much louder than I expected, and I shivered happily as a cool mist lightly speckled across my face against the heat of the afternoon sun.

Not a single person was in sight apart from us, and I was thankful for it as I took a few steps forwards to gaze around.

"I take it you're impressed?" I feel Carter come up behind me, his hands falling to my waist as I take everything in.

"How could anyone not be?" I grin in response, turning my head and placing a thankful kiss to his jaw on the spot I know he likes most. This was truly stunning, and I couldn't help but feel a little bit caught in a dream right now.

"We've never been here before, but we figured you'd like it." He says in my ear, a soft sigh escaping his mouth, "And this way, we get to have you to ourselves." I shivered as he ran a single finger down my back, stopping just above the curve of my ass. "Come," He encouraged me to walk with him, "We brought lunch." As if on cue, my stomach let out a hungry rumble, putting a temporary stopper on the desire beginning to pool in my core. Following Carter to where the other two were currently setting up, my eyes widened excitedly at the sight of the picnic table by a calmer section of the water, Dominic's backpack turning out to be a cooler. While Rowan had led me upstairs earlier to get dressed, he must have packed things for lunch for us all, sandwiches, drinks, and chips being placed down on the table.

"For you." Dominic winks at me, handing over a can of sparkling water and a plate with my food already on it. I happily accepted as I sat down on the wooden bench, Carter sitting beside me with Dominic and Rowan across from us.

"Why thank you." I smile, grabbing a handful of chips from the bag before moving them onto my plate. I never came close to predicting my day turning into this, but I wasn't complaining in the least.

Especially at the soft brush of Carter's knee against mine under the table, his one hand dropping to my thigh just for the sake of touching me. His free one opens my drink, sliding it to rest within reach right beside my plate.

The act of affection was small in size, but I knew it was because he wasn't sure what else to do now that we were all sitting down for lunch. Though I'd never tell him this, it was a little cute to watch.

Sliding noticeably closer so that the sides of our thighs were flush together, I intertwined my fingers to hold the hand on my leg, smiling when I felt Rowan's foot rest just between my ankles.

All of us seemed to be drawn to each other in unexplainable ways, and when our hunger took over the comfortable silence, a certain four lettered word popped into my head once again.

This would be the perfect opportunity to open up about how I feel about them, but what if they don't feel the same way? I suppose this is one of the larger conflicts that has arisen within me, not just because of how secretive they all tended to be, but also because of the fact we were in a polyamorous relationship.

Just because I'm in love with three people at once doesn't necessarily mean I should tell them all at the same time.

Or do I? It's an issue I'm only experiencing now in my head, but is there a right answer? These men are the only things I've allowed myself to want in a very long time, and I wanted things to be special when I tell them the impact they've had on my heart.

Though I don't need to say those three words to prove my love, this wasn't something I was willing to rush or screw up. "You okay?" Dominic tilts his head in notice of me zoning out. I hadn't even realized it.

"Yeah, sorry." I smile truthfully, deciding now just wasn't the right moment. I feel like I'll know when it is—when I'm not over-thinking and simply feeling. Besides, we have nothing but time.

Today felt like proof of that, the minutes passing by both as quick as seconds and long as hours. It felt like we had forever, and even if we didn't, we had now.

"Good," Dominic says through a bite of his sandwich, taking a moment to chew before continuing, "Then eat up. Food is only the beginning of our plans." Little did I know, by plans, Dominic meant shamelessly stripping down to his boxers less than an hour later, toeing at the water's edge.

"What the hell are you doing?" I ask, startled as I look around to make sure we were alone. I knew we were, but I also knew the odds we had the entire space to ourselves on a Friday afternoon was not even close to coincidental. Instead of answering, Dominic offered a boyish grin that made his face light up in amusement and cheerfulness.

"I suggest you start stripping too unless you want to walk back with wet clothes, darling." Rowan sneaks up behind me after disposing of our garbage from lunch.

"What if someone shows up, though?" I argue, not trusting the chances of that possibility. Plus, I had a feeling the water would be ice cold as well.

"They won't." Carter's deep voice says against my neck, his large frame rising from the table, "And you don't know me very well if you think I'd let someone ever lay eyes on what's mine outside of the club."

There was no mistaking the dark promise in his voice as he spoke, and that just about eradicated any last trace of doubt that bubbled inside of me.

"Now strip before I get tempted to punish you." Even under the warm sun, Carter drew a good kind of chill from my entire body, moving to obey his command before my mind could even catch up.

"Yes, Daddy." I tease, purposefully taking mindful steps out of his reach as I pull my shirt from my torso. While I placed that on the ground, I made a point of tossing my bra at him, hating the idea of getting that wet. My underwear remained on though, turning away from Carter and Rowan's hungry gazes in search of Dominic who was now waist deep in the pool of water.

"In." He commands, and I was surprised to find the temperature fairly bearable, likely as a result of the pulsing heat of the day. For that, I was more than thankful, the water licking at my breasts as I got to Dominic's side, showing the clear height difference between us.

I was slightly disappointed when I saw Carter take a seat right at the rock's edge, but Rowan quickly stole my attention at the fact he was climbing a stone-built staircase up to the side of the waterfall.

Seconds later, he jumped off of the cliff right next to us, intentionally soaking me with the splash and leaving my hair in a wet mess.

"Hey!" I yell, waiting for him to resurface before returning the action. He laughed as his head turned to the side, only for his gaze to snap right back at me.

"Oh, you're so going to regret that." Dominic smiles at my side, and when I glance at Carter, I find him happily watching me too in wait to see what happens next. I was already swimming away, though, seeing the plans of retaliation in Rowan's eyes.

"I don't think so." He smirks as he takes two easy strides in my direction, his strong hand grabbing onto my ankle and smoothly pulling me back into his grip.

Dominic offers me no help, but I hear his muffled laughter from behind me.

"Rowan, you deserved it NO!" I jolted as hands were placed on both of my hips, his fingers moving against my stomach where I was extremely ticklish.

Water was splashing all around us, my hair not working to my advantage as we became drenched during my struggle. I helplessly tried to thrash away as I laughed, making an attempt at shoving Rowan's hands from my body and failing pathetically.

When that didn't work and with our fronts so close to each other, I took advantage of his distracted hold as I jumped up using his shoulders as momentum.

Rowan was caught off guard when gravity took care of the rest, my weight plunging his body beneath me under the water. It was a break to catch my breath, but he just as quickly shot back up, not in front of me, but rather behind.

His strong arms wrapped around my waist to keep me with him, though the tickling seemed to have ceased as his body shook with laughter.

"You're such an ass." I still try to shove him off teasingly as Dominic came to my front, smoothing my hair out of my eyes in amusement.

"You warned us about the punching and kicking, but I never expected you to try and drown me." Rowan jokes, referring to our previous conversations about my absolute love for being tickled.

The answer is none. No joy whatsoever.

"That was me being merciful." I giggle as I push my body away from his, going under the water to fix my hair before coming back up.

It was only then I noticed Carter's phone had been taking pictures of us all together, and I childishly stuck my tongue out considering he'd condoned and caught my torture on camera.

Something a lot like a smile spread across his features at the action, and my heart raced excitedly when he tossed the device to the side. It didn't take long before he finally followed our leads, discarding his clothes in a messy pile and walking into the pool.

Though, the decision wasn't due to the cooling effect the water promised.

No, Carter's eyes were dark as he moved in my direction, and I knew there was only one thing on his mind he was seeking out.

Me.

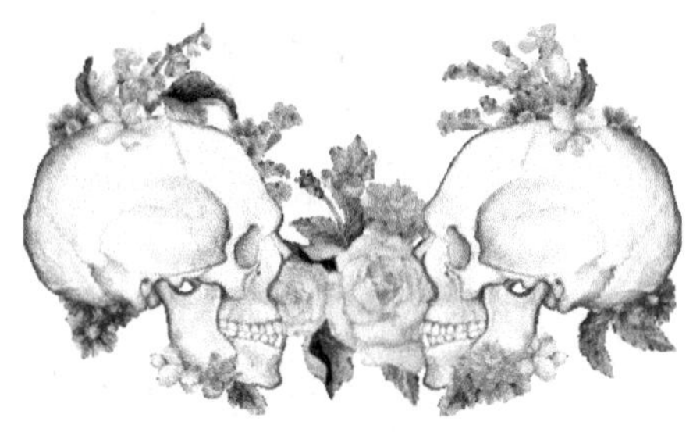

~ Eighteen ~

Hazel

Shit, shit, shit.

I'm in so much trouble. I don't even know how it happened, but one moment it was six thirty and now it's itching seven fifteen, my car only now just parking on their lengthy driveway.

My expected arrival was late by just over a half an hour and I didn't get any responses to my explanation text. I'm dead. Opening my door and forcing myself not to bolt up to the gates, I take the time to smooth out the dark navy coloured fabric of my dress.

The cut ended just below my knee so I didn't have to worry about it dragging, but I had put a lot of effort into my appearance for tonight. I just hope my untimeliness won't take away from that.

With my heels clicking lightly with each step of mine, I make sure to lock my car as I walk up the pathway and to where the guards stood. All it took was one glance at my hand to earn me a polite nod, the gates opening and gaining me entry to what will likely be a long punishment.

My heart racing, I twirled Carter's ring with my thumb—a nervous habit I've recently gained—as I took careful steps to their door. I knew the jewelry piece was some sort of mafia promise ring he gave me, but that information didn't click with me until day two of three when I'd left them.

And now we're here, my body thrumming with nervousness and hesitance. My lateness was one of the top grounds for punishment in our contract, and I knew they were all itching for the excuse as of recently. Hell, I had just given them one on a silver platter.

Raising my hand to knock, my fist does even come close to making contact with the wood before Rowan opens the large door and peers down at me with his blue eyes.

"Hi," I said in a slightly small voice, not getting any kind of idea as to where his head was at right now. I had a huge feeling I was about to find out, though. Inhaling a nervous breath, I watched as a small smirk tugged up on Rowan's lips, the sight more disconcerting than relieving.

All I could do was blink before he was tugging me to him, his hand wrapping tight around my throat as he claimed my mouth with his.

When Rowan kissed, he devoured, and I knew that by the end of the night there wouldn't be much left of me that was still mine. Stealing the air from my lungs, I staggered by the sheer force of his lips before he pulled off, not giving me time to regroup as he guided me to the living room by a hand on my back.

I was more than excited for tonight, but now, I was absolutely terrified as well. At the sight of Carter and Dominic lounged comfortably on their couch, their gazes calculatingly on me, the urge to drop to my knees right here and now felt like a heavy weight on my shoulders.

"You're late." Dominic grins wickedly, his head tilting as his eyes traced over my skin so intently it was as if it were his fingers dragging over the curves of my body. I fought off the shiver threatening to spread down my spine, instead stopping at the other side of the table that now separated us.

"I know, I'm sorry," I apologize, feeling the heat of Rowan's presence skate over my back, "I kind of just lost track of time." That earned me a seemingly thoughtful hum, though I couldn't tell if it was one of understanding or one that had him thinking about all the ways he should punish me. Dominic's gaze revealed nothing, but the darkness in Carter's eyes told me at least they weren't completely upset.

My heart pounded against my chest as the latter gave a short come hither gesture with his fingers, and like a puppet on his strings, I obeyed. Walking around the table to Carter's front, no warnings were given as he pulled me down so that my ass sat on his lap, Dominic grabbing my hair in his fist before bringing me to lay flat on my back.

The two left me sprawled across their thighs, my dress bunching just teasingly past my waist.

hat soon didn't matter, however, Carter carefully tugging at the material until it folded against my stomach, leaving my underwear wide open for their viewing.

The patterning was a slightly transparent white, the lacy designs making the lingerie the most delicate pieces I've ever owned. While comfortable, they were so light it felt as though I were wearing nothing, the matching bra giving a similar effect to my brain.

"These are pretty," A deep, sensual voice sounded from Carter as his rough hand came down to trace along the skin just at the underwear line.

"Mmm," Rowan hums in agreement, my head turning on Dominic's lap to look at him, "Much too pretty to ruin, I'd say." He hadn't moved from his spot away from me, but the power he still clearly held could be physically felt in my core.

"Don't let her come." Rowan orders, my eyes widening slightly at the dominance in that single statement, "I want to play with her for a bit first." Despite his words, his stance told me he didn't plan on touching me himself anytime soon, his feet remaining rooted in the same place.

"It was really just an accident" I insisted, but was cut off when Dominic forced me to look at him, his free hand running lazily over my nipples yet never dipping below the low cut design of my dress.

That in itself was torture, but the satisfied expression on his face showed that he was quite enjoying this. I wanted to tell them it wouldn't happen again, that it really was just a one time thing, but whatever I was about to say was replaced by a sharp gasp from my mouth.

"I got a new toy for you, sweetheart." Carter says with a hint of excitement in his words, my mind circling at the feeling of a vibration tickling my bottom lip where his finger now rested.

Rings are something Carter always wears on his hands—something I've grown very attached to, but the one on his right forefinger was one I didn't recognize.

It was quite simply a black band, nothing more, nothing less, but I didn't miss the small circular knob on the side that was clearly responsible for the low humming noise.

"Do you want to try it out?" He smirks, his thumb swiping across my parted mouth before dragging it down my body and around where Dominic continued to tease.

I knew the question was rhetorical, and I wasn't able to speak anyways as the vibrations met my clit, my back arching only to be pushed back down onto their laps. My lip caught between my teeth as my toes curled, slightly surprised that such a device even existed. What had me more turned on, however, is the intentions behind the

"gift." There were more vibrators and sex toys upstairs than I could even imagine, which meant Carter's ring was not expected to be used often in the house.

Those thoughts made me both love and hate the idea of this, though the first seemed to be taking over as my body ached for more. "While we were waiting for the additional thirty minutes, we came up with an idea as to teach you some manners, darling." Rowan says, and though I'm not able to look at him, my senses track his every movement.

I know he's currently walking past us and looping around to the back of the couch, his two arms resting partially over the dark cushion. Now, I was able to see him. Now, I was able to learn that he too had new toys to experiment with.

Dropping a pair of nipple clamps onto my stomach, I wasn't given the ability to move away as Dominic soothingly stroked my hair, my head being forced to rest all the way down on his thighs. I was well aware I earned every bit of this punishment, though that doesn't make me any happier about it. "Aren't you going to ask us what it is, Hazel?" Dominic smiled down, holding me still when I began to squirm in desperation. While I don't know exactly how Carter's ring works, I do know the intensity is more than enough to notice the vibrations, but not enough to come close to giving me that high I so desperately crave.

My hips gradually rolled to try and gain something more, but Rowan—with a single hand—kept me still.

"It's really quite disrespectful to ignore the men who own you, princess." Dominic lands a punishing slap to my breast over my dress, but a second later, Rowan's removing the material until the entire thing is bunched around my torso. I hear them each take a breath at the sight of my white, intricate bra, my nipples prominently hardened and straining against the transparent sheer.

Their looks alone made me dizzy, but it was the pleased growl from Carter that had my hips tilting again.

"I don't belong to anybody but myself," I lied, wanting to push them just to see what they'd do. A whimper fell past my lips when I felt Carter's hands retreat all together, but I soon realized he was playing with the knob on his ring. When his touch returned, it didn't take my body long to react at all to the increased vibrations, still refusing to touch me beneath my underwear. It wasn't until many minutes later of my torture that Dominic gently slid the straps of my bra half way down my arms, a trail of goosebumps awakening under his touch.

"So far tonight, you've been late, disrespectful, and now a liar." Carter tuts, pressing his finger down hard on my clit as he circled it, "Since you felt above asking, I'm going to tell you how tonight's going to go." Rowan took my distraction as an opportunity to roll both of my nipples in his fingers, a gasp being pulled from my body at the knowledge the clamps had slid off of my stomach and onto the couch.

While he moved his one hand to let go, Dominic happily took his place, each man tweaking and abusing my now red nipples.

"Considering you were thirty minutes late, I think it's fair that we edge you for that same amount of time as you did us." Carter says, his words wrapping around my body like a vice.

No, no, no, no, no.

"Daddy, I'm—"

"Considering you're leaving on Monday, we had the whole night planned out to treat you like a queen as a way to remember us for the next week." He interrupts, dread pouring through me as though it were running in my blood. "But the truth is that you're nothing more than a pathetic little slut," Rowan finished, pinching my breast so hard tears built in my eyes, "Isn't that right, my submissive?" Oh dear god. I nearly orgasmed from his words alone, and I was honestly surprised I didn't.

"Yes, Sir." I replied quietly, tilting my hips upwards in a silent plea for more. None of them liked that response, though. Watching as a blur of movement passes over my eyes, I can't stop it as Dominic suddenly grabs one of the nipple clamps from my side and places it onto the one he's been playing with. I cried out at how fast it all went, and while my body was held almost completely still by strong hands, it didn't stop my shaking as Dominic tightened it the hardest I've ever experienced before.

When Rowan followed suit and the devices began to vibrate, it was almost too much, my orgasm rising rapidly to the surface.

My legs locked up and my mouth fell open in pleasure, but after a few seconds, I realized that consuming high never came. Confused as the effects of the denial crashed through my body, my eyes fluttered open to stare at the man between my thighs who was no longer touching me.

Fuck.

"Daddy, please," I whimpered at the loss of contact, realizing exactly what he was doing. He wasn't lying earlier.

"I can't even be too mad about you being late, sweetheart." Carter smirks, his thumb running up and down the sides of my trembling thighs, "I quite like you like this." I faintly heard the tearing of fabric sound from behind me, but I was too overwhelmed to acknowledge it.

Too much of my attention was on the dark haired man at my front, because while he may not have been touching me anymore, Carter demanded my gaze.

Only once my orgasm seemed to have efficiently ebbed to their satisfaction did things change. The ripped material I'd heard less than a minute ago turned out to be the black cloth of Rowan's now discarded shirt, only a long strip remaining. He smiled as he folded it horizontally twice, turning it into the perfect makeshift blindfold for me to use.

A small exhale pushing past my lips, I complied as Dominic lifted my head from his lap just enough so that his friend could take away my sight. Working surely and steadily, Rowan's fingers kept my hair out of the way as a firm knot was tied in place at the back, my vision effectively becoming encased in a tunnel of darkness. Instantly, I could feel every other one of my senses heightening, the noise of shuffling in specific. It wasn't long before I felt my dress being tugged off of my hips, six hands rearranging me to their taste before I was swept under their desire all over again.

My hips bucked as Carter's ringed finger pressed down against my core, the pleasure reappearing as though it had never been taken away. Every part of me felt hot under their touch, my face undoubtedly flushed in wait to see what would happen. While Carter continued to slowly circle my sensitive clit, I knew it was Dominic's thumbs that gently ran around my clamped nipples, sometimes pressing down just slightly to cause them to painfully pull at my skin. This time, it took me no more than five minutes before that familiar shake returned and their touch retreated.

"Ah, please!" I begged as I suddenly felt cold, even though I could feel the heat of both Dominic and Carter's erections pressed against opposite ends of my body. The one man I couldn't feel, however, was Rowan. I missed his touch just as much as my body ached for him, but the issue with the blindfold was that while I could sense his eyes on me, I couldn't even reach out in his direction. "You don't like it when people make you wait, do you, princess?" Dominic's deep voice responded, but his tone told me he would not be caving to my begging. None of them would.

"Please, I'm sorry!" I tried again, screaming out in frustration as I was brought up to the tip of my orgasm for the third time, just for everything to stop until the flicker died out.

The time between each denial was quickly growing shorter and shorter, my body so sensitive I could probably come on demand at this point. They wouldn't grant me that release, though. It would've been nice if I had at least a valid excuse for being so late, but I didn't. And these men used that to feed their sadistically blissful desires.

"I—" I began, only for my words to be cut off by a thumb slipping into my open mouth, pushing down on the back of my tongue until it became an effort to hold my gag. Somehow, I instinctively know it's Rowan, and the small chuckle in amusement confirmed my thoughts. "I don't remember saying you were allowed to speak, little one." His voice purrs by my face, his thumb pushing father until he has me choking around him.

Carter took that moment to resume his movements on my clit as Dominic did to pinching and tweaking my nipples. Instantly my lips parted wider, and it was then that Rowan said, "Maybe we should put this pretty mouth of yours to better use, darling." I tried to contain the tears collecting at my eyes, only being able to feel as he pulled his finger out and slid it across my bottom lip, wiping away some of the spit that had spilled as though he wasn't about to ruin me himself. Spreading my legs wider for Carter, I relaxed my jaw and parted my mouth in silent invitation for more. I shivered as a hand lightly brushed at the side of my face; a deceiving act of kindness as Rowan lifted my head to the side where I knew he was standing.

Dominic had to reposition slightly, but that didn't stop him from teasing me over and over, his one hand dropping to my stomach just to play with me before slowly sliding his rough palm back up.

I was very quickly becoming wound up all over again, and it didn't help as my tongue darted out seekingly just to be met with the taste of Rowan's precum against my lips.

I couldn't help but moan to myself as I kissed the wet tip of his cock, licking my mouth and in turn gliding across his slit.

A small smile appeared on my face at the fact I knew he shivered under my touch, but when my hands reached out to his legs for balance, Carter ended up grabbing both of my wrists.

Though he didn't stop the vibrations, I felt him move as my arms were forced uncomfortably behind my back, soon becoming trapped together by a single hand of Carter's. The action forced my back into a pleasurable arch, my breasts sticking out more for Dominic's enjoyment as complete control over my head was surrendered over to Rowan.

"Be a good whore and open your mouth," He commanded, his words causing tingles to shoot through my scalp and down to the tips of my toes. Obeying, I took a breath a second before I felt his length push past my lips, more drool already accumulating as Rowan pressed himself inside of me.

My legs tried to press together for relief at the feeling of him, but Carter forced them apart with the hand with the ring, his other being rather occupied from restraining me. When he soon realized this position wouldn't work for that precise reason, I heard the ruffle of clothes as he lifted my ass off of his lap, just to lay on his stomach between my thighs.

My hips were forced to widen as his large frame nestled between them, my body jerking as his ring instantly returned to torturing me. Even with the blindfold, I could practically see his satisfied smirk, knowing there was nothing I could do to take over now. I was completely at their mercy, and Rowan knew that as he pulled back, only to swiftly thrust forward, nearly suffocating me with his cock down my throat.

My hands tried to pull away to steady myself, but Carter's grip remained unwavering around me, allowing gravity to take control.

"You pinch me if you want this to stop." I hear him say, knowing his wrist was more than within reach of my fingers.

The order brought me comfort, and I felt my body submit just a little bit more to their desire at that.

Even with the constant denial I've been receiving. My hips had fallen into a continuous circling motion against Carter's hand, and he let me, seeking out my pleasure myself in combination with Dominic's motions around my throbbing nipples.

Unsurprisingly, it wasn't long until signs of an orgasm hit me again, only this time, my whimper in frustration was muffled and overpowered by Rowan's harsh fucking.

Things were becoming very hard to handle, unable to move, breathe, or speak. As the lack of oxygen started to take effect over my body, blinding hot pleasure appeared in its place. I was on the verge of passing out by the time Rowan ended up pulling out, resting his cock on my warm tongue as I took heavy inhales of air. My face was wet with tears and spit, but I still needed more. I wanted to be able to touch them, to make them feel as good as I do now, but they wouldn't let me. I'm beginning to believe that was the true punishment.

"Such a mess already," Carter cruelly tuts, dipping his head slightly so the caress of his breath tickles my thighs, "I can't wait to see how pretty you look later when you're crying out around our cocks." Bringing the ring back to my clit, a sharp moan spilled from my mouth at the contact, Rowan taking the sound as invite as he thrust back down my throat. Our last night together had truly snapped something in him, because he was no longer restrained as he gripped my hair tight like a leash, holding me still for my destruction.

"You're taking him so well, princess," Dominic praises me, the sound of his voice soothing away the dizziness in my head. Since I couldn't see, having that connection to them kept me grounded and allowed air to fill my lungs, even as I choked and sputtered around Rowan's dick. He began grunting softly from the sheer force of his movements, my mouth trying to keep up with him, but being unable to. I can't recall when, but at some point I had just given up, letting my jaw fall slack as my tongue ran teasingly along the underside of his cock. At the same time, the other two took diligent care of my trembling body, the elapsed minutes slowly bringing pain along with them.

Though I gasped as Carter's soft lips began to kiss along my thighs and hips in contrast, the constant denial and unrelenting vibration of my pinched nipples grew more and more sore with each passing second. I felt completely and utterly consumed, truly becoming a mess under their touch as my makeup smudged, my arousal soaked my underwear, and my whimpers filled the air.

"That's it," The low hum of Carter's voice came from between my legs in encouragement, goosebumps breaking out along my skin, "Twenty more minutes left before we can properly take care of you the way we initially wanted." Twenty?! As in two-zero?

My body screamed out in protest as the vibrations increased on my clit instead of slowing this time, hurting from the intense overstimulation. "Mmmph." I groaned around Rowan's cock in dissatisfaction, my body trying to jerk away as he used that as an excuse to force my head forward until my nose was pressed against his front. No amount of control could have stopped me from gagging around him, but he only seemed to like it more, keeping me there as I fought to struggle away. "What was that, Hazel?" Dominic asks in mock pity, amused and satisfied by my obvious desperation, "Something you wanted to say?" My core tightened at the demeaning undertones of his words, crying around Rowan until he finally pulled me back. Long strings of my saliva kept me connected to him as did his steady grip on my hair, my brain going dumb as I heard him stroking himself with only his tip inside of my mouth.

"Please, I can't handle this," I shook, even though I knew damn well I could. Carter's wrist was more than accessible to my pinch should I need it still, but I wasn't even close to my limit yet. I needed quite the opposite. I needed more.

"This is what happens to bad girls who make their dominants wait for them." Rowan says as power radiates off of every part of him, more tears building in my eyes in response. Any other colour of blindfold and all three would've been able to see how wet the material now was. These kinds of releases tended to be more freeing than any orgasm could promise, and I was greedily indulging in every second, even as I tried to get away half the time. "Stay still, princess," Dominic orders as I squirm continuously over top of him, my thighs practically crushing Carter's head as I sought out my pleasure myself.

I wondered if I'd somehow be able to trick him into letting me come if I pretended for long enough I had it under control? Though I doubted that would end well for me, I couldn't even count how many orgasms I've been denied by now.

All I knew was that my desire branched much farther than just the pleasurable high of climaxing. It was these infuriating men that physically kept me bound to the couch while mentally consuming me from the inside out. Everything was always intense with them as a group, and with my loss of vision along with that, I'm surprised I haven't already shattered completely beneath them.

"Good girl," I hear Dominic murmur as I make an effort to cease my movements, but nothing is able to stop my shaking. He didn't seem to care, though, his priorities set on something that really had me stilling in distress.

The clinking of ice against a glass sounded by my ears, swirling in some sort of drink I knew Dominic had poured while waiting for me. He's always had a thing for temperature play with me, and I remember the cold bite ice brought in contrast to his heated kisses and warm skin.

"Dominic, I—" My words got cut off as I felt a tug at my blindfold, the material slipping away as I was met with bright light and flashes of the men around me. Though my head was still facing Rowan, my heart raced when I looked up to catch his blue gaze staring down at me.

His fingers remained curled in my hair, but his free hand had never stopped stroking himself as I slowly continued to suck on his tip. For a second, I had found myself lost in the hunger in his eyes. For a second, I forgot I was being punished until Carter's hand pulled away at the same moment Dominic brought the ice down onto one of my nipples. My body jerked harshly at the action, Rowan's cock slipping from my mouth as my lips parted in both pain and pleasure, desperately trying to free myself away from the freezing bite at my skin.

"Always so responsive," I hear Dominic say just as my mouth was filled once again, Rowan's taste sliding across my tongue. Before was simple squirming, but I really tried to fight them now, my eyes pinching shut as I gagged and my hips bucked at the ice being dragged around the still vibrating clamps. However, I was no match for one of them, let alone three. I had wanted more, and now I was getting it.

"Please!" I mentally begged, my cries and whimpers not allowing any opportunity for actual words beyond my desperate moans.

I had no clue how much time had passed or if they were even keeping track of the promised half an hour, but I saw Carter's smile out of the corner of my eye when he got the excuse to pin me down.

Everything hurt in the most beautiful of ways, and as Rowan continued to thrust hard into my mouth, I encouragingly let him push my head down when I heard a strained groan fall from his lips. All it took was a single heartbeat before he began spilling himself down my throat, holding onto me tight as I felt his cock twitch against my tongue.

"Such a good girl." Rowan grunted as I choked on his release, trying to pull away but being forced still for him, "Swallow my cum just like that." Dizziness overtook me as I did as he asked, taking him down my throat and sucking away what was left of his orgasm. I moaned at the feeling, knowing I was responsible for it, but when it came to him pulling out and tucking himself back into his pants, things began to move quickly from there. I watched as Rowan fell to his knees before me, only a second before his mouth crashed into mine like an explosion.

With a single kiss, he ignited the fuel in my core and then threatened to become my destruction. His lips may have been sweetly soft, but his tongue was wicked and ruthless, sparking flame and electricity through my blood. I heard a small beep sound from Dominic's watch as he continued to painfully circle my nipples with ice, but I was too lost to think about it. Rowan's kiss burned as hot as my desperation, and when I felt Carter finally release my hands from his hold, they went straight through the blond locks, pulling him closer to me.

These men may have just devoured and ripped me to shreds, but all my body sought out for was more.

A cry tore through me as Carter's hand pulled away yet again, only this time, I was not denied of anything. His mouth latched onto my clit instantly in the ring's place, his teeth grazing me as he sucked hard. I screamed as my orgasm barreled through me in response, nearly falling off of the couch when Dominic snapped the clamps from my sore nipples.

Between that and the way Rowan's mouth moved to my neck, I came apart, my release squirting from me as I soaked Carter's face. It didn't help when he moaned in pleasure, the vibrations going straight to my clit and forcing me under the blanket of my ruin.

Though my every instinct told me to run at the wolfish expressions all three of my men wore, I remained still beneath their gazes. Now partially sitting up, I couldn't help but press my legs tight together at the sight of my release dripping from Carter's twisted mouth and glistening off of his chin.

It didn't help my throbbing body in the least, and when Dominic gave me a light push forwards on the couch, I went straight into Carter's arms. I gasped and shivered as he made me kiss away my arousal from his face, and when it finally ended with our mouths connecting, I moaned at the taste of myself mixing on both of our tongues.

"You will not be late again," Carter asserted against my lips, and when we finally pulled back with my cheeks flushed, I knew that my punishment had ensured that.

"Yes, Daddy." I whispered for only him to hear, resulting in him suddenly picking me up into his arms as my limbs wrapped around him.

"You're trouble." He murmurs, kissing me on my temple before moving us towards the stairs. The action only makes me hold him closer, turning my head to find Dominic and Rowan following close behind.

They both shoot me a wink and a smile as I blush, letting out a content sigh as I let my head rest against Carter's shoulder.

I couldn't wait to find out what they had planned for us tonight, and I wouldn't be surprised if they could hear the excited beat of my heart when we finally made it upstairs. I made the move to get down when we finally made it to the playroom door, but Carter only tightened his grip on my thighs, letting Rowan punch in the code. With the sound of four beeps, I heard the latch unlock, purple lights fading on as it sensed our motion. It has been a surprisingly long time since I've been in here considering it used to be every other day, but I feel like I almost liked it better this way. It made things seem so much more intense now that it's been about a week of staying out.

"Present for us, sweetheart." Carter whispered in my ear, and though it took him a minute, he reluctantly let me down so I could fulfill his command. Doing as he says and walking past Rowan, a breathy gasp left my mouth as he took the opportunity to spank me, smirking at my reaction.

He's the real trouble. Smiling slightly, I walked over to the hairbrush and elastic they'd laid out for me, braiding first before moving to unclasp my bra. It's amazing to think the thought of being naked in front of them used to terrify me.

Now, I embraced it. Sliding the straps down my arms, I couldn't help but whimper as the lace brushed against my nipples, still red and swollen from my punishment.

Though I could feel the eyes of the others on me, I took the time to diligently fold what was left of my clothes, my underwear following right after. I shivered under their watchful gazes, but I didn't meet them as I walked to the door, only to be stopped by Dominic.

"Here." He says in a calm demand, causing me to drop to my knees before him.

The placement left me mostly in the middle of the room, and I didn't waste any time as I spread my knees, bowed my head, and left my palms facing up on my thighs. I was completely open, completely vulnerable, completely theirs. Dominic didn't stick around to wait for me as I listened to his steps walking off, but I was more focused on the way my muscles were relaxing and my mind was clearing.

"Rowan told us you're leaving as of tomorrow," Carter says, questioning in his voice as though he wanted me to confirm it. I knew better than to speak, however. Pleased by my silence, he continues, "How many days do we need to make up for, sweet-heart?" A light exhale passes through my mouth at his words, seeing out of the corner of my eye his large frame walking over to me. He doesn't stop until he's standing at my front, looking down at me for my answer.

"Seven, Daddy." I responded, my skin tingling as I grasped onto the meaning behind his question. They were going to make up for an entire week's worth of scenes in one single night.

"Mm," Carter hums to himself as though he'd thought as such. I wanted to know what he was thinking—what all of them were thinking—but I never spoke and they never offered their thoughts. Instead, I was left in my own head, shivering as Carter's finger dropped down just to my cheek. Never once did he tilt me to look at him, simply touching me to see how I'd react.

"I guess we'll just have to fuck you so hard you'll feel us the entire time you're gone." He says lowly, and while I couldn't see his face, I knew he was dead serious.

The comforting touches were confirmation enough, something they did especially when my limits were about to be pushed. And god was I ever willing to find out what. I forced myself to be still as my core dripped desperately, the contact of Carter's single finger putting me into some sort of trance. I ached for them to touch me—to use me and fill my mind with memories I can use to drown out the ones I'll have to face tomorrow. I wanted all of them, and I knew they would offer me nothing short of everything.

"Stand up and place your hands on his neck." I hear Dominic command from behind me, and on unbalanced steps, I do.

Not even a second later is Carter lifting me yet again, dragging the two of us to the bed where Dominic and Rowan wait.

Correction—where a very much naked Dominic and Rowan lay on either sides of the mattress, an obvious spot between them meant for me. I licked across my bottom lip at the sight of them together, well aware of their trained eyes on me as my body was brought to lay in the middle on my back. Carter was gentle in a way that caught me slightly off guard, but when I felt three pairs of hands setting right to my skin, I knew I was simply happy to have them. They all started slow at first, making me drunk on soft kisses and affection as they made me feel cherished despite the contrasting rough grasps on my arms and legs. The combination was enough to have my back arching in response, both Rowan and Carter taking the hardened peaks into their mouths.

As for Dominic, he silently spread my legs farther apart all the while small bites and soothing licks were planted numerously on my body. My breath hitched at the feeling of his hand then moving down, trailing until his fingers were able to easily slide through my obvious state of arousal.

Being with them felt like the darkest sins of hell and brightest pleasures of heaven, and I embraced both while my mouth parted in quiet gasps of desire.

"You did so good for us earlier." Dominic murmurs in my ear as he continues to tease at my entrance, only to bring his hand farther down so his fingers could run circles around the rim of my ass. I'm suddenly extremely thankful for Carter's text this morning, urging my body to relax and accept what I know Dominic was asking permission for.

I gave him a small nod as the other two continued to play with my nipples, neck, and mouth, and I was a little proud of how I didn't tense up this time as a finger pressed deep inside of me. This was the first time Dominic's ever touched me there, but I let him, moaning while I tightened and then loosened around him. He took his time as he learned this aspect of my pleasure for himself, observing what strokes had me whimpering beside him (which was almost all of them).

Patience was something he executed with me, and when I felt his free hand brush along the side of my face to gain my attention, I sent an answering one down between his legs, taking his cock into my hand. Our groans came in sync with one another at the contact, and though Dominic was currently forcing me to look at him, that didn't stop me from blindly reaching out for Carter and smiling at the low noise I pulled from his throat.

"A week is a long time from now, princess." He spoke quietly, his resolve slightly cracking under the pressure of my hand working up and down his length in deep motions, "We just want to make sure you're taken care of until then." As if to reiterate that, Carter's teeth grazed against a sensitive spot on my neck, no doubt promising a bruise that would last until close to next Sunday. His smug grin at that shared knowledge obliterated any chances of it being an innocent act, however, I wouldn't have expected anything less from any of the three of them. Between his words and the brutal kisses along my body, I felt myself becoming rapidly needier, working my hands faster around the men holding me.

"Fuck, Hazel." Rowan groans from my left, only for me to realize he's stroking himself at the sight of me. Just watching him made my face heat, and then he said the words that had me truly desperate, "Do you think you could take all of us at once?"

Even though my clit was never touched, I suddenly orgasmed around Dominic's finger at those words, whimpering as flashes of images filled my head of the four of us together.

They held me on my back as Dominic continued to stroke me, my arousal dripping down to my ass and used as lubricant. It wasn't until he pulled out entirely did my body stop shaking in pleasure, my hands being removed from their cocks as I was sat upright.

The position forced Carter to move off of me, and when he fell into a kneel at my front, I couldn't help but notice how perfect his posture was.

Apart from the lack of spread knees and bowed head, Carter looked just like me, his ass resting on his heels, his back straight, his hands on his thighs only his were palm down. He looked perfect, and I couldn't help but dart my eyes down to the hardened length of his cock, the silver piercing on his tip included.

"Bend over and take him into your mouth." I hear Rowan tell me, and when my gaze meets Carter's again, he doesn't do anything but smirk.

Taking that as invitation enough, I bent forward on my knees, my ass remaining up as my head lowered to Carter's thick length against his stomach.

I felt Rowan's hands begin to run up and down the backs of my thighs while Dominic gathered my hands behind my back, tying them with a thin rope I hadn't noticed before.

The material didn't hurt, but it did leave me once again at their mercy, Carter now completely in control of my head movements.

Only, Carter's hands never once moved from the tattoos of his thighs. Instead, I gasped as I felt cold lubricant being pressed against my back entrance while Dominic gripped hard onto my braid, forcing my mouth down onto his friend's cock for him. It was so unexpected and unbelievably hot I couldn't help but press my knees together, flattening my tongue over Carter's head and making a point of teasing the piercing there.

Only once he moaned did Dominic press my head down farther, not giving my throat much time to adjust as I felt him slide deeper into me. His girth had me choking before he was even half way down, but none of them cared about that.

As Rowan pressed two lubed fingers into my ass, Dominic yanked my head back, giving me no more than five seconds to catch my breath before guiding me down and holding me there.

My wrists tried to pull at the bearings keeping them together at my back, but they were too precise and too efficient to break through. I was a little confused when I felt something a lot like a small ball being placed into the palm of my hand by Rowan, but it then sparked my memory of hand signal safe words from our contract. It was quite literally a small black squeak toy, but it was more than effective considering the situation.

It was an out if I needed one, however for now I chose to widen my mouth, accepting more of Carter down my throat.

"Do you like this princess?" Dominic cooed as I gagged, tears forming at my eyes from the stimulation. All I could do was moan in response, but it was clear he liked that more than any words could offer.

"Do you like Carter kneeling and still for you? Look at his hands, look at what you're doing to him."

Blinking my eyes open, I watched as his scarred fingers curled into restrained fists on his thighs, forcing himself not to simply thrust all the way up. He let me—he let Dominic take that little bit of control knowing I'd like it, and when my eyes raised to his, I could feel them burning down at me in pleasure.

I watched as he groaned, his rings glinting in my peripheral vision. I wanted to make him come, but it was up to Dominic to decide if he'd let him. Realizing that, I tightened around Rowan's fingers as he continued to loosen me, slowly building up to being able to slide three fingers past the ring of my ass.

This was the first time there hadn't been any slight pain to the process, and after multiple minutes of prepping me, I knew I'd be able to take him now if he chose. For a little while, they simply continued to play with me, slowly working me up as I took Carter again and again down my throat.

I had yet to get him all the way inside, but when I felt the lubed tip of Rowan's dick pressing ever so slightly against my ass, Dominic encouraged me down. Not being able to fight against my bindings, I simply submitted, the first tear in a while falling down my cheek and dripping onto Carter's cock.

That single moment was the tipping point for his restraint, and Dominic sensed that as he pushed my head the remaining inch down forcibly. I was held there as Rowan pressed just the tip of himself inside of me, his hands grabbing onto my hips as he moaned in pleasure.

"Fuck you're tight back here." He said as he carefully filled me up, pulling out and slowly adding a few centimetres at a time with each thrust. His firm grip on my body held me still as my toes curled, more tears escaping my pinched eyes. That was all I could do to keep from breaking, and when Dominic finally gave me the mercy of pulling my head up, Rowan slipped the rest of the way inside, stilling at the feeling of me around him.

He groaned as I clamped down, a whimper coming from me when I was abruptly pulled upright onto his lap. I didn't even get the chance to scream at the change before Carter was on me, his hand wrapping around my throat and squeezing as our lips came together.

The ball from my hand fell onto the bed completely forgotten as he licked into my mouth, demanding I submit to his desire.

My body didn't give me any other choice, aching to obey as I was invaded and consumed, their touch reaching far deeper than my heated skin beneath their fingertips. These men sent me spiraling and I accepted it with welcome arms, melting until I was simply theirs to do with as they pleased.

"Go on and beg for his cock," Rowan's cool voice whispered in my ear, not moving as he filled me to the hilt and kept me there. I was way too far past the confinements of my own brain, and I wasted no time showing Carter how much I wanted him.

"Please, Daddy." I whimpered against his mouth before he pulled back, Rowan spreading my knees wide open for him, "I need you so bad. I want to feel you all at once, filling me up with your come until that's all I'm capable of thinking about." I've never wanted something more, and when my hips were tilted up slightly by Rowan, Carter came forward, gently pushing my knee to the side despite the feral hunger in his eyes.

"You're sure you want this, Hazel?" He asks one last time as his thumbs brush my hips, and my answering moan tells him enough.

"Please," I breathily begged, tilting my neck in submission to show I was all his. My hands were bound, my legs were spread, and I was so wet I knew he could see it, "Daddy, please." My whimpers were cut off as Carter pushed just the tip of himself inside of me, feeling as I was forced to stretch around him. While that had me shaking, Rowan's moan in my ear had me clamping down around them both, my mouth parting for more.

"Breathe and let him in, princess." Dominic came to my side, holding my face in his hands and wiping my silent tears from my cheeks. All I could think about was how they felt inside of me, and I convulsed as Carter released a low noise of absolute desire from his throat, grabbing just about where Rowan's hands rested before thrusting forward a little more.

I doubt it was even a full inch in difference, but it felt like everything as I cried out, trying to rock myself deeper onto him. When Rowan forced me still, though, confusion struck my mind.

"I'm trying not to hurt you." Carter bit out as heavy breaths left his body, taking his time as he drew out, only to push back in. All three of us made noises of pure need as I was slowly fucked into, Rowan's hands shaking slightly as he held onto me.

"Please," I cried as my cheeks turned red in desperation, and when my tear soaked eyes met Carter's dark ones, he held my gaze, closing what was left of the gap between us in a single thrust. All three watched me as my face twisted into an expression where pleasure wasn't even accurate enough of a word to describe the ecstasy I experienced. I was so full it hurt and that only made me wetter.

Nobody moved as Carter's body weighed down on mine, Rowan grunting as he was pressed down too. Dominic began planting light kisses to my jaw as I painfully adjusted to the stretch of them both inside of me, resting back against a hard chest for support. I twitched as Carter moved just the smallest inch to gain a better grip on my body, but I was surprised when Rowan's body mimicked mine.

"You can feel that, huh?" The former gritted as he stilled once again, and it took my brain a long moment before realizing he was talking about his piercing.

Holy fuck.

I never even stopped to think about the fact that they could feel each other through the thin barrier separating them, but the small shake in Rowan's muscles told me they very much could.

"You know I can." He responded, his warm breath spreading across my neck, "I can feel both of you." A shiver danced down my spine at his words, and I knew I couldn't wait any longer. I needed them to move and for Dominic to fuck my throat raw until I was nothing more than a result of their chased pleasure. While no words were spoken, I could tell they understood me as though I had. Offering only a single nod, I trembled as Rowan slid us down slightly, lifting my hips upwards as both he and Carter drew out of me together. My body's instant response was to protest at the loss of their touch, but all it took was a split second before they both thrusted back into me as one person, a cry tearing from my throat.

"Shit." I heard Rowan curse against my neck, but whatever he said afterwards died off until I was consumed by the wordless noises escaping all of us that ventured somewhere between whimpers and demands for more.

Together they built me up towards unimaginable heights, but the one thing that was still missing was the very man kneeling in front of my face.

Our change in positions only minutes ago left me at perfect level with Dominic's cock, and when I opened my mouth to show that I wanted him, he tore down the final barrier between us. Not missing a beat, he slipped past my lips roughly, marking both the beginning and the end of everything.

All three of them moved in on me in near perfect precision, holding onto my body until there wasn't a single doubt as to who I belonged to. These men fucking owned me, and I slowly fell apart around them with every quick, deep movement they encouraged me to take. Nothing would ever be able to come close to what we have, the overwhelming combination of our shared pain and desire only leaving us to burn in each other's flames.

I could feel them everywhere, surges of electricity shattering my nerves and tearing the oxygen from my lungs as though it were their souls slamming into me and not their cocks.

I could hear the sounds of our emotions resonating off of the walls and embedding themselves into our memories. Now, we were all in far too deep to stop what we've started, not just submitting to one another physically, but also in every other way possible.

"Hazel!" Rowan called out to me as he continued to ravage everything I gave over to him, my own cries rising as I felt myself begin to spin out of control. I knew these men were about to push me over the edge in a way I've never experienced before, and I had no choice but to let it obliterate me—no choice but to give myself over to the orgasm scratching and clawing its way through my body.

"Come, princess." Dominic groaned as he pushed himself deep into my mouth, smiling at my struggle, "Let yourself go." His demand shattered my entire being, my body seizing around all three of them as I burst into pieces.

I felt myself clamping down hard around them, pulsing and taking as they claimed me for what I was.

Theirs. As my mind blacked out and my muscles spasmed, I allowed myself to fall limp as Rowan growled into my ear before suddenly stilling and swelling within me. His orgasm spurred mine on as he came inside of my ass, Dominic following and painting my tongue white with his release only seconds later.

We tore each other apart, and for the second time tonight, I gushed around Carter, screaming and crying while he continued to pound into my sore cunt.

As Rowan's arm kept me upright for my ruin, remaining inside of me with Dominic's come dripping down my chin, this moment felt like it could be our forever.

When Carter finally spilled himself inside of me, he did so holding my bound hands with his one, our foreheads resting against one another in the wake of our beautiful destruction.

~ Nineteen ~

Hazel

With our foreheads resting against each other, Carter held onto my trembling body while Rowan undid the bindings at my wrists. I couldn't stop shaking, and though I've never been happier, my tears wouldn't stop falling. I had been torn apart, shattered, and then put back together by these men I call mine, and I wished for this night to never end. Fuck, I loved them so bad it hurt, and as I cried and shook and tumbled, they held onto me like they felt the same way. Even after Rowan and Carter pulled out of me gently, I still felt like I was utterly and undoubtedly consumed by all of them. "It's okay. We've got you, princess," Dominic murmured as he carefully undid my braid, lifting my hands to slump heavily over Carter's broad shoulders. I could feel Rowan's hand slowly rubbing up and down my heated back and his kiss being placed to the back of my head, telling me he was proud of me. I shivered under their praise and sobbed under their touch, hugging Carter close as he brought me to straddle him. I felt Dominic's fingers smoothly running through my hair to help me slowly come down from both the physical and mental highs I just experienced. Most of the time aftercare was just a nice comfort after scenes, but I really needed it right now. I couldn't explain why I was so wiped out, but my body would barely move despite my brain's commands, my tears a constant flow of emotions pouring out of me. They understood this though, possibly better than even me myself. Their loving touches and soft words of approval made me feel safe, and it tethered me in a sense to reality. This was real. I just took all three of them, and in turn of my submission, they gave me everything. Even now, I was never given the chance to feel alone or sad or regret. The real-ization that they weren't leaving struck hard today, but that was the truth. I think I could spend the rest of my life with these men, no matter how complicated or hard it may be. "Hanging in there, sweetheart?" Carter asks as he begins to kiss away each of my tears, placing light touches to each of my closed eyelids before tucking a few strands of hair behind my ears. "Mhm." Was the only response I was capable of, not even noticing both Rowan and Dominic had left until their return. They didn't have to speak to understand each other as Carter's grip tightened just ever so slightly on my body, lifting me up and carrying me over to the bathroom where the other two now waited.

The smell of my bath salts greeted me with every inhale past the door, and it wasn't long before I was being transferred from one pair of arms into Dominic's who was already in the tub. I flinched at the hot water burning against my sore skin, but I was forced to adjust as I was slowly lowered, realizing that the heat felt insanely good on my muscles after the initial burn passed. "Stay." I heard Rowan speak from beside me, but my eyes were too heavy to remain open. So instead, I listened, "We won't talk about it. Just stay." When the realization that he was talking to Carter hit, I was a little surprised as I felt a heavy tension loom over them, one that extended much farther than what happened tonight. It wasn't until multiple seconds later that I heard a slosh of water come from right in front of me, the result of Carter staying as my feet were pulled into his lap. At his touch, despite the exhaustion eating away at my consciousness, I opened my eyes to look at him. There was conflict in his expression, and he refused to look at the men at my sides, but when he felt my gaze, his attention drifted softly over to me. He wasn't angry, I realized. No, Carter was sad, and I didn't know how to take it away. "Just let me hold you." He rasps as if understanding where my mind had traveled to, so I did. While I know he meant more so metaphorically, Dominic still passed me over to his friend, his expression telling me not to push him on this right now. He and Rowan soothingly began washing me while I was held upright by a strong pair of arms, and as the minutes passed, I felt Carter begin to relax slowly. I feared I knew what was bothering him, and like I thought before, I didn't know how to help. Simply deciding that letting them take care of me was the best thing I could offer, I moved with them as gels and body scrubs were lathered over my skin, kisses being planted to my cheeks when they felt like it. Tonight was a lot for all of us, but holding each other seemed to be something necessary for not just myself but for the remaining three as well. We quietly talked as they scrubbed at my body and my giggle echoed off of the dark painted drywall when my feet tickled from the loofah Rowan ran across my toes. My hair remained mostly untouched by the water, but Carter played with it the entire time, combing through the waves as though it were a lullaby for his heart. It turns out it became mine as well, because it wasn't long before I fell asleep in his arms.

I woke up with the top half of my body on Carter's, Rowan spooning my side from behind. A small headache flickered at my temples, but I couldn't bring myself to care much at the sight of a messy haired Dominic half cuddling Rowan as well in his sleep. The sight made me smile to myself as I lifted my head, realizing that this was the first time I've ever woken up with all three of them in bed with me. As consciousness slowly returns to my brain, I very quickly become aware of the pain in my stomach and the soreness of my every muscle, but I forced myself to ignore it for now. My thoughts had more important things to focus on like the fact Carter was one of three I woke up next to. "Hey, sweetheart," He whispered, offering an easy, yet tired smile. I returned a gesture of my own, but my grin dropped a little bit at the dark circles under his eyes and the exhaustion affecting his state. "You didn't sleep?" I quietly ask, the palm of my hand lifting from where it rested on his chest and up to his face. I ran my thumb along the line of Carter's jaw as he softly leaned into my touch, but he didn't seem to care very much about the fact of how underslept he looked. "I didn't want to leave you." I knew he had nightmares as much as I did, but I never considered the possibility that he stayed up all night to avoid them. Did he stay up during our last night together too then? "That's not healthy, I—" I began, wanting to tell him that I understood—that it was okay, but I was cut off by a small hush from his lips. "I'm okay." Carter lies, pulling my chin up until his face is beside mine. I felt warm at the contact—at the feeling of his mouth brushing against my cheek to soothe my worry for him, but I can't help but pull away when I get another uncomfortable pain in my stomach. I wince as I sit up slightly, my eyes going wide at the sight of blood on the sheets. No. "Oh god, Carter, I'm so sorry." I say, closing my legs to try and cover the blood in between them, tears already pricking my eyes. I tried not to cry as I heard Dominic stir from behind me, pushing myself away when I saw the realization passing through Carter's eyes. "Don't worry about it at all, Hazel. They're just sheets." He says at the same time Dominic wakes up. This is so embarrassing, I think to myself as Carter gets out of bed, uncaring that he was still naked from last night. As things clicked with Dominic, he shot me a look when he also stood up, walking over to where I was before sitting down in Carter's place. "It's not a big deal." He says in earnest while I hear the sound of Carter turning on the shower in their bathroom. I can't bring myself to meet his eyes as I bite my cheek and nod, even though I nearly die when I find Rowan awake too, gently pulling the comforter off of his body. That too has blood on it, but instead of speaking, he leans up and kisses the side of my head. "What do you need from us?" He asks, his voice still scratchy from his sleep. The fact they were so damn perfect about this only made me want to cry more. Tampons were ideal. So was chocolate. Though, the part I hated second most was that I was going to have to deal with my family and my period at the same time. The realization had me eternally groaning as I shifted away from the red spot on the bed, not sure what to do. "How about a shower first?" Dominic suggests at my panicking silence, causing me to swallow and remember this wasn't a big deal. Periods happen. Get over it, Hazel. It's not a big deal. "Come here." I hear Carter's voice speak from the entrance as he walks back towards me, picking me up into his arms before I get the chance to protest. I instantly felt self-conscious as I pressed my legs together, but I was carried to the washroom so swiftly, I only caught a glimpse of Rowan and Dominic stripping the bed of its sheets before we were stepping inside.

The warm fog of steam greeted me as I was placed down in front of the already running shower, Carter's hand running down my back as he opened the door for me. "I'm really, truly sorry about your bed." I apologize again, relieved he wasn't mad, but still feeling bad about it. In response, Carter turns and gently grabs my face in both of his hands. "Stop saying sorry for things that are both natural and out of your control." I was going to say more, but my heart skipped at the feeling of blood beginning to trickle down the insides of my thighs, hopping into the shower before this perfect man could notice it. "I'll be down in a few." I say, wrapping my hands around my arms as I let the door sway closed in front of me. Carter's voice was muffled now, but I heard him say something about things being on the counter when I was ready before leaving me to do my own thing. I was appreciative he didn't plan on lingering, knowing that him taking care of me right now would really have my emotions out of whack. Stepping backwards until I could feel the hot water pulsing over my skin, I tipped my head and gratefully welcomed the way my hair grew heavy as it got wet. I chose to focus on that and the fact this shower was now stocked with all of the products I regularly use, rather than what my afternoon entails for me. I chose to forget the fact that in a few hours, I would be back to sleeping in the same bed that's the root of all of my nightmares. Pushing those thoughts off, I took care of myself as I washed my hair and scrubbed some sort of shea sugar scrub onto my legs afterwards. With my skin pink from the heat of the water and my body fully clean, I tapped a button that turned off the shower before racing for my towel. I hadn't even noticed I had been shaking until I reached out for the shower's handle, needing to steady my hand before pushing open the glass door. When I'd finally dried off, I found clothes and an assortment of different menstrual products waiting for me on the counter, tampons included in the combination. Thankful there was at least that, I took what I needed until it ended with me adorned in sweats and a very loose t-shirt, looking about just as great as I felt. Honestly, at this point I couldn't bring myself to care all that much. I had so many other things to stress about, but right now, as much as I dreaded it, the only people I want to see are the three men waiting for me downstairs. As predicted, when I walked back into the playroom the bed was as good as new, no traces of my undesired wake up to be seen. It's a little weird having them see me like this for the first time, but at least I'll be in Detroit all week so they don't have to see me all short tempered and reserved from literally everything. Though, I may just prefer that over seeing my everloving mother and stepfather for the first time in months. I didn't really have a choice, however. I needed to do this for myself so I could hopefully move on, even if it meant facing my demons once and for all. Walking down the long set of stairs, I decided to focus on the more happier reasons for my soreness, the memories of last night spreading through me.

Dominic, Rowan, and Carter—whether they realize it or not—are undoubtedly everything to me. Every single time I'm with them, I feel like I'm free to be who I am and it's the kind of love I used to believe only existed on screen. I don't think right now was the time to tell them, but when I'm back from my trip, I've decided I want to take them on a date. Maybe it's stupid, but I kind of wanted it to be something special and something for me to look forward to. With thoughts of that now in the back of my mind, I forced myself to stop being a coward and venture downstairs, hugging my arms close to my body for warmth. The first thing that caught my attention was the smell of food slowly drifting upwards to my nose, the second being the sight of my three men in the kitchen waiting for me. They didn't notice me for a while as I leaned my body over the railing, smiling as I watched Rowan get kicked out from cracking eggs to the coffee pot where literally all he had to do was click a button. He laughs and makes a crude gesture at Dominic's tease, but it's then that Carter feels my eyes on them, turning his gaze from the sink and up to where I stood. I licked my lips at his shirtless figure as he caught my attention, smirking at my obvious ogling. It was the only thing that kept me from breaking down crying in more apologies, already sensing my decreasing mood. Food helps though. So do the three, half naked men now noting my presence and looking at me with lazy smiles. Seeing them in the mornings—hair still messy from sleep—is probably one of my new favourite things about spending nights with them. I lock this mental image away for later as I waste no time walking down the stairs, gravitating towards Rowan considering neither of us would be let in the kitchen at this point. I honestly found it a little cute that Dominic and Carter were so insistent on babying me and making everything perfect while Rowan tried to butt in just to annoy them. I liked seeing that side of their friendship when it was clear they all saw each other as brothers, no doubt willing to die for one another if it came down to it. It was a kind of love I envied about them, and I suppose that made me lucky to be let into their circle now too. "You feeling okay?" Rowan looked down at me as I was pulled to lean into his side, wrapping my arms around his middle. He seemed genuinely concerned, and I couldn't help but wonder if he's ever been with a girl while she's on her period. The fact he acted like I might drop dead at any second had me guessing not. "I'm good now." I assure, trying to keep comfortably upright despite both my back and stomach cramps simultaneously determined to make my life hell. If only Dominic wasn't a freaking lie detector in human form. Though he didn't say anything, I watched as he slid myself and Rowan two cups of fresh coffee, winking when I gave him a small thank you. I still felt really bad about their bed, but I was being ushered off before I could apologize again, being led away from the kitchen and onto their outdoor patio.

My legs crossed beneath each other as I took a seat on the one couch, sighing as Rowan set down both of our mugs on the table in front of me. "I'll be right back." He murmured as he bent down to kiss my cheek, his finger stroking my jaw once before he turned to leave. I could still feel that touch minutes later, deciding not to care that I was about to burn my mouth as I lifted my warm coffee to my lips. Dominic had added just the right amount of creamer to the drink as a cautious sip slid down my throat, savoring the heat of it as I curled up. It was still a little cold from the usual chill of the morning, but that didn't take away from the gorgeous view of the city beyond their estate, still not used to it despite living here for multiple months now. It wasn't until I heard soft footsteps sounding from behind me that I tore my attention away, my eyes catching on Rowan as my heart stopped. "I know you're too stubborn to ask, so I thought this might help." He shrugs, a warm blanket draped over his shoulder and a hot water bottle in his hands. I didn't even know what to say as he moved to my front, placing the heat to my stomach hesitantly before wrapping the blanket over my body next. I could only watch in awe as his focus dropped to making sure I was warm and cared for, tucking in the sides around my back and toes in a coddling way. When his eyelashes finally fluttered back up to meet my gaze, I knew he saw the tears in my eyes. "Thank you," I say, dipping my head in appreciation and wishing I had brushed my teeth before breakfast for once, "Just... thank you." Rowan's mouth pulled into a small smile as I reached for him to join me, nodding in response to my words, "Anytime, Hazel." Anytime. Maybe it was the changes in my hormones or the fact that this man was simply so good to me, but my heart spiked from the simple action of being pulled into his lap, Rowan's hand looping around to my stomach. He held the heat pack for me so I could just relax on my own the best I could, and while my first instinct would typically be to push him away, I didn't want to. The distancing on my part never came and I chose to let him see this less bubbly side of me, feeling comfortable enough to do so beneath the snug caress of his arms. "Is there anything else you can think of you might want?" Rowan asks against my neck as he leans both of us over to grab his coffee, mine still in my hand. This time when I shook my head, it was genuine. These men were everything I needed. The only thing that made this more perfect was the sight of Dominic and Carter walking through the patio doors a little while later, plates in hand.

They both smiled at me as I gratefully took the food they offered me, my stomach urging me to eat at the smell of the breakfast quesadillas, a thin smear of avocado and diced tomatoes on top. I was well aware of the effort they put into morning meals every day, and though I typically never ate anything until lunch on my own time, only an idiot would pass this down. Thanking them again as they sat down across from us, I picked up the first piece between my fingers and forced down my moan the second the flavours hit my taste buds. This was everything I needed right now, and I realized that I was going to miss them a lot while I was gone in Detroit. I didn't need seven days to tell my mother I was moving on with my life, but I did need that much time to say goodbye. Goodbye to my past, goodbye to my firsts, goodbye to the place that may be the setting of my nightmares, but still my childhood home nonetheless. I knew the next time I returned would be to fulfill my promises I made to myself when I was sixteen, yet despite all of that, I couldn't not think about how much I'd miss them. "What time does your flight leave?" Carter asks not long after I'd finished my first slice of food, dropping my hand to my plate to grab another in distraction. "Just before one." I respond, my heart already beating a little faster as thoughts of this reality kicked in. I refused to show it, but that didn't mean it wasn't there. I was met with a brief silence before he continued, though I didn't miss the way Rowan's one thumb began to rub idly at my thigh. "You're sure this is something you want to do?" Carter says, trying to be casual about it but failing at hiding his distaste at the idea. I wasn't exactly thrilled with this either, how-ever I feared if this wasn't something I did now, I would let it eat at me until I broke again. "I am." Even if my throat is already tighten-ing with fear for the little girl I used to be. He nodded in respect of that decision, but there was a lot worn on his expression that told me he hated it as much as he understood it. Not bothering to add anything more, I bit the pointed corner of tortilla, eggs, and cheese, chewing despite knowing this conversation wasn't done. "We trust you more than anything, princess," Dominic begins, and I know he means every word of that, yet I was waiting for the inevitable but to be added to his statement, "But we don't feel comfortable with you leaving on your own." It was a blow I had expected and was justified, however I didn't know what to say to that. "It's just that we want to keep you safe, and we can't do that with you five hundred miles away from us." I knew they were only being con-siderate, but it flared a little annoyance in me despite it. It was that insecure part of me that worried I wasn't strong enough to handle things myself.

"So what? You're asking me to stay?" I question with a slight edge to my tone, refusing to make eye contact with any of them. Because I couldn't. If I did, they would see how scared I was—how much the idea of facing everything on my own made me feel queasy and small. "No, we meant it when we said we'd support you, darling." Rowan's voice says calmly, not raising his tone or showing offense by my accusation, "We want to come with you, not hold you back." I think the surprise on my face was what lowered Carter's tensed eyebrows, but I couldn't even fathom the idea of even one of them being in my hometown, watching them realize everything I owned was built off of absolutely nothing. Having them shower in a tub too small for even a child to lay in and sleep on the floor because my single bed mattress would only fit one. Absolutely not. Of course, things weren't completely bad growing up, but I wasn't ready for them to bear witness to all of that. I think sometimes there are things better left unseen. "I appreciate it, but I don't think that's a good idea." I say quietly, but I know they heard. I know, because Rowan stopped eating and Dominic was looking at me as though he were reading my soul and I hated it. "I'll be fine," I lie, shifting on Rowan's lap and not caring they could see the fib on my tongue, "I'll call you every night, and it'll be fine." Lie, lie, lie. But if I don't pretend, I'll break like the fragile piece they're looking at me as. Even after they dropped me at Jade's, they insisted they would be picking me up in an hour to drive me to the airport. "You don't pretend, Hazel," Dominic said as he walked me to my door, "Maybe to others if that's what you need to get through this, but never with us." His words haven't left my mind since I left and isolated myself in my room, my packed suitcase sitting in the corner like a warning sign to me. Just say goodbye over the phone, it urged me. You don't owe them anything. I did owe it to myself, though. That might just be the hardest damn part about this. Letting my head hit my pillow, my tired eyes fell shut, if only for a few simple seconds. I needed it to stop—the heaviness in my chest that makes me feel like I can't breathe. I needed everything to stop.

When I was younger, climbing trees used to be my favourite thing to do. Mom never had enough money to buy me dolls or makeup for birthdays and Christmases, but I was okay with that. Half the time, all I wanted was her attention. I remember that January th and December th were the two times of the year she would give it to me. She would drive me around in her small, slightly broken car, and we would go searching for the largest trees I could climb. I didn't care that there was snow, in fact, I liked the bare branches with less things in the way of my reach. She would sit on the grass and play the small radio she won from work years back and play "Come on Eileen" over and over again because it was the only tape she owned. I would climb and climb until I couldn't go any further, knowing all it would take was one misstep and everything would be over. Back then, I didn't care. Back then, mom was happy and dad, while distant, was around too. I was eleven the last time I climbed a tree. That was when the fighting started—the drinking and the crying. God, there were always so many tears. I remember I'd cry too sometimes just because everyone else was, too young to understand it, but I would cry. Day after day, it was like I was in a cycle, all the way up until the day seven men showed up at my door, quietly calm but had my mom shaking and screaming, "Tobias!" I couldn't figure out why, though. I was rushed to my room, but I couldn't stop wondering if they were the same men from The Matrix, adorned in the same black coats and latex pants that looked way too tight to be comfortable. My dad left with them and only showed up for short visits after that, but I was okay because I knew he'd always come back for me. No matter how long he disappeared, he was the one thing that never truly left, even if I couldn't see him with my eyes.

I always wondered if he had been taken to some virtual under-world to fight off the bad guys like in the movies, but when Andrew started coming around the house, I couldn't help but wonder if he was the real bad man. He was conventionally attractive and swooped my mother off her feet after a mere week of flirtatious smiles and charming remarks—ones I was much too young to understand as a child. It was love at first sight as they say, and my mom attempted sobriety because she just loved him too much. But that year when December came around, I did not climb any trees. The lyrics of "Come on Eileen" never played because Andrew believed me much too old to need my mother to escort me like a toddler. I remember screaming that he wasn't my father and couldn't tell me what I could and couldn't do on Christmas of all days. But he took that away from me too. "It'll do you some good to learn some discipline, girl." He spat, and I can still feel the way his scratchy hands felt around my arm—not hard enough to bruise, but I was small and easy to move. "Drew, leave her be." My mother waved her hand at him, but I was too busy trying to fight him off to hear his response. "Pull at the fingers," my father would always teach me, "They're weak. Pull the thumb back and it'll snap like a twig." I tried, but was not strong enough then. "I know what oughta help you." He smiled down at me, so convincingly I almost believed he was being good. He walked me to my bedroom and hauled me to where my wardrobe cabinet stood, small, but it's not like I had a ton of clothes to fill it with anyways. I was confused when he opened it and I screamed when I was shoved inside, not understanding what was happening until the wooden doors closed and I was encased in the dark, a musty smell quickly building up in the small space. "Hey!" I screamed, moving to get out but being met with something hard that kept me locked in, "Let me out!" My feet met the door and I kicked, the wood barely bending beneath the force. I yelled again but froze at the sound of a small chuckle on the other side. "It won't kill ya, girl. I'm gonna go treat your mother nice and good on our date and you'll be let out when we're back." I couldn't stop fighting, though. I hated the dark, and the dust from the floor of the cabinet made me both want to cough and sneeze at the same time. "I'll be good. Please open the—" When there was no chuckle, no sign of life on the other side of the door, I paused. Those few seconds were the calm before the real terror came, where I exhausted myself close to limp as I pounded and pounded to get out. Out, out, out. But as I said, that day, no trees were climbed and no songs were played. In their place, all it left was the dark.

"Hazel!" I was shaken by two hands over top of me, gasping as my eyes snapped open in panic. I was out. It wasn't the tight, dirty walls that surrounded me, it was the walls of my bedroom, Jade hovering on top of my bed. Her curly hair hung around her face as she leaned over, fear in her eyes as she looked down at me, seeming relieved that I woke up. "Jesus Christ." She swore under her breath, her eyebrows loosening as her head hung down, "I thought someone was attacking you." I sucked in a heavy breath, wiping away the moisture that wet my cheeks as I sat up, Jade moving off of me. "Are you okay?" She pants, looking at me as though I were half mad, even though I knew that wasn't what she was thinking. "Yeah, sorry." I mumbled, clutching at my necklace and fidgeting with it as I focused on my breathing, hating I was found this way. It was just a nightmare. It was nothing more than a nightmare. "I... I have bad dreams sometimes. Thank you for waking me." Her eyes tracked the shake in my hands, but she didn't comment on it and I was thankful for that. "Do you want to talk about—" "No, I'm good." I insist, plastering on an embarrassed smile and pulling the sheets off from over my body. So many pretty lies, so little naked truths. "You were screaming to be let out," Jade dropped her eyes at the admission, but it only made me tighten up more. "I know." Was the only response I could fathom, however it was the only answer I was ready to give. Jade and I had gotten impossibly close over this last month of living together, but I didn't have time to open up about my life when the plane I needed to catch was confrontation enough. "Can we maybe talk when I get back?" I suggest, knowing my men would be here soon enough to pick me up. "I think we're long overdue for a spa day." She teases, trying to lighten the mood and I was appreciative for it. The ringing of a doorbell cut off whatever I was about to say next, but I smiled, grabbed a jacket, and prayed to god it didn't look like I was crying. "I'll see you in a few days." I said as I hugged her, clutching onto the handle of my suitcase as though my life depended on it. "I'll miss you, girl." She says, returning my embrace before letting me go, "You call anytime, okay? Day or night." I could only nod in response, not trusting myself to speak anymore.

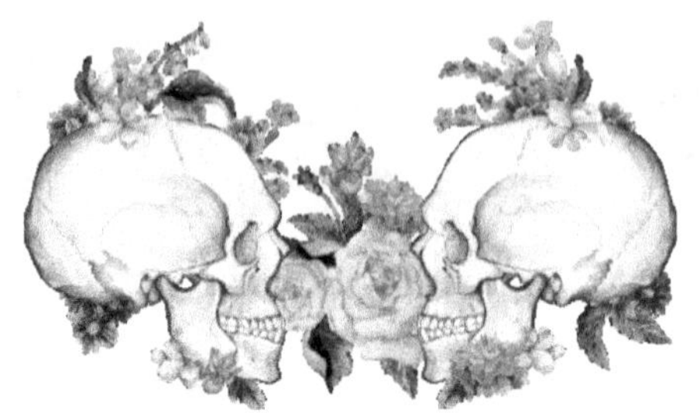

~ Twenty ~

Carter

"So, how are things going with the project?" Vincent asks me, and the smug look on his features makes me want to punch his face in. I have done a damn good job of making sure that's all my father believes Hazel to be. A project. To him, she was nothing to me—nothing more than a disposable pawn to exploit and then end when her death deems itself fit. I hated this game I was playing, but it was one of the very few things I didn't have a choice in. Until my father is buried six feet under, everything would be a game with him. It's up to me to be the better player. "She's playing right into our cards like we planned." I lied, plastering on a cruel smile as though this conversation was nothing more than entertainment for the evening. What Vincent didn't see was the way my fists had balled beneath the table in my lap, my nails digging so hard into my palms I could tell blood had been drawn. I was too numb to feel it, though. I forced myself into a state of nothing, because the alternative is snapping. If I kill my father now, I will only be unlocking a bottomless chest of more complications, ones in which I cannot afford. "Well of course she is." My father chuckles, plopping a grape into his mouth and grinning at how easy I was making this for him, "She may have a sharp tongue, but that doesn't sway from the fact she's still a brainless whore." Do. Not. React. Carter, do not fucking react. I urged myself to think about the brightness of her smile, the green of her eyes, and the sound of her laugh. I went back to our memories of last night and how I think I needed to be held by her too afterwards. Through my unwavering facade of cruelty, I let myself be consumed by the way her soft hands felt pressed against my chest and her lips against my mouth. She was what grounded me, and I just needed to hold onto that for a little bit longer. Hazel would be back soon, and everything would be okay. "As much as your presence is welcomed, I'm sure there's more reason for it than stating obvious facts." I prod, taking a long, slow sip of the whiskey filling my glass and savoring the smooth glide of it down my throat. Vincent's answering smile made my blood run cold, not liking the satisfied look on his face. "Of course." He says, tilting his head and swishing the dark colour of his own drink twice before placing it down excitedly.

Very little in this world scared me anymore, but I was terrified right now—so terrified I worried I might break. "After years of searching, this mission finally has an end date." Vincent shared the news I've wanted for the last five years of my life—the same news I now dread, "September th and your mother's killer will be dead and the bitch will be yours to do with as you please." As long as I make it painful is what he doesn't say. "What do you know?" I question, needing to make a new plan. This was moving much too fast and three weeks was not enough to fix what is already ruined. My father laughs gleefully, and I fear I was not being as convincing as I pretended to be, but when he suddenly stops and looks me dead in the eyes, I knew he was simply amused over his own cleverness and pride. "In three weeks time, Marcus is throwing one last party for his recruits the day before he plans to make his move on us, Roman Ivankov by his side." My eyes snapped up in alarm at the second part, the name of the Russian Mafia leader in pair with Marcus Caddel. "Roman joined forces with a small gang?" I ask, having personally met the brutal man and not believing for a second he would offer his help out of the kindness of his non-existent heart. Vincent loved having this knowledge over me, but I needed to know what the fuck was going on and I was going to make it happen one way or another. "He joined forces with a man who knows how to hide things and a daughter who can provide the family an heir." He shrugged as though this wasn't the worst possible thing he could have told me. My blood ran ice, ice cold at the admission, so frozen and so impenetrable I couldn't move from my seat. "Are you suggesting that Hazel is to be bred off and married to Lev in exchange for fucking money?" I say, realizing my mistake before it's too late. I showed I cared. "My my." Vincent's grin spread like an uncontained fire, burning at my chest and all the way up to my throat, "Isn't this exciting." He looked at me the same way he did when I was still a boy; he looked at me like I was weak. "Tell me the plan and get out." I growl, not bothering with the fake smiles and crude words anymore. If he didn't leave, the world would be seeing a new leader very soon and that was a title I refused to take on today. Vincent made me wait in silence as he took a slow sip of his drink, an intentional act that made me see red. He knew it and smirked in response. "Since everyone will be centralized at a designated point, it'll only require someone to loop the camera footage for an hour, a person to retrieve the wife, and a third to grab Marcus." Rowan, Dominic, me. "And as for the others?" I dare ask, already fearing where this was going. "Gas leak. A tragic accident if you ask me." He shrugs as though he weren't discussing murdering thousands of people. I have no right to act innocent—I've killed more than I can remember to count—but innocents are going to die as a result of his plan. Children, families, waitresses and waiters just trying to do their job. What he was planning was a massacre, and he wanted me to lead it. "If we're going to grab Marcus and his wife anyways, then why do we need Hazel?" I challenge, needing to find a loophole. There's always another way. "This was your plan, boy. Or has your love for her made you as damn stupid as I feared?" The bait. Hazel's going to be the bait to not only plant doubt in Marcus's recruits, but to lure her father straight into our hands. Fuck. "If the plans haven't changed, then why are we having this conversation? The world knows she's in our territory, her father will try to save her. Apart from a date being set, this isn't anything new."

I know my father, and for that reason, I know there's something so much bigger to this than what he's letting on. When that stupid fucking smile of his reappears, I mentally brace myself for the information I'm about to get. This is what I've been waiting to hear, but instead of words, my father just reaches into his suit pocket. He makes me wait as he slowly retracts his hand, a small black box being pulled out with it—one that I hate to admit terrifies me. Popping the case open, he slides the smooth velvet across the table and into my hold. "Being by your side makes the world think she's some temporary fuck toy of yours. A ring however..." He grins, pausing dramatically, "Imagine the amount of media we'd get from one of the world's wealthiest bachelors known for never seeing the same girl twice announcing his engagement after years of rejecting women." I'm going to be sick. "No." I snap, tossing the box back at him, "I'm not marrying anybody, and certainly not the daughter of the man who murdered my mother." When I marry Hazel, it's going to be with me on my knees worshiping the ground she fucking walks on, not one built up of lies and manipulation. I know the day she finds out about her dad and our involvement in his disappearance is going to cause everything to blow up, but I will spend the rest of my miserable life begging her if that's what it takes to get her back. She's my forever and I'm her always. It doesn't make sense, but none of this fucking does. "So you're telling me you're fine having a woman who's not of Italian descent married to the heir of our mafia? Publicly?" Something's not adding up here, and I can tell there's more to this. But of course there is. It wouldn't be Vincent if everything wasn't so damn cryptic. "Obviously not. You'll propose in public, walk her around with a ring on her finger for a bit and then take care of the problem once Marcus is in our hold." I was supposed to play with her heart just to stab a knife into it until the life faded from her eyes. The image of that caused something to change inside of me—something I knew my father noticed. I turned cold. My anger and terror and sadness all numbed into an expression I've mastered over the years of growing up in this life. If I were to be the one to drag Hazel to death's door, then I would become death itself to keep her from passing through. I will become everything I've feared myself capable of becoming if it meant keeping Hazel safe, even if that meant destroying myself in the process. "And if I refuse?" I raise an eyebrow, my voice being forced into a state of cruelty and dominance. It was one Vincent met eye to eye with, clearly infuriated that I would even dare say no. It meant all of his years of conditioning me broke, all by the thing he hated most: love. "I'm invoking your first oath of two in exchange for your friend's life." My father stood, the ring being forgotten on the table. I rose with him, refusing to let even physical stance put him above me. I knew what his words meant, and I didn't fucking care. When Rowan pulled a gun on Vincent last week to protect our girl, he committed an act of treason in the eyes of the Mafia. If it weren't for my deal, he would be dead and Hazel would've been close behind, bait or not.

"You'll propose to that girl, and you will do it in public. If you go against your word, not even our blood will be able to save you." Because he would kill me himself. I understood what he was saying perfectly clear, but I was done being controlled by him. I will fight to keep Hazel protected until I go to my grave, Dominic and Rowan by my side. "Your friends will be getting their own orders soon enough, and it'll do you all good to not push me on this." Vincent says as he walks to the front door, myself following but done speaking to him. A smirk was still worn on his face, smugness in his stance, but what today made me remember was that my father underestimated me. He believes me to be weak and fearful, and while I may be scared, I am anything but powerless. My fear for Hazel's life is what will keep her alive, even if I won't be a part of it. Leaning against the wall and watching as Vincent's hand opens the door, he moves halfway outside before turning back to me. "You will take the girl to that little coffee shop she visits everyday and propose to her there on the th where plenty of people can see." He demands, but once again, I don't respond. I don't even offer a nod. I know this irks him, and I take great pride in that knowledge. He physically doesn't falter, though, maintaining that fake grin of his until it turns into something real—something lethal. "You don't seem as enthusiastic as I am, but that's okay." Vincent says lowly, his tone not matching his words, "Maybe your gift will excite you for the real thing." He stepped away at that, and I didn't waste a second before slamming the door in his face. Like a fucking engage-ment ring makes me happy. It was a death sentence, one in which I still couldn't find a way out of. Angrily walking down the hall and to the living room, my head snaps towards the unannounced open-ing of the elevator doors when the chime greets me shortly after. Nobody stood where my eyes traveled, but in a blink, recognition crossed my face and panic gripped at my heart. Hazel. Running over to the unconscious woman on the elevator floor, her blonde wavy hair splays across her back over the same clothes she left in yesterday. I can't breathe as I crash to my knees beside her body, realizing the pool of blood around her head a second before I see a face I don't recognize. Despite the same hair and attire, the person before me does not have the light dusting of freckles across her cheeks or the cupid's bow shape of Hazel's lips. *Maybe your gift will excite you for the real thing.* I had assumed he was talking about the engagement ring he left behind, but this was so much worse. I was given the illusion of Hazel's death by a bullet wound to the head, only the point was made through someone completely different. This woman was likely an innocent, caught in the middle of my father's "lessons" and paid the price with her life. I was shaking as I remained kneeled on the ground and couldn't move until I heard the sound of footsteps coming from behind me. Dominic and Rowan just got home, and I was about to fucking explode.

Hazel

Nobody is here. Alone for two days, there's been no sign of my mother or stepfather nor a call to explain the absence. At first I was relieved, then furious, now nervous. I was unsurprised when no one showed at the airport for my arrival, but when I walked into a cold, empty house an hour later, I found myself completely and utterly alone. Their lack of attendance was both a blessing and a curse, but it at least allowed me time to become situated and overcome some of my mental barriers without the eyes of others around me. I was especially thankful for it the first time I went into my room, when I dropped to my knees and cried until my eyes were swollen and my nose was stuffy. Now that forty-eight hours have passed, I'm able to bear the weight of it without breaking down. Just barely, though. As promised, I've called Rowan, Dominic, and Carter each day, already missing their small comforting gestures, their laughs, and simply everything that made them them. The thought of simply leaving and going home has crossed my mind a thousand times, but if I don't say goodbye within the remaining five days I have here, I won't allow myself the opportunity to do it again. Just being back is hard enough, and I don't think I'm willing to go through this for a second time just because my mother couldn't be bothered to show up for the visit she herself instigated. Scrolling through my phone and opening the same app I had just closed for the third time in a row, I knew that boredom was eating away at my brain. I was sick of this freezing house and the ugly feeling of it. I needed out. Standing from the couch I was currently curled up on, also known as the makeshift bed I've created for myself, I grabbed my coat from the coffee table across from me. It wasn't exactly cold outside, but it sure as hell wasn't warm either considering it was just past seven o'clock in the evening. Glancing out the window at the still mostly bright sky, I decided against my warmer shoes in exchange for my much more comfortable runners. All I wanted was a quick walk before I retreated back into my nightmares, slipping my phone and some money into my zipped pockets before moving out the door. Like when I left many months ago, the lock was still in shit poor condition, a pathetic false sense of security on the outside of the house. At this point, I honestly couldn't be more unbothered.

Pulling the door hard before I finally heard the latch click in place, I didn't spare the handle a second glance before leaving down the gravel driveway that blended into the path. When I was younger, I remember always kicking at the small stones as I walked, dragging my feet because I liked the sound it made. As a few caught under my shoes now, I couldn't help but think about how un-changed so many things were, even after so much time had passed. That familiarity was what guided me as I walked, catching sight of things from signs to houses that brought back memories I'd forgot-ten until now. I feel like this was the best part of my day so far, and while my intentions were to loop back right about now, I couldn't ignore the sight of the small pub entrance out of the corner of my right eye. I surprised myself as a small grin spread across my face, so many good memories being linked to that place. The owner was always working there in some way, and he took extra diligent care in keeping my teenage self out along with my fake IDs. It always infuriated me because he couldn't give less of a shit about serving anyone else underage, but even once I was bordering twenty-one, it wasn't until the start of January Slash started serving me something more than pop and water. I never pushed him on it after my first failed attempt, and in return he never turned me away from using the place as a shelter to get away from life for a while. Our relationship was weird in the sense we rarely exchanged words with each other, but he kind of felt like my guardian angel growing up when I needed it most. In fact, he even offered me a job when I was eighteen to bartend, hence where I got that experience prior to working at Rush. Now, as I'm standing right in front of the few happy memories I have here, I couldn't stop myself before my feet were carrying me towards the doors against my better judgement. Honestly, I was a little past caring at this point. Walking straight into the warm building, the first thing I was met with was the smell of fresh beer and musk, the sound of conversation and sports from the televisions carrying to my ears.

The small dents and holes in the walls that had been there when I left were now filled or covered by something, and there were a few new staff members I didn't recognize as well from my time working here. A lot seemed to have changed, but so much of it felt like every bit of the escape I craved growing up. "Hazel fucking Walsh!" I hear a voice sound from behind me, turning to find one of my old colleagues, Camilla, headed my way. "Hey Cami," I grin, returning her embrace once she gets close enough. Her short brown hair was the same as when we last spoke and so was her signature eyeliner drawn across her eyes. I offered a genuine smile as I pulled back from her hug, happy to have run into her. "How've you been, girl? Noah around too?" She asks, her eyes scanning the crowd though I could tell she was secretly hoping my answer would be no. So much change. "Not together anymore." I shrug my shoulders, surprised that the admission doesn't sting even a little bit. It wasn't a bad revelation, however. "I actually have someone new waiting at home in New York," I shared, purposefully leaving out the fact that it was multiple someones. "Oh my god, really?" She smiles, leading me over to the bar, "I'm really glad to hear that.

We all thought you deserved so much better." We're in agreement with that for sure. I simply nodded my response as she sat me down on a stool, muttering something about how she had some tables to get to but that Slash was probably around to talk to if I was here to dig. Cami had assumed I was here to get information about my father, and honestly, while I haven't thought about it until now, it was a good idea. Slash knew everything and anything there was to know about things around here, likely including where the fuck my hosts disappeared to. "Well shit." I hear his familiar voice curse from beside me as if on cue, my head turning to rove over the man himself, "Didn't think I'd be seeing you around here anytime soon." "Nice to see you too, Slash," I grin, swiveling in my chair as he walks to the counter to mix up my usual. His movements were as fluid and instinctive as I remembered them to be, sliding a glass down wordlessly before pouring himself a shot. I could already hear his words before he opened his mouth just based on his choice of drink. "Do you need a place to hide, Lyn, because this is the last place you should be if that's the case." Always getting straight to the point with him. Taking a sip of the combination of gin and tonic, I tilt my head and say, "No, but why would you assume that?" Slash poured himself another shot before tossing down that one too, brushing his long, graying hair back from his face. "I heard you've been runnin' around with the Night Reapers." He says lowly so no one could hear, but I was more focused on what he had to say rather than those around us. "I'm sorry, the what now?" I ask, my brow arching at the name I could tell held power to make someone like Slash seem cautious to even speak it. He looked around again before leaning slightly over the counter, his forearms keeping him propped as he finally looked back at me. "Your boyfriends?" He says it as though it were a question, but he couldn't possibly know about them being in the Mafia, could he? I wasn't lying when I said Slash knew everything and anything around, but I didn't believe that extended to me as well. There are eyes everywhere, and I can't believe I haven't been more cautious. How could I have left here on my own when I've been publicly seen with the very men most people fear?

"How do you know about them?" I question before taking another mouthful of my drink. How many people know about me? "Everybody's heard about those men of yours, just very little know who lurks beneath their masks until they see death themselves." Like the masks they wore that night at the hotel after I hid and watched them murder somebody. "And how do you know them?" I repeat, eager for the information I've been too scared to seek out these last few weeks. What he called the Night Reapers were undoubtedly Dominic, Rowan, and Carter, and just the reminder of what they were capable of had shivers trailing down my spine. "How I know doesn't matter, but what does is that you're fucking around with the wrong group of people, Lyn. They're going to get you killed." This time, it was me who was lowering my voice, and it was to a point I almost didn't recognize myself. "I only started living when they walked into my life, Slash. They will not let me die because I have been through too much shit in my life to not get a happy ending, and even when it's my time to go, it'll be by their side." I meant every bit of my truth, and I refused to let anything taint what we had. I was going to wait these five days out and then I would go back home and never leave them again. "What have they told you about their lifestyle, kid? Do you realize you'll never be able to marry them for reasons way bigger than the fact there's three?" I didn't like where this was going, but when I looked into Slashes eyes, I saw he was terrified. He feared for me just as much as I've already feared for myself countless times, his words coming from a place of concern. "Yeah, like what?" I ask, genuinely curious to have this bandaid ripped off. I hadn't even realized I'd finished my whole drink before a second was being poured for me. "Do you plan on having kids, because you would be signing that child up for a hell of a lot of pain if you are. Even if it were with the associate, only the Don has the power to relieve a recruit from their duties? Would you leave the other two just to be with the one?" Slash already knew the answer to that question, though. "You marry Dominic or Carter, do you realize that makes you a figurehead for both good and bad? Do you realize what would happen if even half of the soldiers found out you date women too?" He softened his voice during the last part, but that didn't stop my flinch. "What is that supposed to mean?" I ask, but this time it was I who already knew the answer.

"The Mafia's views are very old and twisted compared to the way life is starting to become now. Hazel, I'm not saying this to hurt you, but you need to wake up before one of my birdies tells me you're dead." He put his hand on my arm, though I didn't meet his eyes as I drank way too much in one go. It burned my throat, but I swallowed it back the tears and frustration I felt. My men weren't like that... but what about the people who were? "I need something strong and preferably in a line." I say, grabbing a handful of the cash I'd brought before sliding it to Slash. I was sick of feeling and needed an outlet. Drinking seemed like a horribly perfect idea. Slash hesitated a second before taking the money and obeying, serving up a line of shots and watching as I downed the first one while making a face at the taste. "You're different since I last saw you." He says, not in a bad way, but the reminder of who I used to be had me drinking another that went straight to my head. I didn't want to talk about my past, though. I wanted to know what was going on, and I was sick of letting myself be in the dark. "My mother and Andrew are gone because of them, aren't they? Because of the Night Reapers?" I take a guess, and his face tells me I'm right. "Showed up a few nights ago and proved their title to be as accurate as the words of others peg them to be. Heidi is out retrieving Andrew's bruised ego and was rumored to be scrapping up some money as well." "They aren't dead, though?" I ask, praying to god my boyfriends respected that even though I'm sure they're itching to kill them. I never wanted my mother dead, but Andrew... he was mine to put out. "Not yet." Slash rubs the back of his neck as he stands up straight, stealing one of my shots for himself, "I heard from someone the leader of the three laughed as Andrew cried on the street in a puddle of his own piss and blood. They promised what they'd just done to him was merely foreplay compared to the hell their girl was going to inflict one day by their side." I froze at that, looking up from where my pointer finger had begun to pick at my thumb nail. "As usual for the Reapers, they struck under the cover of their masks and the night, but I was there as they tossed him on the road and spat on his clothes. Hazel, I might damn well be the only one to know this, but they promised him that death would be a mercy compared to what you would unleash on him one day." My heart stopped as this information overwhelmed me, but Slash wasn't done speaking yet. I feel like I should be furious with them for doing something like this behind my back, but I wasn't. I didn't even realize a small smile had formed until I sensed the small taste of revenge coating my tongue. "What's the last part you have yet to say?" I ask, feeling the fact that I'm very much a lightweight kick in from those three shots alone.

Was it bad I hoped it was something horrible? I wished death upon Andrew with every part of my being, but I wasn't ready to physically follow through yet. As long as he's still alive, Dominic, Rowan, and Carter can have him—though it seems they already have. "There was a fourth person with them that night, Lyn. A doctor." Slash explained, biting the corner of his lip before sighing, "My birdies are never wrong, kid, and I was told once the Reapers were done, they castrated him." Oh my god. I watched as Slash mentally winced at the image, but I was simply in shock. I know they have done so much worse than that, but what they did was no small act. Instead of responding, I simply took another shot while trying to process this news, better yet, process the fact I wasn't revolted in the least. "Jesus," I blew out a heavy breath, slightly angry at myself for not feeling bad when I probably should. But, yet again, Andrew was a terrorizing asshole who brought it on himself. "Yeah, I'm gonna need another round of shots." "Nope, I've already given you more than I should have." Slash rejects my money as I try to buy yet another drink, making me shake my head in discontent. Cami had gotten off her shift about an hour ago, and we've been laughing and drowning ourselves in our problems ever since. "Come on, boss. Let us have our fun." She insists, both of us giggling like his "No" was comedic. Fuck, we were so drunk. "Pleeease," I pouted, pulling out some more cash, "I'm only here for five more days," I added, my words slurring only slightly as I spoke. I leaned with Camilla on the counter as Slash made a face as though he didn't know what to do with us. He was so funny. "The fact you're here is the reason you need to be sober, kid." He says, but I only rolled my eyes at the reminder. "Yeah, yeah. Gotta be on guard for when my alcoholic of a mother decides I'm worth her time, right?" I snickered even though it wasn't actually all that humorous. Slash went to say something else, but I dismissed him with a wave of my hand. He was right. I mean, I was already drunk so why would I need more liquor? "I'm gonna go dance." I decide aloud, grabbing onto Cami's wrist without a thought in the world.

"Patio?" She suggests with a wiggle of her eyebrows, but my body stiffens as I feel a much larger one slide up behind me, a body in which I didn't recognize. My head turned to see a man just a few inches taller than me sliding his hands onto my waist, his head dipping to my ear before I could stop him. "I'll dance with you, babe." He says, but I wiggle him off. "My boyfriends will cut off your dick if you touch me again." I push away, my words barely legible thanks to the alcohol, but I think he got the point. I was just about to go back to dragging Cami off with me before the annoying shrill of my phone ringing went off. I didn't even bother to see who was calling before I put it on silent, hearing my friend laugh at my side as we somehow ended up back at the counter by Slash. "Sit and don't move. I'll drive you home once the crowd dies down a little." He pointed at two stools, not even bothering to ask as two waters and a small bowl of peanuts were placed in front of us. His face was stern about this, but he relaxed a little when I picked up a nut and tossed it into my mouth, chewing with a smile. I watched as he muttered something about me being the death of him under his breath, but he never let me leave as he moved to go serve other customers. The food made me hungry and the salt made me thirsty, all working in one big cycle that made me see things a little less foggily. Cami's head had fallen onto my shoulder a long time ago as we both rehydrated ourselves, Slash coming over to refill the snack bowl twice for us while making amused comments on how we were so going to regret this tomorrow morning. I couldn't even deny it. At this point, all I wanted to do was crash into my bed back in my real home and sleep off these next five days. I thought I would want a week to get the closure I needed, but the truth is that I just wanted out.

Cami's mumbling about how she had to pee brought me out of my head as she stood slowly, groaning at the line up she'd have to wait in. "I'll be here." I say, watching as she drags herself over the bathroom hall and crosses her arms in forced patience. After a few moments, my eyes drifted back in front of me, slipping down to where the wooden bowl of peanuts were as I noticed something off. Where my napkin once was had been replaced by a small piece of paper, my hand curiously turning it over to realize it was a note. "If you don't answer your phone within the next five minutes, princess, what I promised you will no longer stand, and I will be in Detroit quicker than you can hide." My eyes widened and searched on either side of me as to who could have possibly delivered this so stealthily, but the truth is that I was still drunk and my guard was down. It could have been any person here. Fuck. Pulling out my phone, still muted to silent mode, my heart raced as I saw three calls from Dominic, the most recent one being from a half an hour ago. I was screwed. Hovering my finger over his caller ID, I took a breath a second before I hit call, my phone ringing once before I heard the click of him answering. Instantly, heavy breathing sounded through the line, matching my own uneven exhales. "Hey, princess." Dominic's deep voice answered, sending butterflies off in my stomach, "Having fun?" In combination with the alcohol still running through my veins, his words felt like ecstasy. "I am actually." I say, standing from the bar stool and gesturing to Slash I'd be right back. It was too loud in here to hold a conversation over the phone. Stepping just outside of the doors, I leaned against one of the concrete columns that held the patio balcony above. "You're in so much trouble," He warns in a neutral tone, but it was the sounds in the background that made me take him a little more seriously. "What are you going to do, Sir? Punish me?" I say quietly, smiling to myself at the fact he was in New York and I was on my period. He couldn't even make me punish myself over the phone. It was silent for a moment as more noises came before he said, "I am." That was it. Two words were his only response and it had me pressing my thighs together where I stood. "Dominic?" I asked, my face flushing as his answering groan sounded over the line, "Are you touching yourself?" I felt hot as I asked the question, but once the words passed my lips, I knew I was right. I could hear the sound of his fist stroking himself over and over again, some sort of oil making him wet enough for me to know what was happening in my absence. "In my bed with your underwear wrapped around my cock." He moaned, the visual making me bite my lip in desire. I wish I could see him right now, because fuck did he ever sound good. For a moment, I just stayed silent, closing my eyes and picturing how his hand would be working up and down, getting off just by listening to my voice. I shifted when I remembered I was in public, but nobody stood outside except for me.

It was only the two of us, and the fact I was getting so wet it became uncomfortable. "Dominic," I said again, my cheeks heating from the noises his name elicited from him. His breathing fell deeper with every passing second, and I was able to hear as his movements grew more frantic. "Once I'm done talking to you, I have people who are going to take you home, okay?" Dominic says, talking to me as though this was an everyday conversation. "I don't need to be babysat." I argued, my words falling short when another noise of pleasure was pulled from his lips, "And you can't punish me for drinking when you do it too." I knew I was in real trouble when a quiet laugh sounded over the line, but it was barely one of amusement. It was meant to remind me of my place and that he could punish me for whatever reason he'd like. "Your so-called babysitters aren't there out of distrust for you, but rather the people you're staying with. And yes, princess, you're allowed to drink, but that's not why I'm going to punish you. I'm going to turn your ass red because you made yourself vulnerable in a dangerous place without one of us there to protect you." He sounded exactly like Slash. All three of my men had wanted to come with me but chose to respect my wishes anyways. They knew about my history with this place and still didn't fight me on it, even though they saw right through my lies about me being okay. "I'm sorry, Sir." I murmured, amazed at how I found myself submitting to him even from hundreds of miles away. I can tell my words pleased him by his groans, my body becoming intoxicated through Dominic in a way no amount of drinking could offer. "It's okay, Hazel." He says, his hand moving audibly faster over himself at my apology, "You're still my good girl." Fuck. Me. "You like it when I praise you, don't you? Are your legs pressing together right now from the sound of my voice?" They were. Tighter than he knew. I've never hated being a girl more than I do right now, and I could practically picture Dominic's satisfied smirk at the knowledge I would be turned on for the next week straight now with no relief. "Yes, Sir." I admitted, my words dropping to a mere whimper under his affect. My hand reached back to balance myself against the post as I realized he was about to make himself come over the phone, and I couldn't do anything but listen. I could picture him on his bed, his head tossed back against his pillow with the phone to his ear. I imagined his eyes pinched shut with pleasure as his hips bucked up slightly to fuck his fist against my underwear. His cheeks would be flushed and his mouth would be parted slightly, all of this happening because I refused to let him be by my side to do it in person. "Say something to me, princess," Dominic pants, and I know he's getting close just by his tone. I didn't know what he wanted to hear, so I simply settled on the truth. "I miss you."

I heard him hum at my words, a low groan being drawn from his mouth in response. "Fuck... I miss you too, Hazel. You have no idea how much." It's only been two days—it's not like we haven't been apart for longer, but everything is so much different now. Everything I felt for them was so intense it could be overwhelming, and right now, my desire consumed me. "I've stroked myself every night since you left, imagining it was your perfect cunt wrapping around me instead of my fingers. I thought about your pretty face staring up at me, calling out your name right before my orgasm begins to spill down my fist." "Dominic," I whimpered, but he was already coming with my name on his tongue a second later. Even though I wasn't touching myself, my eyes fell closed as though I were, needing to hold onto something as he cursed out a deep growl. I listened as he spilled himself against his hand, and I was panting right along with him. Every heavy breath of his carried through the phone, and I wished so bad I could be there. Even just to watch. Dominic was making me reconsider his offer to stay with me, not because of the sex, but because I simply missed him so damn much. I did with all of them, but the sound of my name pulled my thoughts back to my phone. "I may be your boyfriend, Hazel, and I still plan to take good care of you when you get home, but I'm also your dominant." He begins, however the amused pause on his part told me he wasn't done speaking. My knees were flush together, and my skin was still hot, but what was worse is that I had a feeling Dominic fucking knew it. Waiting for a distraction from my aching body, I squirmed where I stood a moment before he continued. "I suggest you enjoy being able to sit on your ass while you still can, princess." I couldn't even manage a response before he hung up, leaving me wet, unsatisfied, and unbelievably longing for him. Motherfuc—

As though he could hear my thoughts, his sudden text shut me up, my finger clicking on my messages app before my hand flew over my mouth and I looked around to make sure nobody else was around. With a pounding heart, I looked back down at my phone, my clit throbbing at the picture of Dominic shot from his neck down. The angle let me see everything from his tattooed abs to his hand still wrapped around his cock, my light pink lacy underwear soaked in his release. I've received my fair share of dick pics—most unwanted—but Dominic's had me wanting to touch myself right here in the open. I watched as three dots appeared on my screen not long before a second text came through. From Dominic: Five days, Hazel. Five long, excruciating days.

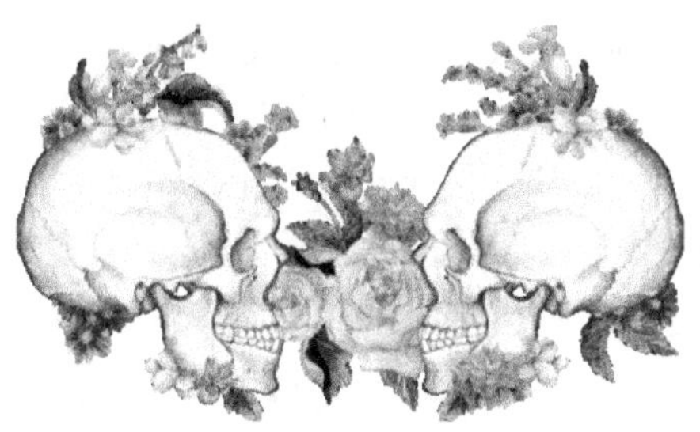

~ Twenty-One ~

Rowan

"She's good?" I ask Dominic as he walks into my office at Rush, Carter already laying back on the long dark couch across from me.

He's been the one watching her most out of the three of us, and I know he was doing it through other people—the twins in specific. Relief flowed through me at his satisfied nod, but I knew he was still here to talk about everything else that's currently going wrong.

Like Carter warned, I received my assignment this morning surrounding Marcus's kidnapping, and based on the tension across Dominic's forehead, I knew he had too.

"What are your orders?" I question as I stand from my desk, taking a seat beside Carter since I knew I wouldn't be able to work while having this discussion. Mine was simple, but this entire situation made me too uneasy to focus nonetheless. Hazel is going to be caught in the middle no matter what angle we come at this at, and that knowledge terrifies me more than I think I'm capable of admitting.

"While you're working on fixing all of the camera footage, Carter and I are going to move in with two separate teams as back up. With Carter's focus on grabbing Marcus, Vincent suspects the wife will be disoriented and attempt to leave in a panic. My job is to knock her out and bring her back to the Base for information if things go wrong with retrieving the main target." Marcus. The same man our girl adores.

I couldn't help it as my eyes drifted over to Carter whose fists were once again curled into tight balls, reminding me of the way he looked two days ago by that elevator.

Vincent was a cruel, cold man, and even though I know Hazel is under close surveillance in Detroit, I still feel sick at how similar that unconscious girl on the floor looked to her. At first, I thought Carter was crying because Hazel was dead, and it was a moment that left us all shaken up despite the truth that she was safe.

"So what are we going to do then?" I ask the question that's been going through our minds since we realized our relationship was so much bigger than just sex.

This was all such a disaster, and as much as I hated Hazel being gone, it was almost necessary for us to work through all of this shit.

Dominic ran his fingers through his hair a nervous tendency of his looking down at his lap in defeat. It was an expression I mirrored, unfortunately having very little say in any of this.

My rights as an associate limited a lot of options for me, and even though Dominic was in one of the highest-ranking positions in the mafia, all three of us knew it was Carter who held the power. He was the one who had the orders of an engagement. He was the one risking the chance of taking on the title of the Don.

He was the one who could make or break everything, and I saw that it was eating away at every part of him.

"I already have a plan." Carter says, his tone so numbing I could see him dissociating his emotions from everything else. I wasn't sure our stories held a happy ending for us anymore, but there was one's who still could.

"You're going to propose?" Dominic says with slight disbelief in his voice, but we didn't judge nor did we interrupt. We simply stayed still, desperate for anything that could shed a little light to this horrible tunnel we've trapped ourselves in. The grim look on his face confirms Dominic's suspicions, and I couldn't help but feel a little despair because of it. This was not how any of this was supposed to be.

"In a little under three weeks, I'm going to take Hazel to Jolene's for lunch. I'm going to ask her to trust me and say that she needs to help me pretend for a while." She's a smart girl, and I know it won't take her long to realize this is about something serious. Hazel will play along perfectly because she trusts us, and it's going to make everything that needs to happen afterwards so much harder.

"And then?" I prob, my heart racing at the noticeable clench of Carter's jaw in response. He's quiet for a torturous moment, and I watch as he shuts everything inside of him down, forcing himself not to feel what he's about to say. I used to fear how effortlessly he could do it, but right now, I was envious. "And then we say good-bye." We say goodbye.

"No." I protest almost instantly as my voice threatens to break beneath the pressure of my fear. From the corner of my eye, I saw Dominic stiffen across from us, but my focus was on the man at my side.

"Goodbye, Carter?" I challenge, "You think letting her go is going to be safe for her after the entire world learns she's to be the future wife of a mafia Don? You've got to be out of your fucking mind."

"Doing this is the only god damned way to keep her alive." Carter snaps, reaching to the tray on the table across from us to pour himself something strong. I was too angry to even want to drink, though.

"She's going to get killed the second she steps out of our pro-tection." I argue, hating how helpless I feel right now. I know I was missing something here, but even if we had people watching her for the rest of her life, I couldn't bring myself to let her go. Maybe that made me selfish, but I would selfishly be hers until death and then some.

"Not unless the rest of the world believes her to already be dead." Dominic says quietly at my front, but it felt loud enough to ring through me until the truth of its vibrations rattled my bones.

No.

"Why are you both so insistent on pushing her away?" I ask, taking Carter's glass from him and drinking it for courage, "Hazel is strong and can handle this by our sides if we just let her in." I knew this, and I don't understand why they're all of a sudden acting otherwise. If I could offer Hazel a normal life with us, I would in a heartbeat, but that simply wasn't the way the world worked.

"You really think she'd still want us after we murder her father." Carter says, and those few words were enough to piss me off.

"Screw Marcus." I shake my head, praying to god they had better reasoning for leaving Hazel than something as stupid as revenge. Why are we even entertaining the possibility of a break up?

"Carter, I'm really truly sorry about your mother, but what's more important here?" I was met with silence as anger and tension spread throughout the room, but I was so sick and tired of being trapped in the unknown. I wanted a plan, and I wanted one that didn't leave all of our hearts broken and lonely. We were all hurting and struggling to cope with how quickly everything has changed, but there was another solution to all of this, it was just one nobody wanted to face.

"Why can't we just let him live?" Why can't the four of us just be enough? "Vincent would never allow it." Carter tries to shut down my idea, but I know he's much smarter than that. The only problem is that it would be up to him to initiate.

"But you could." Dominic murmurs, his eyes moving from his lap over to my friend. As those three words sunk in, I could see the undeniable pain in both of their eyes, mine likely showing the same emotions. I didn't blame Carter for wanting to take the easy way out, but if he didn't take Vincent's place, everything would fall apart.

"You can't kill Marcus and keep Hazel, X." Dominic tells the ugly truth I know none of us want to face. While it wasn't my mother who was killed, I've still dedicated years of my life to hunting this man down for revenge. Losing the chance of his death is something I'm sacrificing too. Carter's jaw tightened in distress, clearing having to restrain himself from lashing out. He was mad at the world, or more specifically the fate he'd have to submit to in order to salvage what's already so damn broken. "Taking Vincent's place is the reason we have to let her go." Carter surprises us all, his voice full of sorrow and remorse. He always planned to take his father's place, and that's what Dominic and I failed to realize.

"On the morning of September 15th, I'm going to propose to Hazel at Jolene's. We're going to walk around and do as Vincent says to give the illusion of obedience, and then I'm driving Hazel to Weston's for the last time." Carter wouldn't look at either of us as he spoke, and I couldn't tell whether I wanted to scream at him for his plans or cry because I wasn't sure that I could stop them. Weston's was the loading area where we kept our private jet, and he just admitted he wanted to ship our girl off the day before everything goes to shit.

"Don't you think she should have a say in this considering it's her whose entire life is about to change because of us? What you propose strips her of everything she cares about and places her in a situation she's not prepared for. At least with us, she could understand—"

"Understand what, Rowan?" Carter cuts me off, "Understand that we're all monsters in our own fucked up ways. That we enjoy killing people who do horrible things, but still people nonetheless." Is it so wrong to believe I think Hazel wouldn't judge if we let down our guard a little?

"What do you think the Mafia is, you asshole?" Though she may seem it, our girl is anything but innocent and does not require to be sheltered. I get that our natural instinct is to protect her from the bad world we live in, but if it came between losing her and telling the truth, I knew what option I'd choose.

"Hazel's the best thing to have ever happened to us, and we messed up by dragging her into our problems." Carter finishes, but Dominic seems to be anything but done with this conversation.

"We messed up nothing." He says with a quiet certainty that left no room for lies, "Above all of this, nothing can change the fact Hazel is related to Marcus by blood and mind. If things were different and we never met her at that hotel, Vincent still would have tracked her down eventually.

We would have been given the orders to kidnap and torture her as both leverage and to send a message similar to what we've been doing now." It was like no matter where things took us, it all led back to the one thing we would never be able to move on from. Her.

"The what ifs don't change anything." Carter argues, and while they maybe don't, it doesn't sway from the fact Hazel was going to be a part of our lives either way.

"Maybe not, but unless you're dead, becoming the Don is an inevitable part of your future, man. We should at least give our girl the chance to decide on her own how she wants things to be." I say, yet once again, I'm being selfish. Hazel would never leave us, and it's going to take dragging her out kicking and screaming to push her away. But, on the other side of things, I selfishly wish I could just lock her up in a life I know could provide security.

"Why can't you fucking see that I'm doing this for her!" Carter snaps, standing from the couch and walking away to distance himself from us.

"Hazel is the one thing in this world that cannot die, and I don't care what it takes to make sure she lives until she's old and gray. On September th, she's going to be placed in a safe house in Costa Rica and will remain there until things settle down."

"Why does it have to be goodbye then?" I question, standing up as well, "Why can't we tell her to lay low for a month or two and then bring her back to us once it's safe?" What has changed so much in the span of two days? The Carter I knew would fight to the ends of the Earth to keep Hazel by our side, but right now he seemed to be doing everything but that. I looked in disbelief at Dominic who continued to remain quiet in his own thoughts, but with so much on the line right now, I couldn't afford to hold back my voice.

"What happened to you promising to be her always?" It was a low blow, one hard enough to show a flinch in Carter's eyes, though I couldn't bring myself to care all that much when he still wasn't letting out the whole truth. Since knowing him and Dominic, we've only fought once and it was about something none of us could recall now.

This, however... I could feel the hostility radiating off of all three of us, and it was a feeling I doubted we'd be able to forget.

"Being Hazel's always doesn't matter much if she's dead, now does it, Rowan?" Carter fought back, my patience thinning rapidly from whatever internal self-hatred battle he was having with himself. If anybody else proposed taking my Hazel from me, they would already be knocked out on the ground. I never thought this would be a conversation we'd be having, but there is a lot about today that has surprised me.

"Don't act like you're doing this for her," I spat, walking over to Carter so he couldn't continue to shut himself off, "You're doing this because you're a coward." We were close enough now that all it would take is a single stride before being able to hit the other, but even though I knew I was the weakest one in this room, I would not accept the future they were trying to create.

"A coward?" Carter says in a tone I've seen people piss their pants over out of fear. Good.

He was finally starting to react.

"I think you're scared and insecure that Hazel's going to finally see every version of you see you for how you truly are and cherish all of the things you've been brainwashed to hate." Dominic stood up at this, ready to intervene if somebody chose to throw the first punch. Little did he know I was just as angry at his silence as I was Carter's words. A humorless laugh left the man in front of me, and it was dark enough to have ice licking down my spine. "Yeah?" He says, tilting his head in irritation, "Like what?" I saw out of the corner of my eye Dominic opening his mouth to stop me from what I was about to say, but he needed to hear this. I was done hiding behind the barriers of filtered truths and even more filtered lies.

"You're scared about what Hazel's going to think when she learns about how you got that scar." I say, referring to the night a knife was slashed down his face, just barely missing his left eye. Everybody who's a part of the Mafia knows the story behind the mark Carter has worn since the night of his sixteenth birthday, and if Hazel were to stay, her finding out would be unavoidable. Vincent raised his son his entire life to believe scars were a sign of weakness—that if you were truly successful, you never would have earned one to begin with. Carter was not an insecure man, but the permanent cut through his eyebrow had him from looking in mirrors because he didn't want to see that part of himself.

"Don't talk about shit you don't understand." I hit a nerve with him, and while I may not be able to see things the way Carter does, Hazel can.

"You finally found someone who loves you, and it terrifies you that you feel the same way." I land the final blow, just for the first physical one to be placed. I'm shoved back so quickly I know the movements were ones of someone who's been trained their whole life, Dominic keeping me upright before slamming Carter back into the wall. "I don't want Hazel dead anymore than you do, but don't take your shit out on us when we're in the exact same boat." Dominic finally cuts in, not allowing himself to fold under the pressure of Carter's dark gaze.

"All three of us idiots fell in love with a woman who deserves so much more, but you can't act like she hasn't chosen us as much as we have her." "Letting her go is choosing her!" Carter yelled, getting under Dominic and shoving him away just as he did me.

"You weren't the one to see her dead on the ground, but I did." Our chests were all heavy with our erratic breathing, and when I looked at my friend—truly looked at him—I found tears of panic and regret built in his dark eyes.

"I know that girl wasn't Hazel, but for five seconds, I thought she was. I saw a bullet wound through the head of the only woman I've ever allowed myself to get close to, and those few moments were the longest of my life." I watched as he slid down against the wall, sitting on the plush carpet of my office as Dominic and I followed in exhaustion. When I walked into the house those days ago and found Carter breaking by our elevator, I knew Vincent's gift was meant to imitate our girl but I never felt the seizing terror that it could actually be Hazel. For the other, however, he had known what it felt like to truly lose everything in a matter of a single blink of an eye.

"The thought of saying goodbye has been tearing me apart, but I would rather watch Hazel grow old with somebody else for a thousand lifetimes than have to relive those five seconds again, knowing I was responsible for it all." Jesus Christ. I wish I could continue to place my anger on him, but I couldn't. Not when I had been so fucking blind to believe he was sending her away because it was the easy choice. Letting go of Hazel was the decision that would ensure things could never be the same— the one that would make everything fall apart.

"She deserves an explanation." I say, trying to hold back my sob and nearly failing. Neither Dominic nor Carter disagreed with my statement, and I almost feel as though that made things worse. Hazel deserves the choice of being able to decide how she wants to live, but we have a choice too. We have the choice of keeping her alive, and just because she's willing doesn't mean she should have to die by our sides because of the future we've been promised to.

This world is unfair and we can only try to make it through each day, saying goodbye being the price of caring for someone so much you'd let them go. I never used to believe in the kind of love Romeo had for Juliet and Noah had for Allie, but that was until I met my own love story, my Hazel, my darling.

"Costa Rica?" Dominic whispers as he hangs his head against his propped knees, a tear that mirrors my own slipping down his cheek. Those two words felt like acceptance, but I don't think this was something I would ever come to terms with, even if I understood.

~ Twenty-Two ~

Hazel

I don't know how I got to this point, but as my feet dragged across the crunch of fallen leaves, I set out to unlock yet another old memory. I've been walking for the last twenty minutes into the forest my mom's house backs onto, encased in silence and my own thoughts as I approached an old barn-like structure that was even more damaged than I remembered it to be.

The place I trained in growing up had wooden boards coated in peeling red paint, ones that hung in awkward angles just like when my father and I found it years ago.

Snow made things difficult in the winter, but the holes made every other season useful, acting as light sources no matter the time of day.

I'd been trained in all kinds of different conditions as a child, but I remember spending endless hours of the nights with my feet light as they shuffled against the dirt ground of the barn, dodging strikes just to pivot and return them. I feel as though this is the only part of my life here I would miss, but I think getting to see it one last time makes things easier to leave behind. Sometimes you need to say goodbye to an old chapter to begin the sequel, and knowing who was waiting for me back home brought excitement over the sadness.

Every day since I left, I've been thinking about date ideas for the four of us and how I should tell them the way I feel. On multiple occasions I've caught myself going over the words in my head, planning out the perfect way to string together those four letters that I can only hope they return.

I feel like I know them better than I do myself most times, and it's a little comforting in the sense it makes me feel safe.

I notice the way Rowan sometimes holds my hand just so he can run his thumb in small strokes against my skin, or how he'll play with my hair when he's bored. Half of the time I swear he doesn't even know he's doing it. And then, of course, there's Carter who shows his emotions so clearly in his eyes, I can feel them holding me even when I'm across the room. Though I'm sure he'd deny it, I don't miss the small glances he always steals when I'm around, watching me even when I'm not doing anything interesting. I used to take Carter's silence for hostility, but it turns out it's simply the only way he knows how to portray things, something I've grown to love about him.

On the other side, however, Dominic used his words for almost everything. His quiet whispers in my ears were continuous when I was with him, always telling me how beautiful I looked or how good I was doing. Yes, a lot of those were similar to things he says to me in the bedroom, but he praises me for everything else too. His gentle words of encouragement were something I never knew I needed until we became so much more, but I planned to tell him— to tell all of them just how much these little things meant to me.

That is, once I was done with Detroit. Taking my first step into the barn, the first sight I noticed was that most of the space around me was covered in dusty black blankets to conceal whatever objects lined the interior. My dad and I used to hide a lot of things out here considering nobody really knew of it, and I'm willing to bet the Polaroids I'd taken with my first partner, Alex, were still hidden behind one of the looser wooden slabs of the wall. I didn't bother checking though considering that had been years ago. I had a lot of secrets hidden within the corners of this place, and the reason I was here was because I suspected I wasn't the only one. My father can hide better than anyone I know, but everybody has a trail no matter how faint it may be.

With my non-existent hosts still gone, it left a lot of time for me to get in my head and go over every last detail of my father's disappearance, branching all the way back to when I was eleven. I had racked my brain over and over again for any clues anything I might have forgotten or missed that could hint to why he left, but every time I thought about my dad, I thought of this barn. Being back here may have been yet another attempt at gaining closure for me, but that wasn't my only motive for this visit.

Taking a breath, I began scanning the area around me. For what, exactly, I wasn't sure, but walking around here was better than remaining cooped up for yet another day. I'm giving my mother twenty four hours, and if she's still a no show after that, then I'm leaving.

I miss my men and Jade and my life in general. I kept the thoughts of them close to me as I began digging through my past, an uneven breath leaving my lips.

Starting with the coverings over the odd shapes against the one wall, I pulled until the dirty sheets came off to expose nothing more than old furniture. Chairs, couches, cutlery sets. There wasn't a single thing to it other than storage. I debated the possibility somebody else found this place apart from my father, though crypticity always has been his strong suit. Moving on from that, I then started looking at the walls, my fingertips dragging across the uneven wood before I stopped and looked behind me. I saw nothing more than forestry but I knew I was no longer alone.

"I get Dominic likes to be a mother hen, but is this really necessary?" I call out, feeling the prickle of eyes at the back of my neck. I've had two shadows following me around this entire week, ones I only noticed that night at the bar a few days ago. "Good eye." The girl I've learned to be as Imani says from behind me, causing me to spin around for a second time today. I wasn't surprised to find her twin Kara right by her side. Working for what I now know are known as the Night Reapers, I learned they don't respond to the Mafia but rather the three men who are destined to one day run it. They are personal to Dominic, Carter, and Rowan, and also known as the Base's assassins.

"Don't you think your talents are being wasted on babysitting?" I raise an eyebrow, my eyes trailing over their all black clothing along with their long hair pulled into braids. Even though they were just standing there, I knew they were fast and precise with every movement they took. All it would take is a blink of my eye, and they'd be able to disappear without a trace.

"We do what we're paid to do. Nobody touches you except for them, and they aren't here." Kara grins from my front, almost hoping someone tries to dare so she can lay them on their ass. Though I like the idea of privacy, I've also liked the twins since I met them drunk when they drove me home from Slash's place. Not my finest moment, but an interesting one nonetheless.

"Well I know you're here. You don't have to hide in the shadows unless you want to." I say, and I receive two grins this time. "If it helps, you can think of us as your body guards instead." Imani winks, moving to my left, "The angels watching over you until it requires us to be otherwise." They undoubtedly had the beauty and grace of angels, but it was the fires of hell that flared within their eyes. I simply nodded in response when I saw they weren't going to slink back into the background, taking a step back to the wall to see if anything could've been hidden behind it.

The twins had silently moved themselves over to one of the couches, plopping down without me even realizing it.

"You should check these cushions at some point." Kara points out as I continue my scan of the wooden boards, not even thinking something could be hidden under or within the seats of the furniture. To say I didn't know what I'm doing would be an understatement. "Is that where you would hide something of importance?" I ask, still working along the walls with their eyes on me in mind. There wasn't a single breath of mine they weren't aware of, and that was both reassuring and unnerving all at once. When no response came, my head turned to where they were sitting, or rather where I thought they were. The couches now unoccupied, my heart nearly leapt from my chest when I turned back to find Imani leaning at my side, that easy smile of hers still across her face.

"If there was something I didn't want others finding, I would burn it." She says before her hand reaches and yanks on the board right beside my head. I didn't even get the chance to move before the wood gave under the force, popping loose along with a lot of dust and crawly things that made me jump back in freight. I hated spiders almost as much as I hated this town. I spotted Kara shooting me a small smirk at my reaction, but I was more so curious about what had been uncovered behind the board that was now useless as it dropped to the ground.

"Yup, definitely looks like something you—" Imani starts, but stops as her head tilts at the plastic baggy she picked up. I catch her eyes slipping to Kara, but she doesn't stop me as I take the item from her to look at what's inside. My mouth parts slightly in surprise as I open the top, multiple IDs and passports filling it, all with my father's face repeatedly across the cards. Jonathan Barkley.

Tobias Walsh. Christopher Michelson. Kieran Sharp. Marcus Caddel. I had to look twice at the last name, seeming familiar but I couldn't quite pin why. I can see why the twins' eyes had widened at this, because it was a discovery I hadn't expected. My father's life was always a mystery to me, but seeing how many different lives he's lived was almost a shock to my senses. I thought back to all those days ago when we spoke in my car, the phone number he gave me still hidden away back home in a place I was certain no one would find. His visit was something I was asked to keep quiet about, and I doubted he wanted anybody to find out about this either.

Shit.

"Is this your dad?" Kara asks, appearing at my side as I instinctively closed the bag but didn't bother trying to hide it. "Yeah, he's been missing for a while now. I hoped that maybe I'd be able to find some sort of clues here, but this isn't exactly a huge surprise to me." I lie, trying to play things off as best I can.

"He's led a pretty secret life, so a few IDs and passports aren't exactly far fetched when it comes to him." The twins' identical faces school themselves into neutrality, but I saw the look Imani shot Kara in something that looked suspiciously like recognition. I made a mental note to ask Rowan about that when I get home.

Feeling the plastic clutched between my tensed fingers, I know there has to be more here. More things that I can't have an audience when discovering.

Though I may be good at sneaking out of places, these two were better trained than I could ever be and would be tracking me until I'm back in Dominic's arms. I suppose the real question now is how do I get that privacy another way? "So which man is the real him then?" Imani asks with a tilt of her head, her curiosity clearly as piqued as mine. She would catch my lie, so I just prayed this was information safe to speak.

"Tobias Walsh is the man I know to have raised me until I was old enough to hold my own." I say, realizing that thinking about my dad made me miss him a little. It helped to know he was alive, but that didn't always make things easier.

"This is actually bringing back a lot of hard memories. Do you think I could have a little bit to myself?" At the reluctant looks I get, I try to really play on my sadness.

"I know it's your job to make sure I'm safe, but is there any way you can do it from a distance for a little while so I can get the closure I need?" I made sure to add just a subtle bit more emphasis on the word closure, knowing it's likely what Dominic told them I was here for considering what I've explained so far. I was betting on the fact the twins didn't want to feel like they were interfering with the whole purpose of my visit, well aware all three of my men would do what was needed to give me what I came here for.

"We'll never stray far." Kara says, and I recognized her tone was one of understanding but also one of hesitance. With a nod of gratitude on my part, I waited until they were genuinely gone, no longer being able to feel their eyes on me. My chest grew a little lighter with them gone, but I still didn't know what to do about the bag Imani found or if I should continue to keep this a secret. I agreed to silence because my dad asked me to, but that was before I began to trust Dominic, Rowan, and Carter with my life.

They would never betray me, and their resources through the Mafia could help assuming they'd be okay with it. My father had given me a business card right before he disappeared from my car, claiming it was the number of someone who could help me with my finances and very clearly hinting that there was money left to me under my name.

I've been too much of a coward to call, because if it's as much money as he's making it out to be, it feels like a goodbye I'm not ready for. He had wanted to make sure I was taken care of, and I feared that meant he believed there was a chance he wouldn't be coming back like he promised. These, of course, were all thoughts I try my best to drown out and shove away, though it makes it hard when my every instinct tells me to dig.

I don't know how Imani knew which board to tug at, but my memory of Kara saying to check the couches popped into my mind as I stared at the furniture to my right.

It wasn't a horrible idea, so I moved there next, my footsteps sounding lightly against the cold floor. Goosebumps had managed to form in a light covering along my arms, but I forced myself not to scream as more bugs scurried away at the tug of the first cushion, quickly tossing it to the floor.

Nothing was under that one so I proceeded to the next one, and the next one, and the next one. My heart was racing at this point, but each time I pulled away a part of the couch, all I was met with was the dust cover smoothing across the wooden frames that kept it together.

Even now, I didn't know what I was looking for, however I was hoping for something a little better than this. I'm tired of being kept in the dark, and I nearly sink to the ground in defeat before I get an idea as the black coloured cambric catches my eye. It could be a stretch, but there wasn't much I had to lose at the moment. Pulling the dagger Jolene bought me as a gift from my jacket, I dropped into a slight crouch in front of the first piece of furniture. I've made good on my promise to her to carry it with me, and I couldn't be more thankful for it now.

Cutting a precise slash through the fabric covering, my mouth parts as I realize my theory has been correct. Two dust coverings were built into the deceivingly old and battered couch, the first one being a fake and the second acting as a secret net to hold more things than I know how to process. If I thought the fake IDs and passports were bad, the sight before me makes those just the tip of the iceberg.

Here, there are contracts, health records, blue prints, and photographs, all things in which shouldn't surprise me, but do. I didn't even know where to begin, so I simply reached out to the first thing I saw: an ultrasound picture dated . I was born in . My brows remained furrowed at the image, but there was still so much more for me to look at, putting the photograph in the back of my mind. Setting it down, I then looked at blueprints to buildings I didn't recognize as well as a few houses as it seemed as well.

There were a thousand questions spurring in my head right now, however there was one thought that battled out over all of the others—the one fact I wished wasn't true. I really didn't know my father at all.

Though my instinct was to cover everything around me up, I didn't trust that Imani and Kara wouldn't come back to poke around in my father's things.

I like them, but I don't know who they are or the reasoning behind their reactions when they saw my father's multiple fake passports in that bag. I had hidden those back behind the wall considering they already saw them, but everything else was stuffed flush into my coat pockets in a way that made it look like they were empty. My business here was done, but my guard was up now. As I stepped out of the barn, the feeling of eyes tingled the back of my neck yet again, but the twins didn't bother to remain hidden this time. I told them on the walk back that I had tried tearing open the bottom of the couch but didn't find anything, and I think I put on enough of an act that they believed my need for silence was due to disappointment rather than millions of questions continuing to form.

There was a lot I needed to figure out, but I could only get through it step by step. Though my mother's house wasn't home by any means, I really just wanted to get into Carter's t-shirt I stole for the weekend and curl up on the couch.

Not much was spoken as Imani and Kara walked me back to the road, disappearing the second they suspected people could see them again back into the shadows. I didn't bother to try and find them this time. I knew they were close. Walking straight into what could be considered a backyard, I led myself around the house until I arrived at the front door, but the sight of a car parked in the driveway had me stiffening. They were home. I instantly felt my throat begin to tighten, but I forced air to pass into my lungs, not allowing me the opportunity to panic or show weakness. I was so much stronger than the last time I was here, and I refused to let myself be anything but. Just take it one step at a time. Pushing every ugly feeling down, I knew the door was unlocked as I walked right in, my heart already racing at the first sight of my mother and stepfather. Swallowing down my emotions, my eyes glazed over Andrew sprawled on the couch, clearly drunk and getting dirt all over my things.

"Oh, Hazel." My mother smiles widely as she notices me, her eyes red and looking even more disheveled than when I last saw her.

"I missed you so much, my sweet girl." My sweet girl. The name makes my stomach churn, hating how happy she looks to see me as though nothing was wrong. It took a few beats before I closed the front door behind me, but the noise seemed to have grabbed the attention of the man currently using my blanket.

"And where exactly have you been?" His words slur as his voice is just as scratchy as I remembered it to be. Just the sound of him speaking has chills running through my body, and it was the kind that made me feel nauseous. A quiet laugh passed from my chest, even though there wasn't a single part about this that was funny.

"Where have I been?" I repeated, my voice low yet anything but quiet. "Is that a serious question, because it's a pretty fucking stupid one if it is." Never in the twelve years that I've known Andrew have I used this tone with him, especially in my mother's presence.

To be completely honest, if it weren't for my men's secret visit last week, I'm not sure if I would have been brave enough to still be standing here. I waited for the lash back—for the inevitable rage I was ready to face, but none of that came. Watching slightly off guard, my stepfather's gaze slipped to my mother's before sitting up slightly on the couch.

"I told you this would happen, Heidi." He shook his head slightly as though he were a disappointed dad catching his teenage daughter sneaking back in on a Friday night. The act appalls me, and I'm already finding myself more and more done with this shitty place.

"Andrew, don't." My mom responds with a dismissive, yet lazy gesture, moving over to the small fridge she owned to grab herself a beer. I still hadn't walked from the doorway, but the direction I could sense this conversation going in didn't exactly seem welcoming. Plus, there were no longer many places I could go now that two other people took up the space. Choosing to lean slightly against the wall instead, I remained tense as Andrew pushed himself upright, the blanket I had been using now half on the floor and half across his legs. It was not something I would be touching again, I knew that for sure. "Her neck is proof enough." My stepfather continued as he shot a disgusted sneer my way, but I let it wash right over me, even though I didn't know what he was going on about.

"I mean look at her. Little miss perfect is whoring herself out for money because her boyfriend probably got sick of the bitch and dumped her."

Was he actually insinuating I was a prostitute? If I thought I was angry before, then the white hot rage pouring through my veins made my previous emotions look like one of a saint. "Let's get two things straight here," I begin, my voice surprisingly steady despite everything else that would make it be otherwise.

"One, though it's funny this is the second time this month I've had to explain this, I am not a fucking prostitute." I don't think he was even listening to me, and that only made my irritation burn hotter. It didn't take me long to realize his accusation was a result of the fading hickeys across my throat from my last night with Rowan, Dominic, and Carter, but I was almost curious to know how he'd react to learning the men who gave me these marks were the same ones who had him pissing himself in fear. "And two, if you call me a bitch again, your tongue will be the next thing you'll lose." I could feel my adrenaline surging through me with each passing second, and as I watched the colour blanch from Andrew's cheeks, I'll admit it's satisfaction that flows through me next.

"Hazel, you apologize right now—" My mother begins, but I cut her off. I'm so fucking tired.

"Do you even give the slightest shit about me, mom?" I ask, crossing my arms over my chest so nobody could see the shake of my muscles. My body's response was one of fear, sadness, and adrenaline, and I didn't want either of them to know I was feeling anything at all. My question caused her to stumble for a beat, but then she was back to scowling as though I was the one completely wrong here.

"You come into my house and treat your family with such open disrespect. It's you, my dear, who should be asking yourself if you care for us." I didn't want to cry—I've wasted way too many tears on these people who don't deserve them, but I was afraid my will to remain strong wouldn't hold up for much longer. It was at this moment I wished I would've put my mindless insecurities aside and invited even one of my boyfriends to come with me, because right now I feel as though I were about to collapse with no safety nets to catch me.

"You're the ones who've been gone for the last five days for the trip you initiated." I argued, and while Andrew groaned on the couch, my mother took a step towards me.

"You're stressing out your father right now. Mind your mouth." He is not my father, but it was a long lost claim I've insisted for years. I wanted to scream that at the top of my lungs, but it would be childish and I didn't want to reveal how much these horrible people had an effect on me. Another humorless laugh left my body, and it hurt as it came out. "I'm stressing him out." I say under my breath, forcing myself to hear what she said so I could let it dissolve away in my head. Of course it's me who's the problem here. Sure, my hosts have been gone for nearly the entire trip without a word, but I'm the one at fault. I'm so done with this place.

"Your father is going through a lot of pain, and—" My mother starts yet again, but I'm so sick and tired of listening to the bullshit excuses that spill from her mouth. There's always another excuse—

another mindless reason that always makes me feel guilty. But this was not my fault. If this conversation was happening even a month ago, my responses would have likely been extremely different compared to what I'm about to say now, but I was done rolling over to things I shouldn't have to shy away from. I came here for closure, and I was slowly getting it, even if I felt a part of myself breaking in the process. "It's funny how you seem to care so much about every goddamned thing in this world except for me." I cut her off, not allowing either of them to talk over what I needed to say.

"Do you not care about how many times this man has hurt me while you were too drunk to help me?" My chest was constricting inside of me, but I pushed through it. This was the one and only time I would be speaking these words, so I just needed to be strong for a little longer.

"Don't talk to your mother like that." Andrew tried to defend as though he were a loving husband standing up for his wife, but it only made my lips curl with disgust.

"What has gotten into you?" My mom lectures like I was disappointing her—like I had no reason to be upset. The first tear fell at that, and I hated everything it represented. I was done, and I didn't know how to repair those pieces of me that longed for the parent that died a long time ago.

"Why can't you just fucking love me?" I cried, needing to physically hold myself so I didn't pass out from the pain. What did I do to become so undeserving of her attention?

"This is ridiculous—" Andrew slurred, and it only made me hurt more. There was no hiding the painful shake of my muscles at this point, however both of them seemed so drunk that I doubted they'd remember this conversation in the morning. I felt my mind curl in on itself as my stepfather stumbled up from the couch, and I wanted to throw up as his eyes met mine. I hated it, but I caved and looked away back to my mom.

"Your perfect little husband broke me growing up, and I came back here to give you a chance to apologize yet you still defend him."

"Hazel—"

"Do you not know how scared I always was?" I yelled, "Scared he was going to hit me again, or lock me in a closet and forget that I was there? Do you not understand how terrified I was that he was going to rape me when I was too weak to fight back." I was full on breaking down now, but I couldn't care anymore. Everything inside of me hurt, and I didn't even try to fight off the signs of me beginning to hyperventilate when I felt them coming.

"You always were such an imaginative kid." Andrew spits as he walks towards me, my body tightening up as I push my back against the wall. My hand was already on the dagger in my pocket, but I could barely make out his features through the blur of my tears and fright. How could I escape this? I just needed everything to stop.

"Get out of my house." I heard my mother shout from my side, and the tears spilling down my cheeks became a continuous stream. Did she not just hear a single thing I said? I'm breaking and it's as though I'm not even here.

"You heard her." Andrew comes close enough that I can smell the alcohol pouring off of him, but it's his presence that threatens a gag from my throat.

"Leave." I felt a part of my brain shut down a little at that, my body still shaking but not being able to associate the emotions to it. I was simply done. Pushing off of the wall, I walked past my step-father, not letting myself feel anything under the smug sneer of his face. It wasn't until I heard my mother's voice that I stopped, my head slowly moving to where her fingers clutched onto the counter top.

"No." She says, the word rasping as she spoke. It was directed towards me, but it was Andrew she was looking at.

"I was talking to you. Go stay at John's for the next few days and cool off?" I was still crying where I stood as my mother moved out of the kitchen and over to the couch, shooting me a half sorry, half exasperated look. She wasn't sending him away for me, though.

She just didn't want to deal with the conflict. There was a long moment where I believed Andrew was going to lash out for the demand, but as I continued to hold myself, something flashed before his eyes. I knew the twins were in the house, ready to step in if anyone tried anything, but based on the way he shifted nervously, I almost wondered if it were because of the message Rowan, Dominic, and Carter had sent him.

They showed him mercy that night, and I had no doubt about it that they would kill Andrew for me the second I gave them the go ahead. Power flushed through me at that, and I think it was the only thing that kept me standing as the man of my nightmares walked around me. I didn't turn as I heard the door slam shut at his hasty exit, nor did I look towards my mother by the couch.

My tears had never ceased, though, and while I felt a weight leave my chest now that Andrew was no longer here, nothing was okay. My heart had shattered and my mind was overwhelmed, understanding that this was goodbye.

The next time I see my stepfather will be with his life draining from his eyes, my mother hopefully taking the hint to disappear herself. Nothing could be the same, but I didn't want to be a part of this life anymore. I wanted to be in the arms of my men, the laughter of Jade, and the escape of photography.

I haven't been the girl from Detroit in a very long time, and I was sick of pretending there was still something left for me here.

"I don't want you in my life anymore." I sobbed as my head hung in defeat, but when I didn't get any response, my head snapped up to the woman across from me—the woman who was passed out on the couch from the alcohol, not bothered to entertain my visit any longer.

The sight destroyed what was left of my old self, and I felt it as Kara and Imani left to give me my space. I was thankful for it too, because I could barely breathe as my hand rested hard against my chest, droplets of my tears being blinked from my eyes and down to my trembling fingertips.

The world around me spun as everything came crashing on top of my body, nausea, grief and despair weighing me down like the chains of my past. I didn't know how to break out, and with my mother unconscious on the couch, my feet somehow managed to carry me to my childhood bedroom.

The reason I've been avoiding the entrapment of these four walls remains the same even after all I've managed to face today, but still I forced myself to close the door. I forced myself to grab the pillow and blanket resting on top of the single mattress bed, just as I then forced myself to the ground, creating a spot for me to sleep now that the sofa wasn't an option. The hardwood felt like knives against my back as I settled down, but the one's stabbing at my heaving chest were way worse. I was going to leave in the morning I knew that for certain but the pain was too consuming to even think about anything other than the reason for my shaking.

My heart was bleeding out slowly with each fallen tear down my face, and it scared me because I didn't know how to stop it.

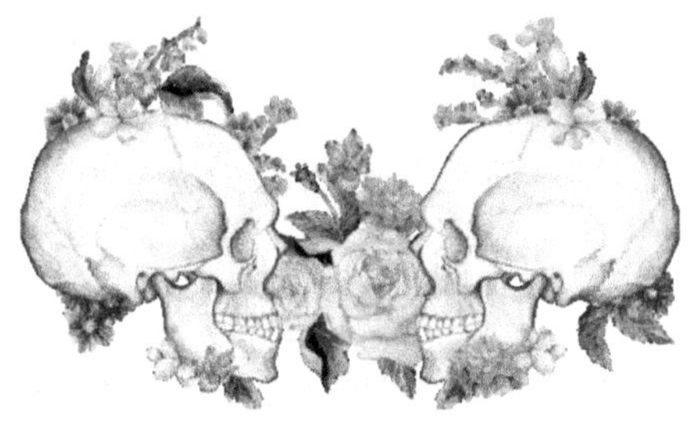

~ Twenty-Three ~

25

Dominic

I broke my promise, and I didn't feel a single ounce of regret for it. I'd received a call about two hours ago from Kara saying something was off, and I was on our jet within the next twenty minutes. All three of us were. My heart hasn't stopped racing since my phone rang—actually, it hasn't stopped since the second I watched Hazel walk through security at the airport a week ago.

I wanted to respect her wishes which is why I exploited the loophole of having the twin's sent out instead to have her back if she needed it, but I've still been on edge for six days now despite that extra layer of protection. On top of the fact Rowan, Carter, and I haven't spoken since our discussion about Costa Rica, everything has been feeling off since the moment Hazel left.

I've missed her so much it hurts, but I could only hope she won't be mad when she finds out we were here to take her home. I know about the IDs and the fact she saw Marcus's name on one of them, but Kara and Imani made it seem as though it wasn't a revelation for her or anything. Hazel didn't recognize the meaning behind that single name, nor the fact it was proof she was unknowingly a Caddel.

Though relief was the first thing I felt because it meant I could keep her with me for a little longer, it was like the world was giving us constant signs to tell her everything that threatens to break us apart. I was still angry at Carter for wanting to let her go, but I don't think I had it in me to be too mad. I've never heard my friend admit to loving anybody—not even his own mother, but he loves Hazel with all of his heart. I know he does, because I do too, and it's the only reason I can't let myself be selfish when it comes to her.

The twins were sent out because I knew they could guarantee her safety since we weren't there, but I don't think there was anything I could do to protect her beautiful heart from the chaos destined to ensue. Hazel doesn't need to get drunk to escape her mind, but she chose to over every other thing she could've done. I wasn't judging her in the least, however it was an observation on top of many others that told me she was slowly breaking too.

Her calls had become forced, and not a single one of us had received a goodnight text to tell us she was okay tonight. Nothing was fine here, but if our girl was going to hurt, she would at the very least have our arms to wrap around her when she shatters. Already off of the plane and well on our way to the address we knew she was at, it didn't take long to realize why Hazel didn't want us to see this part of her life.

Even though this is the second time we've been here in two weeks, I knew this visit had left her stripped bare and vulnerable to the nightmares of her past, her mind the only company she had.

That knowledge was on my mind the entire sprint up her driveway, as well as when Rowan kicked open the cheap door in pair with the useless lock that tried to keep it shut. We were already moving inside when we saw Hazel's mother passed out on the couch, obviously drunk considering she didn't even stir at the noise. I was disgusted at how such a pathetic woman couldn't spare someone as beautiful and bright as her daughter even a little bit of love, but at least wherever her stepdad was wasn't here. It had taken quite literally every last ounce of my control not to kill him a week ago and have him castrated instead, but I don't like the odds of my patience being tested for a second time so soon.

"Dominic." Carter's rough voice pulled my attention to him, his head jerking to the only bedroom door that was closed. I knew our girl was on the other side, but when Rowan knocked and called out to her, there was no response that echoed her name. That was what really scared me.

"Darling, it's us. Can we come in?" Rowan asks softly, but still more than loud enough to hear through the thin walls between. All we were met with was more silence, and it was Carter who slowly opened the door to see what was happening. Though it was fairly dark, it didn't take me long to realize her bed was completely unoccupied and Hazel wasn't there. Shit.

My mind instantly snapped to Marcus and her being taken, moving as I shoved past Rowan and Carter to search the small room. Her bed was bare of its sheets and pillows, and I found myself panicking all the way up until I rounded to the other side of her mattress. Then it was sadness that had me falling to my knees, not fear. "Princess." My voice broke with the nickname, but Hazel didn't even seem to know I was here as I found her crying silent tears, her body shaking and her expression frozen into one of pain. I knew it was the kind that went far sharper than physical wounds, and I hated that things ever got to this point.

Her knees had tucked tight to her chest in what I realized was supposed to be a makeshift bed, but I felt how cold and dirty the hardwood was beneath my legs. It was uncomfortable to kneel against yet alone sleep on as though it were a mattress. The significance in her choice didn't go unnoticed by any one of us, Rowan and Carter now at my side as well. "I'm going to pick you up, Hazel. Is that okay?" I ask, my hands hovering over her but not touching without permission. Her state right now was very similar to one of a sub drop, but I knew what we shared a few days ago wasn't the cause of her tears. Hazel was hurting, and I just wanted to take it away.

"Hey," I say softly when she still doesn't move, forcing myself not to show how scared I am at how quickly everything's changed. It was clear I wasn't the only one going through hell, but unlike me, Hazel didn't deserve a single second of this. She should have parents who could offer her love and support, better yet happy memories she could look back on as an adult and smile about. But the way she was feeling now was something I would never wish upon anyone, let alone a person as deserving as the woman in front of me.

"I need you to look at me, princess." I didn't want to trigger her by touching without permission, but all I wanted to do was hold her in my arms and kiss away her pain until my lips replaced every bad thought in her head. Rowan and Carter let me gently coax her back from whatever state she'd fallen into, and all I could do was offer a small smile when Hazel's tear soaked eyes finally glanced up at me. Her hand reached out and the next second she was in my lap, her body silently shaking from the force of her sobs.

Her head had naturally fallen against the cradle of my shoulder as my fingers ran through her hair, my arm holding around her waist and refusing to let go.

"I've got you." I whisper into her ear, though I wasn't even sure she could hear me. I didn't care if not, because if there was even the smallest change I could offer her support, I would take it. "You don't have to speak, but are you hurt, Hazel?" Rowan asks from in front of me, moving a little closer to rub his hand up and down the areas of her back where my arms weren't touching. The relief I felt when she shook her head no was there, but that didn't change the fact something was very much wrong. My guesses were on her passed out mother, absent step father, or both.

"You-you-y-you-y—" Hazel tried to speak, but she quite literally couldn't manage more than a single word. What she tried to say was muffled by my shoulder, but I was too afraid to scare her by pulling back even an inch.

"It's okay." Carter comforted quietly, kneeling at my left before taking her hand into his. My heart broke in my chest when I caught sight of her nails, the tips of them pink and so short most of them were bleeding. I couldn't see her other one draped over my neck, but I knew the ones hidden would be the same. Nail biting is something I've noticed Hazel's always done when she's either anxious or bored, but it's never been as bad as it was now. This was to the point of actual physical pain, and I knew Carter realized that too as he gently held them between his fingers and lifted them to his mouth to kiss her knuckles. It drew one of the first reactions from her in a long time, and I was almost surprised when her head lifted slowly from my shoulders to look at me and then him. Carter held her gaze as he kept his mouth on her skin, his thumb running across the top of her hand in continuous motions.

"I'm s-sorry." Hazel cried as she hung her head slightly, leaning back into mine and Rowan's touches across her spine. I hated that she felt as though this was something she needed to apologize for, but I hated even more that I wasn't here for her sooner when she needed me. "Nothing about this is your fault." I tell her, kissing her forehead in an attempt to ease the tension from the area. Her face is wet with tears and her nose is bright red from her sniffling, green eyes staring up at me even as she continues to cry. "We're here now, and you're not alone, princess." I say, Rowan brushing some of her hair back from her face so he could play with it until she's calm.

"Whatever happened... I know it hurts. You're allowed to be sad and angry and in pain, but you will never be alone." My hand reached to cup her cheek with my fingers, her face leaning heavily into my touch and allowing me to support her in the way she needed. My thumb wiped away her tears, and even though more replaced them seconds later, I didn't look away from her. Sensory focus is something that had brought Hazel down during her last sub drop, so while Rowan played with her hair and Carter held her hand, I brushed away her tears and showed her it was safe to leave her mind of nightmares with us. "S-she doesn't love me." Hazel rasped as her bottom lip trembled in pain, no doubt referring to the woman who was supposed to be her mother. "I d-don't understand what I ever did w-wrong?"

She sucked in a shuddering breath as though even those few words hurt her to speak. It's because they did, not in the sense of external wounds, but in the tightening of her chest and ache of her heart.

"Nothing, darling." Rowan muttered at her back, kissing her head and keeping his touch there as I watched his eyes close in sadness of his own. Not being loved in the way one deserves is something he knows better than any of us. Though Carter and I grew up in very different environments than him, we did everything in our power to disappoint our fathers by wreaking more havoc than imaginable. Rowan, however... I don't doubt there isn't a day in his life that he wouldn't have striven to shape himself into a person either of his parents would want. He and Hazel were identical in that unfair aspect.

"Sometimes people are just cruel. It doesn't necessarily mean that's the person they've always been with you, but sometimes those you love can die, even as their hearts continue to beat." I see understanding flickering in Hazel's eyes at Rowan's words, and while I feel her cry and shake harder at his truth, Hazel's tears are a story of her own. She cries for the little girl who lost the mother she knew at eleven.

She cries for her sixteen year old self who was almost raped, and then abused to the point where she no longer wanted to be in this world. She cried for every scar she gave herself, and the invisible ones those around her had inflicted on their own. The three of us held her through each fallen tear, and we would continue to once there were no more capable of spilling. This was healthy and something I suspected was long overdue, and though her sobs had rage boiling in my head for the life she should have had, my arms were where she would stay from now on. Despite my agreements from the other night, I wasn't leaving Hazel. I never planned to, and I didn't care if it was Carter's decisions I would be fighting against in the end because of it. Seconds before Hazel fell asleep in my arms, she asked me to take her home. I promised I would, though I didn't move right away from my spot on the ground, Rowan and Carter still by my side.

She sucked in a shuddering breath as though even those few words hurt her to speak. It's because they did, not in the sense of external wounds, but in the tightening of her chest and ache of her heart.

"Nothing, darling." Rowan muttered at her back, kissing her head and keeping his touch there as I watched his eyes close in sadness of his own. Not being loved in the way one deserves is something he knows better than any of us.

Though Carter and I grew up in very different environments than him, we did everything in our power to disappoint our fathers by wreaking more havoc than imaginable. Rowan, however... I don't doubt there isn't a day in his life that he wouldn't have striven to shape himself into a person either of his parents would want. He and Hazel were identical in that unfair aspect.

"Sometimes people are just cruel. It doesn't necessarily mean that's the person they've always been with you, but sometimes those you love can die, even as their hearts continue to beat." I see understanding flickering in Hazel's eyes at Rowan's words, and while I feel her cry and shake harder at his truth, Hazel's tears are a story of her own. She cries for the little girl who lost the mother she knew at eleven.

She cries for her sixteen year old self who was almost raped, and then abused to the point where she no longer wanted to be in this world. She cried for every scar she gave herself, and the invisible ones those around her had inflicted on their own. The three of us held her through each fallen tear, and we would continue to once there were no more capable of spilling. This was healthy and something I suspected was long overdue, and though her sobs had rage boiling in my head for the life she should have had, my arms were where she would stay from now on.

Despite my agreements from the other night, I wasn't leaving Hazel. I never planned to, and I didn't care if it was Carter's decisions I would be fighting against in the end because of it. Seconds before Hazel fell asleep in my arms, she asked me to take her home. I promised I would, though I didn't move right away from my spot on the ground, Rowan and Carter still by my side.

It took a long time before Hazel was able to fully drift off and even longer before her tears had dried, but even now, I could still feel the tremor of her bruised heart against my chest. Whatever her mother had said had broken what hope was left for a relationship with her daughter, and the fact Hazel didn't even want to say goodbye spoke a lot. Instead of meeting her at the airport in New York like we had planned, I was carrying her out of the car and up the stairs of the private jet that flew us here in the first place. I didn't even want to think about what might've happened during the two hours it took to get to her house, but what mattered now was that Hazel was back where things were safe.

She was back with us. I knew there was so much that still needed to be said, especially between Rowan, Carter, and I, but the woman in my arms was my main priority right now.

"I'll go let Marley and Justin know we're ready to take off." Rowan refers to our pilots waiting for their instructions, stealing a long glance at Hazel before turning towards the cockpit. My only response was a quiet hum in acknowledgement, trying to move to the back bedroom but being quickly stopped by Carter. I've been mad at him since he proposed sending our girl away, even if I didn't fight it in the end. It didn't matter, though. All of us have been unhappy with each other since things got complicated and reality settled in. His hand on my arm kept me from walking any further, and I didn't push away as Carter ran his hand over the back of Hazel's head before planting a kiss to her temple.

"Go take care of her." He says quietly, still dragging his eyes over her face.

"We'll talk after." Out of all the responses I expected, this was not one of them, but I didn't let my surprise show as I gave a single nod before leaving Carter alone in the lounge area.

We would be able to argue plenty later, however despite all else, we could at least agree on one thing. Hazel was what was important right now. With her still out cold in my arms, I walked the two of us to the back where she would be able to sleep in peace on a mattress that could give her comfort. If it weren't for her wishes, I would've burned her old one down until it was nothing but ash, but that was Hazel's destruction to claim. I just hoped she trusted me enough to be by her side to light the match.

"Dominic." The sound of my favourite voice brought my eyes down to where a green gaze was looking up at me. Hazel was being held bridal style beneath my fingertips, but the head that was once limp against my chest was now bent back to get my attention.

"Hey, princess." I offer a small smile, pushing open the sliding door and not bothering to turn on the lights to the small bedroom in front of us. There was so much I wanted to say to her, but nothing would come out as she curled close to me when I laid her down on the soft bed. I had planned to leave, not expecting her to be awake until tomorrow, yet the world seemed to have other plans for us. It was mostly dark in the closed off room, and Hazel didn't protest as I pulled the blankets over top of her body. Her luggage was already in the corner waiting for her when she needed it, but I think what was most important right now was that she rested.

I knew airplanes weren't something Hazel was exactly comfortable with in general, so I knew talking about what happened tonight wouldn't do her any good. When she was ready, I would listen to her for as long as she needed and then some, but now wasn't the time.

"We should be back in New York in just under two hours." I say quietly, both of us laying on our sides facing each other. Though it was dark, I could still see the outline of Hazel's form and the colour in her eyes, watching her nod as the first tear since she woke up slipped past her face.

The shining droplet drew a slow trail down her cheek, one in which I leaned in and kissed away silently.

A second fell, and I repeated the action over again, pulling Hazel closer to me as I held her with everything I had. These tears were different from other times these ones were quiet and weren't accompanied by shaking throughout her body. Instead, they were ones of exhaustion. I knew she was tired of fighting, and while she feels as though this is her weight to carry on her own, each tear that I kiss away tells her that it's not. Pain is a part of being human, but I'm going to bear it with her every step of the way, just as I believe Rowan and Carter will too.

"Thank you." Hazel's voice cracks as she speaks, yet another sign of how vulnerable today had left her. Though she had nothing to thank me for, it was her lips I kissed next, my touch a mere whisper against her mouth. A sad smile breaks across my face when I feel her shudder slightly beneath me, her small hands brushing against my left cheek just so she could feel me.

She noticed as I leaned into her touch, just as she noticed what my kiss had meant without me actually having to say anything. I was hers.

It didn't matter if I had to spend hours on a plane just to see her or days doing everything I could to make her feel better. I was her weapon to wield, just as I was her heart to beat and bones to support. I would become everything she needed me to be to get her through this, and I didn't care if there was a price that came with that kind of love.

The extent in which I would go to for her was greater than imaginable, especially during moments like this when it was only the two of us and the words of our silence.

I had no doubt Hazel was fully unaware of the power she held over me, but that was okay for now. All that mattered was the way her body was pressed against mine, proof that we were still here despite all else.

~ Twenty-Four ~

Hazel

I don't remember when I fell asleep, but it was the vibration of a plane's wheels meeting concrete that stirred me from unconsciousness. I knew my men had obliged when I asked them to take me home, however that didn't muffle any of the pain I began to feel the second my eyes opened. My face was nestled against Dominic's chest while his chin rested on top of my head, his one large arm wrapping around my shoulders. He'd held me as I cried last night and he continued to hold me now, only this time he wasn't alone.

Somehow I just knew it was Rowan who was spooning me from behind, his leg pressed in between mine as his own arm wrapped around my waist. I became increasingly aware of how low his hand placement was on my stomach, but like Dominic, he was still very much asleep. "You're up." Carter's gruff voice brought my attention to the corner of the room, his eyes grazing over the three of us curled together on the much too small bed. Something about his expression was cold, though—almost like he was distanced despite being only a small handful of feet away from me.

"Hi." I murmured on the side of caution, but his usual teasing smiles weren't here right now. This felt like the Carter Rowan first introduced me to at the wedding, and it caught me off guard.

"Everything okay?" I ask, feeling as Dominic stirs a little at my front. I can see the line of Carter's jaw harden before he forces himself to let out a breath, but I knew this wasn't the same person who kissed my hurt hands last night.

"We just landed. I was coming to see how you were doing." He says, his tone not angry yet not exactly happy either.

"There's no rush. I'll let you go back to sleep." I didn't miss the fact my question remained unanswered, but I also didn't try to stop him as he left to go back into the main part of the plane. He wasn't upset with me—I knew that, however in previous times when he was overwhelmed, his natural instinct was to distance himself and leave until he sorted through things on his own. I hoped it would be different this time. I hoped he would come to me instead, or at the very least tell me where he was going instead of just disappearing.

To be completely honest, I was too tired right now to let myself worry. There would be plenty of time to do that later, but I just wanted a break from feeling sad and complicated. I wanted to savor the heat of Rowan and Dominic's skin pressed against mine, so I did. I found comfort in the feeling of their snug embrace around my body, and it wasn't long before I felt my mind drifting off once again.

The peace of sleep never found me again, but Rowan did. My eyes had fallen shut multiple minutes ago, but my brain wouldn't quiet now that it had awakened. I'd hoped that a few hours of solid rest would've been enough of a distraction from the raging thoughts inside of me, however twenty minutes of straight restlessness liked to prove otherwise. It seems as though I wasn't the only one to notice this. While my body had remained half on top of Dominic, it was

Rowan's mouth I felt gently pressing against my bared throat. My eyes instantly fluttered shut as a soft exhale left my lips, his touch soothing me with that simple action.

"I missed you." He says quietly as he moves slightly lower, planting another kiss to where my pulse thrummed happily. I missed him too. I wished the words could come out of my mouth, but I was too tired to do anything but urge myself to relax. Sighing, my mind focused on the way Rowan's hand slowly moved lower and lower down my back before smoothing up my spine. It wasn't anything more than a lover's touch, but it felt like everything as Dominic shifted again beneath me. No words were spoken as his fingers started brushing through my slightly knotted hair, Rowan continuing to rub my back without missing a beat. The two of them managed to gently lull me back into a dreamless rest, and this time, it was one I didn't wake from until the following morning.

"—gone." I woke up to the sound of Dominic's smooth voice, my eyes reluctantly opening to find him dressed and sitting on the edge of a bed. Rowan's bed.

"I'm assuming no text?" The latter responded, making me realize my head was resting on a pillow propped on his lap for me. A soft blanket had been laid over my body at some point as Rowan's fingers slowly dragged through my hair, the same way Dominic's were earlier on the plane.

I had no recollection as to how I got from there to this room, but it was still mostly dark so I'm assuming it's only been a small handful of hours from when I last drifted off. "He was gone for twelve days last time. I doubt this will be any different." I hear Dominic sigh quietly, his eyes slowly falling down to meet mine before holding there. I watched as a small smile appeared on his face, but I saw sadness in his features too.

"Carter left?" I conclude based on what I heard, and the unhappy nod Rowan gave me confirmed what I'd guessed. His fingers continued to play with my blonde strands as a heavy breath left his body, something I think was distress being etched across his forehead. I had hoped he would've stayed, but I wasn't mad that he left. Carter promised me he would always come back, and if some time alone was what he needed to face the demons wracking his mind, I would give that to him. He would be back, and I would help him through anything if he allowed me the chance to, even if it was simply being at his side. "There's a lot he needs to work out right now, but I promise he won't stay gone forever." Rowan re-assures, but it wasn't me I was worried for. "He should have at least texted." Dominic argues, and for a moment, we let his words hang in silence. I knew Carter better than I think he realized, and I knew him distancing himself had nothing to do with us and everything to do with how he was taught to feel growing up.

There was so much none of them have told me, but I know Rowan's need for organization is because he had so little of it as a child, just as Dominic didn't have control, and Carter wasn't allowed to show emotion. It was something I would work on with him—assuming that's what he wants—but I don't want Carter to feel as though he has to disappear every time his past comes out to play.

"You should sleep." Dominic murmurs, his voice a whisper against my ear. Unfortunately, I don't think there was any amount of cuddling that could relax my mind this time. Maybe my body, but not the unease that is now coiled tight within my heart. "Is it late?" I ask, my eyes closing simply because they could as I focused on the way Rowan's fingers mimicked a soft massage. The room was fairly dark, but I had no doubt the curtains across the floor to ceiling windows were top of the line at doing their job.

"Just past six in the morning." Dominic answers, moving further onto the bed until he was laying on his stomach beside me. The smell of pine instantly invaded my senses and helped to calm my restless mind, his hand resting on my stomach as he propped his head up right beside Rowan's legs. My chest felt heavy now that I was fully awake again, but they made it better.

They made everything better. With Dominic right beside me and Rowan beneath me, it was impossible to feel alone, even if a part of me wishes that Carter accompanied them.

I was sad—I knew I was—but I also felt as though every minute I've spent with them has slowly been chipping away the parts of me I liked to keep bottled up inside. Even now, as my eyes reopen and flick down to where Dominic's hand is resting against my stomach, I'm not sucking anything in. A habit that I've had since nine years old is slowly fading away because they taught me I was just as beautiful with scars and curves as I would be without them.

No part of me right now wasn't relaxed, apart from potentially my head, but I think that's kind of a given considering the week I've had. I was admittedly a bit overwhelmed right now, however all of it was balanced by the soft touches and sweet words Dominic and Rowan were offering.

Things always seemed a little more manageable with them by my side, and I'm pretty sure it's the only reason I'm not hyper-ventilating anymore.

"Everything okay up here, Hazel?" Rowan asks as his pointer finger gently taps my head twice, my weight shifting so I can look up at him.

"Yeah, I'm good." I say, and my words are truthful too. There's a lot that isn't good in my life at the moment, but right now, I was content just curling up with them and enjoying every second of being back here again.

"Is there anything we can do to help otherwise?" Dominic offers quietly against my neck, his head resting against me as he too re-laxes. The sight was kind of cute, and I saw Rowan smile down at us when he noticed too, his fingers finally moving from my hair over to the side of my face. I wasn't sure if they'd slept at all last night, but they seemed just as happy doing this as they were holding me on the plane earlier.

"Princess?" Dominic's voice drew me out of my thoughts, re-minding me I never answered his question.

"Sorry." I smiled, lightly kissing his jaw before slowly moving to get up from Rowan's lap. "I'm okay for now. I think I'm just going to use the washroom and try to go back to bed." I instantly miss the comfort of their warmth as I slide my feet to the floor, but I can still feel both of their eyes on me as I move towards the bathroom.

"We'll be here." Rowan nods as he adjusts himself on the bed, Dominic moving to lay on his left instead of remaining horizontal across the mattress. The fact that I knew they would was a nice feeling, and I kept that in my heart as I took care of what I needed to do before moving to wash my hands in the sink.

The bathroom was just as bright and open as the rest of the owner's room, but my gaze snagged on the mirror as I saw just how horrible I looked. Every bit of my face reflected the hell I'd been through this last week, and I quietly groaned as the water fell over my shorter than usual fingernails. Just the pressure of gliding the soap over them stung to the point of more tears, though things felt a little better as the dried blood was removed and washed painfully down the drain. By the time I realized I had the sink on for far too long, my hands were shaking yet again, and it took a lot of effort to steady them. Even then, the next time my eyes met my reflection in the mirror, they were glazed over with the tears I begged myself not to let fall.

I was so sick of crying.

"Hazel," Rowan's voice softly called out against the door, and the sound caused me to shut off the tap abruptly.

"Can I come in, darling?" He asks for the second time in twenty-four hours, making me realize just how long I've been in here. My mouth opens to respond, but this time when I blink, things are a little blurry.

I recognize the feeling of nausea a second before it hits, running to the toilet as sensations of throwing up overtook my body. I heard the sound of the door opening as my chest ached from dry heaving, but what was worse was the combination of overwhelming dizziness that made me feel like passing out. When I suddenly found myself in Rowan's arms on the floor, a part of me thinks I did.

"Shh." He gently coos, and it's only then I realize the wetness on my face was a result of my own tears.

"You're okay." No noise would even come out of my mouth as I cried, but my eyes pinched shut as an ice cold cloth was pressed to my forehead in contrast to the clamminess of my skin. Things seemed as if they were passing me in short flashes, and I couldn't tell if I was having a panic attack or not. All I knew is that I wasn't as okay as I thought I was. "When's the last time you ate?" Dominic quietly asks, and I slowly become aware it's him who's holding the cloth to my head. I wanted to speak, but I couldn't even think about the answer to his question.

The truth is that I didn't know, and that seemed to be indication enough that it had been a while. Somehow Dominic figured that out through my crying and shaking on his own, and he was moving before I could ask him to stay.

"He's just grabbing you some food and probably something to drink." Rowan explains, holding both my hand and the rest of my body tight to his chest. I could feel how fast his heart was pounding, and I knew I had scared him despite the calm expression he tried to wear.

This was the third time today they've had to see me like this and I hated it so much it made me cry harder. I broke apart into an absolute mess yet again, and I had no idea when it would stop.

"Are you okay with me picking you up?" Rowan asks as he places my arms around his neck, standing when he sees my small nod against his shoulder.

The cloth on my forehead slips with the movement, but he catches it and ends up carrying me out with one hand while the other holds the back of my neck gently. Each of his touches was delicate and comforting, and I tried to focus on that as he grabbed a blanket from the chair by the window before sitting both of us down on it. Turning me, Rowan situates us so that my back is pressed against his front with my head tipped back on his shoulder.

Only a second later is a blanket being smoothed over me, being tucked in at my sides to keep me warm even though I felt like I was burning up not long ago.

"Thank you." I somehow managed, wishing things could just be easy again. I wanted Carter to not be gone, and I wanted the blissful ignorance of believing my mother might love me to still exist. I didn't want to admit the fact my dad's still missing or think about what all of the stuff I found of his could mean.

There was so much I didn't want, but Rowan and Dominic were all I needed right now, even if a third of their group wasn't here.

"What can I do, darling?" Rowan asks, stroking my hair in a loving way while his other hand wraps around my midsection. I felt inexplicably close to him right now in more ways than one, but the feeling of his touch just about perfectly balanced the feeling of being held emotionally as well. Things would be so much easier if there was just one simple fix to this all, but I knew what I feared was true.

Time was the only long term medicine for my pain. "I just want to forget." I half whisper half cry against his shoulder, and I feel his grip tighten on me just a little more as if pulling me even that millimeter closer would help. A part of me wondered if it did, because like earlier, things slowly began to feel a little easier again. That didn't change the fact I was still uncontrollably crying and shaking beneath his fingertips, but I think this kind of reaction from me was bound to happen at some point.

I used to channel all of my pain into anger to avoid how I was really feeling—the only difference now is that I feel safe enough to fall apart knowing there's already someone there to catch the pieces. There are three someones actually, even if Carter isn't physically by my side.

"Do you remember what I promised you about this window?" Rowan asks after a small stretch of time, his words catching me so off guard every thought of mine paused for a second.

"W-what?" I stuttered through my tears, my head turning slightly to see where his hand was moving the curtain back inch by inch until I could see the glass. It was the very place he promised he'd one day fuck me against, but why he was bringing it up now seemed incomprehensible to me.

"I lied," Rowan whispers in my ear, lifting my hand with his before pressing it against the freezing cold panel.

"I said I would take my time with you until I had you begging for more, but that was a lie." My mouth parted slightly as I felt his warm breath brush across my neck, my tears slowing as my head became consumed by an entirely different emotion. "With glass this cold, I bet you'd be clamping down around me so tight, it would be impossible not to give into everything you desired."

"Rowan," I murmured, wiping away some of my tears with my shoulders as I felt him smile against me. The weight on my chest began to dissolve with every passing second of his spoken fantasy, and I soon realized why he was doing it. He was distracting me like I asked, even though I'd expected more kisses across my forehead.

This method seemed to be a hell of a lot more effective, but now I was turned on and my face was red for new reasons.

"I would fuck you so hard, the glass would fog up and create an outline of your perfect little body taking me like the good girl you are." I nearly shook again when he pulled our hands away from the window, but I didn't miss the fogged imprint our touch left over.

I couldn't imagine how it would feel with my entire body pressed against it when my fingers were cold from those few seconds alone, but now Rowan was having me imagining it with every single part of me. While his distraction didn't take away the dizziness or nausea, it did give me the reprieve I was looking for, and that's why I loved him so damn much.

"Thank you." I say as I turn my head to kiss his cheek in gratitude. I wanted to thank him a thousand times over again for understanding what I needed, but the sound of Dominic's arrival had me looking at the door instead. Don't get me wrong, I was happy to see him walking towards me with a caring smile across his face, however it was the sight of Carter behind him that drew my attention in.

I don't know where he had left to, but it was clear he came back for me even if I could instantly tell something was wrong.

While Carter remained stiff at the door, Dominic walked until he was kneeling at my side, handing me a glass of water and a tray of snacks.

"Go slow. I don't want you to get sick from eating too quickly too soon." After offering a tired yet genuine thank you, I moved to grab a cube of cheese I saw on the plate.

To my surprise, Carter moved with me. As he got closer to where I was sitting, I saw more and more evidence that things were off with him. His eyes looked swollen as his gaze locked on me, his irises as dark as coal. I had no idea where he'd disappeared to these last six hours, but I did know he didn't sleep during that time period. I opened my mouth to say his name, but Rowan's tightened hold on me had me second guessing myself. Instead, I watched as he sat half of his weight on the chair's arm, his eyes darting down to the glass of water in my hand.

"Drink, sweetheart." Carter encouraged quietly, his words rough as though it hurt him to speak.

I knew better than to challenge him right now, and it broke my heart to realize he was putting himself on a constant edge being here just to make sure I was alright.

I saw it in the way his hands clutched onto the cushion so hard it seemed as though he was restraining himself from doing something that would warrant Rowan's cautious hold on my body. It almost seemed stupid because I knew he'd never hurt me, but there were a lot of things that felt off today that I was too tired to question. Obeying, I took a long sip from the glass until almost half of the water was gone, pulling it away only when I saw satisfaction in Carter's eyes. It was the food that came next, and it was a combination of all three of them feeding me while refusing my attempts to do it myself.

"Let us take care of you." Dominic says as he lifts a grape to my mouth, taking the fruit between my teeth before swallowing down the sweet taste. Very soon, I simply gave in, especially to Carter as he fed me in silence. The stiffness of his body never fully ceased, but I knew I was acting as a distraction of his own right now too.

I had no doubt he would be gone again once he saw that I was better, and unfortunately that moment was coming a lot quicker than I was prepared for. I didn't want to admit that the tightness in my chest had fully loosened and that their care had been everything I needed, but it was. Together, my men gave me everything and indeed put back together the pieces of me that I'd previously allowed to shatter, yet I knew there were parts of Carter that were still left broken in the end.

"im sorry" he whisoers for only me to hear before planting a gental kiss to my lips in apology.

I didnt know what it meant, but knowing that the climas of my pain has ebbed, Carter left yet again. this time i knew he would not be coming back until his mind was settled.

the heardes part about it was that i had no clue when that time would come.

Hazel

It has been four days since I last heard anything from Carter, but I feel like at some point enough should be enough. I didn't hold his need to be alone against him, because I truly understand the feeling, however short texts and bland responses weren't enough for me. I'd been gone for an entire week without seeing him, plus these additional four with the exception of the two hour plane ride back from Detroit.

Either way, I was worried, and sad, and I missed him. Carter didn't deserve to be alone through whatever is happening, and today was the first day he initiated texting me, telling me he was safe and just finishing up some paperwork at Rush. His mistake was that he believed I would wait until he got back to his house to see him. While I was still staying at Jade's and had been since I got back, Carter wasn't allowed to just block me out completely and then act like everything's fine when he finally decides to show up again.

I knew he was hurting, and it was the only reason I wasn't mad, but I still wanted to see him, even if he didn't want to talk. My mind had been made up, and as I walked straight past the bouncers at the back entrance, I prayed to God he was genuinely okay and not physically hurt as a result of whatever it is he does during these trips of his.

The usual receptionist, Cassidy, wasn't there as I moved through the lobby, but that was the only thing I'd noticed between the decision of getting in my car and now as I stood in front of the door to Carter's office. Please let him be okay. While I knew the password to the lock, I still knocked as my breath held in wait.

He had to have known it was me because I doubt there are very few people who have entry to this hallway in the club, but the pause had me second guessing if he was even actually on the other side. Debating just walking away, I almost gave up at the same time I heard the click of a lock and the twist of a handle.

My heart skipped a beat as the door slowly opened, but it was the man who answered that had me tightening with uncertainty. Carter's large body leaned against the frame as I took in his appearance—the accurate representation of whatever demons he's been fighting these last few days.

The usual short trim of his facial hair had grown out a little since I last saw him, but it was the darkness of both his irises and under eyes that had me thinking my worry was more than justified.

"I'll leave if you want me to, but I just—" I wasn't even able to finish my sentence before he was pulling me in tight to his body, his arms wrapping around me and hugging as close as he could manage. "I'm sorry." He whispered instantly, his lips brushing against my head as I returned his unexpected embrace. Carter still felt the same, just as his smell was as comforting as usual, but I was no fool to believe he was okay. Most of the time the man in my arms is a closed book, but he lets me see and hear every emotion in his apology. I very rarely hear Carter's voice shake, and it did just now.

"I'm sorry I wasn't there when you passed out. I should have—"

"Shh," I cut him off, just happy he was here again. Whatever angry concern I had on the drive here seemed like something of the past as his grip around me tightened, a relieved but tired sigh leaving both of our mouths. We really do need to talk about him just leaving out of nowhere, but it was clear Carter hadn't just left for the fun of it. If his disorganized appearance wasn't indication enough, then the sadness of his hug was.

"It's been a rough week." Carter lets out a heavy breath of air as he pulls us slightly away from the door, closing it so we could have some privacy together. I really wanted him to open up to me, but I also knew we were both walking on eggshells right now around each other. I didn't want to push him past his boundaries, however this conversation we needed to have was not one that could continue to be delayed and swept under the rug.

"Do you think we could talk for a little?" Carter asks the words I've been waiting to hear for the last four days, and I, of course, nodded and allowed him to lead the both of us over to the dark coloured couch in the corner. I sat beside him while my legs were brought to drape over his thighs, his hands instantly falling to smooth up and down the freshly waxed skin from my appointment yesterday. I know Carter noticed how soft my legs were just as I noticed how rough his hands felt. "You're hurt." I frown as I take his fingers into mine, not wanting to aggravate the bruises across his knuckles.

"I know." He says lowly as I lift his hand to my lips, pressing a gentle kiss to his pain just as he did for me a few days ago. "It's why I had to leave." His eyes didn't leave mine as I slowly lowered his fingers back to his lap. He didn't let go, though, instead interlacing his hand with mine. The gesture was sweet, even if he didn't mean it to be. I think Carter needed my comfort just as much as I needed his, and I was more than happy to give it to him as the side of my head rested against the couch back.

"What happened?" I ask, not just about his knuckles but everything else that led up to this moment. I wanted to know everything he was willing to share with me, and I had a strong feeling it was a lot based on the vulnerable expression he wore across his face.

"I've never really been good at describing my emotions... but I promise I'll try." Carter says, his tone growing a little quieter as his thumb brushes against my knee.

"Do you remember me telling you that my mother passed away when I was a child?" I listened as his voice broke at the sentence, and it was my heart that broke for him when I realized why he'd left —why he didn't want to be around anyone for the last four days.

"Sunday was the anniversary of her death." Carter turned his head away to hide the tears threatening to spill from his eyes, but I knew he was also hiding his anger and every other emotion brewing inside.

His mother didn't just die, she was murdered by the same man he's been hunting for years. I can't remember the name as he very rarely mentions him around me, but I knew his recklessness was a result of the pain this monster caused. "You'd think after almost two decades I'd be able to move on, but the pain never really goes away." Carter says, not resisting as I turn his head to look at me.

"So I make it. That's why I had to leave." I understood what he was saying, but I still didn't get why he couldn't have just told me this. I have a feeling it has a lot to do with how he makes things go away, though.

"What do you do to clear your mind?" I ask, knowing that whatever he does hasn't been enough for him. There was a wild look still in his eyes, and I suspected I knew the answers before they even left his mouth. He's never been in a serious relationship until me, and it was the changing factor in his struggle to forget everything from the past that still haunts his present.

"It doesn't matter." Carter shakes his head as his hands on my legs still. We both knew it was a lie, but things were slowly beginning to make sense for me. I remembered the way Carter trashed his room all of those nights ago after something bad had happened, because for him, it was a release. The fights I'm sure he'd provoked to get bruises like the ones he had was a release. Just as was drinking, and the one thing he couldn't do because of his respect for me.

"It matters when you're wound so tight you can't even look at me after four days straight of solitude." I say, brushing my hand against his jaw but freezing when his one hand grabs onto my wrist. It wasn't painful, but it was strong enough to show I was right. "Rush used to be a place where you could work out your stress on as many women as you wanted without the commitment of either person's feelings getting involved." I state, understanding where he was coming from now.

"Hazel—" "You use alcohol, sex, and pain as distractions, but this year only two of them are there for you to exploit." I continue, knowing after a week of silence, I was finally getting somewhere with him. I could tell by the clench of his jaw and the darkness of his eyes, a very clear shift occurring in his demeanor.

"You may be right, sweetheart, but this is only proving I'm not in control enough to come home yet." Carter gently moves my legs off of him as he tries to create distance between us, but I wasn't lying to myself when I came here with a purpose.

I learned a long time ago what makes Carter tick, and as much as I loved him wanting to protect me, that's not what either of us needed. This last week has been full of me trying to come to terms with things myself, and I was just as on edge as he was, even if he doesn't want to admit it.

"You're not in control because you haven't allowed yourself what you need." I argue, not making any more advances apart from my words and wandering eyes. I've never seen Carter squirm before, but what he was doing right now came pretty damn close to it. I didn't want him to feel like he ever has to hold himself back from me, especially when I can help him forget. The only thing is that he needs a bit of a push, and it was one I was more than happy to deliver.

"I know what you think you're doing, but you need to stop, Hazel." Carter says, channeling all of the dominance I'm familiar with into a single sentence. He rarely ever says my full name, and while my body reacts accordingly to the warning in the form of a racing heart, a taunting smile also appears on my face.

"And why is that, Daddy?" I smirked, taking my foot and dragging it slowly up his ankle. I continued my path northwards until his hand stopped me, his fingers sending shivers down my spine with his touch alone. I knew he believed this was an issue of him not having control, but it was quite the opposite. He had too much restraint, and it was holding him back to the point of him doing every other unhealthy thing possible than accepting my help.

"One of us needs to be intelligent about this, and it's clear you've taken on the role of being a brat instead." Carter says lowly, letting go of my leg despite the evidence of how much I'm affecting him. "If I touch you in the way you think you want right now, I'm not going to be nice or gentle about it."

There was no anger in his tone, but no amount of resistance could hide the tenseness of his body. I wasn't going to force anything on him, however I wasn't going to let him decide what I can and can't handle either. When we wrote the contract together, I signed off on consensual non-consent. My mind hasn't changed about it in the least.

"I don't remember asking you to be gentle, Carter." I purposefully add a bit of attitude to his name as I outright challenge whatever he's convinced will happen if he relies on me to know my limits. "Assuming you're sober, the only damn thing holding you back is yourself and your stupid—" I didn't even get to finish my sentence before a hand was being wrapped around my throat, pulling me towards Carter until I was straddling his lap. A flash of darkness was the only thing I saw before his lips were crashing against mine, devouring me and stealing every last bit of air from my lungs. I melted as his hands pulled my front flush to his, my body melding to his desire and submitting to just how much we missed each other.

A week's worth of longing, sadness and excitement all merged into one long kiss that set my heart on fire. Something inside of me whined in protest when Carter pulled away from me, but his hand remained wrapped around my neck as he felt my pulse flutter beneath his fingertips.

"Are you sure you're okay with this, sweetheart?" He pants against my lips, his hair slightly tousled from where my fingers are still gripping onto. "There's so much more we should probably talk about and I don't want you to feel pressured just because I'm a little stressed."

We both knew he was more than a little stressed, but there was no way in hell I was backing out now that he'd kissed me. I needed this release just as much as him, and I mean something that is so much bigger than just a few orgasms.

"I want you." I say, my words sounding so unlike me and so lust-driven I would've blushed under different circumstances.

"Believe it or not, Carter, I've fantasized about being roughly handled by you since Dominic told me in Brooklyn you were interested in CNC." I think my words might have surprised him a little bit, but when I shifted in his lap, there was no doubt about how much we both wanted this. Leaning forward slightly, I turned Carter's head until my mouth was hovering right below his ear, smiling to myself at his reaction.

"I want you to fuck me like you hate me, and then hold me when we're both too spent to move." That was all it took before whatever little control he had left snapped. A mixture of a groan and a growl built deep in Carter's chest as he pulled me back by my hair, looking at me in the way I'd been waiting for.

My heart raced excitedly as understanding passed through us—understanding of what we were about to do together. I trusted with every part of me that Carter would take care of me, and I knew that because he didn't jump into things and kiss me again. Instead, Carter gently lifted me off of his lap and onto the couch beside him so we could do what was most important for scenes like this.

"Let's discuss our limits."

While the two of us had already signed a general BDSM contract together, Carter and I spent just over an hour doing nothing but talking about our interests all over again. For example, Carter took every tool I agreed for impact play off of the table because he said for first times it can make things dangerous if I'm moving too much to get away. On the other side of things, I said no to blindfolds since I really didn't want to miss a single part of what was about to happen. And, I feared it might trigger me to not be able to see what was happening given my history.

Things that weren't limits normally became them for the night and vice versa—all reasons in which it was so important to communicate beforehand like we are now. I may have been soaked from talking about sex for the last hour with the epitome of sex himself, but after enough time, we were able to also establish an outline of sorts as to what we were going to do. While a lot of tonight would be us acting on our natural instincts, Carter and I discussed a lot of the events that would be taking place as well in almost more detail than my body could handle.

Everything I needed to feel comfortable had been offered, and now, I was currently in our playroom at Rush, alone and practically shaking from how turned on I was. We agreed this would begin with a game of hide and seek of sorts, and with Carter not currently in the room, I was to hide as best as I could in the limited space we had. Considering this wasn't a usual scene, I didn't take off a single piece of clothing as I hid behind the door leading into the bathroom. The thought of Carter ripping them off of my body had me shivering with desire anyways.

I had no idea how long it would take him before he decided to come into the room, but I didn't expect it to be within thirty seconds of me hiding. It was the four digit passcode on the lock I heard first, then the sound of the door opening, closing, and then the sound of unhurried footsteps into the room.

"You know it's quite rude to break onto other people's property without permission, little one." Carter spoke calmly, his dominance flowing over to me from those few words alone. I urged my heart to steady as my hand covered my mouth, praying he couldn't hear the uneven breaths threatening to reveal me. Of course they were naturally louder to my own ear than his, but I was well aware of what Carter's specialty was for work. He knew how to hunt, and there wasn't a doubt in my mind he didn't already know where I was.

"Don't be afraid." Carter smiles as I watch him through the crack of the door, my breath hitching at the sight of the small knife twirling expertly between his fingers.

"Why don't we talk about what happens to bad girls who break the rules?" Despite already expecting the weapon, it didn't change the shocking effect of actually seeing it. Carter handled the blade with such grace and precision it had my knees wanting to buckle, my eyes tearing away from the sight in fear he would sense my gaze on him. He'd wanted me to listen to his footsteps when he first came in, but all I was met with now was deafening silence. I squirmed and shifted under the pressure like a rabbit caught in a snare, and I truly felt like prey when I braved looking back to the room just to find unoccupied space.

"Found you." A deep voice snuck up behind me, and then I was running, trying to slam the door closed as I moved towards the only exit here. I didn't expect the adrenaline to make me feel as good as it did, but a part of me came alive from my futile attempts at escaping.

The beauty of this is that both of us knew how this was going to end, and getting away wasn't a possibility Carter would allow. Gasping at the feeling of a large hand grabbing onto my waist, my front was abruptly pushed against the wall, barely even close to the door as a heavy weight kept me still. Or still-ish.

"Let go of me." I fought against the way Carter's one thigh pressed firmly between my two, my clit rubbing against him as I squirmed. "You think you can disrespect me like this and run away without punishment?" His chilling voice chuckles close enough to my ear that I can feel his exhale in amusement.

"Because let me let you in on a little secret. You can't." A whimper fell past my lips as I was nearly lifted onto my tiptoes from the force of Carter's leg, an intense pressure rubbing against myself from my struggle. There was no question about how much bigger the man at my back was than me, but I was also trained and knew how to get out of a hold like this. I just prayed it wouldn't be something I'd regret, even if I have previous consent to do it.

Feeling Carter's one hand roughly begin to tug at my shirt, I used it as motivation as I reared my head back, connecting with his jaw hard due to the height difference. I smiled as he stumbled back just enough for me to get free, shoving him away as I took a few cautious movements closer to the door. In any other case I would've ran, but for the briefest of moments, my eyes met Carter's and held there.

I took in the heavy rise and fall of his chest that matched my own, traveling up to where his fingers were brushing against the place I'd hit. I'm near certain it will have a faint bruise come tomorrow morning, but it wasn't guilt that had me frozen in place. It was the terrifying smirk that curled across Carter's lips as though he were a little proud of the action... and even more turned on.

Fuck. I tracked the movement the second he took a step towards me, recovering frighteningly quick from the impact when I turned and spun back to the door. There was a little more distance between us this time, but Carter was faster than what should be humanly possible. I only made it two steps before my hopes were crushed, a firm grasp locking onto my shoulder and taking me to the ground. My balance betrayed me as I was forced to grit my teeth as I fell, Carter's pressing weight following me down.

"So quick to run, but not nearly quick enough." He mocked, a hand holding onto my neck and effectively pinning me to the floor. I tried to buck out of his hold, but couldn't, feeling that freeing rush of control transfer over to the man holding me. That's what Carter was doing right now. Despite following along with the scene, he also made sure I was feeling safe in the most subtle ways he knew I needed.

"It's a shame, really." He continued his act of demeaning disappointment, the daze from my cushioned fall slowly fading away into more thrashing and squirming beneath him. I was well aware that my frantic movements repeatedly caused me to rub against Carter's erection at my back, and that only encouraged me to continue my struggles, even once he gathered both of my wrists into one hand and pinned them between us.

The action meant I'd gained back mobility of my head, but Carter made sure to keep well out of my reach now that he'd been hit once. I cried out angrily as I felt the warmth of his mouth meet the sensitive point of my neck, frustrated he'd overpowered me so easily and knew it too.

"Mmm." He smiled against my throat, his tongue darting out before sucking and grazing his teeth against the skin. I didn't want the fight to be over yet, and I most certainly didn't want Carter to know something so simple affected me this much. His smugness genuinely spurred me on as I tried to kick at his side, only to be met with his knees preventing me from even lifting the backs of my legs.

"Get off." I demanded, even though I knew every second of my struggle was slowly draining my already fading remains of strength.

"I plan to." Carter allowed more of his weight to bear down on me, forcing me to feel every part of him that was connected to my body. While his words caused me to flush against my wishes, I couldn't ignore the hard muscle of his front defined against my back, the unmistakable hot length of him pressing against my ass. He made sure I knew who was controlling me, and I let out a mixed, strangled sound when Carter's hips rolled forwards, using my slack and breathless body for his pleasure. "Are you going to be a good girl and let me take your clothes off?" His low voice groaned in my ear, and as planned, I continued this game of resistance by squirming beneath him.

"Screw you." I snapped, my words leading to the tightening grip of the hand around my wrists before I felt Carter's weight ease up a noticeable amount. I was still being held down, but now he had a lot more access to me, his roaming fingertips taking clear advantage of this position. For a moment that's all he did, the shuffling of clothing meeting my ears in time with the uneven beat of my heart. That moment, however, was highly short-lived. Suddenly, I felt something tear at my clothes, slicing through the material effortlessly and cleanly.

"I guess it's going to have to be the hard way, then." Carter says threateningly, but I knew this was exactly what he wanted. One second I was shivering at the sudden rush of air I was exposed to, the next I was being picked up and tossed over his shoulder like I was nothing. I screamed when he slapped my ass perched right over his shoulder, hard enough to have my fists pounding against his back in protest. Just as I went to slap him in return, all of the breath was whooshed from my lungs as I was tossed down onto the large, familiar bed.

The only difference now was that black rope was tied to all four corners of the posts, the intent behind them no doubt to restrain me. Despite my attempts to roll off of the bed and run off, Carter ends up straddling me with his knees resting on either side of my waist, my arms being pulled forcefully above my head.

Though I shouldn't be surprised, I couldn't believe how easily he suppressed every action I delivered at full effort. It was like I was nothing more than a doll for him to manipulate, and with my first wrist skillfully tied up, my testing tug proved me entirely restricted.

"Colour?" Carter asks as he peers down at me, holding onto my second hand but not moving as he waited for my response. My struggle slowed just enough that I was able to meet the darkness swirling in his eyes, but I also saw the affection of my boyfriend rubbing his thumb against my wrist to monitor my reactions.

"Green." I blinked and he was moving again, though the check in showed he was more than in control of himself, his smirk in control of me. It took nothing more than mere seconds before both of my hands were tied apart to the headboard, whatever knots Carter had done holding tight without hurting me in any way. He didn't bother to hide his amusement when my arms tried to tug at the bindings, my chest rising and falling with only my underwear left to cover me.

"Are you going to behave or do I need to tie your legs down too?" Carter questions with a challenging cock of his head, no words able to pass my lips. Instead, I took advantage of the slight space between us as I brought my leg up, kicking out until I met his chest. Or tried to.

Carter moved insanely fast as his fingers wrapped around me, placing my foot to rest against his shoulder as his head dipped down. My eyes never left his as a surprisingly gentle kiss was placed on my ankle, a second passing before his teeth grazed against the bone. He held me still as a place I never expected to be sensitive was teased, shocks spreading throughout my entire body from a single touch.

"So responsive." A quiet murmur was spoken as I squirmed, my leg being placed back onto the bed before rope was promptly tied around there too. I couldn't even fight now if I wanted to, and Carter knew that as his guard lowered and he raised himself off of me. Truthfully, I didn't really know what to do now that I quite literally couldn't resist him, but I already knew somewhat of what was coming next and it had my heart thrumming nervously in my chest.

The glint of the knife from earlier had my pulse spiking as Carter drew it from his pocket, resting the blade across my stomach as his hands shifted to pull off the shirt he was wearing. It felt as though all of the breath inside of me left again at the sight of tattoos and muscle, wanting to press myself up but not being able to.

That in itself was frustrating, although the frustration didn't last long when Carter slowly leaned forward, dark strands of his hair falling across his forehead and partially over his scar. For a moment, I almost thought he was going to kiss me, but then he did quite the opposite.

Failing to notice he'd retrieved the knife between us, I only realized he'd moved when I felt my breasts being freed from the containment of my bra, the center of it now open from a cut down the middle. Unsuccessfully yanking at the black rope in response, Carter sliced both straps around my shoulders as well before tossing the ruined material to the floor. Even if he tried to play mean, I knew he was happy right now, a small trace of the smile on his face he couldn't hide.

It's felt like forever since I last had his hands on my body, and when his head dipped down to take my nipple into his mouth, I cried out his name wishing I could thread my fingers through his soft hair. Keeping his eyes on me, he watched as I writhed beneath him in desperation and pleasure right before he pulled back, smirking at my whimper.

"You're doing so good." Carter encourages as he stops touching me entirely, moving off of the bed and leaving me tied up at his mercy. "But you do look quite pretty like this." Moving the only part of me I still could, my neck craned to see the mini fridge door across from me being opened, Carter's back only straightening after he'd retrieved what was now in his hand. The object was something we'd discussed for a long time before the events that led up to now, but that didn't stop my heart from racing at the sight of the new knife being alternated between his fingers. Knife play was something I've always been interested in, but my past has always stopped me from exploring it.

When Carter first mentioned the idea, I was hesitant, but my trust in him made me feel a lot more comfortable, especially because he took the time to fully talk about it with me. The blade between his fingertips was so intentionally dull, not even simple squirming on my part would cause blood to be drawn. That was a hard limit of mine we'd discussed, but I was okay with light scratches and marks painting Carter's path down my body. The intention of the cold temperature of the fridge was to freeze the knife to the point the steel's coolness could mimic the sensations of actual pain. It was the perfect compromise that would allow me to experience exactly what I wanted while keeping me in the right headspace in the process.

"Though, I do think you would look much prettier with my initials carved into that soft skin of yours." Carter smirked as he gave me the time I needed to take all of this in, slowly walking back to the bed before placing the knife down once again against my front.

I couldn't help the small hiss I let out at how freezing it was, but when Carter moved back onto the bed, this time he wore no shirt and his belt was half undone. He tracked the movement of me biting my bottom lip as I warmed at the contact his presence brought, my hips trying to roll but stopping when they were straddled.

However it wasn't the action that made me squirm, but rather the small vibrator Carter had retrieved, turning it onto a low setting. I couldn't even hear the usual hum of it, but I knew it was on when it was circled ever so lightly over my underwear, Carter smiling before he moved past the fabric until the toy was directly on my clit.

My mouth parted and my core tightened at the sensations, Carter gauging my every reaction as his fingers left with the material of my underwear holding it in place. The vibrations were nowhere near unbearable, but we both knew what came next, and that had my arousal heightened by so much more than I knew possible. Watching the knife move with the rise and fall of my stomach, my heart raced as it was picked up slowly and raised to my neck.

"Stay still for me." Carter says as a gasp left my mouth, his eyes holding mine while he dragged the blade across my right collar bone before moving to the other. My legs failed as they tried to close from the pressure, the pain in combination with the pleasure making me dizzy. Allowing my eyes to fall shut, I simply felt, embracing the sharp feeling of the knife moving down my sternum before veering slightly to the left. It took everything in me not to move, but my eyes snapped open only seconds later when Carter began to trace cold lines around the swell of my breasts, my face flushing to find he's been watching me the entire time.

Though I wanted to hold that gaze, my fear caused me to look down instead as the blade got closer and closer to my nipple, his fingers intentionally gliding the weapon in circles around the hardened peak. "Carter." I moaned, and I think it was the breathy sound of his name on my tongue that caused him to change, dragging the knife right over my nipple and causing me to cry out his name all over again. A second later his mouth was on me, his warm tongue flicking the bud and sucking it painfully into his mouth where he had just threatened to cut.

"Please—"

"You fucking consume me, Hazel." Carter growled as he kissed up my body, his fingers taking over instead as he pinched and pulled a string of noises from my parted lips. Only when he was fully hovering above me did the knife return, this time tracing spots on my stomach and over my hips.

"When you say my name like that, sweetheart..." He continues, breaking to kiss me as our lips collide in pure desperation.

"Nothing else matters."

"Carter," I moaned again, drowning in the waves of his words until all that was left was us—two people who not only found ourselves lost in our touch but in each other. Sensing the change between us, I smiled as the knife was tossed off of the bed with a clatter and the bindings of my hands were undone. Instantly, my fingers found their way weaved through the dark strands of Carter's hair, pulling until a deep groan escaped his lips.

"I need you now." I say against his mouth, my hips rolling up to rub against his hard length just to push the vibrations harder against my clit. It was an overwhelming pleasure that didn't last for long, my underwear being torn straight from my body hastily as the toy fell to my side.

"I know." Carter whispers as he lifts up slightly, undoing his pants while my legs remain tied apart.

"Me too."

Those words were the last he spoke before he was bearing down on me and thrusting himself forward, his cock filling and stretching me until he was as deep as he could reach.

There was a moment—a very short moment—where all we could do was remain unmoving, staring into each other's eyes as our bodies became connected as one. I could feel the twitch of his dick just as well as I could feel the emotion radiating off of the both of us, needing this release more than we needed the air that filled our lungs. We needed the push and pull of everything that led up to being here, and as Carter slowly pulled out, I knew we were about to get that. Suddenly being filled to the brim again, my back arched in sync with the movement of my hand, reaching up and holding onto his shoulder. "Thank you." I heard him mumble into my ear, smiling as I watched every contained part of him become unchained. In a second, everything about us unraveled, my fingers on his shoulder not just holding him but trying to shove him away too. This wasn't just our fantasy anymore, it was a fight to be okay. It was one we fed off of each other to achieve.

"Shit!" I screamed as Carter became unhinged, rocking his hips mercilessly against me as his unrelenting grip held me still for his pounding. He didn't care as my hands pushed out to try and get him off of me, using the momentum of my body to only fuck into me harder accompanied by his sounds of obvious satisfaction. I, however, clenched my jaw, biting back the noises of my own pleasure and instead became filled with the harsh slaps of our skin meeting again and again. "Wouldn't it feel so much better to just give in?" Carter groans, his hand gripping the back of my neck so he could watch my face as I fought him.

"Let me hear you, Hazel." His voice was even huskier than usual, causing me to tighten around him as I shook my head the best I could. I didn't trust myself to even open my mouth, the liquid heat pooling inside of me only expanding with my resistance. Even after that first night with Rowan, I've never been fucked as hard as I am now, and I think it shows on my face as Carter smirks, his head dipping down to take my nipple into his mouth.

My body was still high on the pain of his knife, and when his teeth grazed over me, I broke.

Tears spilt from my eyes as my mouth parted, my heart pounding wildly at the renewed sensations spreading through me. I tried to push upwards to escape the growing knot of pleasure in my stomach, but every failed strain and struggle of mine encouraged me to give in. I knew we were both close as we moaned against each other, my hands giving up at pushing him away and instead weaving through his hair to pull him closer. Carter didn't fight it as I brought his face up to mine, his forehead resting against me as I cried and panted and trembled.

The both of us were absolute messes, our guards completely down and vulnerable as I not only submitted to him, but he did the same for me. I gave in, and it was something you could only experience to understand just how liberating it was. It felt like I had just gained control over the experiences where it had been stripped away from me all those years ago, and when I blinked my tear soaked eyes open, it was the man I loved staring right back at me. It was the sight of Carter's eyes that pulled me over the edge, and it was his name on my tongue that did the same for him.

My body became wrapped up with his in every single way possible as his head nuzzled into my neck, shaking from both my release and everything else that has been eating away at me for the last decade of my life. Somehow Carter understood what I needed when seconds later my feet had been freed from the rope. I didn't waste a second before turning over to straddle him in a sitting position.

I shivered as I felt his orgasm leak down my thighs and back to where we were still connected, but there was nothing sexual about the way I wrapped my hands around his neck and hugged him like I would never get the chance to again. As annoying as it was, I sobbed against Carter's chest when I felt his two strong arms pulling me closer to him, wrapping around my back until we were a tangle of limbs. He held me and didn't say anything as I cried and cried in his embrace, everything about this leaving us stripped bare in the most perfect ways possible. I sniffled at the feeling of wet hot tears streaming down my face, but when they got wiped away, I realized they weren't just mine as I pulled back. Carter was crying too, and it wasn't just a little bit either.

His sadness matched mine as I moved to cup his face instead, resting my head against his while we broke apart together. Nothing was pretty about the way we shattered in each other's arms, and it wasn't a date, but I didn't care. Very little made sense about anything anymore, however there was one thing that did and it was us. Carter knew that I needed special toothpaste for my teeth, and that I refused to eat any kind of seafood. He knew why I was sheltered and kept me close anyways when nobody else wanted me. He kissed my fingers when I was bleeding and broken, and taught me how to love myself again when I wasn't sure it was possible anymore. Carter was my always, and even if he doesn't feel the same way, I refused to live in a world where he's unaware of.

"Hazel, there's something I need to tell you." He interrupts my thoughts quietly, his eyes dropping from mine as he gently lifts me off of him just so that he wasn't inside of me anymore. His tears never stopped, nor did my shaking, but we stayed connected to each other as I nodded silently in response. Whatever it was, we could handle it together. If today proved anything, it was that. Watching as Carter's eyes flicked back up to mine, I didn't move as a single last tear fell, the droplet hitting my hand and breaking apart against my skin.

~ Twenty-Five ~

Carter

Hazel was currently curled up in my lap, her body wrapped around mine as our eyes grew swollen and our cheeks became tear stained. And even now, she was still devastatingly stunning. She was about to tell me she loved me—I could tell just by looking at her face—yet

I couldn't bring myself to feel as though I'd earned that confession from her. I wasn't supposed to fall in love—especially as hard as I did—but even now, I was still falling. I fell as she kissed my cheeks. I fell as her thumbs trailed along my jaw. I fell as she stared at me with the devotion I didn't deserve, and I fell as she hugged me so tight, she became my lifeline. My always.

I couldn't let her go now, even when every instinct inside of me begged otherwise, because Detroit changed everything for not just Hazel, but for Dominic, Rowan, and I too.

She was hurt because I wasn't there when she needed me, and when I'd kneeled to the ground and kissed each knuckle of her bleeding hands, I knew I couldn't be the cause of that kind of pain for her all over again. I would rather die than put Hazel in the state she was in a week ago at her mother's house, but I fear that it won't matter once the truth inevitably comes out anyways.

"Hazel, there's something I need to tell you." I choke out over my tears, repositioning us because what I was about to tell her wasn't something I was comfortable doing still inside of her. I leaned into Hazel's touch as she continued to cup my face, but even that didn't make things easier this time. Rowan, Dominic, and I had fought yet again on the trip back from Detroit, but the option of sending Hazel to Costa Rica for the foreseeable future was no longer on the table.

They gave me an ultimatum on the plane while she was asleep, and I've had nightmares and panic attacks repeatedly these last four days knowing something bad was going to happen and I wasn't going to be able to stop it.

"Anything." Hazel whispers against my mouth, her body still shaking in my hold as she meets my eyes. I didn't know where to start or how she would react, and because of that, I took the coward's way out.

"Let's clean you up first, okay?" I asked, my voice shaking slightly as I did so. The two of us just cracked open an entire history responsible for the tears I haven't let myself spill in almost two decades, but I couldn't stop, especially now with Hazel giving me the comfort I don't deserve but need more than anything. Her silent nod is enough to tell me I have her permission, moving her neck to my shoulder while her legs wrapped better around my waist. On tired limbs, I lifted the both of us from the bed and held her close to me as I walked over to the bathroom to our left. It was slightly smaller than the one at home, but it would be just as efficient to take care of her in the ways that we both needed.

"Bath or shower?" I ask quietly, my feet meeting the heated tile as I slowly set Hazel down. Her response was just as quiet, but I nodded still, letting her use the washroom while I turned on the panel to the shower.

Instantly, water poured from the ceiling, the lights dimming to a deep red colour that was gentle on both of our tired eyes.

Technically it's just past nine at night, but the crying made it feel later for both me and likely Hazel as well.

I absently heard the flush of a toilet and the running of a sink behind me, but the shower drowned out most of the noises, not that it mattered. I was frozen to the spot, staring at my reflection through the water spotted glass door.

The scar that protruded across my forehead and through my right eyebrow was the only thing I could see, the permanent reminder of my sixteenth birthday and why I could never be who I wanted to now. There are some things you can't come back from. This was one of those things.

Anger builds tight inside of me as everything else blurs, memories piling on top of each other until I remember why I can't be with Hazel right now.

"Carter." A soft voice pulls me from the trance I had fallen into, the touch of Hazel's fingers against my back feeling like whiplash to my mind. I was shaking again, and I know she noticed it too. While the feeling of her hand pressed against my skin helped, I wouldn't risk losing control around her ever.

"I think we need to call Dominic or Rowan to come get you, sweetheart." I shook, knowing she shouldn't be here right now. This was a mistake and one that could get bad quickly if she didn't leave. A puff of air left my nose as her touch removed from my back, but Hazel didn't move away like she was supposed to. Instead, she reached around me and opened the shower door, gesturing for me to get in.

There was a hardness in her eyes that told me she wasn't asking, and it was so unlike her it made me smile for a second as I stepped inside now slightly distracted. I didn't have to look to see her getting in behind me, my muscles still strained and my heart tense from its rapid beating. Things were quiet for a while as the sound of the glass door swung closed, but the next time something was spoken, it wasn't from my mouth.

"Get on your knees." I hear Hazel say, her voice soft but not weak. When I turned to look at her in surprise, I found she was being dead serious, watching patiently and waiting for me to listen to her. I tilted my head in confusion as her words settled in, but with furrowed brows, I obeyed.

Kneeling right in front of one of the shower heads, I gave in while water began to soak my dark hair, the rest of my body along with it.

The tile was rough against my knees, but I could barely feel it as all of my attention became focused on where my girl was going with this. Taking my shampoo, Hazel made me watch as she carefully soaked her blonde strands under the waterfall-like stream, lathering my scent into them only seconds later. She kept her eyes on me the entire time as white bubbles slipped between her fingertips, massaging her scalp and doing everything I should be doing. But still, I didn't protest as she ordered me still, stepping back until the water flowed against her body, the finished shampoo coursing over her shoulders, down the curves of her breasts, across the planes of her stomach, and along the insides of her thighs.

All Hazel was doing was standing there, but her heated gaze was like a physical caress as it held on me. Staying perfectly still for her, I waited until she was conditioned too before she took the first step towards my lowered body. Surprisingly, in the time it took Hazel to take care of herself, my trembling had managed to ease to a manageable extent, my senses sharpening on the sound of the water, the sight of her body, the feeling of the ground, and the scent of my shampoo being poured into her hands all over again.

"Tilt your head back." She ordered so I did, craning my neck so that when her fingers first touched me again, the soap wouldn't drip into my eyes.

"What we have, Carter..." Hazel begins, running her hands through my hair, "It's a two way street." She never once broke eye contact with me as she shifted closer, my mouth planting a single kiss to her stomach to show I was listening. To say I was sorry.

"You keep hiding yourself from me, and that's okay, but you're not allowed to leave anymore without a note." Hazel says, no longer asking.

"I will never force you to talk, but you can't treat me like something fragile and incapable of handling things by your side." She is not fragile or incapable—I have never doubted that—but there's so much she still doesn't know. It was the reason I wouldn't let myself indulge in her love, even if this entire thing was my fault. I didn't speak as Hazel continued to brush her fingers thoroughly through my hair, falling into her touch now instead of retracting from it.

This wasn't her fault, and everything she was saying was right.

"I know something bad is happening with work whether you'll admit it or not, and one day I won't let you shut me out about it anymore." I tensed at her words all over again, but she was tipping my head back this time herself as the bubbles from my shampoo were gradually washed away back into the drain. My instincts wanted to protest the idea of her knowing anything more than what little we've told her, but I know that's not fair to either of us. Especially to Hazel.

"I'm okay if leaving is what you need to handle what's going on up here." She whispers, tapping her index finger against my head, "But maybe one day... maybe one day you could take me with you."

I let my eyes shut as the last of the shampoo is finally washed out, her hands already reaching for the conditioner as a few tears slip past, hidden by the water also dripping down my cheeks. But she notices. I don't know how, but Hazel sees me for how I am right now, bringing her fingers back to my hair instead of pressuring me to speak.

"You don't really know the extent, Carter, but I can fight." She says, my eyes reopening to look at my beautiful girlfriend above me,

"If you want to go into a ring with me, I'll fight you. If you want to drink, let me be your partner." Hazel washes the conditioner from her hands before moving to hold my face instead, my teardrops sliding over her fingertips.

"If you want me to stay home for a week so you can use me in every way you need... then I will be whatever kind of submissive you need to get you through this." How did I end up with someone like her? What did I do to deserve a person so understanding and as perfect as Hazel? I watched as her head remained tipped down, taking care of me in ways I didn't even know I needed. Usually with us, things were the other way around, but if it weren't for her, I probably would have spiraled again for another whole week.

"You're everything to me, Carter." Hazel kneels down too, still holding my face as water drips over our bodies.

"I hate it when you're in pain, so if I can help, just let me help you." A shuddering breath racked through my body as so much emotion poured out of me, everything I've tried to keep hidden breaking like a dam. I don't like accepting help from people because that means acknowledging things are wrong, but Hazel figured it out on her own. It doesn't matter that she doesn't know the specifics—she's holding me through everything and refusing to let go.

Tonight wasn't going to end anytime soon considering all that I wanted to tell her, but there was something that couldn't wait that I had to do first. Until Hazel, I didn't know if I could feel this way again, so many pieces of me having been broken away as a teenager, but she makes everything easier.

She makes me feel like I have a voice above all, and a heart below the layers of fucked up memories that make me who I am. My entire life has consisted of trauma, money, and influence, but none of that matters if I grow so cold I can barely recognize the person I used to be before it all. I learned how to run before I could walk, but Hazel makes me feel like I can finally take things step by step. She makes me feel alive—like when I'm with her, nothing else can hurt me.

"Hazel." I cry, pushing away the now dark strands of hair that are stuck to her face, her eyes looking up at me through her own wet lashes.

She was so selfless, so beautiful, so... her. She was the one thing I would never regret having in my life, and because of that, I stopped running. "I love you." I whisper as I hold her face, her hands mirroring mine. I watch as Hazel's fingers move to wrap around my wrists just to have that contact, and when I see the most breathtaking smile appear across her face, we fall apart. I don't know who moved first, but it wasn't long before her lips were pressed against mine as I opened for her, my body rocking back until I was pressed against the cold wall. Hazel had straddled me, her hands sliding into my hair as she pulled me back from our kiss, her cheeks flushed with happiness and a mixture of her previous tears.

"Say it again." She says against my mouth, her green eyes holding on mine as the same relief I'm feeling swirls within them. "I love you, Hazel." I say, kissing her in between words.

"I love you so goddamn much it hurts." So much that I will do anything—become anything, to give her the life she wants and deserves.

"I love you too." She grins softly, but our hands turn frantic when she says the words that set me aflame. No matter how close we were, it was no longer enough as I pulled her into me, crashing my mouth to hers.

The slip of our tongues against each other was passionate yet needy at the same time, the water falling down over us making everything perfectly messy. I groaned as Hazel's hips rolled down to meet mine, her body gently rocking against me in desperation to be together. I never knew I needed to hear those three words as badly as I did, but there was no going back now and I loved it.

"Lift up a little." I panted as Hazel's hands held onto my shoulders, gripping tight. The next time she came down, it was with my cock fully inside of her. She was still sensitive from earlier, but I knew she liked it even more because of that.

Moving my fingers to Hazel's hips, I held her as she rose up on her knees before softly coming back down, repeating the same movements again and again. This was nothing like the fucking from earlier—she was making love to me, and for once, I didn't try to take control. I let Hazel decide the pace and angles, watching as her mouth parted and her eyes looked down to where we were connected. She looked so pretty right now, and I watched as recognition crossed her eyes at not where her body met mine, but the red lines painting her breasts and stomach with my marks.

"Is that..." Hazel inhaled at the sight of my initials written across her hip, and when she looked back up to see my possessive smirk, I felt her tighten around me.

"You're mine." I mutter into her ear, loving the way she cries out in response. I still don't take over, though, letting her consume me as I fall to the mercy of her touch. I wanted Hazel to take what little pieces I had left of myself and make them hers, exactly where they belonged.

This was a moment that changed so many things for the both of us, but when it got to the point where Hazel was too lost to continue on her own, I pulled her forward to rest against me. Her head fell happily against the crook of my neck as I planted my feet on the ground for support, using my hips to rock up into her. Our movements were still slow, but it was the depth that made the pleasure so dizzying. My muscles flexed around her with every whimper that came from her mouth, and I simply kissed her wet hair while my fingers ran over her back.

"I love you." I whispered again, fully triggering her orgasm as she tightened around me with trembling legs. My release followed instantaneously with hers, groaning into her neck while I filled her with my cum. The feelings that came with it flooded over the both of us, but if this is what it feels like to drown, then I never want to know what it's like to reach the surface.

Hazel and I stayed in the shower together for at least an hour after the fact. Taking turns caring for each other, we remained under the water until our fingertips were wrinkled and the water grew gradually colder. When she finally insisted it was time to dry off, we did that for each other too, my hands spinning Hazel to face the mirror to see what I saw. She was breathless as I ran the towel over her smooth skin, down her legs and back up to where the small initials X.A.

were showing against her left hip. If I angle my head to the right, I can also see the faint bruise of where she'd headbutted me earlier. Hazel blushed as I smiled at the thought of carrying her marks on me, faint scratches also across my shoulders from when she rode me earlier in the shower.

That was one of three times we'd fucked during that—in my opinion—too short time span under the water.

"Don't look at me like that." Hazel grins as our eyes meet in the mirror, amusement flashing in her expression.

"My body needs a break." Rising to my full height, I brush my hands across her arms as I pull her back to me, kissing the top of her head and breathing in the combination of my shampoo mixed with her smell. I listen to what she says, but that doesn't stop the fact I've never been more thankful that I destroyed her underwear than I am now.

"How about movies and snacks instead, hm?" I suggest, my heart warming at how much she clearly likes that idea. Don't get me wrong, the sex is always great when it comes to Hazel, but the intimacy of getting to be with her afterwards will forever be my favourite part. Even though I didn't want to, I forced myself to pull away at her nod, opening the drawer to our left to grab out two of four robes for us to curl up in. I could barely take my eyes off of her, and that only got worse when the most beautiful smile appeared on her face as I wrapped the soft material around her body.

"Mia regina." I say ever so quietly, pressing my lips to Hazel's forehead and tying the belt around her waist into a large bow. Dominic said he'd gathered that she understood Italian just by observing her when Vincent was around that one day, and I knew he was right when her eyes lifted to mine.

Shrugging on my own robe, I see a fire in her gaze as she greedily takes me in. It doesn't fade as I make my way right back to her, placing a hand on her lower back before dipping my head.

"You always have been." I pull her closer when she quite literally shivers from my words, her legs pressing together all over again. It seems that my girl likes that name. "Come on, sweetheart." I nod my head to the door as we begin to walk out of the bathroom together. "If I don't get you under the covers, I'm going to take you against this counter instead." I watched as Hazel's eyes grew wide and a blush appeared on her face from my words, laughing even though I was very much serious. I still don't think she knows the effect she has over me, but one day, she will.

"You still owe me the movie night you promised." She giggles as she takes my hand into hers, leading us back into the playroom and over to the fairly messy bed. "And probably some new lingerie too." Hazel adds at the sight in front of us. Picking up a shred of what used to be her underwear, she knew I was being smug as she tossed it to the floor with a shake of her head.

"You liked it." I playfully kissed her cheek as we both crawled back into bed, her robe riding up dangerously high before the covers were mercifully pulled over the both of us. "I did." Hazel agrees with a smile, tugging me closer as my arm wraps around her shoulders, her head resting comfortably against my side. No words could describe how happy I was right now with her like this, my hand reaching to the desk beside us where a remote lay. It didn't take long for Hazel to begin looking around, noticing the fact there was no television in the room, but my smile only widened as I pressed the red button on the remote. Instantly, a faint vibration grew beneath us, green eyes turning to me in question before a shiny black object rose from the foot of the bed where the storage bench was.

"You're kidding?" Hazel says, a chuckle escaping me at the way her mouth has dropped open in awe. It was so unintentionally adorable I wished I could take a picture to keep it forever, but when her gaze turned back to me, it was even better. Her damp hair had begun to fall into loose curls as it dried, and she was just too damn perfect to look away from. "How's this for your movie night, sweetheart?" I winked, pulling her closer to me and listening as a happy sigh left her lips. Something that was way too quiet for me to hear was muttered in response, but it sounded a whole like the same three words that won't leave my mind

"Carter?" Hazel whispers down to me, faint sounds of background music playing from the television.

"Hmm," I hummed, my eyes remaining closed as her fingers ran through my now dry hair. About thirty minutes into the movie I had gotten up to get us snacks, choosing to settle in between her legs this time instead of beside her. My head currently rests comfortably against her stomach with her thighs on either side of my shoulders, a long forgotten bowl of popcorn to our left. At some point Hazel's hands had made their way to my hair, and I've been the calmest I've ever been since.

"I just wanted to see if you were asleep." She says quietly, brushing some strands away from my face to play with. There were probably a few times where I had nearly slept from her touch, but I was wide awake now with her pretty eyes staring down at me. Bringing my hands to run up and down the outer sides of Hazel's legs, I tilted my head to look at her better.

She blinked at me through her long, dark lashes, her right cheek pulled slightly between her teeth—something I know she does when she's deep in thought. I noticed her nails had grown out only a little more since I last saw her, but overall, she seemed a lot better since that night in Detroit.

"What are you thinking about?" I ask as I study Hazel's face, squeezing her thigh gently to remind her I was here if she wanted to talk. She stopped biting her cheek, but I couldn't tell if it was curiosity or worry that drew both of our attention entirely away from the movie.

"It's just... well you've never fallen asleep around me before, and I thought you might have just now."

"And you're wondering why I haven't?" I take a guess, giving a small smile to show I was fine with her question. Her small nod confirmed my thoughts, and while this was something I had wanted to tell her about tonight, I still didn't know where to start.

"It's not my business. You don't have to share anything you don't want to, but I was just thinking I should probably go home later so you're not spending the entire night awake just to stay with me again." My hands didn't stop moving against her at her words, however my heart did start to beat a little quicker. I could already feel sweat building along my forehead slightly as I fought off the memories I always tend to relive at night, yet a part of me somehow knew Hazel was already aware that I have nightmares.

"You're not going anywhere." I say quietly, tightening my hold on her almost for support and trying to focus on the feeling of her fingers running through my hair. I know our experiences were very different in their own ways, but somehow it made it easier knowing of all people, it's Hazel who could unfortunately understand.

I sighed as I tried to figure out how to tell her why I can't sleep with others, but all I could think about was that I was sixteen too when a part of me I still haven't gotten back was taken.

"Do you remember what I told you about my initiation?" I ask, sensing her confusion before she silently nods in response. "There wasn't much question about whether or not I was going to pass it. As the Don's son, it was pretty much a sure thing." Focus on her hands, Carter.

"It's tradition to celebrate what people believed me to be as the future of the Mafia, so it wasn't a surprise when I was driven home to be surrounded by everyone important in our world. Dominic and his family were there along with hundreds of other guests who were nothing more than strangers to me." I took a long deep breath before I spoke again, but somehow, this was a little easier than I expected. Every time my chest started to tighten, it was Hazel who gave me the air I needed to continue. She was quiet and only listened as I took the time to gather myself, and I think a part of me just fell in love all over again because of it.

"After my mom... it's fair to say I wasn't a very well behaved kid. And Dominic, he was always by my side to create the mischief I needed to ease my mind." We both smiled a little bit at the image of that, but it was short lived when I began to speak again.

"He quite literally saved my life in ways I don't think he knows about even now, but his importance in my life was something Vincent noticed too well. Dominic and I grew up together, and when I—fuck, when I started to develop feelings that weren't allowed, my father intervened in ways."

I couldn't finish my sentence, but I knew Hazel understood what I had just admitted. I don't think even I have come to terms with the majority of my childhood, but loving my best friend led to so much of my father's disappointment towards me both then and now.

"The after party was when only people close to our family remained gathered—when the more important gifts were offered as acts of servitude towards me considering I would one day be in charge of everything." Acts of servitude I never wanted or asked for.

"Closer to the end of the night, there was a toast to the greatness that would one day follow with my leadership." I curled my lips in disgust, remembering all of those details much too clearly.

"And the drink that was handed to me had been slipped with GHB without my knowledge." My eyes fell shut as Hazel's hands froze in my hair, but I couldn't bring myself to see whatever emotion was strongly worn across her face right now.

"It wasn't until about fifteen minutes later I began to feel it in my system, but with it combined with the alcohol, it hit me really hard." I could already feel my throat begin to tighten and my mouth dry just talking about it, even when I felt her fingers try to soothe me. "I think Vincent was intentional in keeping Dominic distracted elsewhere then, because he knew he'd realize something was off, and there was no one there to help me when two women approached me." With a tear falling from my still closed eyes and down my cheek, I stopped hiding. "Nobody questioned it when they led me away, saying they were there to show me what it meant to be a man as an initiation gift from my father. But Vincent didn't do his research. The one was a hired prostitute, but the second was the sister of a man whose blood I had been soaked with only hours previously by my own hand."

Taking in a shaky breath through my nose, I at last looked at Hazel to see her crying quietly with me, her own eyes shut with sadness as her head rested back against the headboard.

"Vincent couldn't stand the fact I liked Dominic, and when the drug had me nearing unconsciousness..." I had to stop as a sob threatened to rack its way past my lips. "The sister knew the consequences of killing me, so instead she left me permanently scarred as a reminder of what I did to her brother." I let my tears fall this time as I reached for Hazel's hand, kissing her palm to show I was okay. I hated that she was crying for me, even though I was too.

"I've had a long time to try and recover from it, but some things just don't go away." I say, squeezing her fingers with mine.

"Dominic found me, though. There's a lot of parts about that night I still can't remember, but I do know he was the only reason I got through it, even when I wasn't able to think straight for a couple of days afterwards." This was the part I never wanted to tell Hazel because I didn't want her to fear or hate me, but through the blur of tears in her eyes, I saw the same burning hatred in her I still feel sometimes. "The doctors weren't sure for a long time if I'd ever be able to see out of this eye again after that night, but they said I was apparently lucky. The whole thing was covered up, but I wasn't done with any of it." Watching Hazel carefully, I just knew by looking at her face I could tell her everything. Sometimes there were no pretty parts to stories, but that was okay.

"The price of that night was paid with their lives, and though I was young and irresponsible then, I still feel very little regret for my actions." Sighing and turning onto my stomach to see Hazel better, I was relieved to find she wasn't upset with me from my confession. Because of that, I continued.

"The only problem is I paid a price too." Reaching up to wipe some of the tears from her face, I offered a small smile, even though there was nothing happy about this.

"In some sick way, I can't feel another man's touch now intimately because it hurts too damn much to have the reminders of the things that had been taken... the things... the things that—"

I couldn't finish my sentence, and this time, as everything went deafeningly quiet, I knew I wouldn't be able to.

"Carter." Hazel's voice spoke shakily for me, taking my face into her hands as she sniffled from the tears that matched mine. She looked like she wanted to tell me she was sorry I had to go through that. That she didn't hate me for those women's deaths, and that she loves me either way. I prayed it was all true, but when she pulled me over her and flipped me onto my back, there was no doubt that I didn't need a god to be reassured. I felt the weight of Hazel's body purposely pressing down on top, hugging me as her head nestled against my neck.

"Thank you for telling me." She spoke through her tears, my arms wrapping firmly around her and taking in everything she gave. "It may not always seem like it, but you will never be alone again, Carter." Letting my eyes close, I just let everything come out. Yes, I still focused on Hazel's smell—the feeling of her skin against mine and the sound of her pained words, but I also let a little bit of myself heal by talking. I guess what she said had been right. With my girl held tight in my arms right now, it was impossible to feel alone.

"I love you, always." Hazel softly whispers against me, giving me back a piece of myself that I have needed for eighteen years too long.

"I love you too, sweetheart." I cry, feeling my heart beat not just for her, but for us. "Always." That night, not a single nightmare had found me. That night, I fell asleep with Hazel by my side.

Hazel

"You have to promise you won't freak out though." I bite my lip mid smile as I turn my head to look at Jade. Even with my words, she seems like she's about to explode with interest and blatant curiosity.

The spa day Jade had promised me before my flight to Detroit had been decided to happen today, or more importantly, right now.

"Girl, this is my calm." She laughs, shaking her head as the colour settings on her pedicure bowl change along with the jet pressures. Honestly, apart from the excited look in her eyes, I'm pretty sure the both of us were one second away from just melting into these seats and never moving again. It's been way too long since I've gotten my nails done, and in combination with the lotions and different gels, my body was practically glowing from all of the pampering.

"Remind me again to thank Dominic for this after you spill whatever it is that has a permanent smile across your face." Jade not so subtly prods, but I can't help but agree to the first comment. We had planned to go out to the nail salon this afternoon together and then grab a bite to eat, yet two women showed up at our door instead saying they were a mobile spa service sent here at the request of Mr. Sawyer. I hadn't even told him our plans, and yet here they were saying they had been paid to be here until : for whatever we wanted. I love that man.

Speaking of which...

"It's... I guess I'm just really happy." I grin, my mind going back to that night with Carter for the millionth time in the last multiple days. I'm not going to lie, so much of me broke along with him when he chose to open up about his past, but I was admittedly thankful I could understand things a little better now. I meant it when I told him he would never be alone again, not just with me, but with Dominic and Rowan too. And when Carter eventually fell asleep in my arms, I knew that what we had would be forever.

"Things are just going really good for me right now." I say, not bothering to try and hide my blush of happiness at the admission. "It's crazy to think about, but I think these men are it for me." In some unreal way, the idea of spending the rest of my life with them feels like a dream that is very quickly becoming a possible reality.

"Yeah?" Jade smiles, clearly more than happy for me. "You know, I think you're it for them as well." I don't know why a part of me is shocked by her words, but I guess it's just easy to forget they were all friends as well for years before I came into the picture. Everything about New York has just felt natural for me to settle into, and while Rowan, Dominic, and Carter didn't come into my life softly, I can't think of having things any other way.

On top of bartending at Rush, I've still been able to keep up with photography considering I shot yet another wedding two days ago. Jolene's become a mother to me, and with Jade as my best friend, I've been able to grow closer with Mila on the side. The only reason she's not here right now is because Jade said she wanted my help surprising her with something. And though I've only been able to meet up a few times with them, a slow friendship has also started with me, Aaliyah and her husband Issac. Everything about New York has become home recently, especially when it came to the three men I couldn't keep my mind off of. "A part of me feels like we're going too fast, but an even bigger part wishes that we never slow down, you know?" I say, nodding to the lady who's finishing the last of my manicure when she gestures to the kind of hand lotion I want to use. It felt good to have average length nails again, even if they were just acrylics.

"I get it. Honestly, Mila's the only woman I've ever gone slow with when it comes to relationships, but sometimes moving fast is better if you know what you want." Something about her words reassured me, and I'm quite thankful for it. I think fast just simply works for us.

"And what about you?" I ask, suspecting I already know what Jade's been planning to ask her girlfriend for a long while. "The newly copied key on the counter wouldn't happen to be for a certain someone, would it?" Their one-year anniversary is coming up in a week, and I couldn't be more excited for the both of them. For Jade, I think Mila is her everything just as my men are for me. I watch as the kindest smile on her face appears, and I know I'm right. "I wanted to talk to you about it first considering you live here too, but..."

"You don't have to ask me anything, Hails." I cut in when she trails off, already knowing where she was going with this. "My living here shouldn't affect your decision of asking her to move in at all."

She lets out a soft breath at my words, visibly allowing the weight of her worries to escape along with it. It was clear she was worried about bringing up the idea to me, but I don't think she realizes just how much I want this for her too. Things are getting pretty serious with them, and while I'd never tell her this, I've already come to terms with the fact I'm probably going to be moving out soon myself.

"Really, because I don't want you to feel like your space is being invaded by bringing another person in?" Jade says, speaking a little louder as the lady working on her fingers turns on one of the tools to begin shaping her nails. My eyebrows raise slightly in surprise that she'd think that I'd be against this, but I could tell she was overthinking this just as much as I do other things. I know she's dominant behind closed doors, but right now she is being the cute, nervously excited girlfriend I know Mila isn't going to say no to.

"It might actually just be the two of you by the end of the month." I explain. Whether the possibility of moving into the mansion is where things will take me or if I end up in some small apartment around town, I want to give the two of them the space they deserve. Mila's never expressed having a problem with me living here, however I'm sure things would just be easier with me in my own space.

"Are things getting to that point with them for you too?" Jade asks, hinting at the thought of me living with Carter, Rowan, and Dominic. While I can't exactly just invite myself into their house, it's still something I could see happening in the near future. Biting my lip, I nodded as I lifted my hips from the seat I was on, pulling down the waistband of my shorts slightly to show her where I'd spent the main portion of my Friday afternoon. After Carter had fallen asleep with me there, I'd gotten a bit of a chance to look at where his initials had marked my skin. I'd been wet just looking at them, and the memories that were brought with it was enough to tell me I never wanted them to fade.

"You didn't." Jade gapes, her mouth quite literally dropping open at the sight of the small design of black ink on my left hip. Smiling, I nodded. "It's called an ephemeral tattoo. The lady who did it says it'll last anywhere from nine to fifteen months if I care for it properly, and then fade away back to my normal skin like a temporary tattoo." It really wasn't a hard decision for me to make. It's not permanent, and while the needling still hurt like a bitch, I've had it for a few days now with no regrets. "Are you going to say something?" I grinned at her reaction, knowing she wasn't judging as she stared.

That's one of the reasons why we're friends.

"Two things." Jade begins, looking up from the tattoo and back to my eyes. "One, I suggest you prepare yourself because after

Carter sees that, he's going to tie you to his bed and never let you out again." I laugh at that, but I know she's probably right. Hell, I'm almost counting on it.

"And two, I hope you know Rowan and Dominic's initials are coming next when their dicks get jealous and demand to mark you themselves." For a small moment, I just stare at her in complete silence. Her seriousness is laced with the humor of an amused friend, but when she's the first one to crack a smile, we both burst into a fit of giggles like a couple of teenage girls.

"I can't believe you just said that." I laugh, doing my best to keep my hands still from the happy shake of my body. When I glance down, I find the two women doing our nails wearing small smiles as well at our conversation.

"You can't tell me I'm wrong, though." Jade counters, giving me a look that dares me to challenge her knowing damn well I won't. "The best kinds of love tend to carry no limits." The girl named Ayaka says, skillfully finishing up the final touches as she gives me a knowing smile. I didn't tell Jade about the I love Yous that Carter and I had shared multiple times since Thursday, but I'm sure she's derived enough from the fact his name is currently carved into my skin. All three of my men are currently away for business right now in France since something they apparently couldn't tell me came up, however I've already finally figured out a plan to tell Rowan and Dominic how I feel too.

They get back on the tenth which is a Friday, meaning the days for our scenes are going to be decided by Sunday.

Once Rowan lets me know his and Dominic's nights, I'm going to take each of them out myself instead as a surprise and tell them then. However the rest of our evenings play out can still be their call, but for now, I just let myself relax with my best friend at my side.

"That they do." I say in agreement, lifting my hand and smiling at the pretty shades of red that are now painted across my fingers. That they do.

~ Twenty-Six ~

Hazel

Feeling a large body press up against my back, I stiffened before I realized who it was, relaxing into the deep voice that had my core tightening with desire.

"Miss me, darling?" Rowan's lips brushed just below my ear, my body spinning to face him in excitement at the knowledge he was finally back, the other two likely close by as well.

"No more week-long trips." I smile in response, hugging him as his own arms wrap tightly around me. My tone was teasing, but between my visit to Detroit and theirs to France, I didn't want to spend another moment away for a long while.

"Agreed." He nods, kissing the top of my head before pulling me back slightly so he can look at me.

"How could I not when I have a girl back home who dresses as beautifully as this?" Bringing his fingers down to the thin strap of my dress, he toyed with it as his eyes roamed down the indigo blue fabric until his hands followed. Dominic had asked for me to meet them at Rush tonight for their welcome back, so I figured I may as well have some fun while I waited. Not bothering to hide my blush at his compliment, I stayed still as Rowan walked around to my other side, a hand dragging from the nape of my neck all the way down the exposed skin of my back.

"I take it you like it?" I say just to break the intensity of his stare, suddenly becoming highly aware of the fact I wasn't wearing a bra—yet another thing that left me more vulnerable to him. My heart skipped as Rowan's one large hand curled around my waist dangerously low before pulling me back flush to his body. His breath was against my skin in an instant. "Oh I like a lot of things about it." He offered a sinful grin that made me entirely compliant when he began to move our bodies against each other in time with the music.

"For starters, I like that I can feel you heating beneath my touch yet shivering from my words." A breathy sigh left my mouth as my head tilted slightly against him, his one finger moving my chin until I was looking at the bar. Seeing Carter and Dominic watching me with unrestrained hunger had me excited, but finding Riley trying to cover up her anger at their blatant dismissal of her also brought a sense of smug possessiveness to me. "I also like the way all it's going to take is a single tug of this dainty little string to get you completely naked for me later, the teasing thong I know you're wearing likely thin enough to just tear off along with it." I gasped and my heart sped as I felt Rowan play with said string, well aware he was right to say I would be bared to him in a second if he went any further. And the entire time, Dominic and Carter watched me, trying not to overly react considering we were still surrounded by a club full of people.

"But you wanna know what I like most, little one?" He asks rhetorically, because when I'm suddenly spun to face him, I know I'm about to find out.

"I like that I can do this." Subtly kicking my feet apart, I licked my lips as Rowan's leg filled the space between my own. Just like that, what was left of my tension unwound from my muscles, my skin coming alive as his hands cupped my hips surely. He kept things innocent for no longer than a minute before he was encouraging me to grind against him, my fingertips grasping onto the collar of his absurdly fancy suit, the silken underside feeling rich to the touch.

"Should I make you come just like this, Hazel?" Rowan asks, his breath hot on my neck and his hands gripping tighter with each discrete roll of our bodies. I hid my whimper into the material of his suit, but the invading smell of his cologne didn't help to relieve the heat between my thighs. None of them let me touch myself while they were away, and while memorable, the orgasms Carter had given me last Thursday had not been nearly enough to keep me sated all week.

They had wanted me needy and begging, so by the time they were back, everything would feel heightened for me. God did they succeed. With the press of the crowd and the tingling vibration of the music thrumming beneath me, I knew I was so responsive because of the continuously denied lust pooling in my stomach.

Teasing me was Rowan's cruelly effective form of foreplay, and while this was a game I more than enthusiastically participated in, it was their turns to be driven mad with desire now. Reaching my arms up to hang over his wide shoulders, I smiled when I felt Dominic join us at my back, my leg brushing forwards until it was directly against Rowan's crotch. He shuddered under my touch, and when that single action told me he was ready to move off to somewhere more private, I knew I was about to be in trouble.

Feeling Carter's body join us next, I let myself be danced between them in a haze of excitement, waiting until Dominic finally made the first move to leave before I let my defying revenge take over.

"Let's get out of here, princess." He says just loud enough for me to hear over top of the music. "We missed you too much to share you any longer with the eyes of those around us." Rowan slipped his hand into mine with the clear intention to pull me away, but when my feet remained still on the spot, his eyes met mine in question. Dominic realized what was happening the second his gaze locked on where I stood, and Carter's knowing expression was much too enthusiastic for my sense of control. "You edged me for an entire week just because you made the decision to go to a different country last minute." I state, my body growing more turned on with each challenging look I got from them.

"Now you just expect for me to be at your beck and call when you finally decide to come back?" My inner brat was thriving off of every last second of this moment, and when I made use of Rowan's hand by pulling him closer, I rose on my tiptoes and said in his ear, "You're not the boss of me." Once those words left my mouth, I knew there was no going back. Rowan's smile was the last thing I saw before I was being picked up and tossed over his shoulder like a sack of potatoes, his hand resting firmly against my ass. I'm pretty sure it was to make sure my dress didn't ride up and expose me to everybody in this club, but I still had to wrap an arm around my chest to make sure my boobs weren't flashing people either. With it too loud to hear anything he might want to say, I looked up to see Carter and Dominic right behind us, quietly talking to each other while looking at me. They were talking punishment, and I was soaked because of it, however my racing heart almost wished I had even one drink tonight just for a little liquid courage.

"Don't think Dominic's forgotten his promise of reddening your ass from what happened in Detroit." Rowan says the second we make it past the VIP doors and down the hall where I know the playroom is. I catch a glimpse of Cassidy smiling when she sees me, but two large men very quickly flood my view of her, their conversation breaking off when I see Carter not joining us.

While Rowan continues down to the end of the hall, Carter moves into his office with his door shutting behind him. What the hell? The movements of walking quickly stop as Dominic loops around the two of us to punch in the passcode to the playroom.

When I feel a hand running up and down my slit where my panties are now soaked, I know it's because Rowan's preoccupied with that. A shiver racked its way through my body at the action, but the sight of Carter walking back towards us had me tensing, not because of the dominant way he carried himself but because of the box he had concealed by his large hand.

"We really did miss you, princess." Dominic's voice hums in my ear as the door opens, Rowan setting me down and holding me upright for a second as I regain my balance. That's the only kindness he offers me, though. When both men step away and Carter locks the door, I know whatever punishment I've earned myself is about to begin.

"Present at the foot of the bed facing away from it." Rowan says, taking the small mystery box and tossing it onto the bed. "And keep that pretty white thong of yours on too." I didn't try to challenge him on this as I felt Dominic come up to my back, tugging at the string around my neck for me without even having to ask. The cool brush of his fingers down my skin brought goosebumps to my arms, but the warmth of his breath contrasted it entirely.

"Keep the heels as well." With that, his touch was gone, the top half of my dress falling before gathering at the curve of my hips. It took a little encouragement as I shimmied the material the rest of the way down, making a show of it as I stepped out and bent to pick it up. Not wanting the surprise of this to be ruined yet, I made sure to casually shield my left side when all I had now was the white of my shoes and underwear.

Well, that and the tattoo they have yet to see. Forcing myself to keep my focus on what I was told, I folded my dress and placed it on the counter, making use of the brush and elastic as I tied my hair back into a neat braid. I've gotten a lot better at it with practice, but it also meant less time to prepare myself for the hell I know I just caused. When I obeyed the final task and knelt as I was told, any regret that I might have had faded at the sound of Carter's sharp inhale through his nose.

They all saw the tattoo, and whatever ideas they were previously thinking had just been put on pause. With my head bowed, the only thing I could make out were shadows and faint outlines of them, but it felt like forever before I could see any actual movement. My heart sped even more with it, though. Listening to the sound of drawers being opened and closed, I forced down the urge to look up or shut my legs to relieve the tension brought with the silence of footsteps carrying my way. When polished black shoes at last came into my vision, I let out a shaky breath knowing it was Carter.

"Get the cuffs." The words came out as a deep, gravelly command to the man now at my back. I didn't resist as Dominic pulled my arms behind me, cold metal wrapping around my wrists until my hands were bound and resting above my ass. The touch left as quickly as it came, leaving me even more exposed and forcing my back into a deeper arch. The black ink across my hip was completely on display, and when a finger hooked under my chin to get me to look up, I was met with a savage sort of sensuality I've never seen before. Carter was going to utterly and absolutely consume me.

"Spread your knees." Rowan's voice sounded in my ear, not even realizing they had slowly inched their way closed until he'd spoken. There was an obvious change that had happened in him, though, too. If I could see Dominic, I'd bet he would be sharing the same sort of possessiveness Jade had warned me about a few days ago. In combination with my words from earlier, I knew I was in for it. Listening, I opened my legs while holding Carter's burning gaze, the heels of my shoes digging into my skin in a way that kept me grounded from the intensity I was already feeling.

"Stay just like that, princess." Dominic directed before standing, the motion stirring the air and sending a chillingly sweet breeze across my bare skin. I did my best not to squirm or really do anything more than just show compliance now, but it was hard when Rowan and Dominic moved behind me, the faint sound of them getting onto the bed catching my ears. Carter gave them only a single glance and a nod before his attention returned to me, and I was lucky I was already on the ground because the passion in his eyes would've knocked me over otherwise.

My tongue darted over my lips as Carter slowly dropped to a crouch in front of me, still fully clothed and entirely overpowering. I was still as his gaze slowly traveled down from my mouth, to my neck, to the hardened peaks of my nipples, to the spot I know brought this reaction from him.

"Is it permanent?" He asks quietly, his eyes lingering on my hip while his hands continue their path down.

"No, Daddy." My breath hitched when his fingers slid to between my thighs, deftly moving my underwear to the side until I was completely on display for him.

"It'll fade in just over a year." I forced my eyes to remain open when his thumb brushed over my clit, another two digits sliding up and down my dripping slit.

"A year is a long time, sweetheart." Carter says almost re-strained, but I knew this was him trying to decide what this meant. Nothing. Everything. I was all in.

"I know." I pant, my toes curling as two thick fingers pushed inside of me with ease, already coated and slick with my arousal. His eyes flicked up to mine at my words, followed by a small pause. Then, whatever was holding him back snapped. I all but gasped when he pulled out, slamming back in with a force that had him holding onto the back of my neck to make sure I didn't fall back-wards. Angling himself in the perfect position, Carter stroked my spot again and again in the most delicious way possible. This was for my pleasure alone, and with everything centralized in one spot, I could barely think about the fact Rowan and Dominic were still behind me doing god knows what. Were they touching themselves? Were they upset their names didn't mark my body too, or were they just watching, deciding where they wanted theirs to be? "You do realize what this means, don't you?" Carter tips my head to look at him, his fingers never slowing down inside of me. When his thumb rejoined the mix, I damn near fell apart right then and there.

"Yes." I moaned, my hips rolling in small circles in time with his movements. I couldn't move much because of the way my hands were cuffed behind my back, but that didn't stop the way my body began to build to a heightened tremble.

"It means you're ours." He growls, tightening his grip on my neck as his hand sped up against me.

"When you come, we're going to spend the next hour punishing you for earlier, and then we're going to take turns showing you just how much we missed you and this pretty little cunt." A whimper was pulled from my mouth as my body leaned forward slightly, Carter's knees shifting until mine were forced to open more. The angle of his fingers changed along with it, breathless noises escaping me as a result.

"We're going to fuck you like our whore and love you like our girlfriend until you're so sated, you'll never want to leave our beds again." That part was whispered into my ear, and as I felt Carter's lips brush against me, my orgasm rose straight to that dangerous edge.

"Come." I hear Dominic say from behind me. The reminder that he and Rowan were watching as Carter fingered me almost brutishly was my tipping point. Groaning quietly, I let them take it all as my orgasm uncoiled in my stomach, dragging me under until it felt like my body was going to explode. The entire time, Carter held my face, watching my every reaction until I soaked his hand. "Good girl." He murmured, only pulling his fingers away when I neared overstimulation.

"You're such a good girl." He'd said it with such desire that I shivered under the praise, my knees pressing together all over again when a gentle kiss was placed on my forehead. It was so contrasting to the release I'd just experienced, I couldn't help the way my heart fluttered, my body still shaking as I heard footsteps from behind me along with the tug of zippers. Following the path of Carter's hand with my eyes, I watched as he first undid his belt, the dark blurs of Rowan and Dominic joining him appearing in my peripheral vision.

I had no idea what they were going to do next, but god did I want to know. The way he was looking at me now threatened to make me come undone all over again, but all Carter did was force my legs back into place with one hand, pulling his cock from his pants with the other. The glint of his piercing was already covered in precum as a small amount of it dripped down the length of him, my mouth wanting his taste across my tongue. He seemed to have very different ideas, though.

My eyes narrowed as Carter's fingers came back to between my thighs, dipping inside of my now slightly puffy slit while holding my eyes. At first I was confused, but my lips then parted in humiliation when I saw him gather my orgasm that was still leaking out of me before bringing his hand back to his length. All I could do was sit there when he repeated the process, paying no attention to the fact I was extremely sensitive or the redness of my cheeks because of my embarrassment. Squirming on my knees, my body tried to follow when Carter abruptly stood, his cock now wet with the release he'd brought from me.

Only a second later was Rowan taking his place, shirtless and his eyes a little bit wild. My thighs hurt from being in this position for so long, and my clit throbbed when a thumb drew three lazy circles over it, but that too soon stopped, Rowan's only use for me being the arousal between my legs. He did the same thing as Carter until could hear the slick glide of his hand when he stroked himself, not saying anything before standing and moving back to make room for the third.

This entire thing was degrading in a way I didn't know I could experience, but I couldn't act like I wasn't turned on at the sight of both Rowan and Carter's long fingers wrapped around their cocks, the veins of their arms.

"Hazel." Dominic's smooth voice drew my attention away from them, walking until he was stroking himself right in front of my face.

"Open your mouth for me, pretty girl. Stick your tongue out and get me nice and wet." Thankful at least the humiliation of earlier could be gone—even though it had me soaked all over again—my lips parted in a silent invitation to do with as he pleased. "Don't swallow. I want to see your spit and my precum dripping down your face by the time I'm done with you." If my mouth wasn't already open, I feel like it would've dropped from his words. Outstretching my tongue for him, I didn't dare move my head as he ran his tip over me, tasting him in the ways he wanted. Dominic was typically a man of praise—pretty much the opposite of Rowan and a portion of Carter—but when he didn't push more than the head of his cock past my lips, I looked up to find demeaning eyes staring in return. It was so unlike him it had my heart racing a million beats per second, but when he smiled down at me in a cruel, warning way, I swear those feelings tripled.

Things were fine for a little while, however it wasn't long before my mouth started to water and I struggled to obey the command of not swallowing the saliva quickly pooling under my tongue. This was humiliation in an entirely new way, and the false hope he'd given me made this all the more punishing as I began to squirm on my knees. Allowing a shaky breath to leave my body, I stilled when Dominic's fingers reached to brush against the side of my face, softly tucking a loose piece of hair behind my ear.

That kindness faded almost instantly, though, his hips thrusting forward and my throat protesting the sudden movement. Instinctively, my arms tugged from behind my back only to meet the biting clasp of the handcuffs keeping them bound. "I really did miss you, princess." He whispers, pulling out as quickly as his touch came. My eyes watered as a string of my saliva remained connected to his tip, Dominic's large hand fisting himself as he used that to get himself off.

"Please." I whimpered, just to be gently hushed by Rowan's quiet reprimand. My body begged for the relief it never got as Dominic took a single step back, just for the other two to take three forward, forming a slightly curved half circle around me. "Stay just like that, sweetheart." Carter groaned from my left, my head turning to find him fucking his fist just as Rowan and Dominic did the same thing. While I was knelt down at their feet, they were touching themselves, their cocks glistening from either my arousal or my tongue. The act was so belittling—so overpowering, I couldn't help but bite my lip to keep from pressing my knees together all over again.

"Look up, Hazel." Rowan encouraged, his body slightly to my right.

"Look at what you're doing to us." Just the sight of me was getting them off, and I realized what was happening a moment before Dominic's head tossed back and the muscles in his body tensed, a low noise being pulled right from his parted lips. With my tongue darting out at the sound of my name under his breath, the first spurt of his release dripped down his fingers, the second hitting my cheek and then my lips. "Fuck." Carter swore quietly as his hips rocked into his hand, Dominic's orgasm no doubt triggering his own. It was demeaning, but I loved it when he too came on my face, his movements continuing in time with Rowan's until all three of their pleasure was painted across my skin. It has to have been one of the hottest feelings in the world to know that alone was enough to push them over the edge, and with my face now a canvas of their dominance, I knew it was something I'd want to experience again in the future. Hearing their groans and seeing them come apart was motivation enough, and while it was messy, I felt powerful as I took each of them into my mouth one by one, cleaning them until they were satisfied.

"You did so good." Dominic said to me afterwards, going back into a crouch in front of me as Rowan left to the washroom, Carter unlocking one cuff from my sore wrists. I blushed at his words— or more so the sincerity in them—footsteps soon sounding as a still half-naked man walked back towards me, a seemingly damp towel in hand.

"Can I?" Rowan asks, looking down at my covered face with a small smile. At my nod, he didn't waste time bringing the cloth to my forehead, my body learning it to be wet with warm water. There was almost something intimate about the way he cleaned me too, his focus genuine and unhurried as the towel was wiped gently across my cheeks, my chin, and then further down to my breasts. At the same time, Carter took care massaging the hand that didn't have the cuffs still attached, even though I wasn't uncomfortably sore from them. I wasn't about to turn away their care, though, and I sure as hell wasn't about to put an end to their words of praise either.

"Give me a kiss." Rowan says once he's done with the towel, bending at the waist until his face was hovering over mine. I had to stretch my posture just slightly, but I practically melted at the feeling of his lips, the minor strain more than worth it. The kiss in itself felt like a form of aftercare, and I truly needed it when Carter grabbed my face next, followed by Dominic and his soothing touch. Everything about the way they were holding me right now felt languid and calming, and it was that that told me my punishment was going to be something new and likely very painful. I did kind of seek it out, though.

"Why don't you go see what Carter retrieved from his office, princess?" Dominic says against my lips once he finally pulls away, tipping my chin to the side before standing the both of us up. I had to grip onto his arms at how weak I felt from kneeling for so long, but when my eyes finally connected with the bed, my body stiffened.

"Go be a good girl and grab three for us." Rowan smirks at my reaction, brushing up beside me before giving a gentle push towards the mattress. I wanted to protest—to tell them no fucking way, but I did sign off on rubber bands for impact play, even though I'd straight up said the idea scared me a little. Or a lot. None of the men said anything as they waited for me to gather my confidence, however Carter did spank me after too much overthinking had elapsed.

It got me moving as I nervously bit my lip, crawling onto the bed to fumble with the thin cardboard box they were contained in. I could feel their eyes on me when I felt the rubber between my fingers, but I didn't allow for too much more hesitation, gathering three bands as I was told.

Once the box was shut again, I moved off the bed, finding all of their shirts gone, but their pants now done up all over again. I knew what it meant, and I also knew this was going to lead to a lot of new sensations for me whether it was something I'd want to try again or not. Taking Dominic's open hand as words enough, I placed the first elastic into his palm which he took almost too excitedly. Carter was the same, but when I handed Rowan his, he grabbed my wrist before I could pull away.

"Don't be scared." He murmured, tugging me slightly closer as he turned my arm over. Letting myself be handled by him, he positioned me so my palm was facing up, placing the band back into my hold.

Standing still with tense curiosity, I watched as Rowan's index finger pressed the bottom of the loop to my skin, the one on his other hand pulling at the top of the rubber as it slowly stretched upwards. I knew what he was going to do just by the glint in his eye, but he didn't pull far before releasing it, the band snapping against my palm before bouncing off. Though it didn't hurt as much as I feared it would, I also knew this spot wasn't as sensitive as other parts of my body that now tingled with renewed anticipation.

"That was one way we could do it." Rowan said, picking up the elastic from where it fell to the ground before repositioning it like he did before.

"If we stretch it farther and angle it like this..." He let go of the band yet again, this time a hell of a lot more taunt than the last. "The pain increases." I pulled away when the sharp nip of the impact snapped against my skin, my mind amazed yet worrisome at how the simplest of changes could lead to it genuinely hurting and leaving a noticeable sting behind. As if sensing this, Carter smiled as he took that same hand, bringing it up to his lips before pressing a soft kiss to the skin. I couldn't help but now imagine his mouth soothing the pain elsewhere, and both that and Rowan's demonstration brought me some inner peace. I was comforted by the fact I was no longer going into this completely blind, and when it soon led to Dominic scooping me up and laying me on the center of the bed, he winked before pulling my arms above my head and tying them up to the headboard.

That's why the cuffs were never fully removed.

"Remember that you're the one in control." He says as he moves to unstraddle me, checking to make sure the restraints weren't causing me any pain. While they weren't like the padded cuffs they usually used, the cold threat of them was also the whole point. Nodding to show him I wanted this, I tried not to squirm too much when Rowan took one foot and Carter took the other, both undoing intricate clasps of my heels and finally giving me relief after the long night I'd spent in them. They no doubt noticed my sigh in contempt at the sound of them hitting the floor, and they allowed it because I'm pretty sure there was going to be an entirely new kind of pain soon. At least this kind likely includes pleasure as well.

"I like seeing you all tied up like this, sweetheart." Carter says as he moves to sit at my left side, Rowan on my right, and Dominic now in between my legs. My back arched into his touch as his hand ran all the way down my front, lingering on the spot where his name now resided. "Since you were so good for us earlier, we'll be nice and leave these on for you." He continues, the tips of his fingers slipping just slightly under the waistline of my thong and teasing the skin there. When his touch retracted, that's when I grew aware of the bands still in their hands.

"Maybe Dominic will even let you come if you please us enough." My eyes shifted to him at that moment, but as he got closer to my heat, my knees were forced to spread more in accommodation of his large body. I wanted to beg for them to go easy, but they all knew I'd intentionally sought out the thrilling high of being punished. Since they knew me that well, they also knew just how to put me back in my place, and it had everything to do with learning the patience I didn't have.

"She always has been such a pain slut." Dominic says in response, talking about me like I wasn't even here.

"She might not even need me to come with what we have planned." My hips rolled up slightly at that, but my entire body froze as Rowan's hand rose to rest against my rib cage, the elastic against my skin looking just like it did during his demonstration. His eyes traveled to meet mine at my body's tenseness, but I couldn't help it. I'd expected him to just pull the rubber back and jump right in, but all he did was smile as Carter moved to lay on his side, turning my chin before capturing my lips with his.

He wasn't soft in the way he kissed, but every movement was still slow, leaving my body desperate for more with every passing second. With my eyes shut, I could only assume it was Dominic's hands running up and down my thighs, Rowan's doing the same thing to my side. Their fingertips were teasing and left goosebumps in their wake, but just as Carter deepened the kiss, Rowan let the rubber band pull back, snapping it hard against my skin.

I jumped at the unexpected impact, but it was soon followed by a moan when I felt Dominic's leg press in between my two. My squirming caused my hips to rock up, my clit dragging directly against his pants as another snapped against me, this time at my waist.

"Fuck." I whimpered, but Carter's mouth swallowed the majority of my curse, his tongue twirling against mine in the most sensuous of ways.

"Does that feel good, little sub?" Rowan asks teasingly, the feeling of his finger brushing my nipple a flash before the band was being pulled taunt. The cuffs made a ringing noise as I tugged at them helplessly, trying to turn on my side only for a warm, wet mouth to latch on around my breast, Rowan's tongue soothingly running over the hurt he'd just caused. That fine line between pain and pleasure mixed into a tidal wave of sensations that washed over me hard, my body riding that edge because I had no other choice but to. It was the reason I cried out when Carter pulled away, his lips trailing along my jaw instead. "Answer him, Hazel." He whispered into my ear, drawing a tremble right from my legs. I couldn't even remember what he'd asked, the dizziness consuming me when it was Dominic this time who pressed one against my thigh. "Please—" I cried, not even knowing what I was begging for. It didn't matter either. Everything was so overwhelming—so damn good—it made the week of edging feel like a mercy compared to this. There was no escaping their intensity, and the cruelest part is that I had no desire to do so either.

"Answer me, darling. Does this feel good? Do you want more?" Rowan's voice was a breeze against my hot skin, and even when I saw Carter positioning an elastic on his side of my body, all I wanted was more.

"Please, Sir. Please." I begged, nodding my head as though they wouldn't be able to see the desperate mess they've reduced me to without it. He smiled at that, but there was very little kindness in the expression. With him, Rowan was all degradation, and I knew just from that look he was going to use my need against me. "What are you saying please for, little one? You know how to get your release." He shook his head, moving with Carter as the two of them sent sharp stings through my nipples at the same time. A strangled gasp was wrenched from my lips as all three of them took advantage of my state, touching and pleasing me by stripping everything away piece by piece.

"You're so pretty when you cry." Dominic coos as the first tear slips down the side of my face, the drip of it being a release in itself that I've come to need. It felt so good to just let everything go, and that's exactly as I did as instead of fighting the pain, I let it become a part of me.

"There you go." He placed a hand on either side of my hips, guiding them as he slid me in circular motions against his thigh. That friction alone was dizzying, but the only thing I was capable of taking was what they were willing to give. It felt like too much and not enough all at once. With every sharp feeling of the rubber bands came bursts of need, and just seeing my men around me, comforting me through the punishment, created an indescribable desperation that ached to be fulfilled. "We've got you, Hazel." Carter murmured, paying extra attention to the hardened peak being rolled between his fingers painfully.

"We'll stop when you come." My legs tried to press together at the sight of my nipple being taken into his mouth while Rowan played with the other, but all I was met with was Dominic's thigh and the elastic he still had yet to use. I hadn't paid close enough attention earlier when Carter told me they would be nice and leave my underwear on, but when I felt a firm thumb beginning to run circles on my clit, I feared I now knew why the thin barrier was to be seen as a kindness.

"You can't." I moaned as my hips shifted, my core still being rubbed hard against Dominic.

I knew what he planned to do, but telling him he couldn't do something was the absolute biggest mistake I could've made right now. His eyes said it all in addition to the fact Carter and Rowan were now doing everything they could to stimulate me to the point of breaking.

"But you're doing so good." Dominic says, my watering eyes holding on the way he threatened to send my body into overdrive.

"Just hold on a little bit longer for us, princess. I'll even kiss it better afterwards." I whimpered but didn't safeword as his hands moved to place the rubber band right on my clit, my thong feeling like nothing as the other two stopped to simply plant distracting kisses all over my skin.

"Do you want this, Hazel?" Dominic still asks, holding my eyes while Carter and Rowan practically worshiped the upper half of my body. I did want this, but I was still allowed to be terrified by the build up. "Yes." I panted, tossing my head back to rest against the soft pillow against my neck. I let my vision be blanketed with darkness as I put all of my trust in their hands, something I know they didn't take lightly.

"Yes what, brat?" I began to breathe harder.

"Yes, Sir." I corrected, bracing myself for the shot of pain I was expecting. I waited, but it never came. I could still feel Carter and Rowan's mouths on me, their tongues licking my nipples before grazing me with their teeth. Even Dominic's touch remained, but still, nothing happened.

"Keep your eyes closed." The latter spoke as if he'd just predicted what I was about to do. The squirming got worse for me as I swallowed, my heart racing, but the longer I waited, the more sensitive that area seemed to become. Suddenly, I could feel the warmth of Rowan's breath playing on the tip of my nipple just as I could feel the faint throb of my clit beneath Dominic's rough thumb. Hell, at this point I could feel the way Carter smiled against my neck, now focusing his attention there—or more specifically the sensitive points that had me whimpering. Waiting. Needing. "Please, please." I begged, but the answering voice was nothing more than a low chuckle, turned on in cruel amusement. Instead of a verbal response, my mouth parted on a breathy inhale as I felt two thick fingers slip easily past my thong and sink deep inside of me. My already closed eyelids pinched slightly at the sound it made from my wetness, but just based on the way they curled upwards told me it was Rowan who was fingering me at this excruciatingly eased pace.

"Are you ready for your punishment, sweetheart?" Carter whispers before nipping my ear, groaning quietly at the sight of my tears in submission.

"Yes, Daddy." I spoke just as hushed, letting my arms go limp from where they were bound. While I couldn't see him, I knew Dominic didn't miss that act of acceptance. I could tell just by the way Rowan sped up his fingers a little quicker and Carter's hand moved to my stomach to not only comfort me but to also keep my body pinned down. This was so going to fucking hurt. With my eyes closed, I continued to wait, falling into the pleasure of their touch until I felt my orgasm at last starting to appear.

Already, this one felt different than the last—stronger and a hell of a lot more exerting from the constant sensitivity. I knew I was about to come just as my body started to lock up, my knees trying to close in as Dominic waited a beat. Another. And then I felt the unforgiving bite of the rubber band. I fell apart instantly, but this fall was anything but graceful. I damn near screamed as my release gushed from between my thighs, my knees trembling as Rowan's hands pulled away just for Dominic to dip his head down, his tongue swirling around my clit until everything broke apart. They were right in their promise to make it feel good, though if it weren't for Carter's hand on my middle, I would've bucked right off of the bed.

"I love you." He whispered for only me to hear, kissing my temple as a river of tears ran down my face, my hips twitching because Dominic's mouth was still on me. He numbed the sting with his tongue just to bring forward the nip of overstimulation, my entire body feeling as though it were floating in the best kind of relief possible.

I really did miss them, and though this was mostly just fun and games with us, I wasn't lying when I said I didn't want to spend this long apart anymore. Just by the way they held and kissed me made me believe they felt the same way, and once my hands were untied entirely, they held me a little more, all of us coming together into one consecutive hug. My body almost became cocooned by their much larger ones, actually saying hello for the first time since they came back.

"Hi." I smiled with my cheek pressed to Rowan's chest, Carter's hand rubbing my back and Dominic's fingers intertwining with mine. I heard their smiles when I pulled back just a little, brushing some of my hair back despite most of it still being strung together in one long braid. It soon didn't matter, though, when Carter began to unweave the strands anyways, tossing away the hair elastic until he was fully able to run his fingers through the defined waves. "How are you feeling?" He asks after a pause of us just relaxing into each other. Mentally, I felt amazing, however I would be lying if I said my body wasn't hurting. Now that I've mostly come down from my high and the adrenaline has faded, I could definitely feel the effects of those bands.

"Sore." I sighed, moving to cross my legs under me for better comfort. "Sore and tired." Still, though, I didn't regret a single part of it. And with the way they're looking at me right now, I can confirm it was definitely worth it. "I guess it's a good thing we have a solution to that then." Dominic winks from my side, kissing the top of my hand before moving to get off of the bed. I could tell he was already in aftercare mode just by the way he held himself, but I didn't want that quite yet. I was sore, but my body was greedier for something else.

"I want to take care of you too." I say, pulling him back towards me as my fingers moved down to the very obvious bulge still in his pants.

"All of you." My voice drops to a lower octave at that, seeing the heat pass through his eyes, and likely the eyes of his friends as well.

"You just spent a lot of energy, and the three of us have jet lag from the time differences. I appreciate it, but you should sleep, princess." Dominic smiles, however I know he's doing this for my sake and not his. Not willing to give up just yet, I rose to my knees so there wasn't so much height between us, twisting from Rowan until my other hand rested on the back of Dominic's neck.

"What if I told you I'm not very tired anymore?" I ask, already feeling myself grow wet between my thighs all over again.

My thong was twisted and positioned in a very uncomfortable way after all that we've done so far tonight, but I also saw it as an opportunity as I rocked backwards on the bed, the two men at my sides giving me the space to do so. Their eyes never wavered from my body, especially when my thumbs hooked under the waistband and began to pull until my underwear was around my knees.

The little show I was putting on for them worked, and I grew in confidence when I let the fabric go, sliding smoothly down my legs until my one ankle was the only thing keeping it connected to me. "Don't you want to make me feel good, Sir?" I grinned in a way that promised trouble, and when I spread my knees apart ever so slowly, I knew I'd won. Dominic pounced first as he ripped away the little bit of the thong that remained hooked around my ankle, settling right between my legs where I had tempted him to be. I couldn't even help it as my quiet giggle in satisfaction escaped my mouth, more than happy with this change as his belt came undone for the third time tonight, his cock in my fist the next second. It took very little encouragement to guide him to my entrance, but there was nothing rushed about the way Dominic slid into me until his hips were flush against mine.

There was something almost gentle in the way he drew out, and it caught me so off guard that I gasped lightly when he thrust back in, just as he had before. The two of us were slightly off centered on the bed with me on my back, but my mouth remained in a slight part as Dominic took me slowly and thoughtfully in a way I hadn't expected.

"Does this satisfy my princess?" He smiled when a soft moan left my lips, and I knew he felt just how much my body reacted to those words alone. Leaning up and taking advantage of the close proximity between us, I kissed him in a way that matched the feeling of what we were sharing right now, rolling my hips up to meet in time with his.

"Yes, Dominic." I whispered against his mouth once I eventually pulled away to breathe, using his name because we all knew he wasn't fucking me right now.

No, Dominic was making love to me, and when I felt Rowan and Carter position themselves to lay on either side of our bodies, they simply watched and held my hands until I slowly came apart once again. There was something so intimate, so incredibly open about the way we all were connected right now, that when Dominic's orgasm was triggered by mine, I knew I was going to spend the rest of my life with these men. If I didn't, I couldn't see myself being able to have even the smallest fraction of happiness that Rowan, Dominic, and Carter brought from me.

Ironically, I've never felt as safe, as loved, or as beautiful as these three make me, and even with all of those things aside, it didn't matter because it all came down to them. To us and everything we shared.

Whether it's hundreds of miles to Detroit, thousands of miles to France, or a unit so much bigger it took weeks to travel, we would always come back where we belonged and that was with each other.

After Dominic kissed me one last time, Carter took his place. I smiled when his thumb held my hip in a way that touched his tattooed initials across my skin, making some crude comment about how he was going to make it permanent one day. The craziest part is that I wouldn't even protest if one day was right now.

I knew I wasn't the only one who felt how vulnerably perfect this moment was that we shared, and when it came down to Rowan on top of me, my left hand in Dominic's and my right in Carter's, I didn't care about dates anymore. At the end of the day, we didn't need fancy, planned ideas to tell each other how undeniably and unconventionally in love we all were. We could see it in our eyes, feel it in our touch, hear it in our breaths. It was like everything we'd been through together all led up to this moment, this minute, this second. The only thing that mattered was us, and it was my whisper saying I loved them that caused Rowan and I to fall apart one last time.

With our hearts breaking open, we combined all of the pieces of ourselves both good and bad to form one soul, one body, and one love.

Our love.

~ Twenty-Seven ~

Hazel

I swear I could cry from how happy I am, the reassurance that they loved me back burning true not just in their words but in their touch as well. In fact, I did cry when Rowan scooped me up into his arms similarly to the way Carter did a week ago, just holding me and failing to hide the biggest smile on his face. For the first time in twenty three years, I think I finally understand what it feels like to have a home, and while I'd always imagined it as a house with four walls, it turned out to be the embrace of three men instead.

No words could describe the way I was feeling right now, but content was a pretty good second.

"I love you too, darling." Rowan whispers into my hair, the warm press of Dominic's body appearing at my back.

"And I hope you also know my name is being tattooed onto your ass now whether you like it or not." I pulled back teary eyed as I laughed, and as if for good measure he grabbed a handful of my backside playfully yet more than serious at the same time. It felt so good just seeing all of them happy like this, and I damn near choked on air when Carter tried to tickle the side of my body his name was on, falling back into a fit of giggles as I tried to kick him in retaliation.

"I hate you." I gasped when the other two ganged up on me as well, my hips trying to twist away from their touch.

"Liar." Dominic smiles when he ends up pinning me down on my back, kissing me because we both knew what was true. I don't think I'd ever truly experienced a love like ours until now. It was so easy to just get lost in all of them, and I feel like that's what happened for the majority of the night that led to us all naked in the hot tub off of Dominic's room, almost a bottle into the champagne Rowan popped open.

"Come on, you have to tell me something." I laughed when Carter suddenly pulled me into his lap, the blue lights colouring the water fading to a faint purple. My head easily rested against the hard muscle of his shoulder, but it was more than comfortable with his hands wrapping around my middle. I almost became breathless when his thumb slowly stroked over my left hip, but he wasn't even looking as he did it. The action just seemed natural now.

"Well I could tell you how beautiful you look right now." Dominic smiles in full sincerity, his eyes thoughtfully dropping down to my lips as I squirmed until Carter was forced to tighten his arms around me.

"I could tell you that your smile is one of my favourite sights or the fact that the little blush across your cheeks right now makes me want to do very sinful things to see if I can make it deepen." He was teasing both me and Carter as he let out a pained groan, forcing my movements to stop all together. We were done with sex for tonight, but I had to bite my cheek to stop from smirking at the fact Carter's dick very clearly didn't get the message.

"He likes you, okay?" He chuckles, kissing my cheek before resting his chin on my shoulder from behind. I can't help it as I happily snuggle into him, rolling my eyes at the fact he just spoke about himself in the third person.

"Does he have a name too?" I tease, splashing water when both Rowan and Dominic grab my feet. I thought they were trying to tickle me again but when they just propped my legs on their knees, I sighed as they started to massage me. It felt as close to heaven as things get and I nearly wanted to give into sleep from all of the tension being loosened from my body. The key word being nearly, because I was much too happy right now to cut this short.

"He responds to a lot of things as long as it comes from your mouth." Carter winks, nipping my ear when I laughed at his horrible innuendo. Shaking my head, I relaxed into his chest until I was able to look at the stars above us, a faint fog created from the clouds. We were far enough out to miss the busy lights of the city, though. I only realized how far we'd strayed from my initial question when I realized it had partly been an evasion tactic on their part, and while I wasn't mad in the least, I was persistent.

"For real, though." I say, closing my eyes as I let the hot water surround me up to my neck. "Why did you have to go to France last minute?" It wasn't a planned trip and it wasn't for Rush either. I'm starting to come to better terms slowly about the whole Mafia thing, but whether it was ideal or not, it was a huge part of their lives. I can't change it, however that doesn't mean I don't want to learn still. They'd promised me that we could talk when I was ready, and I think I was now if even just to be able to understand them better. I could feel the intensity of Rowan's stare especially at my question, and based on the small pause of silence, I knew they were all choosing their words right now.

"How much do you want to know?" He breaks first, staying true to their agreement. I knew if I directly asked, Dominic and Carter would answer too, but I didn't care who it came from as long as it was the truth.

"I don't want you to shelter me." I shake my head, tucking a slightly dampened piece of hair behind my ear as I readjust myself. "I meant it when I said I loved you. That includes these parts too." Even if I feared it would one day be the cause of a lot of complications for us. I watched as Rowan nodded once—the act so small you'd only be able to notice if you were looking for it—but he nodded nonetheless. It was clear all of them wanted to protect me, and I loved them for it, but we all knew that wasn't their decision to make.

Them choosing to talk told me they respected that.

"When you search our names, you'll hear about Rush and the strains of hotels and casinos we own, but those provide very little to our actual worth." Rowan started, moving up from my foot to my leg to massage.

"It's the hotels that house some of the most wanted criminals as a hideout and the casinos meant for dealings where the players spend large and go home with larger." My mouth stayed shut as he spoke, simply listening even though I wasn't sure what this had to exactly do with France. I could tell it was important, however, just by the way Carter's thumb continued to run over my hip as a nervous impulse he needed to relieve. "I've always been good with numbers, and that's why I can understand cheats without a second glance just through observance. Either way, people have to pay up at some point and that's when Dominic tries to talk. He reads people and when he finds they're ingenuine, stubborn, or straight up crooked, Carter comes into play." Tilting my head to the side, I looked at him as I regarded the new slight cut along his chin— barely noticeable but still there. Had that been from France? Did he hurt the people Rowan called cheats? "We've only ever shown you the... well behaved side of us, but we have a reputation pretty much everywhere for what happens when you cross the line in our territory." Dominic adds after a second, and I knew he was still trying to soften things for me. "What happens?" I ask. "When someone crosses the line?" I had a feeling I already knew, but I didn't fear their answer. At this point, I'm fairly sure there's pretty little they'd be able to tell me that would make me scared of them. Carter tightens his hold on me just as his mouth falls down to my ear, his breath a whisper against my neck.

"Like Rowan said, people have to pay up somehow. We give them three days to gather what's due. When we find that hasn't happened, their life becomes a statement instead." My breath held as he spoke, and it may make me fucked up, but I couldn't help but feel a little warm at the idea of them taking what's owed to them themselves. I would never accept it if it were innocents being killed, but the thought of them getting their revenge—making those who've double crossed them regret even thinking it in the first place...

"Careful how you're looking at us or we might believe you to be a little more like us than we thought, princess." Dominic's eyes flash with something, because he knew the light flush of my cheeks had nothing to do with the champagne. Shifting yet again on Carter's lap, I didn't say anything for a moment considering this was all very new waters for us to be in. When I first found out about the mafia, I was more mad that they hid it from me than the fact they were in it themselves. I know there's still loads of things I don't know about them yet, but I want to.

"So that's what happens when someone steals from you?" I raise my eyebrow, Carter keeping a hold of me as I lean forward to grab the bottle of champagne.

"Among other ways." Carter says against my neck as I refill my glass, but he didn't add more and I think I was fine with that for today. To an outsider's eye, the fact I wasn't trying to run in the opposite direction of them all right now might make me seem crazy, but while I'm kind hearted, I never said I was good. I'm not running for the same fact I didn't stop them from killing that man at the hotel. I'm not running for the same fact that one day I'm going to kill Andrew, and when Carter's ready, I will offer to help him kill Vincent too.

Sometimes there's not always good and bad, heroes and villains. Sometimes there are just two sides to differently similar stories.

"Can I ask you one more question?" I ask, a laugh mixing with my gasp when my feet were suddenly tugged forward until I was positioned into Dominic's hold with my legs over Rowan's. The tips of my hair dampened from the stir of water, Carter somehow looking even hotter from watching me from that slight distance. "You can always ask us anything, darling." Rowan says, his hands smoothing up and down my legs as an excuse just to touch me. They were all a little more intimate as they held me, their words sweeter when they spoke. I think it had everything to do with my confession and the fact that what we had wasn't going away anytime soon. It was a good feeling, and I think it was one we were all a little high off of right now.

"It's a little random and it might not even matter..." I kind of trailed off as I leaned into Dominic's front, exhaling as his hand came to play with my hair. Hopefully it wasn't personal or saddening, but I knew the mafia wasn't exactly any of their first choices in career paths. I wanted to know more about what they dreamed of— in a life where the world wasn't so complicated.

"Nothing will ever not matter when it comes to you, Hazel." Carter says, moving to sit beside Rowan as he holds my eyes. He meant every one of those words, and the sincerity in his gaze made me blush a little bit. I loved how they never shut me down when I spoke. It was something so small, but so big to me.

"This is just imagining, but if the Mafia never existed and you could choose any job you wanted, what would you want to do?" I know this would never happen, but that didn't change the fact I wanted to know what their aspirations were. Your dreams are always a huge part of you whether you get to live them or not. Just by their eyes I could tell my question hadn't been what they were expecting, but when I watched a small smile appear on Rowan's face, I knew no boundaries had been crossed. "I've always been good at drawing, and if I could, I would open my own tattoo studio." He admits, surprising me enough for him to chuckle a little.

"How did I not know this?" I grin, slightly amazed because one, Rowan doesn't have a single tattoo on his body, and two, I've never seen him draw anything before. Though there also hasn't exactly been a lot of time recently for me to learn these things.

"Half of our ink was done by him." Dominic says, lifting his arm from the water before tracing his fingertips across his skin. "This one's my personal favourite." I tipped my head down to look over the design of a raven with its wings outstretched, the design residing on the top of his right hand above his pointer and middle fingers. While small, I couldn't help but furrow my eyebrows in question about the fact the bird was cut into several pieces as though a knife had slashed clean through the image multiple times.

"Why is it split up like that?" I ask curiously, noticing the way he shivers slightly when my own fingers start to touch the intricate design. It started with me watching and ended with me holding his hand, only making things all the sweeter. "Ravens and crows are both seen as bad omens to most, but they're also birds of high intelligence and adaptability." Two things that Dominic had in every way. I waited for him to continue as his free hand wrapped around my stomach, my side still pressed to his chest and my head resting under his chin. Rowan smiled at me when I glanced at him but I could see the tiredness in his eyes from that single look alone.

I didn't even know what time it was here, but I know it's probably late. "Hazel." Dominic says to break the soft silence, lifting his fingers to run through my hair. "It's a reminder that even those of the highest intelligence and most efficient adaptability have limitations. My mind is a weapon, but it's not one I use without thought." My eyes widened slightly as I looked back at the tattoo in an entirely different way, one in which I never would've expected. The raven represented a part that made Dominic who he was, and there was a type of vulnerable beauty in that that made a part of me fall for him all over again.

"Thank you." I say after a small stretch of quiet, feeling just a little closer at what he'd shared. Now I wanted to ask about every tattoo and so much more when I knew we should all be sleeping. I could already feel my body slipping away, even though my mind was far from settled. If I had things my way, I would've fought the feeling harder. Only, Carter was the first to notice my decline in energy followed by my tired yawn into my hand.

"How about we talk more tomorrow, darling?" Rowan suggests when he realized next, squeezing my leg with the hand he just was previously running up and down my skin. I quietly groaned the second he tried to move away so I could get up, shaking my head in a weak protest. I know none of them were going to let me stay up though now that I'd shown my exhaustion.

"If you sleep I'll tell you about the time Dominic almost killed me with a potato." Carter says suddenly as he lifts himself from the seat below, water rushing across his skin all the way down to the hard length of his cock.

"What?" I asked in a slight daze, licking my lips before realizing I was ogling. When I guiltily looked up at him, not fighting the fact the other two stood with me in Dominic's arms, all he did was smile because he knew he'd won. Damn it. Carter's promise was so ridiculous I wanted to know more, and now I was caving when I was lifted gently out of the hot tub, my muscles loose from the aftercare we all gave each other.

"Good girl." Rowan whispered in my ear when he stepped out with me, the praise making me melt just as much as the gentle kiss he planted to my cheek afterwards. I felt all warm and tingly right now as my head rested against Dominic's chest, but that soon led to me being transferred into Rowan's arms, the other two moving into the bedroom and leaving us behind. The way things happened felt natural, however I still raised an eyebrow in question when Rowan sat me down on the edge of the tub, his body spreading my legs and taking up the space between them. My breath hitched when his pointer finger hooked under my chin, slowly tilting my head up until I could fully see him and everything he was feeling. "I love you, Hazel." He whispers as he slowly leans in, keeping his eyes on me until I could feel his exhale across my mouth. "I've loved you since I first dropped to my knees and kissed you in front of that mirror and likely even long before that." I didn't even blink before his lips were against mine, soft and inviting and full of an affection like no other. I think we both fell for each other our first night together, but nothing compared to hearing the words across his tongue and feeling the passion flowing within his touch. Just like that the world faded away and a new sliver of myself became mended after so many years of being broken. "Rowan." I spoke his name simply for him to hear it—to show that I was his as he was mine. "I know." He said, understanding what I was too tired to say. He knew because he felt the exact same way. "I know."

I haven't left their house in two days, and while I wouldn't yet consider it moving in, I did end up having to go to Jade's to grab my computer because they didn't make it sound like I was leaving tonight either.

Telling them I loved them was no small thing for me, and with everything else that was happening, they refused to let me wander anywhere without them somewhere close apart from the bathroom. Just spending the weekend with them has let me see an entirely different side of them, and it was one I could definitely get used to. Like seeing Dominic in the morning with messy hair in the kitchen, cooking us all breakfast and fussing over me like a mother hen. And then there was Carter who no matter what got up at the ass crack of dawn to work out in the gym downstairs, coming back sweaty, hot and delicious. However Rowan the most like me, sleeping in and spending the first hour of consciousness cuddling and drinking the coffee we took turns making. His voice was always so tired in the mornings, and there was nothing quite like him whispering I love you in my ear when we first woke up.

It's fair to say I feel like I'm on cloud nine as of recently, and while I woke up alone today, I had no complaints because it was accompanied by the delicious smell of something filling my senses from downstairs.

I smelt bacon, and that was encouragement enough to force me out of Dominic's bed—the one I fell asleep in last night. At some point in the night I faintly remember Carter coming in to spoon me from behind without a single word, but his side was cold when I woke up and I'm not actually sure that Rowan slept last night. Something to do with finishing up something for work and considering he didn't specify, I assumed it was mafia business. If it weren't for Dominic joining me in his bed after I'd taken a long bath, I don't think my mind would've calmed enough to fall asleep. I couldn't pin it exactly, but yesterday felt a bit off with all three of them, even though nothing coherently seemed wrong. Maybe it's wishful thinking, but I hoped that if something was truly wrong, they'd come to me now if they needed it. I suppose I'll just have to wait and see. Walking out of the room wearing the silky pajama set Rowan had picked out for me the night before, I smoothed down the uncombed strands of my hair with lazy movements.

The smell of breakfast only got stronger the farther I got down the hall, my stomach rumbling with interest in response. "It's my dad." I hear Dominic's voice speak from the main floor, strained and clearly unhappy at the continuous ringing of his phone. I just make it to the stairs when I see him stepping out onto the balcony, the sun of the day already bleeding deep into the sky.

The last time I checked my phone it was just past noon, my body very clearly in need of the sleep after Dominic kept me up all night teaching me the never ending wicked things he could do with his tongue. I could still feel him from the soreness that followed me into this morning.

"Darling." My nickname echoes off of Rowan's tongue at the first sight of me, my eyes peering over the railing to find him reading in a chair just off of the living room with plenty of windows to light the pages of his book. His office was right across from where he sat, the separating wall a mixture of glass and dark wooden frames in theme with the rest of their house. It was clear this slightly hidden corner was his space, but god did the sight of him dressed in dark gray sweats with an even darker toned shirt feel inviting. Rowan had stuck to lounge wear for today, and I liked that more than I'd admit.

"You look happy." He smiles as I make my way over to him, trying to sit at his side only to be pulled straight into his lap. The first thing he did was kiss me lightly, the contact short and sweet but the caress lingering with the feeling.

"I am." I say as I twist to let my legs drape over the arm of the chair, my head falling happily against Rowan's waiting chest. "You sleep okay?" The question slips from my mouth at the sight of the dark circles under his eyes from either a restless sleep or no sleep at all. He'd said he'd been working on some important project that couldn't wait, but I had at least figured he would've gone to bed at some point.

"Yeah, I just think the jet lag is still catching up to me." Rowan answers, moving his book into his left hand so he could hold me better with his right.

"Carter went to Jolene's for coffee but he should be back in fifteen or so if you're hungry."

I was but I didn't mind waiting a little either. Being cuddled first thing when I wake up is something I'm never going to pass up.

"Okay." I mumble as I let one of my hands rest against his stomach, my head against his shoulder. "You can keep reading. I'm just going to try and wake up." Even as I said that, I could feel myself slipping away again just from the warmth of his comfort. When my eyes closed and Rowan reached over to our sides, I sighed when a fleece blanket was placed over our legs, making sure to tuck it in around my feet so I wasn't cold. God, I love this man. "Okay, Hazel." He says, and while I can't see him, I have a big feeling he's probably smiling down at me right now. It was tempting to open my eyes just to see that, but when I heard the shuffle of a page being turned, I knew he'd gone back to his book. It felt so good being able to do things like this, and whatever tension I thought I'd felt yesterday dissolves along with my worries. I feel like things have been looking up for us a lot lately, and I planned to enjoy every blissful second of it. I don't think I fell asleep again, but I could still faintly hear Dominic talking on the balcony the next time I opened my eyes, the sight of Rowan finishing the last page in his book appearing right before he closes it entirely.

"Did it have a good ending?" I smile tiredly, no signs of Carter meaning he's probably still gone. I couldn't tell if I wanted him or the coffee more. I guess it doesn't matter when I'll soon have both anyways.

"Good, but not happy." Rowan eventually answers and I nod because I get it. It's typically books like those you tend to think about for days if not weeks afterwards. I wanted to get back into reading when I have the time, but I've been so busy as of late there hasn't exactly been a lot of opportunity to just relax on my own time. I'm sure the need for space will come eventually, but I'm perfectly happy right now having movie nights with Jade and spending time with my boyfriends.

"Fair." I say, shifting myself so that I'm sitting up a little more.

"Why don't you put it away and grab new ones for both you and me? I don't have to leave for work until four thirty." Something that looked a lot like appreciation in Rowan's eyes flashed at my offer, but I was starting to understand the little things just as they had for me. While I struggled with small spaces sometimes, Rowan had a need for organization in almost everything.

It ranged from things as simple as the dishwasher being organized in a specific order to the shoes at the front door having to be in line with the mat. It's subtle, but I know he wouldn't be able to just put his book down on the table for a few hours and go put it away later.

"I love you, darling." He says quietly as he tips my chin up for a kiss, an action I'm more than compliant to. Grinning afterwards, I pull away as I reluctantly slide off of his lap, keeping the soft blanket wrapped around my body for warmth.

"I love you too." I tilt my head, fully taking in his attire and biting my lip at how good he looked. I might have been liking it a little too much as a low chuckle leaves his body, the kind that makes it hard not to press my legs together over.

"Sit. I'll be back in no more than a few minutes." Rowan taps his index finger against the cover of his book as though it irritated him he had to put it away. I suppose my staring probably didn't help that much.

"I get to stay in your special chair?" I tease with a contained giggle because in all of the times I've been here, Rowan is the only person I've ever seen occupy it. Like I said, apart from his room, this place was where he liked to relax.

"There is nowhere in this house that isn't free to you, darling." He says, only making the first move to walk away when he sees I've sat down and gotten all cozied up in his spot. Even then, his steps were backwards so he could continue to look at me.

"Noted, Sir." I threw back with no other motivation than to get him to hurry, my laugh echoing when I heard him murmur the word insatiable under his breath. It clearly worked when he tore his eyes away from me at last, heading towards the elevator at a much quicker pace than what he would usually walk. I felt so good to be able to tease him like that, smiling like an idiot because I knew no one else was watching.

It was just me now, but even in a house this big, I felt anything but alone.

Pulling the blanket just a little higher over my body, I pulled my phone from my pocket to check the time, finding that Carter was taking a lot longer than what Rowan said he would. I was about to call him just to make sure he was okay when my eyes connected to the wallpaper of my dad and I together when I was still a kid, my smile turning into a different kind at the memory. It was days like these where I wished I could see him—where I'd be able to tell him all about my relationships because I know he'd still be happy for me despite being with three men instead of one. In fact, I'm sure he prefers it that way since there are more people to protect me even though I don't need it. The last time I really looked at his face was when I found those passports of his in Detroit, but I ended up giving everything I found to Rowan because I knew if anyone could help, it would be him.

We hadn't really spoken about it since, though, however I'm not exactly sure if he's had a ton of time to look into it yet either. Curiosity brought my eyes from my phone to the partially glass wall of his office, and I wondered if it was that that kept him up last night. I hoped not because I told him it wasn't the biggest priority right now, but when I looked at his desk, I couldn't help but notice the dark gray envelope sitting there with the same clasp as the one I'd given him. Everything I found was in there, but he told me he was sending it away to one of his men for prints. Had there not been any results and he didn't want to disappoint me? It was a sweet thought, but there was one thing I wanted to see again and that was the ultrasound photo I haven't been able to stop thinking about since I saw it. The date stamp just didn't line up, and my curiosity got the best of me as I put my phone down, neatly placing the blanket onto the seat of the chair. Rubbing my eyes as I stood, I took a few steps towards the office door, thinking about the fact Rowan just told me there was nowhere I wasn't allowed to go. Anyways, these were my files I'd given him, but my hesitation was about what I was going to find.

Surely he would've said something if he found a clue of importance, and I couldn't tell if that realization disappointed me or not. I wanted to see my father again so badly, but I knew he was alive. When it comes down to it, that's all that matters to me. Finding Rowan's door unlocked, I pushed it open with my attention zeroed in on the file.

The string clasp of it was already undone, and with a steadying breath, I opened up the top to find the contents of my father's belongings in there.

The items were of varying shapes, but there was more paper in here than what I remember there originally being. With the desk being mostly empty, I used the space to start pulling out pieces, the first stack of paper containing a series of fingerprints to names I didn't recognize, all connected by a single paperclip. Setting it down, I made a note to go back to that when the next thing I found was what I was looking for, only this too now had a clip. Pulling out the ultrasound photo dated , my mouth parted in a silent gasp because of the photograph attached to it.

The sight caused me to stumble, a man sporting the same bright green eyes and blonde hair as me, both distinctive features given by my father. The image itself was clearly taken from the internet considering it was bordered by the text of a high school graduate, class of.

His nose was slightly crooked as though it had taken a hit or two throughout the years, but this man was disturbingly similar to me.

A different mouth but the same hair. A different nose but the same eyes. The man named Cameron Monet looked similar enough to be my brother older by two years, the son of my father but not my mother. The question was why did Rowan have this and why didn't I know? Shakily putting the image down and forcing myself to breathe, it was the passports and IDs I found next, simply dumping all of them onto the desk to save time. A frown marred my face as I picked the closest one to me up, my father's face connected to the name Jonathan Barkley only seeming more confusing than the last time I saw it. Sure, it's not a huge surprise to learn he led secret lives, but were children really a part of it? I jumped at the sound of the front entrance door opening and closing, likely Carter coming home, but I was too transfixed in everything else to care. Picking up the next passport, my head tilted at the name Marcus Caddel appearing in a bold font across the top, but instead of pausing in thought like last time, I froze in horror.

Before me was the alias that felt familiar when I first read it and had my heart sinking in recognition now that I've seen it again. My hand shot out to grip the desk when I felt myself fall forward slightly, but not even that could ground me at the fact I'd heard this name before and not in a good way.

"My mother was murdered shortly after I turned seventeen?" Carter had said.

"The man we've spent years hunting will die by my hand one day. Marcus Caddel will know what true pain feels like, just like I did thanks to him." No.

Carter had told me that a few days before I found his room destroyed, before he kissed me, before he held me, before he told me he loved me and nothing would ever change that. But there was no way he saw the background on my phone and didn't know, no matter how different my father has changed his appearance to remain hidden. My entire body shook, unsure what to do, but it soon didn't matter when I felt the eyes of others on me

. "Hazel." Rowan spoke my name from the door of his office, but it was not the same way he said it when he was reading only minutes ago. It wasn't until I turned I realized I was crying, but seeing Carter there too made it worse. Dominic came next, and when he tried to move towards me, he quickly stopped when I took two steps back.

I thought I knew what betrayal felt like in Detroit when I told my mother I didn't want her in my life anymore. But this... this hurt so much fucking worse. "You knew?" I say, my voice breaking on the last word as I barely manage to keep myself standing upright. I hated the feeling of my tears wetting my cheeks and the way each inhale became harder to take, but it was the guilt—the confirmation in their eyes that I hated the most.

"My god, you knew?" I said again, this time not as a question but as a painful accusation. Everyone knows the idiom of being stabbed in the back, but I never actually expected to feel the physical impact of it in my heart.

"I know this looks bad, I know it does, but please put down the scissors, Hazel." Carter says, panic clear in his eyes where my fingers were gripping at the blade. I hadn't even realized I'd picked them up. I knew what he was thinking and it hurt as I listened, dropping them to the desk along with the sheets of secrets that had just been uncovered.

"You need to explain what the fuck this is right now or I'm leaving and I won't be coming back." I demand, my voice surprisingly steady despite what my actions are showing on the exterior. I doubt I could actually follow through on that last part, but I couldn't tell what I needed most right now. Answers were the most obvious thing that came to mind, but I really just wanted to be held by the only people I can't have near me right now.

"Okay." Dominic says, his hands shaking as he raises them slightly.

"Let's go into the living room and we'll tell you everything." I knew he meant it, but I shook my head anyway. My grip on this desk was the only thing keeping me from collapsing and I wasn't about to get one of them to pick me up.

"No, you'll tell me here, starting with how you know my father." All it took was a single glance to see they didn't want to have this conversation, but that's tough shit. I wasn't about to give them an opportunity to hold me or make me feel better because I'm not sure I'm capable of getting the answers I need otherwise.

"You should sit down, sweetheart." Carter says with genuine concern, but I didn't want to hear it.

"You're not in a place where you have the right to tell me what to do." I shoot back, though I do lean against the office chair slightly from the overwhelming waves of dizziness and nausea.

My expressions hardened despite my tears still flowing. To be honest, it didn't even matter. I waited in a tense silence for the explanation I was owed, and I forced myself not to feel sad at the fact Rowan's entire body was nearly shaking where he too leaned against the door frame for support.

"You want to know everything?" Carter asks, tipping his head down slightly in acknowledgment that this was what I wanted, even though it's a discussion that never should have needed to be had. My silence was my answer and it was one that was going to change everything. My dad is Marcus Caddel, father of myself and my half-brother Cameron Monet. Vincent killed my uncle Marcus's brother and in revenge, Carter's mother was murdered when he was only seventeen by strychnine, a poison that is more than lethal in even the smallest of amounts. He did this as Tobias Walsh, and when the entirety of the Alcazar family sought out retribution, my father became Christopher Michelson, then Jonathan Barkley, then Marcus Caddel.

For years, he's hidden under an umbrella of false identities, meeting Cameron's mother Ivy two years before meeting my mother Heidi and having me.

They don't know anything more than that, but they knew where my father was going to be. Dominic, Rowan, and Carter had been ordered to kidnap and make a statement out of the man who raised me, and they've known who I was since I met Vincent for the first time by that elevator.

"You held me." I shook my head, my fist balled and rested against my chest as though it could make the ache go away.

"You held me when I cried, worrying my dad might be dead or hurt or alone when you knew this whole time he wasn't!" I may have just been stating facts, but it was the only thing I could do from breaking. Losing them was a loss I wouldn't be able to recover from, yet how am I supposed to continue on when they plotted my father's murder while telling me they loved me.

"Is this why you haven't killed Vincent?" I ask, my words directed straight at Carter. He killed those women but not the man who sent them there. Why?

"Because you needed him to get to my father?" It was the only explanation I could think of, but I feared the truth would be so much worse.

"If Vincent dies, I'm going to be caged into a life I never wanted." Carter says, and while my heart aches for him too, that doesn't erase everything else.

"But you admit it? You've been trying to kill my dad even after all we've shared. After I told you how much he means to me? That he's the only family I have left?" A lone tear falls down his cheek, but I'm too fucking tired to care.

"No." He takes a step towards me, physically flinching when I move away. I knew it was too good to be true.

"Fuck, yes, but that plan stopped after I realized what you were to me."

"And you think Vincent would just let my dad go after everything? All of you seriously believe he won't do everything in his power to ensure his death with or without you?" There was no way in hell they could think that was a possibility, and even if they weren't the ones to pull the trigger, they would be the ones handing over the firing gun either way. Hearing all of this was a kind of pain I didn't know I could experience, but my vision started to switch between being in and out of focus after enough time had passed.

My body felt like a dam very quickly being rushed at in surges, and I was no longer sure how much longer I could last before breaking.

"No we don't believe that." Rowan says, but there was a kind of numbness to his words that felt like the knife being twisted. "There's only ever been one other way to ensure your father gets out of this alive, and I promise you I will make sure it happens tomorrow."

What does that even mean? I wiped furiously at my cheeks when more tears flowed, and it took my arms physically wrapping around my body to keep from moving closer to them.

"Please, Hazel." He cries with guilt, and I wish I could say that made me feel better, but it didn't. Not in the least.

"Please let us make this right. Tell us what you need and we'll make it happen, just don't leave." His last beg came out as a desperate plea, and it was my undoing. I broke as I fell to the ground, sitting against the desk leg with my hands over my face and my knees pressed to my chest. I didn't move away when I felt Rowan and Dominic come to my side, but their touch against my skin didn't feel the same. What they didn't understand was that they'd already given me everything I ever could have needed just by being them. No actions could take back what was already too far gone. Even if they don't plan to kill my father now, they had when I was well in love with them, foolish enough to believe my happily ever after had finally found me. "I'm sorry." Dominic whispers in my ear, but I'm barely listening when Rowan gently pulls my hands away from my eyes, his gaze focused on my shaking body where our fingers were now connected.

"There is no place in this world where people won't be able to find Carter and Dominic, so tomorrow I'm going to kill Vincent and flee to a safe house in Costa Rica until the dust settles." Rowan tells me, surprising me with my eyes shooting to the son of the man in question. Carter hadn't left the door since I first flinched away from him, but a lot has changed since I last looked. The only thing I could see through his hardened expression was disgust, not for me but for himself. His arms were crossed and his eyes were entirely on me, but if he was bothered by Rowan's words, he didn't show it.

"We were going to convince you to come with me, and I was going to tell you everything once we got there to ensure both of our safeties together. I know there is no amount of apologies we can give you to make up for the lies we told, but I promise you I will fix this." I didn't stop him as his hands lifted to cup my face, but my vision was too blurry to even make out more than the shapes of his white blond hair I had been playing with only minutes ago. His words should have reassured me, so why am I only feeling so much worse? I didn't want Rowan to have that burden because I know his rights as an associate are very little compared to the ones Dominic or Carter has.

Those two could kill Vincent and get away with it, but Rowan... he would be hunted down for the rest of his life if he were caught.

How did things go so wrong so quickly? I could feel Dominic's shaking body beside me, trying to put up a good front but failing to hide the absolute terror in his eyes at the thought of me leaving like this. Rowan's given himself the task of fixing things that we all fear are irreparable and Carter has gone so cold it hurts because I know he's falling apart silently on the inside.

We all were. I was so fucking mad at them, so mad, but my mind couldn't help but travel to so many other places now as the dots began to connect together.

My uncle died before I was even born meaning this all began before I became a factor. I wanted to be able to scream just to be able to communicate something, but there's one truth that no one wants to talk about and it's the fact my father is Marcus Caddel.

From the shadows he allowed himself to be beaten down just so he could rise now.

He killed Carter's mother just as Vincent killed his brother, but that also made him smart in some sick, perverse way. Nobody goes years hiding from any mafia, and my dad has managed to do so my entire childhood. There was more to this than I think any of us knew, but they were all morons if they believed my father was una-ware of the uninvited guests he'd be having at his party tomorrow.

And while changing the plan behind Vincent's back could work, it's only when I realize how unbelievably tense Carter is that I remember the other fact no ones talking about. If Vincent dies, Carter is going to become the Don of the Italian-American Mafia.

My eyes widened at him to realize what that means, because he's going to be the uttermost powerful leader of the three crime families and hold the responsibility of the title along with it. The Mafia was not a world I grew up in, and I don't even know a fraction of what the position entails, but what I do know is that it's a life Carter doesn't want. He told me that the morning after he'd traced his initials on my hip a week ago, saying it would be like a prison sentence with nothing more than a pretty cage.

That was the same morning I'd promised him that if things ever came down to him being forced into the position, I would run away with him to the ends of the Earth if that's what it took. Rowan and Dominic would be by our sides, and we would never have to look back again. In a better world, that could be a reality. In a fair world, people like Vincent would simply cease to exist. But this life is not better nor is it fair. All we have is the chilling grasp of reality that leaves one option, and that is to survive.

"I need to go." I sniffle as I push myself up from the floor, or at least try to and fail. "I need to go." I say again as though I was trying to convince myself of that. They didn't help me up. Dominic gently grabbed my hand and Rowan kept a hold of my face, but the new kind of pain across their faces wasn't out of pity but out of regret for the fact they weren't going to let me leave.

"It's not safe for you to be gone right now, princess." Dominic shakes his head, and even though I'm furious with them, I can tell forcing me to stay wasn't something he wanted to do. Truthfully, I didn't really care.

"Let go." I cried as I pulled myself away from all of them. Thankfully, to this they listened, even if it looked like it hurt them to do so.

"I'm going home." The worst part about those words is that I thought this was the only home I ever needed. I didn't seek them out this time and instead used the desk to steady myself upwards, standing even as sobs threatened to wrack my body. I knew I was about to start hyperventilating soon, and I didn't want to be anywhere near here when that happened. Thinking back to how broken I was and still am over everything that happened with my mom, I feared I wasn't going to be able to recover from this kind of loss after the true reality of this all sinks in.

"Please—"

"Don't." Carter cuts Rowan off, and his tone actually startled me for a second before I looked over to find him shaking despite his expressionless face. He's not looking at either of us right now, but I'm pretty sure he's aware of things as small as the heavy breaths currently leaving my body.

Everything about the way he stood caused an icy cold wave of acceptance to wash over me, because even if I somehow found it in myself to forgive them, things could never be the same now.

I'll admit, as much as they could've just come clean, this wasn't only about me anymore. Maybe it makes me stupid, but I really do believe they'll do everything they can to keep my father alive. If they wouldn't, then Carter wouldn't be standing like everything was going to be stripped away from him, both me and his freedom of a life without the confinements of being Don. Though hating them would make everything about this so much easier, I couldn't, not even now. Trapping himself in a future like that is something I'll never wish upon him, or Rowan and Dominic because I know they'd be just as stuck as him. "My father is smart enough to work through things on his own." I say, lifting my chin slightly just to cause more tears to trickle out of the corners of my eyes.

"If you chose to kill Vincent—any of you—don't do it for me. That's not what I want." It was the only thing I would ask of them, because I wasn't going to give them the illusion his death would make everything okay again. I don't know if anything could.

The air stirred around my body as Dominic stood followed by Rowan, but neither of them tried to reach out to me this time when I took a heart shattering step forwards. I refused to look at how they were feeling, so I chose numbness instead, waiting for Carter to move out of the door frame.

"You want to go back to Jade's?" He asked in a horribly deafening way, however I knew he was doing it out of respect for me.

"Yes." I bit my cheek as my bottom lip quivered, my mind very quickly becoming a mess of emotions I already knew would consume me the second I was alone. I felt Rowan's shuddering inhale as though it were my own lungs breathing in the devastating tension, but I couldn't look away as more tears fell down Carter's face.

When I forced myself to stop being a coward, I looked at Dominic first, finding his hands curled tight at his sides to restrain himself from going to me. Something passed through us when our eyes connected, and the force of his pain was strong enough to nearly make me fall down all over again. It didn't matter that it was their fault they lied. This was tearing all of us apart, and I hurt for them just as much as I was angry that they caused this.

"Okay." Carter said, and that was it. Nothing was keeping me here but myself. There was still so much—too much—I had to process, namely the fact I was unbelievably upset and torn from my father's involvement in this too, but right now the only thing that mattered was us. Carter, my always, Dominic, my everything, and Rowan, my forever.

This felt like goodbye, and when I took a second step towards the door, this time I didn't stop.

~ Twenty-Eight ~

Rowan

This was worse than any fate death could bring. I felt her slipping away from us the second she saw that file, and again when she walked out the door crying with her hands wrapped around her stomach. We should have told her, but we waited too long.

There's only us to blame for this, and fuck, to say we were paying the price was an understatement. Losing Hazel was the worst kind of pain I've ever experienced, but it was the fear that came with her absence that made it so much worse. She was supposed to be safe in Costa Rica right now as a temporary vacation, the three of us planning on how to get around the assignment we're supposed to be religiously preparing for. Instead, I'm currently sitting outside of Jade's house, tapping my foot nervously on the concrete step at the feeling of eyes of me. I've felt them since I stayed here all throughout the night, neither Jade nor Hazel leaving the house once. My instinct is very rarely wrong, but I've also never been more distracted and off balance than I am now.

I wasn't here to plead for Hazel's forgiveness, I was here to ensure her safety. It was the least I could do at this point. Whatever Dominic and Carter were busying themselves with wasn't my problem. So, I stayed where I was with strained eyes, my body cold from the night and my face swollen from the tears not even I could fight off from spilling. I promised to respect Hazel's space the second she chose to walk out our door, but I had no doubt Vincent was well aware of our... was it a break up? The thought sent yet another wave of terror straight into the blood in my veins, however I couldn't allow myself to falter.

Vincent knows Hazel's here, and I would rather die than have him lay an eye on her one more time— Smash! The sound of glass shattering into a million pieces had my heart stopping, the windows being the first thing that comes to mind. I had people all over the property, but I wasn't about to chance wasting the time to circle the house. I went to the only thing I could think about, and that meant going in.

Finding the door locked when I tried the handle, I grabbed the key I had in my pocket as a precaution, not wasting a second before moving inside and drawing my gun. It was eerily silent inside, but my quick scan of all of the windows proved them to be intact. Hazel had a window in her room, though, and that knowledge terrified me.

"Leave her alone, Cal." A voice comes from the kitchen, my body spinning to find Jade crouched on the floor with broken porcelain at her feet, the colorful designs of what used to be her glass in a pile of small pieces.

It was a mug. Hazel's okay. Vincent would never go after Jade because of who her parents are, but the woman I know who is just across the room is exactly the kind of person he would target.

"Out. You're not welcome here anymore." Jade points to the door, wiping her hands against her thighs as she stands to her full height. I don't know what Hazel told her, but I know Jade would defend her to the ends of the Earth just as I would. It's good, I thought. At least she's not entirely alone. Her words still hurt, though. I was at fault for causing Hazel pain, and as she should, Jade sided with her. We may have been friends for years, but I would never forget the way she was looking at me now. "I just want her safe, Hails." I say, but she's already shaking her head as she physically shoves me backwards.

"You don't get to call me that anymore." She hits me again, not to hurt me but to let out that little bit of anger I know she hasn't been able to relieve.

"Don't you realize what you've done to her?" I didn't miss the way her voice had dropped to an angry whisper, just as I didn't ignore the aching in my chest as a result.

"I need to see her. I don't want—"

"I don't care what you do or do not want." Jade interrupts.

"She's sleeping because she was up the entire night shaking on the bathroom floor. She came home silent and the second the front door closed she collapsed to the ground. Rowan, she didn't get back up for three hours." Not a single breath left my body as Jade spoke, my eyes facing the door to Hazel's bedroom but my ears trained on every horrible thing I was told—every horrible thing I was responsible for.

"I didn't go to work today because she won't eat and I ended up sleeping on the couch outside of her room last night because she kept waking up screaming from nightmares. She knows you've been outside since yesterday, and yes, she has gotten every single text message Dominic sent her in apology. Hazel doesn't want to see you, and after everything, I think you at least owe her that." Jade winced slightly when she saw tears start to fall down my cheeks all over again, but it was because we both knew she was right, even when we wished she wasn't. I didn't know if what happened yesterday was Hazel breaking up with us, but I felt the grief of it either way. We should have told her everything a long time ago, yet our selfish cowardice only left despair in the end.

After she'd trusted us with her father's belongings from Detroit, it was I who had the task of looking into the prints and IDs. The ultrasound picture of Hazel's half brother Cameron Monet was the worst discovery of them all, though. I knew how to research, and while Hazel would never admit it, I knew a part of her despised that her father was never a permanent figure in her life. Sure, Marcus was there, but he never stayed for any more than a few days to make sure Vincent's people didn't link him to his family. Ivy was different, though. They met two years before Hazel was born, the pair having a one night stand and never hearing from the other again.

Marcus didn't even know he had a son until Cameron was thirteen, but it wasn't a coincidence he and his current wife ran into each other again.

Turns out they both have a mutual agenda, and that's the downfall of Vincent MacGuire and everything he stands for. While Marcus was away hiding, leaving Hazel behind, he got to raise the boy—Hazel's brother—in the ways she never got to have.

There was so much we should have told her, but the conflicting part of ourselves didn't want to hurt her in that way either. It didn't make our secrets right, but it also didn't come from a bad place either. I would give Hazel the time she needed even if it killed me to do so—but I would never give up on what we had—have. God, please let it be have.

"Quite frankly, I have no opposition to having extra eyes on the house considering who you are, but I'm not risking her passing out again from spiraling if she sees you in here." Jade's arms cross over her chest, and I know it would take physically moving her to get to Hazel's door. I knew when I wasn't wanted, and the daggers shooting my way were more than indication enough.

Nodding my head once, just enough to show I heard her, I wiped at my eyes as my fingers came away wet. There was so much I would say if I could right now. I would say I was sorry. That even though Hazel didn't want anything to do with me right now, and rightfully so, she would always have a home with me. I'm not one to carry regret, but hurting her will forever be the one thing I'll never forgive myself for.

"Make sure she keeps the acrylics on." I whisper the only thing I can think of as I slowly back away to the door, even though every instinct in my body tells me I need to be with her. Even though I have no right to wish this, I can't stand the idea of her hurting anymore than what we've already caused. "What?" Jade asks, my question catching her off guard, but I only shake my head as I open the front door of her house. "Don't let her bite her nails." Not waiting for a response, I stepped outside and gently shut the door, locking it behind me to be safe. I didn't know you could grieve somebody who was still alive, but when I sat back down on the cold, unforgiving concrete step, I felt like I'd lost everything. However despite that, while I didn't deserve it, I found peace in the fact she was at least asleep now, hopefully dreaming of a world where everything didn't hurt so damn much.

Hazels

I wasn't sleeping

I can't breathe. My body won't let me breathe. I can't think or talk or speak because I know the second I do something, I'm going to shatter. Jade thought I already did, but she was very much wrong. After what happened in Rowan's office yesterday, Carter let me leave, but he refused to let me drive.

I was pissed he had his driver take me home at the time, but looking back, I probably would've caused an accident considering the state I was in. He didn't say anything to me as he opened the car door, but he didn't close it even once I was inside. For a moment, he had just looked at me before tilting my chin up to meet his eyes. I didn't want to, but I did, hating to see his tears that mirrored mine.

"It's okay if you never forgive us—if you never want to speak to us again, but I will promise you this. Your father will not die, even with the past I've had with him." I know that promise hurt him to say, and even if I didn't want it to, my heart still bled for him at the fact he was willing to give up years worth of work and resources because of me.

The truth is that I was mad at my dad too. How can I even look at him again without remembering the way I held Carter on the anniversary of his mother's death because he couldn't take it anymore? I was caught in the middle of two incredibly horrible situations, but I did know this. If my dad—if Marcus Caddel intentionally murdered Carter's mother out of revenge—I wouldn't speak to him again.

"Please close the door." I'd said quietly over my cries, but I knew he heard me. The metal of the car soon became a physical barrier between us, but he listened. Now I was here, my hands gripping hard onto the bathroom counter as I stared at my reflection in the mirror. My eyes were a bright green, even more prominent than usual because of the red puffiness of my face.

My hair was frizzy from the way I brushed out all of the knots in anger just a few minutes ago, but the one thing I couldn't stop from seeing was the way I wouldn't stop pacing.

There was so much about this I still didn't understand, but the only people who could give me answers were the three people I refused to talk to. If it weren't for Jade, I don't think I would even be functioning at all right now. If you can call this functioning. Dominic has stopped texting me, but I knew Rowan was still outside.

For what reason, however, I didn't know.

On top of that, it was impossible to not feel on edge with everything around me so broken. While I don't believe my father is foolish enough to be caught off guard at his own event, thoughts of if he was okay invaded my mind again and again. Things can always go wrong, just as they are ever changing. The world is cruel like that, and half of the time you just have to hold on and pray for what you can.

Unfortunately, I wasn't in one of those moods. Waiting has made me restless, and even though I thought I might pass out from the food I haven't eaten, I knew one thing. I needed out. Turning on the bathroom sink, I repeatedly splashed icy cold water over my face as though the nip of it would dull the nagging ache in my heart. It didn't, but at least I was a little more awake than a few seconds ago.

Drying my skin hastily with a face cloth, I tossed the material onto the counter as I spun away and slowly dragged my feet back towards my bedroom. I had to force down my dizziness with each tired step, but I think I just needed to get out of here for a while—to get away from them. Everything, and I truly mean everything, hurts.

I couldn't even breathe in without my lungs burning with the same sense of loss I feel in my heart, so I needed to leave. But, there was still one person I had to speak to, and I prayed with every part of me that she wasn't in on this too. That discovery would be like the last tap to a web of breaking glass that causes everything to fall apart, but if I'm being honest, I feared I was already there.

"Hazel?" I hear Jade's soft knock at my door, probably having heard me getting up for the first time in hours.

"You can come in." Came my reply, but I didn't even recognize the sound of my own voice layered with so much of everything I didn't want. Instantly my door opened, a slow and hesitant entrance, but one nonetheless. Jade's eyes were on me, or more so the fact I was actually out of bed. In her hand was a large cup of coffee, and if the circumstances were any different, I would've smiled at the sight. She can't even stand the smell, so I knew she had to be really concerned about me to make it anyways.

"Hey." She says as she takes a step into the room, looking to find me rummaging through my clothes and failing to actually choose something to change into. I watch absently as she sets the mug down on my bedside table, my eyes catching on my alarm clock beside it showing : p.m. I hadn't even realized how late it was.

"Thank you." I nod appreciatively, but I hope Jade knows that I'm thanking her for so much more than the coffee.

She has been more of a friend to me than I could ever ask for, and I was going to miss her so damn much when I leave.

The truth of the fact is that Rowan was right about one thing. I wasn't safe here anymore. I wasn't going to live off of them in one of their safe houses, and staying here in a house surrounded by guards / isn't realistic either.

The only way out was taking that part of my father within me and hiding until not even Carter's tracking could find me.

I didn't know what to do, but I wasn't ready to see them yet just as I was nowhere near ready to say goodbye. And yet, I still feared that was the only option I would soon have left. A weird sense of deja vu filled me as my hand grasped onto the steel handle of The Horizon Cafe, opening the doors for what could very well possibly be the last time.

The familiar fresh smell of baked goods welcomed me with my first step in, but even that just didn't feel the same this time around. Rowan was gone when I left Jade's to come here, and I was still deciding whether or not it was a relief or yet another thing to stress me out.

I'm still waiting for that moment when everything falls apart from beneath me, and I wondered if the way Jolene's eyes met mine would be that tipping point. With my walls up, I watched as the older woman tensed, her gaze assessing before tension lined the soft wrinkles across her forehead.

Whispering a hurried sentence to the employee I've come to know as Pablo, he nodded once before taking over what Jolene had just been doing. I couldn't tell if her reaction was because I visibly looked like hell or because she'd been expecting me, but I suspected I was about to find out.

"Who do I need to pay a visit to for this?" Was the first thing she said once she'd rounded the counter, not paying any mind to the fact we were surrounded by customers—a few of which definitely heard the threat in her tone. It was so normal I felt, if only for a second, I could breathe again without the weight of everything else around me. When all I was able to do was shake my head and pray Jolene would understand, she gently yet firmly gripped onto my forearm until she was leading us away to the back.

There it would be quiet, and like everything else, I found myself wondering if it was a blessing or a curse. Nothing was spoken when Jolene opened the door to the same storage room I'd helped her organize mere weeks ago, but I suddenly hated the silence that came with it.

"Are you hurt?" She asks after a small stretch of time, her eyes flicking over my face down to the clothes Jade had to pick out for me since I couldn't do it myself. She's been everything I've needed and more, but we both knew why I needed to leave. Jolene was my last goodbye before them, and it was taking everything in me to formulate an audible response.

"Not physically." I managed, but when she pulled me into her arms and hugged me, I wasn't strong enough to stay up. Gently, Jolene guided the both of us to the floor, pushing away a box so we could rest our backs against the wall. I cried as she brushed my hair back behind my ears before simply holding me and letting me fall apart.

She had to have known who caused my pain, because there was no chance in hell Dominic, Rowan, and Carter wouldn't be by my side right now if I was sad from anything else. I hated the truth of that, but there was no denying it no matter how painful it was.

"It's just... I don't know w-what to do." I sobbed, Jolene's comfort becoming a life line I wish I never needed. As she held me, I had a feeling she knew why I was crying, but I didn't have the energy to push her away right now. I took that comfort and held it close to me, accepting that things could never be the same now that so much had gone wrong. I was leaving, so I took this moment to try and give myself the closure that felt impossible to gain, but still, I tried.

"You already knew?" I sniffled, not wanting to hear the answer I was already expecting to come. Marcus or not, Jolene has been like a mother to me since I moved to New York.

The problem is that none of them held secrets out of ill intent, which is why for now, even though I knew it was all a lie, I let myself pretend I was okay.

"I figured it out when Carter came in for coffee the other day." Jolene admits, but she was unapologetic in her words.

"To say I was surprised is an understatement, but you can't let this beat you down, my dear. Not yet." I didn't stop her as she turned my head to look at her, her touch loving even though her hand shook just slightly

. "You're allowed to be in pain, and I hope you give those boys hell, but they are the safest place you can be right now. Believe me when I say a lot of shit is changing today, and if there was any time to make an attempt on you, it would be now."

My eyes dipped down as I wiped some of my tears from my face, exhausted and so incredibly drained.

Someone had followed me here to the cafe, and I have a strong feeling Rowan will be waiting outside for me when I leave.

I forgave them within days of learning they were in the Mafia, but this is so much different in ways I haven't even processed. They lied to me again, just as my father did for most of my childhood.

I'm so sick of everyone around me thinking I can't handle things. Most of my reaction now is based on the fact of so many secrets being kept at once, but if they had just told me, a lot of this could have been prevented. Or at the very least minimized.

"The time to shut down is not yet, no matter how hard it may be." Jolene shakes her head, but I can tell she's just as hurt by this. Dominic, after all, is her nephew. I think she understood where so much of this betrayal was coming from because of that, but that didn't make it any easier in the end.

"I know." I whisper, knowing she's right, no matter how unfortunate that may be. Vincent is after me right now, and he is not a man to be trifled with. I may have caught him off guard that one day, but I make no mistake it was because I was a woman and he's a moron. He will not underestimate me again.

"It's just, I'm terrified that if I see them again, I'll forgive them for everything." I say, taking a deep breath and forcing myself to continue.

"I'm not staying away to punish them, but how do we move on after so many lies? How can Carter even love me when my father..." I couldn't finish my sentence but Jolene understood. She gave my knee a squeeze with a sad look that speaks of a kind of wisdom that can only come from age and experience.

"How can you love Carter when he has a father as vile as Vincent?" She counters, causing my heart to stop. I know I shouldn't feel this way, but admittedly, I've felt a little guilty too about all of this. Before I knew my father was Marcus, I'd hoped with every part of me the men I loved would get their revenge, even if it meant killing the person who has caused them so much grief. I love Carter despite his blood, but I can't imagine it would be easy for him to reconcile with who mine is.

"Relationships are complicated, my dear, but blood will never equal the child. I don't doubt for a second that those boys don't love you with everything they have, even if they were idiots in keeping things from you." The problem is that I already knew all of this. It was because I still loved them it was killing me to stay away. Things just weren't as simple as forgiveness anymore, though. Rowan,

Dominic, and Carter were supposed to be ambushing my father's event right about now, and the consequences of resisting will be life changing. Jolene will forever be the mother I never had, and despite how I'm feeling at this point, she was right. I couldn't run blindly—not that I planned to—but there are probably eyes everywhere I go now. Sometimes, no matter how hard I try to escape the harsh truths that reality brings forth, the only real option is to face it and learn how to adapt.

"I—"

"Hazel!" The sound of my name interrupted what I'd been about to say, though it wasn't that but rather the voice that said it that had me stiffening. Carter's tone was one of panic, and it was the only reason I didn't try to act as though I hadn't heard him.

"They're here." Jolene says, but there's something about the way she now holds herself that makes me suspect she wasn't talking about the man who calls my name again. She was stiff, and Jolene always had a usual flow to herself that was graceful yet firm when needed. This right now was tense, and it was the threat of something else that caused her to stand with me and open the door with caution.

"Jo, have you seen—" Carter starts but his words stop when he sees me, just the sight of him becoming a punch to my gut. Truthfully, he looked like hell too, but unlike me he had a cut that was long and fresh across his forehead, dirt smeared across his left cheek.

"Sweetheart, I know you're mad, but I need you to come with me." Carter says, desperation clear in his tone. Something was wrong, yet I could still hear the customers happily eating at their tables.

"What's wrong?" I ask, not resisting when he grabs onto my hand before whispering into Jolene's ear. He told her they would talk later but that she shouldn't leave the cafe tonight. I admired the way she didn't show any fear or panic, but I still didn't miss the frown she gave at Carter's rough appearance. Looking out the window where I could see cars moving normally down the street, I furrowed my eyebrows as I tried to find something that was wrong but couldn't.

"Carter, what's happening?" I ask again, a little louder to pull his attention to my words. There was something sad about the way he looked at me in response, however it was what he said next that had my stomach clenching with nervousness. "You were followed here and it wasn't by one of us." That was the only explanation I got before Jolene slipped around the both of us, whispering something she assured only I could hear on the way past. Carter was already too busy moving to notice, but there wasn't a single word I'd missed. "Remember who the real villains are." Plural, not singular. I barely even got the time to comprehend that warning before I was being pulled forward, Carter's body discreetly yet very distinctly shielding my body with his.

Something had happened outside, and I wasn't even able to turn and see Jolene one last time before my hair was being whisked backwards from the wind. There was an unsettling kind of chill to it, however, that wasn't there when I first walked through these same doors. It caused the hairs on the back of my neck to rise, but when my eyes connected with Dominic sitting in the passenger seat of a pickup truck, my heart dropped at the sight of his white shirt torn and soaked with splatters of red.

I didn't fight them when they drove me to their house, and I haven't said a single word since I discovered the fresh blood hadn't been Dominic's. The drive back was awkward but after learning there had been a man working for Vincent waiting for me in my car, I didn't have much desire to talk.

In combination with the stress of everything else, all I wished to do was sleep in hopes my dreams could let me escape if even for a few minutes. We were all completely and utterly exhausted, but I was too tired to care about the sideways glances I got from Rowan or to ask about how the cut got across Carter's forehead.

There had been so much unresolved tension in their car it'd felt like a blessing the second I stepped out into the parking garage, walking myself to the elevator knowing the other three were following behind. It was Dominic who placed his hand on the scanner to gain access, soon controlling our ascent to the first floor where the doors opened with a ding a few seconds later.

Like the car, I was the first one out.

My steps were hurried because I could feel the fissures of my heart expanding with each sharp breath, but when a hand wrapped around my arm, everything around me exploded.

"Hazel," Rowan pleaded softly as he tugged me back, and the second I spun around to meet his chest, I wrapped my arms around him no matter how hard I wanted to push him away.

The problem with love is that it can never be black and white, but that's what makes it all consuming in the ways no person can come back from.

I hadn't lied when I said they were my everything, and as I felt Rowan's hands pull me close by my back, I realized that my pain wasn't weakness.

There was a certain kind of strength in vulnerability, and I let them see me for what I was. A little bit broken. A little bit scared. Forever theirs just as they would be forever mine. This wasn't me forgiving them for their lies but merely accepting things for what they were. As I finally let myself fall apart in the place I felt safest, I gave into Rowan's touch knowing we didn't need to figure out any solutions right now.

While nothing about this was simple, I found comfort in the fact we were all here, somewhat okay but most importantly alive.

"I'm so sorry, Hazel." Rowan cried, holding me as close as our bodies would physically let us.

"I'm so fucking sorry." I could hear the pain in his words, and as hard as it was to understand this moment couldn't last forever, we were pretending as though it would.

With Dominic and Carter at our sides, I felt okay again, even if it was temporary.

"I know." I whispered against his chest, my words slightly muffled by the material of his shirt. It didn't matter because I knew he heard me.

Yesterday, Rowan had told me the ending of his book was good but not happy.

Right now, that felt a lot like our story. For better or for worse, these three men have taken the person I was and helped me to become a person I didn't believe I had in me. Before them, I wanted a love story like the ones I saw in movies and read in books, but what they don't often tell you is that even those scripts are flawed.

It was them who taught me it was the mistakes that meant it was real.

I may still be furious with them, but we could worry about everything else later.

Right now, I just wanted to let ourselves be together, even if it turns out our happily ever after isn't as in reach as we'd hoped it would be.

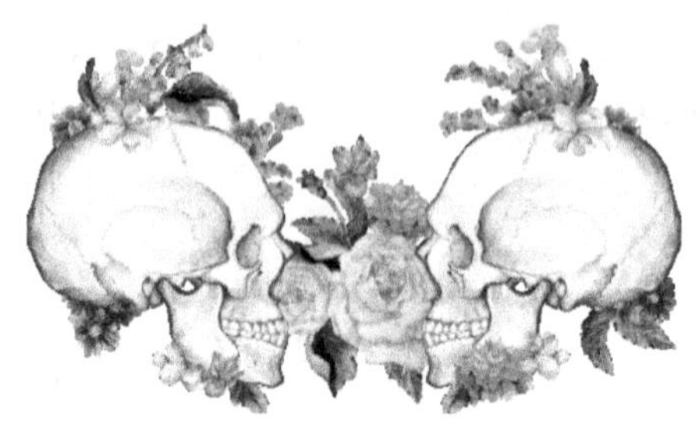

~ Twenty-Nine ~

Dominic

Looking out at the night sky of New York, I couldn't believe how much of it was the same.

The lights of the buildings were still aglow and the dark still brought a peaceful kind of quiet, but it felt like so much had changed for this one thing to remain so constant.

I was supposed to be asleep right now, but I simply couldn't, my mind too restless to allow me even a minute. Hazel was back, but not really.

She was distant and so sad.

Watching her break apart in Rowan's arms earlier made me jealous for the first time in our relationship, because I've never wanted to hold her so badly.

She was in pain, and it was our fault.

Being overwhelmed in every way possible, I was on my own until the sound of soft footsteps made me suspect I wasn't the only one restlessly thinking about the things to come next.

Turning away from the railing of the first floor balcony, I found Hazel standing quietly at the patio doors, waiting for permission to join me.

She would never have to ask, though.

My answer would never change.

My nod was combined with a tired sigh, but I didn't wait to see if she would act on the action.

I already knew she had when I felt the heat of her body move to my side, copying my position and resting her forearms against the glass fencing.

For what felt like forever, we were both quiet, staring out at the landscape yet fully attuned to the other's presence. It was she who spoke first, because Hazel was well aware my silence was me giving her the control as to where she wanted to take this. If only either of us knew.

"I feel so small seeing the city like this." She says after some time, brushing back a piece of her hair behind her ear. Not turning my head purposely so I didn't have to see what she was thinking, I simply listened to the sound of each of her breaths. We were so close right now her arm was flush against mine and that on its own had my heart racing in response.

"In a good or bad way?" I asked, my voice rough as I spoke. It sounded as though my throat was raw from screaming, probably because it was. When I could see her shift in movement at the question, it caused me to brave looking over at her. When I did, I found Hazel's eyes already on me. My heart clenched in a way that was proof of how much I was hurting, but I still chose to keep that bit of distance between us. I didn't have the right to feel bad when I could've stopped it.

"I haven't decided yet." She admits, looking down at where our hands were nearly touching. The desire to go to her was strong, but I just don't think her mind was as ready as her heart was.

I didn't want to push her or make a move to get closer, but at least she wasn't completely pushing me away. That had to mean something, didn't it?

"And what about everything else?" I whisper next, willing every ounce of control within me to go at her pace, even though I could see how much it was slowly killing her too. Hazel had no idea how much I wished I could lie and tell her everything would be okay between us, but the truth is that I wasn't sure if that was a promise I could keep. If she could, I know Hazel would tell me that she wasn't bothered by the fact her father killed Carter's mom—that she could fully trust us again to not keep secrets from her after promising for a second time we wouldn't. But that's just not the way it was, and that was the issue.

"I don't know." She shrugs her shoulders helplessly, however it was the response I'd expected all the same.

We made sure her father was safe—the price of that is yet to be determined—but even that wouldn't be enough to fix the things that were already so damaged.

Even though it's clear Hazel wants to forgive us, she doesn't know how to because we betrayed her in a way that isn't as easy as simply moving on.

She just learned she has a brother and a whole other family she doesn't understand, and while she's mad at us, I know half of her feelings are directed towards her father too.

Taking in the tiredness of her eyes and the slight trembles of her posture, I could tell this was eating away at her for more reasons than the obvious fact we kept secrets that weren't ours to keep.

"I know that I need time." Hazel says after a small stretch of silence, but I don't miss the way she turns so she's facing me more openly.

I would give her as long as she needed, even though we don't have any left to spare.

It didn't matter.

I would give her anything she wanted if it meant soothing the pain I caused her. Hazel surprised me when she slid her hand across the railing and slowly intertwined her fingers with mine, but I made no move other than to accept, too afraid to scare off what was happening.

"I know that I'm hurt and angry and sad..." She continued, "But I also know the reason this hurts the way it does is because I still want you three above everything else." My heart stopped when her eyes finally looked back up at me, feeling as though the world itself had stopped within a single moment.

Neither of us looked like ourselves right now, but we were still us, just a little more complicated.

I completely stilled as Hazel took a single step towards me, tears beading in her eyes but not falling down the rosy pink of her cheeks. She planted a hand right on my chest where my pulse thrummed nervously, and then she tilted her head up so I could really see her.

I could see the light freckles across her nose only visible at this proximity, and the curve of her jaw I've spent hours studying in past times when we've cuddled.

I look at the slight tint of brown you can see around her pupils before it fades into a bright green, before looking down to her mouth where the dip of her cupid's bow reminded me of all of the times I'd spent kissing her there.

Hazel was a canvas of memories I would never be able to forget, and if the time comes one day where she decides she doesn't want us anymore, I know that won't change a thing for me. I will never be able to love anybody that isn't her again. "Dominic." My name rolls off of her tongue in a current that has the power to bring me to my knees, and when I raise my hand to cup her cheek in the way I've been wanting to, she utters the words that tear me apart.

"I still love you." I watch as her eye tracks the tear that falls down my face before pulling my head down to hers, resting her forehead against mine as her sad exhale passes across my cheeks. Like I said, this wasn't forgiveness, but it was an understanding, one in which that left me both whole and destroyed all over again.

"I love you too, princess." I whisper against her lips, despite how strained and heartbreakingly mournful those words were. "There will never be a world where I don't." There was a pause.

A beat.

A second.

And then Hazel rose on her tiptoes that remaining centimeter before her lips brushed against mine, the feather light touch intangible yet so incredibly strong. She stayed like that for just a moment, and it was then I realized what this was.

One more kiss— one last kiss, that was going to destroy me the second she pulled away.

Another tear fell from my eyes as I let Hazel hold me, but when her's began to mix with mine, I moved, grabbing her by the waist and pulling her into me until she was clinging onto my shirt as though it were a lifeline.

With our eyes shut in sadness, we seared our time's end in the same place our story began—the place where she kissed me for the first time and took my heart as her own.

When the inevitable came and we eventually pulled apart, our foreheads rested together as they had so many times before. Only it was not the uncontained, intimate act it had once been.

This time, it felt like goodbye.

"Please, Hazel." I begged her one last time, but in the end, it only brought us both more pain to hear it.

With her hands still clutching tight to my shirt, I cried as she gently removed them, her bottom lip trembling from the unforgiving weight of our end. Her voice cracking, I closed my eyes as she whispered what I knew was a decision.

The last decision.

"I can't." And despite the fact we were still standing together side by side, we both broke apart in each other's absence.

Hazel didn't come to bed when she all but pleaded to be left alone on the balcony afterwards.

I could still taste the faint hint of cherry against my lips from the very kiss that in fact drove me to my knees, but it just wasn't the same knowing it would be the last time I'd experience it.

Since then I've been lying awake for hours in my room, debating between whether I should give her the space she asked for or try to promise yet again we could find a way to fix this.

That we weren't over.

Thoughts of if she was still on the balcony flooded my mind, wondering if she was cold or if she needed something. We'd set her up in one of the guest rooms at her request, but what if, what if, what if. I didn't need to look in a mirror to know that my eyes were red and puffy, lined with dark circles from my lack of sleep.

I missed her already, and every time I think I can handle the thought of her leaving once the dust settles, my body proves myself wrong. Please don't let this be the end.

Please let this be some fucked up nightmare I can fix by simply opening my eyes.

Only when I did, everything still hurt. Giving up on any hopes of finding sleep tonight, I pushed myself up onto my forearms, my denial being my only aid in succeeding in even that.

I was going to go see Hazel, because I couldn't live with the idea of her feeling alone, even when it was my fault—

"Dominic!" I heard Rowan's voice yell in panic a second before the sound of something large smashing traveled to my ears, my hand grabbing the gun in my bedside drawer as instinct took over.

The first person I thought of was Hazel, and I could only pray she'd gone back to the third floor where her bed was for the night. Whatever was happening was from the level below me, and I needed her safe.

There's no way someone could have gotten into the house, but if it were Vincent, I don't even think our own wards could keep him out.

"Fuck!" I heard Carter curse this time, but when I ran down the hall and over to the stairs, all I saw was something in my friend's hand before the glint of metal caught my eye. One of the wooden bar stools was broken into splinters on the ground, however the second it was obvious there were no real threats in the house, there was only one other reason Rowan would be looking like he was dying.

In Carter's hand lay a metal ring, the one he'd gifted to Hazel as both a tracker, and an engraved symbol of our power that almost guaranteed her safety from everyone but those foolish enough to cross us. The only question now was where was she?

"Carter." I try to coax as I tuck my gun away within my clothing, moving down the stairs as I then notice the slightly crumpled piece of paper in Rowan's hand.

Denial clawed away at my mind at what I suspected it to be, but I needed to calm the third of us down before he fell into one of his episodes that took weeks to bring him out of.

"He took her." Carter growled as he paced, his hands pulling at his hair so hard I feared he might pull it out.

"He had to have. She's smarter than to leave like this. She wouldn't have taken this off." His thoughts came out as one jumbled stream of words, but all I could think about was the way my throat was tightening and my hands were shaking as I got to Rowan's side. He didn't even look at me, grimly handing over the sheet of paper that had Hazel's handwriting on it. I didn't understand. While we had her car brought to our driveway from Jolene's, there was no way she could even step foot off of the premises without us being alerted. Rowan balled his fists as he silently looked at the ring clasped between Carter's fingertips, leaving me with no other choice but to read what I already feared.

To Dominic, Rowan, and Carter... I really don't know where to begin this, but I suppose apologizing is a good start. I know you wouldn't let me go on my own, and that's why I had to leave, no matter how much I appreciate the space you were all willing to give me. I promise where I'm going will keep me safe, but there's too much happening right now for me to stay here.

Clutching the paper between my hands, I looked up to make sure what I was reading was real.

That Hazel had left us and didn't seem like she was coming back.

Rowan was quiet in the way he showed his fear, but Carter looked like he was about to tear the world apart to get her back.

I had a feeling that's what would happen as I looked back down to the letter, continuing where I left off.

The truth is that I have secrets of my own, namely the fact I saw my father a month ago when he snuck up on me in my car. He spoke of a man, one who had been hunting him since before I was born.

Now I know that was Vincent. That wasn't all, however. He also told me to stay with you three, because he knew love when he saw it and trusted that you'd be able to keep me safe when he couldn't. But this couldn't be true. Marcus has been trying to break us down from the inside for decades, and yet he speaks of loyalty.

He's had every opportunity to take Hazel and marry her off to Lev Ivankov to fulfill his bargain, but he left her with us instead.

I didn't understand.

Why would the enemy leave his daughter with the man whose mother he killed? It was then I realized something I didn't know if Carter had figured out through all of his frantic pacing, but I did, and it changed this entire game. He asked me not to say anything, but what much does it matter now with everything so messed up? Hazel's letter says, but if she were here I would tell her it matters. That everything that has to do with her does. Something came up tonight, and I knew I had to go, and not just temporarily.

Maybe in another life what we had could've been forever, but we live in a fucked up, unfair world. There are some things I need to work out on my own, but I hope you know I will never forget you three. You were the only things I'd ever truly chosen for myself, and I think a part of me—no matter how far I go—will always belong to you. Maybe one day we'll meet again, but for now, this has to be goodbye.

"Sincerely Hazel." I whispered the last two words, urging myself not to tear the paper in two out of sheer and utter pain. I was angry, and hurt, and sad, but above all else, I was fucking terrified. Fear is an emotion we have beaten out of ourselves from day one in the mafia, but I'm pretty sure I was having a panic attack right now because I quite literally couldn't breathe. My instincts told me to fight it—to leave now and track Hazel down before it was too late, but it had been hours since I last saw her on the balcony.

She could be anywhere right now, hurt or even... no. Her being dead would never be an option. I didn't realize I was shaking until Rowan clasped a hand on my shoulder to steady me, but still, he refused to look in even my direction. Was I the 'something that came up'? Was our kiss the reason Hazel's in more danger than she could ever understand? The thought tore me apart, and I was surprised I hadn't thrown up yet based on the nausea hitting me like a train. "What could have come up?" Carter spits, pulling at his hair again as tears welled in his eyes.

"She promised us she'd stay in her room as long as we gave her space. She—"

"Carter." Rowan tries to carefully get his attention, sensing the spiral he was going down. He's been different since Hazel, but I think we all forgot for a while what this other side of him was like. It started with the denial, the pain, the panic, and then the rage, and I could tell he was teetering on the edge of the first three. If he gets to the fourth... fuck, he needs to not get there. I was caught between calming him, and resisting the impending levels of dizziness taking over, but there was only one thing that mattered here and it had nothing to do with any of us. It hasn't been since Hazel walked into our lives, and we risk everything if we cave to the fear eating away at our hearts.

"Saverio, fermati." I say in Italian, using the name his mother used to call him before she died—a name he hasn't heard in years thanks to his father. In English, I said, Carter, stop, but I knew he wouldn't listen to me otherwise. His dark eyes connected with mine almost instantly, pure anger swirling within the black irises now focused on me. It was hard because I could see the tears he refused to spill, but we had too much to lose risking all of our energy on our emotions.

I had his attention now, and that was good enough.

"Rowan, we could still find her if she's with her phone. Look at any texts, calls, or transactions she might have made with it. I'm going to talk to security to figure out why we weren't notified of her absence." It was usually Carter who called the shots, but I wasn't letting that happen this time. Not when in this state his only idea would be killing people until we found what we needed. We all paused for a short second, two sets of eyes staring at me in understanding. We knew that this wasn't something we could risk fucking up.

This was it, and we only had one shot at making things right. The second Rowan moved, I did, putting Hazel's letter on the kitchen counter before gauging all of my options. Carter didn't give me the chance to do that, though, before I was suddenly being pinned down by his hand at the back of my neck.

"What did you say to her, Dominic?" He asks the second we're alone, my face pressed against the cold marble countertop with his grip unwavering. I could already tell Carter was feeling backed into a corner just by the way he shook, but this wasn't the first time we've fought and it sure as hell won't be the last either.

"We have more important things to worry about right now." I argue, trying to hook my leg behind his to catch him off guard but he was terrifyingly focused in his hold. Feeling his mouth come down to my ear, he gives me the opportunity I was looking for. Using my hand instead, I hooked my elbow around his head to off his balance, pushing away and getting out of his reach in mere seconds. "

You don't think the fact you were the last one to see her holds any impact on where she might've gone?" Carter growls, coming back to his full height and rounding on me.

"Rowan would've said something, but I can practically see the guilt in your eyes." I couldn't argue with that, but every second we fought was a second we could be using to find Hazel.

"You want a lead? Call Jade. Hazel can't make it far without any of her belongings." I say, trying to distract him even though I'm sure Rowan's already on it. We were walking a very fine line here, and it was only a matter of time before one of us teetered over the edge. The other reason that I didn't want to talk about this is because an even greater part of me feared Carter was right. That I was the push that drove Hazel away from us for good. "If I find out this happened because of something you said, Dominic, I swear to god—"

"What, Carter? What exactly are you going to do?" I shout.

"In case you've forgotten, none of this would've happened if you weren't so insistent on all of us keeping secrets!" Only a second passes before I know my words got to him, and it was in a way I already found myself regretting. I watch as Carter throws the ring he'd just been clutching onto so tightly somewhere into the living room where neither of us could see the metal anymore.

The motion caused a tear to fall from his eye, but I don't think he even noticed it happened when he shoved me with a force he's never used on me before. I didn't see it coming until my body was thrown to the ground, because I had finally pushed him too far with the blame all three of us bore with great remorse.

My head slammed against the back of the couch before all I could see was Carter storming out of the house, tense and in so much pain. He was gone before I could even utter a word, and I feared like Hazel, this time he would not come back.

~ Thirty ~

Carter

She left us. Hazel was gone and her note made it sound like she wasn't coming back.

Because of that, I wasn't either, at least not the same man I was when I was with her. I wanted to believe Vincent was responsible for this—that there was no way she would take off my ring—but she did.

No, my father didn't force her to leave, because he was currently waiting for me at the Base, and only he knew how to get into our house undetected.

The timing was too short to have gotten back here undetected, and Marcus had bigger plans than grabbing his daughter right now.

It was true Dominic, Rowan, and I kept him out of harm's way, but when I got to the Base with every intention of letting out my anger, I was shocked to find Heidi Walsh—Hazel's mother—tied to a chair in the basement with her mouth gagged shut.

Already waiting for me, Vincent gave a smug smile that even after all of these years still made my skin tingle in discontent, motioning for me to join him in front of the two way glass. I'd come here to fight in the rings below to let off some steam, but instead I learned that the assignment yesterday still went through as planned with replacements for the three of us already ready to go.

But like Hazel warned, Marcus had seen them coming.

Vincent and his men caught Ivy Monet, Marcus Walsh' decoy who was now dead, and none other than an incredibly terrified and tired Heidi.

"What is she doing here?" I ask, hating that I was distracted enough to get myself into this situation. I can barely think right now, and just the sight of my father's face makes me see red. Crossing my arms as I take in the bloodied disaster of a woman in front of me, I can't even feel pity for her knowing how much she's hurt her daughter. I didn't like the fact Vincent had her, though.

"I'll admit, Ivy was quite smarter than we'd expected. She escaped before we could get her down here, but it wasn't for nothing. We found this whore about a block away, drunk and talking about how she needed to speak with a man named Tobias Walsh—that he could save her relationship with their daughter." My blood ran ice cold as I continued to stare right ahead, refusing to react at the mention of Hazel. I swear to god, if Vincent had anything to do with her disappearance I would kill him with my own bare hands.

I know Rowan and Dominic are out there looking for her right now, but I knew I would be no help to them in the state I was in right now. If there was any chance of me getting Hazel back, there were things I had to do first that couldn't wait. Humoring Vincent for just a little longer was one of them.

"And what use is she to you?" I question coldly, focusing on the way Heidi's arms trembled so hard you could hear them against her restraints.

While I didn't feel pity, she would be of no benefit whatsoever to whatever plan my father was already stirring up. That I knew for sure.

"Alive, she's useless, but I know I've taught you better than to assume that's what we need her for." Vincent smiles, sharply turning to his left before placing his hand on the door handle into the room.

He wanted to use her as a message, but for what, I still didn't know.

Narrowing my eyes as the bulletproof door is pulled open, I don't even wince at the instant sounds of Heidi's high pitched shrieks, used to much worse occurrences than that. In fact, in this moment I almost felt numb to this entire situation.

"I see Hazel gets those pretty lips of hers from her mother—" Vincent starts, but he should've known better than to even speak her name.

The rage I still carried from when he called her a pet surged through me, my feet moving on their own accord. I stepped inside, and for the first time in my life, I swung at my father fulled by nothing other than sheer anger.

It was a mistake.

With nothing but disappointment, Vincent had a gun poised at my head before a second could even pass, chuckling as the metal door closed behind me. Heidi's sobs were muffled by her gag, but I was intensely aware of every aspect of my surroundings the minute I knew he could've killed me if he wanted to. I let down my guard and caved to my emotions, an action that will cost me my life if I'm not careful.

Staying still and waiting to see what will come next, I don't bother to try and hide my disgust as Vincent's lips curl into a smile that makes me sick.

There's no point in faking things with him anymore, so I dropped any act that remained and instead lowered my eyes to him.

I wished I were Dominic right now to tell what he was thinking, but when Vincent tutted under his breath at me, I can honestly say I didn't expect it when he stepped away.

The gun lowered from my head but not before grinding the metal into my skin, right along the scar that cut down my eyebrow.

My body stiffened at the clearly intended action, but I refused to show any kind of response that would fuel whatever game he was playing right now.

When Vincent saw I wasn't going to try and attack again, he fully removed his contact from me, spinning towards Heidi instead.

"You broke our agreement, son." He speaks quietly, even with his eyes on the woman in the chair. I didn't move as Vincent trailed the gun down Heidi's face instead, lingering the barrel against her lips where spit soaked her chin.

Her eyes moved to me where she silently pleaded for my help, but all I could think about was the way I had to hold Hazel on the dirty floor of her childhood home after what her mother did to her.

Maybe a few days ago I would've been inclined to help Heidi, but I could already feel myself slipping back into my old self. Why should I care when the only thing I've ever wanted is gone because of me?

"You should be thanking me for not killing that associate you call your friend by now, because you broke our deal. You do remember what that means, don't you?" Vincent taunts, suddenly bringing the gun down on Heidi's cheek until her ear-curdling scream filled the room.

I didn't react at the way blood began to trickle down her face from the new gash, but I also didn't expect to feel... regret? This was merciful compared to what Vincent's capable of—compared to what I myself have doled out, so why did I all of a sudden feel the need to stop him?

Our agreement stated that if I broke the two debts I owed, Vincent would be allowed to kill either Rowan or Hazel in repayment, but Costa Rica was our plan against that. It never happened, and now Hazel is gone. I should've forced her onto a plane if that's what it took to get her out of here, because my voice was now turning into a deadly sort of calm, the cruel hands of horror gripping onto my very soul.

"Where is she?"

"I don't know what you're talking about." Vincent smiles, his arrogance dripping off of him in a way that left me unfeeling. Or maybe I was simply feeling too much.

I knew from the first night I met Hazel—from the night I took care of her in that hotel room two months ago—that I would be anything she needed to make sure she was okay. I may not have realized it then in the way I do now, but I have always been hers. She managed to unravel the walls I had no choice but to create growing up, and I would not let anything stand in the way between myself and her safety.

"I'm sick of the games, Vincent." I practically spat out his name, showing him my nonexistent respect for everything he was. "If you don't tell me where my—"

"Where what, son?" He interrupts me with pride, throwing his gun to the floor before wrapping his fingers around Heidi's throat in warning.

"Where your girlfriend is? Where Lev's pretty new fuck toy is?" The clearly hungover woman's face quickly turned a dangerous shade of red as her body tried to buck away from her restraints, desperately trying to get away from Vincent's grasp. It was no use, though, unless I tried to stop it.

My father expected me to lash out at his words—depended on it, but I refused to let him control me anymore. But if I do nothing, Heidi will die, and I haven't decided if I want that yet or not.

"She's gone, Carter." Vincent laughs, and I can't stop myself from shifting this time.

"You really should tell your pet's brunette friend to keep her phone better protected, because it was almost too easy to lure Hazel away from you with a mere handful of texts." Heidi's face was an ugly shade of purple now, and I could tell she had no more than half a minute left before it would be too late.

"Quite frankly, I think I did you a Favour, son. Family reunions always have been my favorite type of gatherings." I was silent for a moment as I simply stared at him, terrified at what he was implying. If he were telling the truth, that would mean... fuck, that would mean Marcus has her instead.

"You're lying." I tried to call his bluff, but all it took was looking at his face to know he was dead serious. He sold Hazel out to his greatest enemy to punish me for falling for her.

It couldn't be true. She couldn't really be gone.

Vincent didn't say anything as he waited to see what I would do, that god awful smirk still plastered against his face. In his eyes, I will always be the pathetic man who wouldn't fit the mold of his perfect soldier, but the truth is I can't bring myself to care anymore.

I raise my head as my father pulls his hand away from Heidi's neck in annoyance, her weak yet frantic coughs instantly filling the room.

She didn't know it, but it was only fueling the uncontained fire inside of me.

The woman was alive, but barely, and as demented as it may make me, I felt a little satisfied knowing she got to experience that fraction of what she let her daughter go through.

Honestly, I think my newfound calmness on the exterior is because of how much I was hurting about the possibility that Hazel may truly be gone, and when Vincent brought his horrible eyes on me again, I let myself plummet over the edge of no return. Pulling my gun from my pocket, Vincent's still on the floor from his outburst, I aimed it straight at his head and kept my arm steady like he trained me to.

He didn't let a single one of his emotions slip past his calculated demeanor, but the eyes staring back at me were not my own. The dark shade of mine came from my mother, his a dulled blue that had me tensed even after all of these years.

"I wondered when you'd finally gather the courage to try and do this." Vincent says in the manipulative way I was more than acquainted with, not moving an inch even as he takes a step towards me.

"You and I both know you won't do it, though I'll admit, I'm quite interested to see where this will go." It was my turn to smile this time, and if Vincent were a smarter man, he'd know there was no part about my intentions I was lying about. Feeling as though I was holding my breath, I let out a soft exhale—the last one before everything would change. Becoming the Mafia will never be something I'll want, but I desire Vincent's death more. I didn't have Hazel to consider any longer, and when I tear the world apart to get her back, I'll make sure she can be happy again. That's all that will ever matter to me. Taking these seconds to process what I was about to do, I switched my index onto the trigger of my gun, ignoring Heidi's cries in the background. I was done. It was only now Vincent seemed to realize this.

"Every story needs a villain, Carter." The man who was my father only by blood spoke, chills running down my spine even now. I knew, however, that this was simply another one of his games—his tactics. I would no longer allow myself to be an expandable piece on his board, so I took everything that made me weak and hid it deep within myself, allowing the man I used to be to come back out to play.

"Maybe," I shrug.

"But I'd rather it be me than you." Hazel told me to only do this if I wanted it for myself, but the truth is that this is for us. For the first time since I've known my father, I watched him shift in caution before his eyes glanced at where his gun was on the floor. There was no way for him to grab it in time, though.

This may not be funny, but I laughed humorlessly at the situation we were in, because after all these years of him hurting and training and forcing me into a life I never wanted, the only way to escape was to sign my freedom over in another way. Vincent's arrogance was the fatal mistake he couldn't fix, but this was not me winning anything.

"Just you wait, Carter. One day, you're going to—" I pulled the trigger. He would get no last words, because there was no kindness in the bullet that became embedded within his skull. I saw only a single flash of fear in the eyes of the man that left me so fucked up, but I held his gaze as he fell backwards to the ground, watching as the life drained from his face. Vincent MacGuire died within seconds by my hand, and it wasn't enough.

The sound of the gunshot rang through my ears, but it was quiet. Heidi screamed and started shaking her head, terrified that I had just killed my own blood and didn't shed a tear while doing it. He will never see the light of day again, so why didn't I feel satisfied? Why wasn't it enough? I knew from the time I was sixteen this day would be inevitable—that I would eventually seal my fate with a single action, and yet all I felt was more anger. I couldn't think about what I'd just done or what Vincent had claimed during his final conversation. It was over, but the only thing I felt was even more trapped than when I was still in the chains of his manipulation. Fuck!

"Please." Heidi's brittle voice shakes from where she sits, and it only causes me to slowly shut my eyes, forcing myself to take a slow breath. "I just wanted t-to fix things with h-her." She begs, unknowingly saying everything she shouldn't be.

"Hazel needs—" "You don't have the right to decide what she needs!" I shout, cutting her off abruptly as a sensation similar to drowning consumes my lungs. Heidi flinches at my hard tone, but I don't care. Not after the way she hurt my always. "You don't have the right to keep secrets or determine what's good for her... and you most certainly can't give her what she needs." I shake, walking towards the bound woman and taking my gun with me.

"You don't deserve her!" She wouldn't meet my eyes as her body tried to curl in on itself, but she didn't get to act like everything would be okay.

Hazel gave her everything, and her mom chose herself instead. She wasn't allowed to feel sad when she could've stopped everything. "You didn't love her in the way she needed, and now it's your fault she's gone." I felt a splash of water hit my hand, opposite to the one raising the gun unflinchingly, but I didn't look to see where it came from. The only thing I could think about was the dead man on the ground and the woman who broke Hazel growing up. She didn't deserve to live. Not after all she's done.

"Please—please don't do this!" Heidi cries, red streaks of her own blood staining her pale skin from where Vincent hit her, but her begging was useless. Just as I now was, chained to a future I could never escape.

"You hurt her." I state, bringing the gun up and letting the barrel rest against her clammy forehead.

"You wasted the chances given to you. There's nobody to blame for this but yourself." Stilling as Heidi tilted her head up, meeting my gaze, I felt my chest become constricted at the resemblance I saw between her and her daughter. A vision painfully similar to Hazel looked at me with tears running down her cheeks, blood tainting the once clear droplets. I've never hated anything more than I do right now, and the fact I knew I wasn't going to pull the trigger only made it so much worse. "Please," Heidi whispered as one last plea, and with my back facing the two sided mirror, I lowered my hand and shot twice, two bullets breaking the binds that held her captive in the chair.

She jumped in fear from the loud bangs, and for my third and final shot, I blew apart the camera in the corner behind me that monitored all activity in the interrogation rooms. Not that it really mattered.

Nobody here that could see it would be stupid enough to cross me Carter MacGuire the new Don of the Italian-American Mafia.

I just became one of the most powerful men in the world, and unfortunately for everyone else, I planned to use it to destroy the people who took my everything from me. I planned to use it for revenge.

~ Thirty-One ~

Hazel

Two Days Ago - Jade: Hey, are you okay?

Me: Yeah, why?

Jade: You just never came home from Jolene's, so I wanted to make sure you were okay.

Me: Shit, sorry. Things are a little crazy right now. Carter was waiting for me at the Cafe, and some stuff happened that led to me ending up back at the mansion. I'll tell you everything the next time I see you. Everything good on your end?

Jade: Yeah but I definitely think we could use another talk at some point. Things are just feeling off right now.

Me: What's going on? Do you want me to come back?

Jade: No, it's okay. You have enough things to worry about right now.

Me: I'll be fine, I'm worried about you. What happened?

Jade: I asked Mila to move in with me over dinner tonight.

Turns out she's moving to Ontario to live closer to her parents and already has all of the documents she needs to get there. She doesn't want me to come with.

Hazel: Hails, I'm so sorry to hear that. Are you at the house? I'll come meet you wherever you are.

Jade: Yeah I'm home... but I just don't understand it. I thought she loved me better than that. Do you think we can have a movie night with some snacks? I could really use a distraction right now.

Me: Of course, I'll be over as soon as I can. I should be there in about .

Jade: Thank you. I really appreciate it.

Me: Like I said, anytime. And that's how I got to being in my car, the flash of Carter's ring on my finger allowing me right past the guards without a second glance. I would be back, but I just know Jade has to be heartbroken.

Truthfully, I think I was a little too.

The kiss I shared with Dominic tonight nearly killed me, and after I all but begged him to go, I fell apart right there on the balcony until I wasn't able to cry anymore.

It's been about an hour since then, and even thinking about it still hurts. So, I just stopped, turning up my radio loud until it was strong enough to muffle the thoughts that tore away at my heart. I knew I would see Rowan, Dominic, and Carter again soon enough, but I had to be smart about this, not just for my safety but also for my emotions.

I feel like I could fall apart at any moment right now, and I don't know if they'd be able to save me this time. With my dagger clutched tight in my handthe gift Jolene had given meI parked my car in Jade's garage to keep hidden, checking my surroundings before getting out.

I locked up straight from there, not letting my guard down for a second until I was in the house with the door closing behind me. The first thing I noticed was how dark it was inside, the only light coming in being from the unclosed blinds and the television that was currently aglow.

On the couch across from it slept Jade, her dark brown curls tied up in a bun with a blanket draped over her body. I'd tried to get here as quickly as I could, but I could imagine she was exhausted from the stress of what I'm assuming to be a break up. It's honestly a wonder that I wasn't out cold already too.

I think I just had too much on my mind right now for sleep.

Giving her a sad smile since I knew she couldn't see, I grabbed the remote that was on the table in front of her, powering off the TV so she could rest while the night still allowed her to.

My first instinct was to stay on the chair beside her to be there when she wakes up, but the logical part of me tells me I should probably go back to the mansion. There hadn't been nearly enough time yet for me to forgive them for the secrets they kept, but I knew being with them was the best thing I could do for all of us right now. If putting aside my feelings is what keeps us all alive right now, then that's what I'll do.

"How did things get so messed up?" I sigh under my breath, walking into the kitchen to where we keep our pens and grocery lists. I didn't want her to feel like I didn't show, but maybe I could come here in the morning with Carter after his usual workout to check in. I think I might need Jade just as bad as she needs me right now.

After scribbling out a quick note for her, I tossed the pad of paper onto the counter where she could see it in the morning.

I wished I could stay, but alas, I walked into my room instead to pack some of my personal items I knew I would need to tide me over these next few days. It was the right thing to do, so making sure I was quiet enough to not wake Jade, I grabbed my headphones, the book I'd just started recently, and a heavier jacket to keep me warm. I'm sure there's more I'll need depending on how long I end up staying, but this should be good for now.

With the items either in my hands or tucked away in my pockets, I opened up my bedside table for one last thing. Retrieving the box of assorted chocolates I'd bought last week, I made sure the kind Jade liked most were still in there. It wouldn't make up for what I'm sure she's feeling right now, but chocolate could never hurt. Slipping on my jacket and glancing around the room one last time for anything I might need, I sighed as I turned back to my door. I hadn't even realized having my hands full was a mistake before I saw a flash of black to my right, the figure of somebody large coming up to my back.

I spun around instantly as the items from my arms dropped, the sound of chocolates scattering on the floor, but my dagger was in my hand within seconds. Whoever was in the house very clearly didn't belong there as I stared into the face of a masked person, and I didn't wait as I swung out, meeting the abdomen of my target. The grunt of a man had me darting out of his path as he let out a cry of pain, but my adrenaline had my heart spiking as my hand grabbed out to the handle.

"Jade, get out!" I screamed, hoping to wake her up, but I wasn't given the chance to do the same before two more people were advancing on me, another man accompanied by a woman.

"Blyad!" The person I cut shouted, a heavy... Russian accent layering his words?

"Jade, run!" I tried again as I was forced away from the door, but no matter how good I was with a blade, I was outnumbered and extremely rusty. My skin prickled as the man clutched his now bleeding stomach, and when his eyes rounded back to me, I was absolutely terrified.

"She's his, that's for sure." The woman spoke, pulling something from her pocket that had me swallowing nervously. With her hand steadily clutching a needle filled with something I sure as fuck didn't trust, I pulled my arm back with the dagger in hand. The man beside her was very intent on staring at the ring Carter had given me on my finger, but I cut him off before he could speak. "I may be outnumbered, but I won't hesitate to throw this if you don't get out of my house right now." I threatened, my eyes moving from the serum to their friend very clearly in pain.

"And it's going at the big one too." I wouldn't miss, but I never had the chance to anyways. A deep chuckle came from behind me before I could even realize there was a fourth, the sharp prick of a needle piercing my neck before I could do anything to stop it. "Why are you laughing, you asshole? This bitch cut me." The Russian man cursed, but it only made the person behind me appear more amused.

"She's my sister, Lev. I'd be disappointed if she didn't." Sister? I panicked and struggled as two arms grabbed at my body, but within five seconds, the injection caused me to be too weak to keep a hold of the dagger. Three seconds later, I could no longer stay conscious, one last breath leaving my mouth before everything faded to black.

The first thing I noticed when I opened my eyes was the painful throb of my headache. The next was the fact the dulled light in the room I woke up in felt too obscenely bright, everything around me spinning.

"That will be all, Cameron." I heard the blurred voice of a man close by, but I was too out of it to depict anything more than fuzzy outlines. I heard a door click shut only moments later before I was able to tell I was laying down on a white bed with the sheets pulled over my body.

My mind urged my hands to move and push me up, but every-thing felt too heavy and too sluggish to leave the comfort of the warm blankets. Lifting my head ever so slightly from the pillow it was resting against, I was able to notice the single light above me actually had a gentle flicker to it, only noticeable if you looked close enough.

"You're awake." That same male voice from earlier spoke, but this time when I looked in the direction of the sound, I swear my once racing heart stopped beating all together. My body was still coming down from whatever drug I had been injected with, but there was no doubt about who the man in front of me was.

"Dad." I say, my throat painfully dry and scratchy, but I knew he heard me nonetheless. My father was right in front of me, wearing the same glasses I remember him wearing when I was still young.

"It's good to see you, kid." He smiles as he stands from the chair across from me, coming over to sit on the edge of my bed. The entire time I was silent, forcing myself not to flinch away or freak out over the fact that I didn't feel safe. For the first time being around my dad, I was scared.

"The dizziness is from the propofol we gave you to get you here. I'm sorry there wasn't a more... civilized way in such short notice, Maddie." He Marcus says, and instead of returning his grin, I put every single bit of my strength into sitting up in case I needed to protect myself.

"Everything's going to be okay. I'm going to explain everything."

My elbows almost collapse under my weight as I push myself up-right, but I manage, scooching back until I was able to lean against the wooden headboard. So much has changed since I last saw my father, and while a part of me wanted to go into his arms and hug him in the way I've wanted to since he left, I refused to be lied to any longer. I needed answers and I needed them now.

"Where am I?" I ask as I look around the room now that I'm more awake, noticing for the first time that there wasn't a single window in this place. There was nothing personalized and no colour other than the red lettering of an alarm clock sitting on the bedside table. It looked like a cleaner version of a prison.

"We call this the Keep." My dad explains, opening his arms as though this were a luxury.

"You're free to decorate this room however you'd like once we get you settled in and relaxed." Under control and tamed. I think back to the man Lev that I'd slashed with my knife and the detail that my brother was also there. Fuck, he'd been in the room with my father as I was waking up before he was sent away. I couldn't explain it, but everything felt off here. Things were more than definitely wrong.

"Where am I?" I ask again, hoping he can tell from my tone his answer wasn't the one I was looking for. I wanted to know how long it would take for me to get back to New York where I belonged.

"San Diego." He says, wincing slightly at my tone and sensing he had a lot of damage control to take care of. That didn't help me to settle in the least.

"There's so much that you don't know about, but you're safe here. You're back home." No. My home is in New York, no matter how mad I am at Rowan, Dominic, and Carter. Right now, I would give anything to be with them again, secrets be damned.

"I didn't realize it took drugging and forcing me to get to a place that's my so-called home." I countered as a very obvious frown marked my face, my pulse nervously beating against my chest against the clothes I've most certainly never worn before.

"Tell me what's going on. You owe me at least that." I say, praying my reactions were just my paranoia talking. My father's sigh sent chills up my spine, and not in a good way. I wasn't scared of him physically hurting me, but rather about what all of this meant. There's no way the men back at home would let this happen without some sort of intense form of manipulation involved.

Either way, I didn't care what my dad wanted to call it. I was kidnapped and didn't want to be here. "It's understandable that you're feeling overwhelmed. I know this is a lot, but the answers you seek are easier shown than described." He shakes his head as he extends his hand out to me. It's a very long time before I accept.

If that's what it takes to get me out of this room, then it's an easy price to pay.

"I needed to be able to get you somewhere alone so we could talk without the ears of others around us. Nowhere is safe anymore." My father says, opening the door into the hallway as the both of us stepped out, halls upon halls of identical entrances lining the pathway.

"Well apart from here of course." He adds at the last second, shooting me a smile I'm assuming that's supposed to be comforting. I was pissed though, and nothing he could say could fix that. Not right now at least.

He's been keeping just as many secrets from me himself, and I'd hoped he'd be able to repair the distrust I now have, but so far he was failing. Because of that, I chose to stay silent and take in my surroundings instead, scanning for any possible exits I can get out of at night. I still haven't even processed the fact we were in San Diego, however I don't exactly have a choice but to accept it right now.

"The last time we spoke, I told you to stay with those three boys you were seeing"

"Am seeing." I interrupted, wishing I could just take everything back.

All I could think about right now is that I said goodbye to Dominic, and now I was trapped here with nowhere to go. When my father stared blankly at me, I added, "They are my boyfriends, and I plan to see them right after..." I began, but very quickly trailed off when the nervous tick I'd acquired over these recent months was very different from what I was used to. "Where's my ring?" I ask, trying not to make my voice shake over the fact Carter's gift was gone. All he did was try and persuade me forward, and that made me even more scared.

"Dad, where is my ring?" I repeated, my voice shaking this time as I spoke. I promised to never take it off. It was the only thing he's truly ever asked of me, and it wasn't on my hand.

"Did you know he had a tracker in it?" Is his only response, but it was confirmation enough. Somebody took it, and now the only thing that brought me comfort in this shitty place was gone.

"Yes, I trust him. And even if I didn't, it's not your call to take it away." I didn't stop my father as he directed me down the hall by a pushing hand on my back, but the newfound tightness in his jaw told me he was growing tenser by the second. A lot of things have changed in the six months he's been gone, and I was no longer the obedient little girl I was before he left. I learned that from the men in my life who bothered to love me the way I needed, and my father didn't seem to be pleased by it.

"Would you still trust him if I told you he's now the Don of the Italian-American Mafia?" He says once we're behind a new set of closed doors, only this room appears to be an office with a computer sitting on a desk. If it weren't for his words, I probably would've taken the time to look at it. But the only thing I could see was New York and the only thing I could hear was Don.

"What did you say?" I ask, my voice deathly quiet with fear and a shit ton of anger if this wasn't some messed up joke. The reality of it not being one was too destructive to even think about.

"I know it's hard to realize the people who loved you can be"

"You don't get to tell me how I feel!" I say, my hands shaking at the thought of Carter being the Don of the Mafia. This couldn't be true, because he would never be happy again in a life stricken by forced duty and appearances. He doesn't want that future. He never has. "Carter killed his father yesterday morning after he and his friends realized you were gone. You would've already been on a plane over here with your brother during that time, though." A trip I couldn't remember because I was unconscious at his order.

Oh, and whoever this Cameron Monet was, he was not my brother.

I was horrified for Carter, not even able to imagine how he must be feeling right now. As much as he'll never admit it and I'll never say it, I know a part of him has always longed for Vincent's approval.

It was the little boy inside of him who still grieved the life of having parents who couldn't give less of a shit about you. I know, because I long for it too.

No matter how much my mother has wronged and hurt me, the reason I don't want her dead like Andrew is because some stupid, minuscule hope of mine is that she's not gone yet. That there is still some good left in her. No, I don't want her dead because I will still grieve her as though she were everything to me, even when I was treated like nothing. "And whose fault is that?" I accuse after a moment of thinking, walking further into the room for the sole reason of placing some distance between us. I'm not sure if my dad realized it, but he's hurt me too. In his own way, he was hurting me now, and I didn't know what to make of it.

"The MacGuire's have been after our family for decades, kiddo. I'm not playing the innocent, but things can't just stop at Vincent anymore."

"Why not?" I raised my hands along with my tone in defeat, so exhausted from all of this. I wanted to go back to a week ago when I was still happy. When Carter, Dominic, and Rowan weren't locked into lives they hated and myself the truths that had me coming apart at the seams. I stared at the silvering strands of my father's hair, and the circles under his eyes that hadn't been there the last time we spoke, and I wished we could go back to when not having him was lonely but manageable.

The sound of his exhale was carried across the room to where I stood, my hands clutching my stomach right over where Carter's initials were. At least that couldn't be taken from me.

"Why aren't they knocking on this door finding me right now? Why do I feel like if I try to leave this place, you're going to force me to stay like one would a prisoner?" He flinched at my words, but didn't deny any of it, confirming once again that I was right. He wouldn't let me leave, even if it's what I wanted.

"Let's sit and I can show you why you can't go back to those precious men you think love you." Marcus practically spits at the last part, and I say Marcus because this was not the man who raised me. No, this person was driven by vengeance and that means something else had to have happened that made Vincent's death no longer cancel out my uncle's murder.

"I don't" "Hazel, sit down." He demands, and there's no use in arguing when I'm admittedly feeling sick anyways. Though, his tone did have me on edge either way.

Listening, I sat in the chair across from the office one, my dad occupying that seat once he saw I wasn't going to try and run. This entire conversation had me biting my tongue in irritation, but I just wanted answers... and a clue as to how I can get home. Tracking his movements as he typed something into the sleek black computer in front of him, his eyes met mine, looking just as tired and regretful as I'm sure mine do.

"You're right." My father says, nodding his head only once before leaning back slightly.

"I can't imagine how you must be feeling right now, and I'm truly sorry that you got caught in the middle of this disaster. I really did believe Carter was a good man for you despite his father." And that's the part I didn't understand. What did he do to make my dad so distrustful of our relationship? I thought having Vincent dead was what everyone wanted. None of this was voiced however, because I'm slowly learning the less I talk, the more other's take the silence as an opportunity to fill in the gaps.

This time was no different, and instead, it seemed to even calm the edge I could tell we were both on right now. "You were aware I was throwing a party for the entire organization in celebration of finally being able to make our move on Vincent, but what the MacGuire's didn't realize was that their ambush was essential to that plan." I didn't question how the hell my father knew I was aware of that information.

"I could tell just from those few minutes of watching those men to know that they were in love with you, and I counted on them calling off their assignment on that night of the 13th.

However we could've still managed if they hadn't. Either way, it was much easier to handle their stand ins considering we had ones of our own." We, as in my father and the wife I had to learn about from Rowan.

Was my step brother there too, the one who's been alive for two years longer than me that I had no idea about until now? I forced a deep breath in through my nose to calm my senses, because I could already feel myself cracking from the inside out again. There was no way I could risk letting my guard down in a place like this, not with so much on the line.

"Vincent killed the person who was imitating me and kidnapped Ivy while I was trying to get to you, but when he realized we had something that could bring the entire Mafia down on him, he came to us instead. Ivy got away with promises of a deal we get you in exchange for a kept secret." Isn't that what this whole thing came down to? Secrets. I didn't want to hear about the stepmother nobody bothered to tell me about, or the deals that made me feel like nothing more than a bargaining chip.

My ring was gone, and it was he who took it. I couldn't care less about contracts with Vincent, even though it was my curiosity that kept me listening.

"Pulling back our forces in agreement, we were anonymously contacted about your protective jewelry, and how Carter, Rowan, and Dominic would never believe you left unless it was taken off. We had a professional learn your handwriting so the note looked real"

"Note?" I cut him off, my eyes widening as my body shot up from my seat. I couldn't stay quiet about that, because my father was making it sound like I chose to leave them for good. Like they might believe I didn't want them anymore. "There's a lot more you still need to know. You'll understand why we did what we had to do once I finish explaining." He tries to defend himself, but this was a line that couldn't be uncrossed. My dad was speaking like I wouldn't be going back, and like hell was I going to accept that.

"Explaining what? The fact that the people you look down upon were here for me when you weren't?" I say, thinking of every moment I had with them that led up to now.

"That you took me away from everything that made me happy just to take away my choice again by bringing me here? Why would you work with Vincent anyways if this entire thing is about killing him?" My dad tracked the way I brought my hands down to rest against the desk, a cover up for the fact I was dizzy from standing so abruptly, but I was too angry to care what he thought. None of this made sense.

I've taken care of myself for almost a year without him and now he thinks he has the right to be my father again? To keep me grounded here like I didn't know what was best for myself. It was bullshit, and when he closed his eyes to collect himself, I spun on my heel and turned to leave.

I didn't even care that I knew I wouldn't succeed.

"It was until your boyfriend abused his use of power within minutes of collecting it." My dad stops me in my tracks by nothing more than his words alone.

He was talking about Carter, and I didn't care about whatever he did to get on my father's bad side. I promised to be there the next time he needed an escape, no matter what, and I was currently thousands of miles away.

"Well at least they don't hold me against my will to make me listen." I say, tears welling in my eyes but I was too damn stubborn to cry right now. I refused to.

"I need to speak to them, dad." I tip my head, exhausted from recent events. "Just let me make a call to let them know I'm okay." Carter would never believe his ring would leave my finger at my own free will. He had to know something wasn't right. The way I left things with Dominic was a different story, but I would at the very least say goodbye to the other two as well. I don't think my heart could handle never seeing them again.

"Would you still want to be with them if I told you they're the reason your mother's dead?" My dad questions coldly and then everything goes quiet in my head. The pounding of my headache and the loud scream of my thoughts all ceased, everything channeling into one single statement.

"What?" I say, my voice cracking from the dryness of my throat. His fists shook where they were balled against the table, and the intensity of his expression told me he wasn't lying. This wasn't some game to keep me here. I received a small look of sympathy from him, but my father never was one to soften the blow with me.

I felt like I couldn't breathe as he typed a few things into his computer before spinning it around to face me on the desk. While I was practically across the room, there was no mistaking the terrified look of my mother's face partially cut off by the broad shoulder of Carter's body. "No, he wouldn't do that." I shake my head as if the action could take the image away. He knows how much it would hurt me for her to die. There's no way...

"Press play." My father demands. I wasn't sure if it was the adrenaline or the denial that made me want to prove him wrong, but my feet were carrying me over to the desk before I could prepare myself for the horrible possibility he described. His eyes closed with pain as I did as he asked, however mine were unblinking as my finger pressed down on the keyboard to begin the video feed. The quality was awful, but I knew who the two people were just as I knew it was Vincent who was dead on the ground.

"You hurt her." Were the first words that were spoken through the screen, and if I could see Carter's face, I knew it would be guilt I'd be seeing.

"You wasted the chances given to you. There's nobody to blame for this but yourself." He continued, and a sickening feeling filled my stomach at this. My father believed these words were being spoken to his past wife, but I knew Carter better than that.

Those words were directed at himself and the regret he felt for hurting me. I watched through blurry vision as a gun was raised to my mother's forehead, tears and blood flowing rapidly down her cheeks from where she was held captive.

I waited with every part of me, hoping he would walk away. That he wouldn't do what my father told me he does.

"Please." A desperate whisper left the woman's mouth one last time, and I almost felt relief when Carter dropped his hand down, the gun leaving with him.

The wide frame of his body blocked the sight of my mom from her shoulders down, but I didn't need to see when I heard the two deafening bangs of gunshots. I watched as her mouth parted in a shout as her body jolted, and I didn't look away when Carter turned until he was looking directly at the camera that captured this video. I looked into the darkness of his eyes before he raised his hand for a third time, aiming directly at the lens before shooting and stopping the feed entirely, my heart along with it.

There was a sharp ringing in my ears as I stood there in shock, but I could still hear him when my father said her body was found this morning, dead from the two bullet wounds to her heart and stomach. I couldn't stop myself as I collapsed into the chair I'd previously been occupying, and within seconds, I could feel my panic attack seizing my lungs and ripping at my chest.

Every bit of denial I held had been diminished by a single minute of a recording, and again when I learned Carter had dumped her body at the back of a hotelthe same one where we first met. My mother's death had been a message, but I didn't know what exactly it was yet.

Was he trying to punish me because he believed I actually left him? "The plan was always to have Carter kill Vincent because only he was capable of achieving it, but Heidi was caught in the middle in ways we still aren't sure of."

I think I'm going to be sick.

"Where did you get this?" I ask, heaving air into my lungs as my knees curled up to my chest on the chair. Even now, I wanted to refuse to believe this, because this was something I would never be able to forgive, no matter how much my heart aches for the three men still in New York.

"Ivy managed to pull this from their base before it could be deleted from their receivers. To make a long story short, Vincent broke into your friend Jade's phone when she was sleeping to get you out of that mansion. I sent a team out to retrieve you while Lev Ivankov, the man you put in the infirmary, took your ring and composed a story that would make it seem like you ran." A small bit of pride appeared on my father's face about the dagger part, but I didn't seek it out in the way I once did growing up. Now, it was a reminder of everything I couldn't save.

"With you on the jet over here, Rowan was the first to realize you were gone. He and Dominic have been out looking for you ever since, but Carter is seeking revenge in the form of a rampage. I know this is going to be hard to hear, kiddo, but his true colours aren't the same ones he showed you." And that was the part that kept me from accepting all of this. It wasn't a mask Carter wore with me, but he's so skilled at wearing them to everyone else that that's all the world has ever gotten to see. I felt as though my head might explode from the gears turning with this new information, but it wasn't until I went back to the beginning that I started to question things from a new perspective.

This wasn't about Carter and I, this was about his mother and my uncle. This game of revenge was born of grief, Marcus for the loss of his brother and Vincent of his wife. But then again, why would Carter kill my mom when this entire thing could've just been over? It didn't make sense.

Every conclusion I could think of led back to Vincent, so what was I missing from the night his wife died seventeen years ago? There was one question on the tip of my tongue I've been asking myself since I learned that my father was Marcus, and I knew I couldn't cave to the cowardliness that tempted me to keep quiet. Too much rode on the answer.

"Did you kill Carter's mom?" I asked, my nails digging into the palms of my hands as I awaited my father's response.

His green eyes held a glint of surprise I was unfamiliar with as the words left my mouth, and when he closed the lid of his computer shut, he touched my arm as he said, "No, kid. I didn't." Just like that, the final piece of a very complicated, very jagged puzzle fell into place. There was only one other possibility as to how she died, and it had everything to do with the secret my father was telling me about earlier.

"But Vincent did." I say, my chin lifting to fight against the disgust welling in my eyes. I didn't need my dad's confirmation. His silence was answer enough, because what I've failed to realize this entire time is that Carter, Dominic, and Rowan have been living a lie for almost two decades of their lives, their efforts wasted to a man trying to cover his tracks. "Come in." I hear my father say over the firm knock at the door I'd failed to hear over all of my thoughts. It didn't matter because all I could think about was the fact Carter's destruction was a closure-less feat now that this revelation had been uncovered.

"Hazel." The sound of my name brought my attention back to the man in front of me, my body twisting to see who was currently joining us in his office.

"I want you to meet my business partner Lena Garvin." He says, but I wasn't listening anymore.

My body froze as a woman walked in with confident strides, taller than me by a few inches even without the heels she wore now. Not a single imperfection marred her beautiful olive skin, her dark brown hair straight and ending at just above her shoulders. Everything about her radiated power, her demand for attention clear in the black of the eyes I know I've seen before. If I wasn't already sitting, I would've fallen down.

"I don't understand." I break out of my stupor just to be met with realization the kind that rewrote this entire narrative. This woman was the secret powerful enough to blackmail even men like Vincent MacGuire, and it was clear she'd succeeded just by the lethal smile she wore, identical to the one I've already seen on a younger version of herself.

The secret is that Carter's mom is alive, and she is currently standing right in front of me.

~ Thirty-Two ~

EPILOGUE

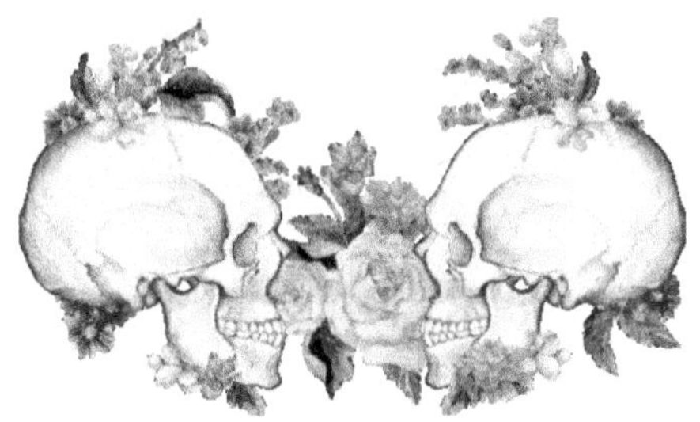

Hazel

I didn't expect my hands to feel as cold as they did, despite the warm feeling of blood dripping down the length of my fingers and the red that wasn't my own painted in splatters across my face.

I wasn't one to hold much regret over my choices, though.

Today was a moment I've been waiting for the last eight years of my life, but even I'll admit, I will never come here again. "You can't get rid of the memories, Hazel, but you can replace them with better ones—ones that you can control." My father had said to me right before I made the decision to fly out here to Detroit.

The potent smell of gasoline burned my nostrils more and more with each passing second, but I didn't stop, not even as Andrew's screams began to ring in my ears. In fact, the sound only encouraged me.

"That house is your prison for as long as you give it the power to be so." This was me taking back everything that has been stolen from me for far too many years, even if it meant sacrificing another part of myself in the process. Smiling as I watched Andrew's expression of fear turn into pure and utter terror, I circled the chair he was tied up in, pouring a path of fuel until it surrounded him at his feet.

"You know, I heard somewhere that being burned alive is the most painful way to die." I say, tossing the can of gasoline across the living room of my childhood home. Or at least what was left of it. Andrew's body trembled as he looked up to meet my gaze, and while he tried to appear stoic, I knew it was only a matter of time before he broke for good.

"I'm going to kill you for this." He threatened, spit flying from his mouth with each new word, but I didn't even flinch. With his blood already across my skin, I couldn't care less. This was going to end the same either way.

"No," I shook my head as I slowly reached into my pocket, retrieving the small knife I'd stolen on the trip over here. Positioning the blade over his right hand, I leaned into his ear as I ever so slowly let the edge break past his flesh.

"I survived, and after tonight, I'm never going to pay another thought over the waste of life you are." Striking true, I exhaled as blood spurted from the palm of his hand, yanking back the knife before retreating my touch all together

. I wasn't sure how I would feel coming here again since my mom, but satisfaction was a pretty accurate description for how I was feeling right now.

My body thrived off of the regretful screams Andrew let out from my ministrations, but what was to come would be so much worse for him.

It would be everything he deserved, and maybe after this, just maybe, I could breathe again without the heaviness of each painful inhale that was barely keeping me alive. As I slowly backed away, making sure to not step in the trails of fuel I've lined all over this house of nightmares, I paid no attention to the desperate final pleas of the man being left behind.

There would be no sympathy for a person like Andrew.

Not a single ounce resided within me when I walked out of the place I was raised in one last time, and while I could still hear his cries from the bottom of the old wooden porch at the front, I knew nobody would come. Neighbours may question the noise, and authorities may question the destruction, but nobody would look into a case such as my stepfather's, especially not in the poor side of town his skeleton would be found in.

Only hours ago, my dad told me that if I did not desire the memories here, to make new ones.

That was exactly what I intended to do. Drawing a single match from the box in my pocket, I watched as I lit just the tip until flames danced right before my eyes.

The weapon itself may appear small, but it took away all remembrance of the prison this house once was for me. Soon, it would be burned down until it was nothing more than a pile of ash.

Glancing at the bricks of crumbling concrete and the slabs of loosened wood, the world before me didn't seem as scary as it previously did. The heaviness in my chest remained as did the ache in my heart, but not even the past was strong enough to control me anymore.

Tossing the match at the blocked entrance and stepping away, I revelled in the quiet second that came before the sound of gasoline catching fire met my ears.

With a blink, this entire abandoned street became painted with hues of orange and red, the silent promise on my tongue remaining that this would be the first and last time someone died by my hand.

Andrew's screams were instantly muffled by the roaring of the flames around him, but it wasn't guilt that drove the vow I knew I couldn't allow myself to break. From this night forward, I would never kill again. Not because it was wrong. Not because it was dangerous. But because I fear I liked it, a little too much.

9 787046 063961